A Powe

The Face
of
Fear

A POWERS AND JOHNSON NOVEL

The Face
of
Fear

R.J. Torbert

TWO HARBORS PRESS, MINNEAPOLIS

This story is a work of fiction.

ISBN: 978-1-938690-77-8
LCCN: 2012923928

All characters and events in this publication, other than those clearly in the public domain, are fictitious, and any resemblance to real persons, living or dead, is purely coincidental.

Copyright © 2012 Entertainment 21 Corp
A Powers and Johnson Novel; The Face of Fear
All Rights Reserved
The moral right of the author has been asserted

All rights reserved, including the right to reproduce this book or portions thereof in any form

Ghost Face is a Registered Trademark of Easter Unlimited Inc. Fun World. All Rights Reserved.

Ghost Face protected under copyright registration Fun World Div. Easter Unlimited Inc. All Rights Reserved.

Zombie Cryptic Mask protected under copyright registration Fun World Division/Easter Unlimited Inc. All Rights Reserved.

"I'm Missing You" lyrics protected under copyright registration. R.J. Torbert. All Rights Reserved.

Follow @RJTorbert on Twitter.

TWOHARBORS
WWW.TWOHARBORSPRESS.COM

Acknowledgments

This book had to be written. This story played out in my mind so many times throughout the years that it needed to be finally put on paper.

Roseann:
You are beautiful inside and out. No one has more loyal friends than you. It is a reflection of the type of woman you are. Thank you for your understanding and patience during the writing of this book.

Shannyn:
This is for you. Never, never give up. If you can envision it, feel it, and desire it, then it is a dream that is attainable

Sharyn:
You are loved, and I hope this makes you proud.

Henry:
You are everything a father should be. Thank you.

Dear Mother:
It was you who always said, "The only people that fail are those that try." I miss you.

Gina:
I miss you, baby sister.

Alan Geller:
How would history be if you did not stamp your approval on the design and development of the mask that has become the "Icon of Halloween" in stores, films, and now books around the world? You are the genesis of all that has become.

Stanley Geller:
You have always said, "No matter how well you do something, it is always second best. There is always a way to do it better." Keeping that in mind, I want you to know I gave it my all.

Kevin Cronin:
A terrific cop, a good teammate, a wonderful man, a great friend.

Jason Lash:
Front and back cover design.
Your support and encouragement was appreciated during the past two years.

Andi Wolos:
A good person and a hard worker—thanks for proofreading the first draft of this book.

Allan Longobucco:
You are my greatest source of laughter. Thank you.

Ken August
Your support, enthusiasm, and encouragement during the writing of this book is greatly appreciated.

John Valeri   Tim Wagstaff   Rodrigo Kurtz   John Klyza
Your devotion and dedication in promoting Ghost Face on your websites is not only appreciated by me but fans worldwide of this mask and the movies associated with it.

Thanks to the following:

My Twitter followers—you are amazing.

As well as:

Jennifer Siff	Sid Bluming	Andrew Dell'Olio	Joey Zee
Frank McGovern	Ki Ceniglio	Jef Workman	Joanne Kowitt
Jerry Kowitt	Scott Tillchock	Joel DeGregorio	Joseph Santospirito
Robert Chapman	George Lynagh	Kathy Daley	Maria Robison
Rickey Roth	Kathy Tillchock	Nada Marjanovich	Katherine Healey
Adele Glimm	Ralph F. Brady	Paul Pappas	Paul Kampmeyer
Robert Healey	Kathleen Healey	"Aunt" Mary Cuomo	Isora Gozley
Loren Santospirito	Sean Moran		Patricia Riggs
Marquerite Zangrillo	George Zangrillo	Gordie Brown	Peter Cook
		Meghan Rief	

Entire Staff of Z Pita

Mayor Margot Garant
Your enthusiasm and support is greatly appreciated.

Brittany Tillchock
You are a talented young lady. Thanks for your help as administrator for the PowersandJohnson.com website and The Face of Fear Facebook page.

Port Jefferson Free Library, Port Jefferson, Long Island
Where this book was written.

Finally, to Wes Craven:
His first words to me when I showed him the summary of my story were: "Wow! You really thought about this." A true gentleman, a gracious man, a legendary director.

Saturday, June 4

Deborah loved relaxing in the back of the home where she grew up in Belle Terre, Long Island. It was at the end of Cliff Road surrounded by a wall and metal gates. It may have seemed like a prison to some, but the walls and gates insured privacy in the upscale community of Belle Terre. Long Island, as most would think, is just that: a long island located in Southeast New York, east of Manhattan.

Deborah was so close to everything yet still had the privacy of being alone in the country. She could close her eyes and soak in the sun or open them and look out at the beautiful Port Jefferson harbor. There was nothing like watching the boats on the water and the rest of the activity to give her a level of relaxation that she never tired of. Most of the time she would bring a good book and a newspaper to read until she took a short nap.

She was blessed, and she recognized it. At 26 years of age she couldn't have asked for a better life other than losing her mother at the age of 13. Her dad was more than a dad; he was a father in the true sense of the word. William Lance was involved in his daughter's life in every way, even during what most parents considered the terrible teenage years. He would often say the hell with the people who would say the terrible twos or threes. It was the ages 16 through 18 that he found most challenging in raising a young woman. Even during those years William Lance was there for Deborah in every way, including when discipline had to be given.

William was rich in finances, but more important, he was rich in friends. From the time Debbie as her friends called her, got her first cell phone, she was required to call her dad at least once a day no matter where he or she was. If she missed a day, she would lose her phone for a week and have it replaced with a GoPhone. His words stuck with her after she lost the phone the first few times. Her father would say, "Until you are responsible to another, I want to hear from you once a day. This way when I don't, I know something is wrong." Little did he or she know, those words would ring true.

Robert Simpson, her father's assistant, came out to bring her an iced tea on this late morning day. "Unsweetened iced tea with cranberry juice, Ms. Debbie."

"Thank you, sir," she replied.

Robert placed the glass down next to her lounge chair on the round table and bent down closer to her and said, "It's just the way you like it," as he smiled.

Deborah took off her sunglasses and put her hand on the back of his neck and brought him closer for a kiss. Robert moved his hand over to the bottom of the bikini, where Deborah stopped it.

"Are you crazy?" she laughed.

"Oh," he replied. "It's been a while, baby. I miss you."

"Well, it's going to have to wait a little while longer. We can't hook up while my dad is home," she replied.

Robert shrugged his shoulders and replied, "He won't notice anything."

Deborah pushed him away, saying, "No, sorry, I can't. I'll be back tomorrow while Dad is playing golf," as she gave him a wink.

She made a good decision, because her father came out back a few minutes later to check out the scenery. He gave his daughter a kiss on top of her head, which was Robert's cue to get some work done in the house. Debbie told her dad she would see him the next day before going back to her place. She was on her way to meet her best friend Patty and see a concert in Bridgeport. She planned to stay over with her relatives before coming back Sunday afternoon on the Cross Island Ferry.

"OK, sweetheart," her father replied. "Just be careful, and don't forget to call your dad tomorrow." He kissed her again.

She smiled and said, "Yes, Dad."

The Cross Island Ferry crosses Long Island Sound between the city of Bridgeport, Connecticut, and the Long Island village of Port Jefferson. The 90-minute ride allows pedestrians, vehicles, motorcycles, trucks, and buses of all sizes to load onto the ferry. Riding the ferry in the summer saves time and gives riders a chance to relax and soak in the atmosphere or read or even sit in the bar for a drink.

Debbie gathered her things and sent Patty a text saying she would be taking the 4:00 pm ferry to Bridgeport and would meet up with her to have dinner at 5:30 before the concert. She went up to the bedroom she grew up in and smiled, as she did every time she entered it. Her father had kept everything the same since she moved out on her own. She always thought that once she and Robert were married, she would be back living in the guesthouse with him, so no matter what, this was her home and would always be her home. Many people have called it the Pink Mansion, the Lance Mansion, or the Pink House, but to her it was home.

She went into her walk-in closet and started looking at things she could possibly wear for the concert that night. She had so many clothes that she had left many of them in her home in Belle Terre when she moved out. Her life was always very private and low-key, even though her father had been in the public eye.

By the time she showered, got dressed, and put her makeup on, it was already past 1:00 pm. Debbie felt like having lunch down in the village before catching the ferry, so she asked her father if he wanted to join her at Z Pita, many locals' favorite casual eatery.

"Forget about tomorrow, Dad, let's have lunch."

"Sure," he replied.

"But only if you're buying," she replied, laughing.

He shook his head. "Some things never change."

Debbie drove to Z Pita with her Dad following. Because she was taking her car onto the ferry, he needed to take his own vehicle which was diamond white Corvette, he called it his favorite toy. They walked into Z Pita and sat for lunch at table four. It was ironic because the two men sitting at table three, Detectives Powers and Johnson, were going to be a part of her for the remainder of her life. No matter how long or short it would be, it was these two that would have an important role in her destiny and yet now, this second, they were just two men sitting close to her space while not even giving them a moment's thought.

The Z Pita building was the original firehouse in Port Jefferson Village, but now it was a 900-square-foot restaurant that had 20 tables inside. If you didn't make a reservation for dinner, most likely you would not be at one of the 20 tables. The chalkboards on the front sidewalk facing Main Street listing the specials gave it a distinctive, unique look. Once you came inside, the small café was divided by a wall. The owner Joey Z kept one side for families and the other side just for adults. He opened the place in 1998 and had been busy ever since. He earned it. The service was top-notch and the food was delicious. The historical pictures of Port Jefferson Village only added to the charm. Upstairs, above the restaurant, he rented out the apartment to Detective Powers, who was sitting three feet away from Debbie and her father at table three.

When lunch was finished, Debbie kissed her father goodbye as she got into her 2010 burnt-orange Charger and drove down Main Street, took a right on East Broadway, and turned left into the ferry parking lot. The attendant asked her if she had a reservation and assigned her to lane 4 after she replied that she did not have one. Debbie pulled her car around and drove into the lane, shut her engine off, and waited until the vessel named *George Washington* pulled up to the dock next to Danford's Restaurant and Hotel. She turned the key just far enough to listen to the radio station 106.1 BLI without turning the engine on and began to send a few texts. One of them was to tease Robert Simpson: "keep your pants on, I will attack you tomorrow. It will be worth the wait." She did not get her reply from Robert before they started loading the ferry.

The huge vessel hit the dock at 3:12 pm. It took about 15 minutes to unload the vehicles crossing over from Connecticut and another 12 minutes to load up the cars going to Bridgeport. Across the street was William Lance. He hadn't told his daughter he would not leave until she drove the car on to the boat. She was an adult now, but he was still her father. It would not change the way he worried about her. Debbie turned her car on and started driving up the ramp to load onto the boat. Her car disappeared from view once she was inside. As the ferry employee directed her, the young woman pulled into the last possible space on the north side of the large boat. She turned the key to shut off the engine and instead of getting out of the car, she took out her hairbrush to fix her hair and take inventory of her belongings in her pocketbook. Inside she found little post it notes that she kept from her father. He would leave her notes, sometimes serious, and at other times, humorous but she always kept her favorites. It was times like this when she was alone that she would read them. Yet, she was not alone. 4 vehicles in front of her in the row next to her were 3 occupants who had interest in what Debbie Lance was doing. One of them got out of the car and walked upstairs to the pursor's office to pay for the ride across the sound. When he reached the window, he bought a ticket for one vehicle and 1 occupant even though there were 2 others with him. The man went back to his vehicle as his partner left his seat and went up to the purchase window and also bought a ticket for 1 vehicle and 1 occupant. When he came back downstairs to meet up with his other companions, Debbie Lance was still in her car going through her personal effects. The 3 of them became restless as they got out of the car and started looking around to see that almost everyone had gone upstairs to the air conditioned seating to relax, pay for the ride or go to the restaurant bar or sit on the top deck. One of the men walked past Debbie and received a smile from her as he walked by her window. He was actually enjoying the suspense and the thrill over what he was about to do. The young woman put all her belongings back in her bag and was so preoccupied that she was startled by the loud ship horn of the ferry which occurred everytime it left the village. The sound was so loud it could be heard throughout the entire village, even inside the buildings if it was quiet. Debbie laughed at herself for being so frightened by the sound. She opened her car door still with the smile on her face as the man who had just walked by her window punched her in the side of her cheek and she quickly fell over unconscious. Within seconds his two accomplices ran over as the keys were tossed to them. The trunk of the car was opened and Debbie Lance was thrown inside. The man who struck her promptly sat down behind the wheel of her car and started unpeeling a banana. He only became annoyed when he realized the radio in the vehicle would not work while on the ferry.

    He looked over at his partners and gave them a thumbs up as they returned to their vehicles.

    Debbie never met Patty for dinner, and she wasn't at her seat when the concert started. With no replies from Debbie to texts or phone calls, Patty finally called Robert Simpson to tell him that she never met up with her and that she was worried. Robert looked at his watch and saw 8:06 pm, which meant more than four and a half hours had passed since Debbie drove onto the ferry. Robert ran up to the main house and gave William Lance the news that his daughter never made it to Connecticut. William Lance called his daughter's cell number, to no avail. He tried to remain calm but with his over protective emotions about her, he decided to call in favors with the Suffolk county police department who in turn connected him to the FBI. Normally it would require a much longer time to have elapsed before their involvement but the ferry did cross state lines and courtesy would be given to the former Suffolk county executive.

He knew she boarded the ferry to Connecticut because he had witnessed it. William dialed Debbie's number five times, and it kept going to voice mail. Each time he left a message to call him. Questions kept entering his mind. What could have happened on the boat? Did they find her car? She wouldn't run away, would she? Was this a kidnapping? He had visions of someone throwing her overboard on the Long Island Sound. He shook his head to try and clear his thoughts, but they wouldn't go away. Down the hall he could hear Simpson dial her phone and leave messages. William Lance was getting concerned. If something happened to his daughter, he would not have a reason to live anymore. He did not want to overreact, but he knew his daughter. There was no way she would have committed suicide, so the only explanation was that something happen to her. He tried to think of other options that could have happen but there was not many, especially when there is only a certain amount of space on a large ship over the long island sound.

During his term as county executive, he was the chief administrative officer of county government. He was elected for four years and had a high approval rating when he decided not to seek reelection from the voters of Long Island. His expertise on budgets, program services, and labor relations proved to be what most considered an extremely successful term during his tenure, however it was his relationship with the police department and its force that created the quick response that was given to William Lance.

    Special Agent Jack O'Connor arrived at the door within the hour. Though he was not convinced foul play was involved, he took information from both William Lance and Robert Simpson as to Deborah Lance's trail. He then drove to the Cross Island Ferry, which was getting ready to close for the evening, and realized there was no way to verify that Debbie had in fact took the vessel other than her father being a eye witness to her driving on to the boat. Only a reservation would have been documented proof that she was on the boat once she checked in. He knew then it was going to be a long weekend.

Sunday, June 5

Special Agent O'Connor was back at the Lance house Sunday morning, and it was clear because no one had heard from her that there was a mystery surrounding the disappearance of Debbie Lance. The FBI agent had already been informed that the Charger she was driving was found about a half-mile from the ferry. He ordered the car to be impounded immediately for forensics to go over it. Still, the possible scenarios were a concern. Anything could have happened on the water, or after the car was driven off the ferry. Regardless of how it happened or why, Debbie Lance was nowhere to be found.

William Lance had called in a favor and requested help from the Suffolk County Police Department. As a courtesy to the former county executive of Suffolk County, the current administration called the police commissioner, who in turn called detective lieutenant Kevin Cronin to send someone out to the house. Although this was not a murder case yet, Cronin recognized this was a special inquiry that needed attention. He sent detectives Paul Powers and Bud Johnson to Belle Terre to speak with the FBI. As they were approaching the mansion on Cliff Road, Agent O'Connor was leaving and asked the detectives to meet him at the security building, which was located about a quarter-mile down Cliff Road near the entrance to the Belle Terre community.

When they got out of their vehicles, O'Connor was not friendly and immediately demanded to know why two Suffolk detectives were intending to go to the house.

"This is being handled by the FBI. Let me make that clear," he said.

"Hold on," Bud Johnson replied as he held up his hands. "Don't shit your shorts."

"What?" O'Connor replied.

"Listen," Paul Powers interrupted. "We're here as a courtesy to the Suffolk County executive. All we want to know is information and to offer any help we can and take a look at the evidence so far."

O'Connor looked at Bud for a moment and started to calm down. The agent reviewed the chain of events and the evidence to date with the two detectives. "She actually had boarded the ferry to go to Connecticut. As of now, how she disappeared off the ferry is the big question."

As he spoke, Paul Powers had many thoughts in his brain as to the possibilites. O'Connor continued, saying, "We believe it's likely to be a kidnapping. Bridgeport police found her 2010 Charger abandoned a half-mile from the ferry in Bridgeport." Agent O'Connor thanked the detectives for their offer but told them the agency would handle it.

As the three men parted ways, O'Connor noticed Bud Johnson looking behind him and, as Johnson opened his car door, yelled to him. "What was that about?" O'Connor hollered.

Bud replied as he got in the car. "I like to look at asses."

"Oh," Agent O'Connor answered. "A comedian on the case, just what we need."

Ignoring the banter between Bud and O'Connor, Powers called the Bridgeport Police Department for information on the abandoned car. As they drove off toward the ferry, Paul spoke. "I want in on this case. Listen, it's Sunday. I'm going to get on the ferry, and I'll see you in the office tomorrow. I have to refresh my memory on a few things." Bud knew there was no talking Paul out of things once he started with his theories. Paul got out of the car and walked over to the ticket office, paid cash, and waited to board the next ferry to Connecticut as a pedestrian. "See you tomorrow, partner," he said to Bud.

Paul rode the ferry back and forth twice Sunday and again on Monday. There was still no word on the whereabouts of Debbie Lance or any communication from the potential kidnappers. The more he thought about it, the more he became obsessed with what happened to Debbie Lance. He started pushing numbers on his BlackBerry to make calls. First Rachelle, then Allan, his high school friend who was now head of security in Belle Terre, and then Timothy, the co-owner of Timothy's Bar and Grill, a bar and grill on Main Street in the village. He set up a meeting to talk to them. He had a plan. They set a time when they could all get together Wednesday evening, unless the case was solved by Tuesday.

He walked up the stairs to his apartment and played his messages back. Kevin Cronin's voice boomed over the machine. "Paul, it's me. Listen, your visit yesterday was a courtesy call. Let's not get tangled up with the FBI unless we are asked. After all, this is not a murder."

As Paul undressed, the messages continued, and it was Kevin Cronin again. "Off the record, I don't believe it's fair of me to tell you what to do with your own time. I'm a firm believer that preventing murder is more important than solving a murder." As the call disconnected, Paul smiled. The detective strongly felt he knew how Debbie Lance had disappeared. Why she had disappeared was another story. One look at the Pink Mansion, and he assumed money may be the motive.

Paul had grown up in the Village area of Port Jefferson and grew to love it so much that when his father moved to Florida, he stayed. He could not afford a home in the Village but was lucky to find the apartment above Z Pita restaurant. During his years of growing up and going through the police academy, Paul rode the ferry hundreds of times back and forth to Connecticut. The one thing he noticed as a cop was the lack of security on the ferry. He was never stopped while carrying a gun and was never stopped when he had a shotgun in the trunk. He had other concerns about the lack of security and realized those same concerns could be the reason that whatever happened was pulled off, most likely while the ferry was on the water. He knew if someone was going to get killed or kidnapped, it was very possible to accomplish it on the ferry, and he felt confident he could prove it.

Wednesday, June 8

The evening was cold for June. Usually Paul would just wear a dark T-shirt when he went out for the night. He was so used to not wearing a jacket that he suffered in the cold when not wearing one. As he entered the bar, he could see Timothy, Rachelle, and Allan sitting at the far table. He studied their eyes as they conversed. Something amused Rachelle, and she continued to giggle at whatever words were coming from Timothy. Paul found her laugh attractive. He noticed how her eyes sparkled when she laughed. His concentration was broken when Timothy let out a laugh that sounded like Santa Claus, except he said "Ha, Ha, Ha" instead of "Ho, Ho, Ho."

A couple at the second table from the wall began to argue so loudly that the entire bar turned their heads. It ended quickly with a slap to the man's face before the woman ran out of the bar. The man she left behind, shaken and embarrassed, looked around with a nervous smile and then stared down at his drink.

As Paul approached his three friends' table, he smiled at Rachelle and appreciated it when she reciprocated with her Julia Roberts smile. "Hi there!" she said with a hug. Paul acknowledged Timothy with a polite hello and gave Allan a hug. "Thanks for coming," he said. "I asked you to come tonight because I need your help."

Timothy, Allan, and Rachelle knew what it was about. There was no doubt it was about the kidnapping at the Cross Island Ferry. Paul believed it was time to get some additional help even if it was not through normal channels. Timothy, as much as he annoyed Paul, was the self-appointed "mayor" of Port Jefferson, as the co-owner of Timothy's on East Main Street. It was a popular hangout for all the locals. Rachelle was the hostess and co-owner of Z Pita restaurant, which Paul frequented for many reasons. But it was Rachelle he had become attracted to over the past few years.

She was 5'5" tall with eyes the color of the Pacific Ocean and the perfect figure to match. She started as a waitress at Z Pita while going to school and became so interested in business that she combined her interest of writing about restaurants and local happenings in the Port Jefferson area in the local paper, *Port Jeff Now*, or the *Now*, as it was commonly referred. Her writing talents won her awards, and she was most proud of the article "The History of Drowned Meadow," which was Port Jefferson's original name. This was due to the business district becoming a marshland that flooded with every high tide. The name was used until 1836, when it was changed to Port Jefferson. The *Now* promoted her to writing more serious articles about the quiet village. Her business acumen was so well respected by Z Pita majority owner Joey Z that he offered her equity in the restaurant to insure she would stay with him during her goal of being a respected writer on Long Island. He also hoped it would encourage her to stay even after she established herself in journalism. Rachelle was so busy with her goals that at the age of 28 she had not been out on a date in more than two years. Paul thought that was a waste, but he was happy there wasn't anyone in her life. He held out hope that they would eventually have an opportunity to know each other on a different level.

At 29, Paul moved up fast in the Suffolk County Police Department. He became the youngest detective sergeant of the homicide squad in Long Island's history at age 26. He worked day and night on his cases when he was not at the gym. He knew it was because he did not have a family of his own that he had the time to focus on his cases. He was at the peak of his physical and mental conditioning.

Paul told the group his thoughts on the case. Though Debbie could have disappeared once she reached Connecticut, he felt that it happened somewhere over the Long Island Sound on the vessel itself and believed he knew how it was pulled off. Since this was being handled by the FBI and it wasn't a murder, it wasn't Paul's case, but progress was going nowhere. It was odd to him that she had been gone four days already with no leads. He decided to work on his own time. He rode the Cross Island Ferry back and forth five or six times, studying every possible way she could have driven onto the boat to never be seen again.

He asked Timothy to keep his ears alert and eyes open at the bar that had his name on the front sign. The people involved in the kidnapping had to be local. William Lance was not well known outside of the Long Island area, plus they were apparently comfortable pulling this off on the ferry. Allan was head of security in Belle Terre and had been Paul's best friend since junior high school. Married with two children, life was difficult on a security officer's salary, but his wife Ann worked as a freelance artist, which helped make ends meet in the expensive little village. Even with Allan's job and his wife working, it still would not be enough to afford Belle Terre if it had not been for his inheritance from his parents.

As drinks were served at the table, Paul explained to his three friends that he felt strongly about how the job was pulled off and asked if they wanted to take a ride with him on the ferry Saturday. He would show them. All three of them were intrigued enough to say they would meet him on the 9:00 am ferry. Paul said they should meet him at the pedestrian walk-on area. They said good-bye, and Paul offered to walk Rachelle home. She lived up on Prospect Street in a little house at the top.

Paul had walked Rachelle home from the restaurant a few times after closing during the past year. He could never understand why it never went further than wonderful talks, walks home, and even her sitting down with him at Z Pita when he was alone, which was often. She usually stayed up front at Z Pita and decorated the place during the holidays. It was Joey who constantly walked around and around to make sure everyone was happy and the staff was working.

Z Pita had become a local favorite because of Joey Z. It was not just about the good food and good service. He had turned the place into something very comfortable. He was famous for constantly walking around the two sides of the restaurant making sure everything was going smoothly not only with the customers but with the service. Even his business card, which said ATHENS TO ROME underneath his trademark Z Pita logo, had the words "a friend you haven't met" underneath his name on the card. He had turned 217 Main Street into a place to come back to over and over again. The word *owner* used to be on the card, but when he gave Rachelle 3 percent ownership to stay on, he was respectful to update his card to say *host*. Joey Z, with

Rachelle's help, kept the standards high.

"I believe," Paul said, "you writing about this will help put an end to this quickly." Paul gave Rachelle a quick hug as they walked up the hill to her home, as if to say, "I'll keep you warm." Rachelle liked Paul and was comfortable with him. She always felt safe around him, knowing he was a marksman with a 9mm Glock.

"Why are you so interested in this?" Rachelle asked Paul.

"It's my nature as a cop," he replied. "Plus something isn't right. There's more to this than someone being kidnapped, and besides, you want this town to be safe, don't you? Nothing like this has ever happened since the Belle Terre murders over 20 years ago."

"I suppose so," she replied. "I guess I should be excited about writing the story you want me to do, but I guess I'm a little nervous about it."

"You don't have to do this," Paul answered. "I just thought if you write about it, we may draw whoever is responsible out."

Rachelle laughed and said, "Paul, it's been all over the front pages since it happened."

"True," he replied, "but not including my theory, which I'm going to show you."

They reached the top of Prospect Street too fast for Paul. Paul loved the way the wind brushed Rachelle's hair in front of her eyes. It was almost an awkward moment, but then Rachelle's younger sister Madison opened the door to break it up.

"Hi, Paul! How's it going?"

"Going great, Madison," he said, as he looked at Rachelle.

"Good night," she said, as she hugged him.

Paul thought maybe he was beating a dead horse trying to be more than friends. As he reached the sidewalk he heard Madison's voice from the window. "Good night, Detective Powers. Thank you for walking my sister home." *Clunk,* he heard the window shut. Madison was an interesting character. Her voice tone was half-childish when she thanked him, but he knew her well enough to know she was sincere in her expression. She was Rachelle's younger sister at 26, but 5'9" and a dance instructor, she was in perfect physical condition and always protective of her older sister. She had Rachelle's blue eyes but a totally different personality. She would talk to anyone about anything, maybe because she talked with kids all day and couldn't wait to talk to an adult. Paul walked down the hill to his apartment above Z Pita and was so tired he fell on the bed with his clothes on, turned on the television, and fell asleep within a few minutes.

proved many times during chases how deceptively quick he could be when he had to.

"Let's go, my partner-in-law," Bud yelled at Paul. "The world is a fucking mess, and we have to clean up some of it. Come on. There are assholes out there waiting to make us heroes."

Paul turned to Bud as he closed the bathroom door. "Give me 10 minutes," he said, shaking his head. Paul thought at least Bud would keep him young.

While Paul was in the shower, Bud walked around looking for something to read. He loved to read, because he loved trivia. He always told Paul that all his trivia knowledge was one day going to make him a rich man at one of the game shows. He picked up Paul's CD collection. He laughed as he looked at CDs by Taylor Swift, The Corrs, Jewel, and Pink and began talking out loud to himself. "Cop in homicide, and this is what he listens to? What a disaster." His attention turned to the clothes on the floor. "He's a fucking slob!" As he laughed at his own statement, his eyes moved over to the corner of the room and saw the Ghost Face mask hanging on the coat rack. He smiled and pretended to take out his gun and pointed his finger at the mask. "Go ahead, fuckface, make it easy. You always wore that costume to hide your fat ass. Yeah," Bud laughed at his own jokes and continued to amuse himself as he walked throughout Paul's apartment. He found more CDs on his bureau and had a comment for every one. Jewel: "She's hot"; Pink: "Wouldn't want to get in a fight with you, baby"; The Corrs: "Don't know you but would like to," as he looked a little closer at the three sisters. At the bottom of the pile he found Olivia Newton-John and shook his head in disbelief.

As Paul came out of the bathroom with a towel wrapped around his waist, Bud held up the Olivia Newton-John CD and said, "You have got to be kidding me, man. What's this about?"

Paul just shook his head and said, "When is the last time you heard her music? There's some stuff she's done you'd be surprised at. I don't think anyone sold more music than her in the '80s, so respect that."

"Yeah, yeah, yeah," Bud replied. "Man, I'm so jealous of your chest, look at you," he said, as he went toward Paul.

"Stay away, you freak," Paul snapped. "You are one crazy guy." Bud laughed as there was a knock downstairs.

Bud yelled, "Come on up." It was Rachelle, and she came up and was surprised to see Bud there.

"Oh, I'm sorry, Paul. I thought it was just you."

"It's OK," Paul replied. "What can I do for you?" He still had only his towel on, so Rachelle was a little distracted, never having realized the good shape he was in. Detective Powers, at 29, was in peak physical condition. He worked out four times a week when it was possible, and when he did, it was intense. Paul was 6'3" and 200 pounds, with a six-pack stomach, and Rachelle was having a difficult time staying focused. Dark hair, blue eyes, and full lips made the scar on the left side of Paul's cheek barely noticeable. The scar was from an altercation with a drunk who had suddenly pulled a knife on him and caught him on the side of his face. It was a mistake he would never make again.

Madison ran up the stairs yelling for Rachelle to hurry up. "I've got to go!" she said, mounting the stairs. "Oh!" she said, noticing Paul.

Bud, still holding up the CD, yelled, "What the fuck is this, Grand Central?"

Paul held up his hand, saying, "Wait, hold on, Rachelle. I'm sorry, Bud seems to create a circus wherever he goes."

Rachelle seemed a little overwhelmed from Madison wanting to leave. She smiled and said, "Listen, I wanted to speak to you about Saturday, but there's no time. Let me see you later. Is it OK to stop by later?"

Paul smiled and said, "I'll be downstairs for dinner. Sit with me, and we can talk."

"Oh," she replied, looking a little disappointed.

"OK. I'll see you later," Paul said, turning to get dressed.

Just then there was another knock. It was Joey Z, who opened the door and yelled up the stairs, "Hey, Paul, if you don't mind, the fire marshal is here. Can he take a look upstairs?"

"What the fuck?" Bud said. "This place is a damn zoo. I'm leaving. I'll wait for you in the car. And get some fucking clothes on, will

Thursday, June 9

It was 8:06 on the digital clock when Paul opened his eyes. His gaze roamed his apartment as he lay there. He thought it was a pretty decent bachelor pad. Originally it was two small apartments when Paul had moved in five years earlier, but after two tenants in the other apartment had payment problems in quick succession, Paul suggested to Joey Z that if he made it one large apartment, he would stay for five years. Joey liked how conscientious Paul was in paying his rent, and having a regular customer in the restaurant who was a cop was only icing on the cake. It was safe to say that Joey Z considered Paul a man he could trust. He quickly revised the apartment to suit Paul.

As Paul continued to adjust his eyes and convince himself to get up, he looked at all the things in his room that shaped his personality. The CDs on his bureau consisted of Taylor Swift, Pink, Jewel, The Corrs, and Olivia Newton-John. He liked female voices when listening to music. He found he relaxed and enjoyed the songs more than when listening to a male voice. The photos on his bedside table were of his mom, who had passed away when he was 28, and his dad, who was forced to retire as a senior buyer at Woolworth when they closed the stores down in 1997. His father was full of anger when he lost his job at 48 and had to start over in middle management at K-Mart, where he worked until he was 60.

His dad, Anthony Powers, always liked to tell the story of what he felt destroyed Woolworth. He had planned to attend the stockholders meeting when the new upper management changed the name to Venator, which means *hunter* in Latin and a type of Roman gladiator. This proved to be a disaster, and eventually the name was changed to Foot Locker, after one of its successful specialty stores, in November 2001. Anthony Powers was a proud man, and it hurt him greatly to watch what was once a great company be completely ruined by "outside" management brought in by the chairman. Anthony claimed if he had the talent and patience, he would write a book of not only the fall of Woolworth but its secrets that lay dormant to this day.

Lying there in bed, Paul thought maybe arranging an interview with his dad and Rachelle might be good to facilitate a possible article for her to write and to allow his Dad to get things off his chest. But then again, it had been well over a decade, so maybe it was something to leave alone. Besides, would anyone really care, anyway? His eyes rolled over the far wall to a shirt hanging upside down from the corner of a picture, his pants on the floor from the day before. The coat stand in the corner of his room had the famous Ghost Face mask hanging from it. He loved horror movies and had received the mask as a gift on a routine visit to Fun World after a local Dunkin Donuts was robbed by someone wearing the mask. It was there that he met the owners, who were gracious enough to give him a souvenir. Paul smiled, thinking that he had no idea where his coat was, but he never took his mask off the rack.

He got up to take a shower, when he heard the knock and entrance of Bud Johnson, his partner of two years and a guy he had disliked immensely when he was first assigned to him. Bud grew on Paul, and even though his personality and looks reminded him of the actor Jack Black, in fact, if you put his photo next to one of Jack Black, the resemblance was uncanny. Paul respected his work ethic and considered Bud a man of great integrity. The only flaw Paul had to get used to was Bud's language. He had the vocabulary of a truck driver, but somehow it fit him. Paul watched his language and rarely used profanity. His father raised him with the belief that the most intelligent people in the world never curse. It was something Paul never forgot and was conscientious about into adulthood.

"Hey , my partner!" Bud yelled as he ran up the stairs. Paul was five feet from the bathroom when Bud greeted him with a big bear hug. Paul learned to just smile and accept that this was Bud. Full of life, humor, half the time singing lyrics to songs that somehow he remembered with ease. He could hear a song from the past and tell you the artist and the year it was a hit. Once in a while he was off by a year or two, but it was rare. Bud was a bit chunky at 5'11 and 220 pounds, but he could still run with the rest of the slim guys. He ya?" he said as he pointed at Paul.

As he went down the stairs Madison said, "He's kind of cute for a chubby guy."

"Come on, Madison," Rachelle said as she grabbed her by the arm.

Paul smiled at Rachelle and said, "See you later." Then he yelled down to Joey Z, "Let me get dressed, and you can bring him up, Joey. I've got to get to work." He got dressed and ran down the stairs, and Joey went up with the fire marshal. He jumped in the unmarked police cruiser with Bud at the wheel.

"What's going on?" Bud asked. "You got a fucking social club going on."

Paul replied, "It's quiet, really, it just seems to change whenever you're around."

"What's up with the girls?" Bud came back with. "Rachelle's sister is a cute one—tall, firm, nice ass."

"Stop!" Paul yelled.

"And Rachelle," Bud went on, "you have no clue. She wanted to stop by later, and you tell her you'll see her downstairs when you have dinner? You're working too much."

"She's a friend," Paul answered.

"Yeah, and you are an ass," Bud replied.

"Let's drop it," Paul answered.

Bud just shook his head and turned on the radio. Paul's thoughts were on Rachelle. He liked her, but his problem was he was afraid of rejection. If she didn't have the same feelings, their friendship would never be the same. He didn't want to lose that. He loved how hardworking she was, between working at Z Pita, writing articles, and holding a mortgage for a home. She co-owned the house with Madison. They had lost their parents to lung cancer three years earlier. First their father, then their mother one year later. The sisters both worried about eventually getting lung cancer, but their parents' doctor told them their mom and dad had died of smoker's cancer, the result of smoking for years.

Paul's thoughts were interrupted when Bud started singing a song by Lady Gaga when it came on the radio. It was something he loved to do with her songs. He just liked to sing, period. It seemed he knew all the words to so many songs. Paul was OK with Lady Gaga, but he thought he would like her better if Bud wasn't so crazy about her.

They reached the precinct in Yaphank, and Kevin Cronin, the precinct detective lieutenant, was waiting for them. "Get in here," he said, waving to Paul and Bud. As they entered Detective Lieutenant Cronin's office, he didn't even wait for the door to shut behind them. "Paul, I know we spoke about this before, but I want to reaffirm to stay off the Lance kidnapping case. Thanks to the FBI, we have enough problems." It bothered Cronin that Paul just stood there without saying anything. As he continued to speak about the status of active cases, he knew Paul well enough to know that was going to be an issue.

"What's up? Let's hear it."

"I know how they pulled it off," Paul replied. Detective Lieutenant Cronin stood up and said, "Who are they?"

"That, I don't know yet," Paul replied, "but I rode the ferry five times since the kidnapping, and there is only one way it could have been done."

Cronin looked at Bud. "And you? I guess you know about this?"

"Nah," Bud replied. "I'm only his partner. This is the first time I'm hearing anything about this."

"OK, sure," Cronin replied. "Stay away from this," he said, looking at Paul.

Paul left the office without assenting to the directive, and Cronin recognized it. He respected Paul's instincts and thought he would give him a little time and see how this would play out for a few days.

"Bud, go take Paul to breakfast and see what's going on."

Bud answered back, "No problem. It's my favorite meal of the day."

"Always a comedian," was Cronin's answer. "Don't forget about the bad guys!"

Bud and Paul drove to the local Coram Diner because there wasn't enough time to go to Bud's favorite place for breakfast, Maureen's Kitchen. Paul ordered a cup of coffee and a bagel while Bud got a four-egg-white omelet with a side of sausage and bacon.

Paul looked at what he had and said, "Why don't you get a side order of a rack of lamb with that?"

Without missing a beat, Bud answered, "No, no, no, I'm on a diet. You know, you can come to me if you want to know where the best food is."

Paul sat there shaking his head as Bud went on about food. "Maureen's Kitchen for breakfast, except for the whole-wheat pancakes, which are the best at the Station Coffee House in Port Jefferson Station. One of the servers there—Brittany is her name, but I call her Sunshine—is the nicest young lady who can make anyone smile.

Paul tried to interrupt. "Are you finished?"

"No," Bud replied. "I can't forget about the Greek Salad at Z Pita." Paul began to laugh, as Bud was on a roll. "Café Spiga in Mount Sinai has the best Italian food and they have this female singer on the weekends with such a beautiful voice."

"Her name is Cathy" Paul replied, "And she is the daughter of the owner Leonora, who is a great lady, always walking around checking to see how everyone is doing. The Giordano family has done a great job with the place"

Bud seemed surprised that Paul knew of the place.

"You really are an expert when it comes to female singers, you are a strange dude Paul Powers."

Paul was amused and said. "Yes, and you are definitely the food expert, but this explains why you have so much gas in your system." There was no comment from Bud as he just smiled and took a sip of his coffee.

There was silence for a few seconds until Bud spoke again. "Seriously, Paul, what the shit is going on? I know you're up to something. We have a job to do, and you're distracted with something else. Let me tell you, we need to discuss it, and don't tell me not to worry about it, because I am. You never know when you need your partner to have your back, and if you're falling in love with this chick, just move in on her and get it over with."

He was going on when Paul interrupted him and said, "Bud, listen it's not the girl, it's the Lance kidnapping. I'm sure I know how they pulled it off, and I'm going to show a few friends Saturday. I want Rachelle to write about it in her paper. We need to put the heat on them."

"Whoa, partner," Bud exclaimed. "This is FBI shit. Don't get involved with this fucking mess, man!"

"Bud," Paul replied, "I just can't. I just don't think it will get resolved unless I get involved. The FBI is not sharing anything with us, and quite frankly I think she's still here on Long Island and would not be shocked if she's in the Port Jefferson area."

"Come on," Bud replied. "OK, listen, I'm in. I want to see your theory and keep an eye on you. This FBI agent Jack O'Connor can be a prick, especially if he finds out we're poking around." Bud had a puzzled look on his face. "Are there any cops that are not fucking Irish?"

"I guess it's in our blood," Paul replied. "Come on," he added, "I've got a ton of paperwork to do."

When they got back to the station, Detective Lieutenant Cronin called Bud into his office.

"Are things OK?" he asked Bud.

"He's fine," Bud replied. "Don't worry about a thing. He's got me for backup," he added as he left the office.

"That's what I'm worried about," Cronin said out loud to no one but himself.

Rachelle thanked Madison with a kiss and an "I love you" as she got out of the car to her *Now* office. They always had a close relationship, but it had gotten even closer when their parents died within a year of each other. They never said goodbye on the phone or in person without an "I love you." Rachelle loved writing for the *Port Jefferson Now* paper, and she loved Z Pita. She felt blessed doing two things that she loved to do. Her boss at *Now*, Steven Anderson, was a good boss and treated her well. She always waved to his glass wall as she walked by, and he always greeted her with a smile and a wave. But today he waved at her to come into his office.

"Yes, Mr. Anderson?" she said as she came in.

"Rachelle, I have an assignment that I think is perfect for you. You wrote such a beautiful piece about Port Jefferson history that included the Revolutionary War period that we think it would be a great read to have an article about Philadelphia, 'the Birthplace of Freedom,' and how there is any correlation with the war and the founders, if any, with Port Jefferson. I want you to feel it and live it. Which means you would have to stay in Philly over the July 4th holiday and not only write about the history but the events going on down there."

"It sounds great!" Rachelle replied. "Let me check with the restaurant to see if Joey Z has it covered with me gone for a few days. I assume I can bring someone with me on this trip?"

"Yes, yes, of course," Anderson replied. "Let me know in the next week or so." Rachelle went to her cubicle and, as she sat down, a big smile came across her face. *Philadelphia*, she thought. She had read about it, the most historic square mile in the United States, and to stay there for a few days with all expenses paid sounded exciting to her. The first person she called was Madison.

"That's wonderful. Let's talk later. I'm in the middle of class. Love you," Madison said, and then there was a *click* as she hung up. Rachelle sat down at her computer and started writing about Timothy's' Bar and Grill. She had been there many times with it being so close to Z Pita, she thought it was time to write an article for Timothy. The article was finished within an hour. She called Timothy's Bar and Grill "the place to be for casual drink and food, especially for burgers and fries." Rachelle credited the success of the bar to Tim's hard work and enthusiasm to have a fun, casual place for "talk, dining, and drinking." The row of flat-screen TVs across the bar was a favorite for those who became regulars. Some nights you could not get in, and other nights it was a comfortable, quiet place for a conversation.

She gave the article to her editor and left to walk the half-mile back to Z Pita to get ready for the lunch crowd. As fate would have it, Rachelle was five minutes into the walk when she heard a car horn. She turned around, and Timothy had already pulled his Kona Blue Mustang convertible to the curb. He said, "I know you're going my way."

Rachelle laughed and got into the car. "What a gorgeous car," she exclaimed. "This color, I've never seen a blue like it."

"Thank you, Miss Robinson," Tim replied. He pulled up to the curb between Z Pita and Timothy's Bar and Grill, right in front of Yogo Delish Frozen Yogurt, and as Rachelle was getting out of the car, Timothy went for it. "Rachelle, would you like to have dinner with me sometime?"

"Well," Rachelle replied, "I think that would be nice. Let's try and set it up sometime between all the work."

"Call ya next week," Timothy replied, with a look of relief on his face. Rachelle walked away with a smile that turned into confusion as she entered Z Pita. Timothy drove to the back parking lot, known as "Trader's Cove," and walked to Timothy's Bar and Grill. At 32 years old, Timothy Mann was feeling good about himself.

Friday, June 10, 6:00 pm

Paul walked downstairs, out the back door, turned right, walked about 25 yards, and turned right again into a small alley that eventually led him to the sidewalk on East Main Street. He turned right again and reached the front door of Z Pita to have dinner. It would be easier if he just walked through the kitchen when he came downstairs from the apartment, but that was a big no-no with Joey Z. He would have no part of casual walk-throughs his kitchen. Rebecca, the young hostess, was on duty for the evening and gave Paul his standard table in the room, which was table three. Within minutes Tina came by to take his order.

Out of nowhere, Rachelle jumped quickly into the other chair at the table, with her huge smile and said, "No date tonight?"

Paul smiled and said, "You're always working." He was shocked he said it, and Rachelle was taken by surprise.

Oh, this certainly has been an interesting day, she thought, reflecting on Timothy asking her out and now the humorous remark by Paul. "Friends make safe dates," Rachelle replied.

"Yes, that was what I was thinking," Paul shot back.

Rachelle wanted to change the subject and asked, "What are you having for dinner?"

He answered, "The black bean wrap with grilled salmon and artichoke hearts." It was his creation and favorite dish. Joey even put it on the menu as "The Powers Special." It came with sweet potato fries, and the meal did pretty well with the patrons. "Are you ready for tomorrow?" Paul asked her.

Rachelle answered, "All set, my friend. See you at 10:00 am."

"OK," he answered, "I'll say good night before I leave." Rachelle was working until 11:00 pm. Normally Joey Z would close the place, but Rachelle was taking most of the day off on Saturday for the ferry ride to Connecticut and back. Paul ate his dinner and was amazed at how busy the place got. Z Pita had an extremely loyal following in the local community. He grew to be very fond of the servers in the restaurant during the past few years, from Tina to Rebecca to Donna to Bobby and the rest of the staff, and still Joey Z always gave credit to Rachelle on her hiring practices. Tina served his dinner and asked a trivia question as she did, and Paul told her he wanted her to meet Bud.

"He is the trivia master, and you two would have a good time," he said.

"Bring him in," Tina replied. She had met Bud many times when he was with Paul, but the conversation had never gone beyond normal cordial greetings.

Paul finished his meal and said good night to everyone, including Rachelle. He wanted to hug her good night, but his shyness and insecurity got the best of him. As he walked out the front door, his thoughts went to the next day. It was time to put some pressure on the case. There was a woman who had been held in captivity for almost a week, and nothing was happening…at least as far as he knew.

As he walked around the back of Z Pita, he could smell the food being cooked in the restaurant. He climbed the stairs, got to his room, and pushed the voice-message playback. It was Bud, and he was singing the lyrics to "Always On my Mind" and then stopped to leave his message: "Sorry, it's all I could think of. I don't recall the lyrics to Jewel, Olivia Newton-John, or any of the other female singers you love. I'll pick you up at 9:30 am, my partner. I told Detective Lieutenant Cronin we will report in around 2:00 pm tomorrow, that we have a lead. Somehow I'm not sure he believes me, but I'm with you, friend." Paul heard the *click,* and the answering machine said, "End of messages." He smiled and went into the bathroom to wash up for the night.

Saturday, June 11

Bud kept his word and came up the stairs at 9:30 am. "Don't you lock your door? Shit, anybody can just open up and make themselves right at home."

"Yeah, yeah, yeah," was Paul's reply. "You worry about everything." Bud and Paul walked down to the ferry, and there was Allan, Timothy, and Rachelle already waiting for them by the pedestrian area for walk-ons. It was easier to be a walk-on than deal with the long line of vehicles that always filled up the ferry, plus it was a lot less expensive.

They all got on the boat and Paul immediately brought Bud, Timothy, Allan, and Rachelle to the lower vehicle deck to watch the cars drive onto the ferry. They all were quiet as Paul stated his theory. "OK, look at the cars loading onto the massive boat. The attendant is giving directions on when to stop. Look at the woman in the Honda. Watch her get out of the car. Look at everyone around her. No one is paying attention to her. I would also be willing to bet she doesn't have a reservation like most people, that's the key. All they're concerned with upstairs in the purser's office is that the vehicle is paid for before you leave the ferry. Now, let's follow her. You'll find she'll go to the purser's office and pay for the ticket." Within minutes the woman they were following went to the window and pulled out her credit card.

"They have her name," Timothy said.

"Yes," Paul answered "but not if she had paid in cash."

"What does that have to do with kidnapping her?" Bud interjected.

"Patience," Paul answered. "What would happen if and when they got her near the car they dragged her, threw her in the trunk and had an accomplice drive her car off the ferry? No one would know the difference."

"Come on," Allan replied.

"I'll prove it to you," Paul replied. He looked at Rachelle, who was taking all of this in. "Rachelle, write this theory in the paper and say we are going to reenact it on the ferry."

"I can't do that," Rachelle remarked. "The ferry will not allow it, first of all, but I can write something that may put a scare in the kidnappers."

Paul answered, "We know Debbie was on the boat, her father watched her drive over the ramp on to the boat. I think it would be helpful to us if we take a look at the possible scenario. If its in the paper, it may or may not give the kidnappers pause or doubt. If not, at least we made public a security risk on the ferry. It may be a long shot but they may even get sloppy or even release her knowing we have figured out how they did it. That is if they haven't already killed her. The ferry reached Connecticut, and the four of them got off and then went back on the return ferry to Port Jefferson." Paul began thinking out loud as they were going back to Port Jefferson. "Why bring her to Connecticut? She had to be on Long Island."

"Hey," Bud interrupted his thoughts. "The FBI told us she was going to a concert."

"We need to know more," Paul replied. "Something isn't right. We have to get involved somehow."

"And I have to get a burger," Bud replied. "Hey, Rachelle, how are the burgers at Z Pita?"

She laughed and said, "You are a funny guy, Bud Johnson."

"Yes, that's what they tell me. Right, Paul?"

As the boat docked at Port Jefferson, Paul could hear that laugh of Timothy's again. He looked over and he saw him put his arm around Rachelle for a second, which caused his heart to skip a beat.

"You are fucked up," Bud said, looking at Paul. "You're going to let this guy move in on her?"

"We're just friends," Paul said as he looked away at the Long Island Sound.

"There is nothing better than being in and out of bed with a friend," Bud replied. "Don't make me lose respect for you," he said as he walked away.

Paul grabbed his arm. "What's that supposed to mean?"

"I know you, Paul; that's all I should have to say. Get some rest; starting tomorrow we have the late shift for a week."

Paul walked over to Rachelle, Tim, and Allan. "Timothy, please keep your eyes and ears open in the bar, especially once Rachelle's article is printed," he said. "Allan, I stand by what I said about whomever did this is local. Just be aware, and keep your eyes open."

"OK," Allan said, "but I'm not sure why you have me involved."

"Because I've known you for over 20 years, and I trust you, that's why," Paul replied as he hugged him. They walked off the boat, and Paul could see Tim and Rachelle walking ahead, as if they wanted privacy. Paul got the message and stopped for a minute as if he was waiting for Bud. As he walked slowly, Bud caught up to him and said goodbye.

Paul had a chance to see how beautiful Port Jefferson was. There was no comparison between it and Bridgeport, the other destination of the ferry. Although he had lived there for many years, he never tired of the village and it always gave him pleasure to just stop and look around. One day he counted 24 restaurants within a two-minute walk from Z Pita. He didn't remember why he had the time to find out, but he always remembered that number.

Paul reached the top of the stairs above Z Pita, when his cell phone rang. It was Detective Lieutenant Cronin asking him to stop by the office. There were some things to be discussed. Before he left to go to the office, he sent Rachelle a text that he would see her the next Saturday at the ferry and to please get her article printed for Tuesday's edition. Rachelle received the text downstairs and was puzzled by the distant nature of Paul's words, but answered him and said OK. Paul just shook his head and, as he lay on his bed, decided he needed an attitude adjustment with Rachelle before he destroyed a wonderful friendship. It was difficult, but Paul forced himself off the bed to drive back to the precinct.

William Lance was by the phone waiting for instructions about his daughter. It had to be about the money. Lance was a self-made millionaire who had started and then sold a chain of 8:15 convenience stores. They were like 7-11 stores, except 7-11 is open 24 hours a day. The 8:15 stores were like an office convenience store. Everything for your business needs with the hours 8:15 am to 8:15 pm. It was a huge success and quickly grew to 24 locations all over Long Island in 20 years. He sold the 8:15 convenient stores for $47 million, then went on to become Suffolk County executive. He retired at 55 and bought the famous Pink Mansion up in Belle Terre once owned by a famous Contessa.

Special agent Jack O'Connor was with Lance and had been very accessible during the week that had gone by. He also knew that the likelihood of getting Debbie Lance back was unlikely. The kidnappers didn't seem to be in a hurry to get this wrapped up, even for the money. Debbie's car was found a mile from the Bridgeport Cross Island Ferry, which meant that from the time she drove off the boat, she was kidnapped within five to twelve minutes of driving off the dock. O'Connor questioned William Lance hard about why he was targeted. Someone close, on the inside, had to be involved. Everything was moving so slowly.

O'Connor's thoughts were interrupted when a call came in from a Connecticut number. O'Connor used his hands as a countdown to William Lance as to when to pick up the phone. Five, four, three, it seemed forever as Lance watched his fingers count down to one, so O'Connor's team could get in place.

"Hello," Lance answered the phone.

In a voice that sounded like a cross between John Tesh and Vincent Price, the reply was, "Three million dollars by Sunday, June 19th to be left in the trunk of a car that will be on the ferry's 10:00 am boat to Bridgeport, the George Washington. There will be a yellow Honda Accord on the ferry. We will get the key to you during the week. You will drive on the boat, get out, find the yellow Honda, open the trunk, and put the money in the trunk. When the ferry arrives in Bridgeport, you will drive off the ferry and drive back to Long Island. Do you have any questions?"

"Ah," Lance replied, "how do I get my daughter back, and I can't liquidate $3 million worth of cash so fast. Please give me more time."

The calm, evil voice on the other end replied, "You will get her back, dead or alive. You have until the 19th, no more. It depends on whether your friends at the FBI decide how involved they want to be. If we see them on the ferry, you will get your daughter back dead, guaranteed."

There was silence on Lance's end. "That's right," said the caller. "You don't think I know the FBI is involved with this? New York to Connecticut ferry? Give me a break. We will get a key to you." The line went dead.

O'Connor's cell phone rang, and the man on the other end told him the call had been traced to a McDonald's on Boston Post Road in in Orange, Connecticut.

"Wait," Lance yelled at O'Connor. "Are you trying to get my daughter killed?"

"Listen," O'Connor answered, "her only hope is if we find them. If you pay this ransom, I don't think you will get her back alive. The more time that goes by, the less likely this will work out."

Lance just sat down and put his hands over his face. O'Connor hesitated and sat down next to him and asked, "Is there anything you're not telling me? We need to know everything if we're going to save her. What happened to her mother?"

"We divorced when Deborah was six; she lived with her mom until her mother got sick. She was 13 when she lost her mother and has been with me ever since. She graduated from Stony Brook University and has been a teacher at Mount Sinai Schools for only a year."

"Why her?" asked O'Connor. "There has to be more to this than money."

"Excuse me, sir, dinner will be served in 10 minutes."

"Thank you, Robert," Lance said as O'Connor looked at William Lance's assistant, Robert Simpson. He was muscular, good-looking, and 37 years of age, though he looked younger.

"How long has he worked for you?"

"Twelve years," replied Lance. "I trust him with my life, and he loves Deborah. He would never hurt her. He's almost as torn up about this as I am."

"Mr. Lance," O'Connor replied, "can you get ahold of three million in cash by Sunday, June 19th? Eight days from now?"

"Yes, I could get it tomorrow," he replied. "I've always worried about what's been going on in this country, so I keep cash aside on the property."

"Three million in cash?" O'Connor replied.

"Yes," Lance answered.

"And how would they know to ask for three million? Tell me. What are you not telling me or forgetting to tell me? Who knows about the cash being hidden somewhere on the property? Also, if you had the cash on the property, how did you know to ask for more time?"

"Three people," answered Lance. "Deborah, myself, and Robert, and it was Detective Powers who told me to delay and ask for more time."

"Why does Simpson know about the cash?" O'Connor asked.

"In case anything happened to us. I wanted him to have it." O'Connor looked even more puzzled and had a look on his face that told the former Suffolk County executive that he thought he was an asshole without even saying it.

"Did you do a background check on him 12 years ago?"

"Yes, of course," Lance replied.

"Show it to me. Besides, we're going to check it out ourselves. As for the cash, are you sure it's still there? Check it out, and do it now." He called for Agent Summers, who was in the next room. "Let's get the guys together and get a plan on what we're going to do on the 19th."

Paul arrived at the precinct and immediately went into Detective Lieutenant Cronin's office. "Where's Bud?" Cronin asked before Paul even shut the door.

"Not sure. We said goodbye in Port Jefferson this afternoon. We have the late shift all next week."

"What cases are you working on?" Cronin replied.

"No murders in the past 32 days, so we've been working on a couple of cold cases from 2004 and 2006."

"Keep me posted. I may have you and Bud help out on a couple of robbery crimes if they need it within the week."

"What about the Lance kidnapping?" Paul replied.

"What about it?" Cronin replied.

"The FBI is going nowhere and…"

"And what ?" Cronin interrupted him. "Paul, you are a good cop, but stay away before you get all of us in trouble. She's in Connecticut, across state lines, and there has been no murder."

"How do we know there is no murder?" Paul shot back.

"Dismissed," Cronin replied. Paul just stood there until Cronin looked up at him with a look as if to say "What are you still doing here?"

As Paul opened the door to leave, he said, "She's in Port Jefferson, not Connecticut," then shut the door just in time because Detective Lieutenant Cronin jumped out of his seat and was at the door within seconds.

He yelled in the squad room for everyone to hear. "Get your smart ass back in my office now!" Paul stared at him, dropped his papers, and slowly walked back to his office. "Shut the door!" Cronin bellowed. "Explain yourself before I send you home for good."

"Detective Lieutenant," Paul replied, "she is in Port Jefferson, somewhere."

"Do you have proof?" Cronin replied.

"No, but I will very soon."

"What are you doing?" Cronin replied. "No, wait, I don't want to know. Are you breaking any laws?"

"No," Paul replied. "Give me one week, I will prove within seven days the kidnappers are from this area. Everything went down too smoothly. Just give me a week." Cronin stared at him and gave him his famous stern look that no one liked to see.

"Paul, you have one week. Keep Bud in the loop, and make sure you keep him around for backup. Most important, stay away from the FBI."

"Yes, sir." Paul replied.

"Dismissed again," Cronin replied. "And this time, no remarks when you're walking through my door. Go home, enjoy tomorrow. You have a long week ahead of you."

Sunday, June 12

Seven Days Until Ransom Due

Rachelle sat down at her computer Sunday morning and wrote about the theory of the Lance kidnapping. The headline read "The Port Jefferson Kidnapping—Local Police Detective's Theory." She wrote about Paul's theory on how they kidnapped Debbie and how they got away with it. She wrote about how the Cross Island Ferry never checked vehicles getting on or off the boat and never checked bags from pedestrians walking on or off, not to mention metal detectors for guns and bombs.

She wrote how Debbie Lance drove onto the ferry, was most likely thrown into a trunk of another car, and another person drove her car off the boat and left it on the side of the road in Connecticut. Whoever kidnapped her, paid for her vehicle in cash, allowing anyone to drive it off the boat. With no reservation, there were no names, and there would not be proof if her father had not witnessed her car loading on the ferry. All they cared about was that the number of vehicles on the boat matched the number of tickets sold on the boat. Rachelle criticized the security of the ferry to the extent that she demanded that security cameras and a security system be put in place to avoid this kind of event from happening again. The ferry had what looked like cameras on the boat, but no video was recorded the day Deborah disappeared. She continued writing to tell her readers she would be on the boat Saturday to reenact what local officers believed was how the kidnappers pulled it off. She surprised herself because she had just told Paul she couldn't write it, but she did just that. As she put the finishing touches on the article, she sent Paul a text asking if she could stop up at the apartment before she started work at Z Pita. He replied right away to stop over.

She arrived at Paul's door, knocked, and ran up the stairs. She greeted Paul with a hug and said, "I'm sorry to stop over. I know you didn't think you would see me for a week."

Paul laughed. "Don't be silly, Rachelle. What's up?"

"Please read my article and tell me if anything comes to your mind." He sat down and read. Her writing was so precise and so descriptive he felt like anyone reading it would feel like they were a witness to it.

"Nice," Paul said. "Lets see what happens, if anything. Maybe something, maybe nothing,but I have a feeling something will happen.

"Paul," Rachelle replied, "I know what you mean, but if this goes to print for Tuesday's edition and people from the Cross Island Ferry read this, what's to prevent them from stopping us from doing this reenactment? The kidnappers have already accomplished what they wanted. They have Debbie Lance."

Paul thought about it for a moment and suggested that it would be impossible for the ferry to make adjustments within four days. He said, "I wouldn't be surprised if they're already making adjustments, Rachelle. They know something occurred on the boat, and they're going to try and fix it fast to avoid the criticism. Now your article will be the icing on the cake. They have Debbie, but I want them to think I know what happen. I want to put doubt in their mind before they kill her"

"So, you're fine with this?" Rachelle replied.

"Yes," Paul answered, "it will be fine. It's time to ruffle some feathers. Besides, your article may even save her life if she's not already dead. If they know we're on to them, they may hold off killing her to avoid a murder rap."

Rachelle paused, looking at Paul, and replied, "Will I see you later downstairs for dinner so we can talk more about this?"

"Yes, of course," Paul replied. He gave Rachelle a hug and whispered in her ear, "Everything will be fine. See you in a couple hours." He kissed her forehead, which surprised Rachelle. She felt close to him and she didn't want to leave, but she ran down the stairs to typeset the article. Paul looked around the apartment as he stood alone and spoke out loud: "Things are going to change around this town very soon."

Rachelle finished up her article and made it in to Z Pita by 4:00

pm to prepare for the Sunday dinner crowd. Joey Z was ready to leave when she got in to relieve him. Joey Z was a man of 59 years of age who was one of the hardest-working men Rachelle had ever seen. He bought the restaurant known as Z Pita 20 years prior. It was Port Jefferson's first firehouse station which is why it had a historic landmark plaque on the sidewalk in front of it. Joey Z had also purchased the building that housed the other famous bar in town, Billie's, well known for its oversized drinks and burgers. He was rich in real estate but always complained about the hours he worked. After a while, everyone took his complaints with a grain of salt. They all knew he loved coming to his restaurant, and the customers appreciated seeing him constantly walking around to be sure everything was going smoothly with both customers and the employees. He taught Rachelle to be the same way, and she was, with few exceptions. When she saw someone she knew, like Paul or Madison, she would sit with them for a few minutes before their meal was served.

Rachelle checked the reservations and the tables requested and made sure table three was left open for Paul at 6:00 pm.

Paul arrived at 6:05 pm, and Rachelle sat with him for 15 minutes before his food was brought to the table. It was the first time in quite a while that they spoke about things other than the kidnapping. She had the most beautiful smile to Paul. He wasn't long into his dinner when Timothy walked into the restaurant and was going over his and Rachelle's schedules to get together. Paul tried to ignore it and looked down at his dinner when Rachelle walked over to him. Tim looked over at Paul and gave him a wave, and Paul gave a meek smile in return. Paul left a note for Rachelle to call him when she was ready to walk up the hill to Prospect. She didn't get out until 11:00 pm, and it was a chance to see her again. Plus he figured if something was going on with Tim, she wouldn't call him anyway. At 11:10 he got a call from her, and he met her at the back door as she was locking up. It took less than 10 minutes to walk her home, and again there was Madison. As usual, as he walked away, she said, "Thank you, Officer Powers, for taking care of my sister."

As the door closed behind her, Madison looked at Rachelle and asked, "What's going on with you two?"

"We're just friends," Rachelle replied. "Besides, Timothy asked me out."

"Oh, good," Madison replied. "Then you wouldn't mind if I gave Officer Powers a go?"

As she started to walk away, Rachelle grabbed her hand and with a tear in her eye said, "Please don't, not now."

Madison looked puzzled but said, "OK, but there is a time limit, big sister."

Rachelle smiled and said, "Well, at least you know who the older one is."

Monday, June 13

Six Days Until Ransom Due

Rachelle received an email from Steven Anderson at about 8:30 am praising her article. It was going to press, and it would be on the front page of the *Port Jefferson Now* paper for Tuesday's edition. Her ambition and desire to be what she described as a "real" writer was only challenged by the fact that she actually and truly enjoyed working at Z Pita and felt she also had a future there with Joey Z from the way he treated her. He let her do whatever she desired in the casual eatery, with his easygoing personality. There was never a problem when she wanted to put a woman's touch in the place. She never mentioned it, but her thoughts would not let her forget that she also enjoyed the human interaction with the customers, particularly the regulars.

She laughed to herself when she thought that maybe she should write a book on the things that had happened with customers at Z Pita alone. She never knew what was going to happen once the day began. Most customers were terrific and polite; however, there were always a few that went against the grain. The staff had always been carefully selected, and it showed. The regulars had told Rachelle that dining at Z Pita for 15 years or more, there was never a long wait to get someone's attention for help. Between the young staff and the experienced staff of Tina, Rebecca, Melissa, Emily, and Bobby, not to mention Joey Z walking around, it was difficult to find a reason to complain. Rachelle continued to laugh as she found herself trying to convince herself that she wanted Z Pita in her life as well as a writing career. Her thoughts were broken by a phone call from Timothy.

"Hello, beautiful Rachelle," she heard as she answered the call.

"Hi there," Rachelle answered.

"How's your day going?" he asked.

"Well, since it's only 9:00 am, I would say not bad," she laughed.

"Well, good," he replied. "I was just calling to see if we can work something out this week to get together, maybe tomorrow night to celebrate your article coming out?"

"Umm," she replied. "I can't tomorrow night, but why don't you come into the restaurant tomorrow morning and we can look at our schedules. I'm sorry I didn't have time earlier, but it was hectic at work."

"Sounds like a plan; no worries," Tim answered.

Rachelle disconnected the call and turned on the television to relax a bit before taking a shower. She surfed the channels until she found Suze Orman. She loved learning from Suze and found it very amusing to watch people try to get her approval for a $10,000 vacation. Her iPhone rang again, and it was Joey Z seeing if she could make it in by 11:00 that morning. He had an unexpected problem at his house, and he was adamant about who was in the restaurant when he wasn't there.

Rachelle pushed the button to end the call and spoke to the television. "Sorry, Suze, I will see the end of your show one day." She jumped in the shower and made it to Z Pita by 10:30.

Rachelle's day always went quickly when she was at the restaurant. Being the hostess/manager and seeing the regulars during the day made a 10-hour day seem like five hours. The weekdays were mostly supported by the regulars, while the weekends saw more out of towners.However, what Rachelle liked best about Joey Z was that if any of the regulars wanted a table on the weekend, he would work them in, no matter what. This particular day, Rachelle had a chance to see many regulars, such as Dennis and Mary Ann, Steven and Julie, and Cassie and Matt. A day like Monday at Z Pita would give Rachelle the conflicted feelings she had about what she wanted from life. As those feelings continued to give her pause, Paul walked in, which startled Rachelle, who promptly dropped the dishes she was carrying.

Tuesday, June 14

The *Port Jefferson Now* paper came out with the theory behind the kidnapping on the front page, and it resulted in many compliments and calls to the *Now* office, including one from the editors of *Newsday*, Long Island's biggest paper, which had one of the biggest circulations in the United States. It also caught the eye of John Winters, a strapping six-foot muscular 48-year-old man who lived up on Thompson Street. He called his brother Mason, who lived next door, to come over. Mason was over within minutes.

John threw the paper at him when he walked in and yelled, "Who's talking?"

Mason looked at the front page and said, "What do you mean? This is a guess, a theory."

"Really ?" John replied. "They also got most of it right! Some theory! Get the group together and have them meet us tonight at Timothy's Bar and Grill for a few drinks."

"How about dinner at the Village Way?" Mason asked.

"What are you, fucking crazy? We won't be able to hear ourselves talk if they're having karaoke night," said John.

"OK, OK," Mason replied. "8:00 pm, Timothy's Bar and Grill."

John read the article three times. He had heard of Rachelle Robinson before but had never paid much attention to her. He decided he would give her attention now. The article named Detectives Powers and Johnson but did not name the two locals who would be involved in doing the reenactment Saturday on the ferry. Mason called Wayne Starfield, his brother Kyle Winters, and Phil Smith to meet them at Timothy's Bar and Grill at 8:00.

Starfield replied, "Who's with the girl if I come?"

"Tie her to the bedposts tight. You'll only be gone for about an hour."

As 8:00 approached, Wayne tied Debbie to the posts and whispered in her ear, "I'll be gone for about an hour. If I come back and it looks like you made any attempts to escape, I'll slowly take your clothes off and rape you until dawn in every which way. Do you understand?"

Debbie, shaking, nodded her head in acknowledgement, whimpering in terrifying cries that were muffled by the heavy cloth tied over her mouth. William Lance's daughter was so terrified of being raped and tortured she was not going to attempt anything.

The appointed hour of 8:00 came quickly. John and Mason walked in to see Starfield and Phil waiting for them at almost the exact table Paul spoke to Rachelle, Timothy, and Allan the week before.

"Have you read this?" John asked as he sat down. "The whole town is talking about this."

"Yes," Starfield answered, "but there's nothing we can really do about it."

"The hell we can't," John replied. "The article is close to what happened. If we don't stop her, she could lead everyone to us." The crowd at the bar interrupted their discussion with loud laughter and high fives.

"What's going on?" John asked the waiter.

"Timothy, the owner, is one of the locals written about in the paper in regards to the Lance Kidnapping, and he's telling customers some fun theories," the waiter answered. John's eyes widened as he looked back at his table of friends. "We should pay him a visit tonight," he said.

Sitting at the table, if anyone paid attention to them, they looked like a bunch of rowdy characters from a movie. Starfield was 5'5," missing teeth, and had long blond hair and beard. Phil Smith, although 5'8," had a menacing look with a heavy mustache and long black hair. John, at 6'4," was husky with a potbelly but was clearly the leader by his body language. Mason, the younger brother, was 5'9" and thin, with short blond hair. He was no match for John intellectually or physically. Phil took a sip of beer as he stared at John.

"Why are we here in a public place discussing this instead of your house." Although it was a question it didn't sound like one by the sound of his voice. John resented the comment and gave Phil a returned stare that had daggers in his eyes

"Because I like the beer here, and besides, look what we learned about Timothy over there just by being here." They had a couple more beers before leaving for the evening.

Timothy closed up the bar at 1:00 am, which was normal for a Wednesday night. As he got to his car, he pulled out his keys and heard a noise. As he turned around he was tackled. On top of him was the famous mask from the movies, but it was different. It was silver, and it was wrinkled. Tim was subdued by two others, who also had the same—but different—mask. One was gray with cracks in the mask, and the other was a straw-looking Ghost Face.

"What do you know?" came the voices behind the silver wrinkled Ghost Face mask. Timothy could not speak fast enough for them, because he was going into shock. The silver wrinkled Ghost Face mask came down and stabbed him in the stomach.

"So," one of the attackers stated, "you think you know everything about the kidnapping?"

As Timothy lay there with blood starting to come from his mouth, the three attackers ran off as their sick laughter filled the night. Timothy pressed his OnStar button from his key ring, and within minutes the police and ambulance were there.

Paul and Bud heard the call on their radio and rushed to Mather Hospital to meet the victim. When they brought him in, Paul was shocked to see it was Tim. They rushed him to surgery but it was too late, Timothy had bled out. Bud grabbed the ambulance attendant and the first officer on the scene.

"What did he say?" Paul asked, walking up to the trio.

"He kept saying, 'Ghost Face mask, wrinkled, kidnapping, Zombie, Scarecrow' over and over again," ambulance driver said.

Bud looked at Paul. "What the fuck? Why? What does Ghost Face have to do with kidnapping?"

Paul replied, "We're going to find out." The detective put his hand on his forehead clearly upset over the murder of Timothy. His thoughts were interrupted by his partner.

"Shit," Bud replied. "I don't want to get involved with this Ghost Face crap. What does 'wrinkled' mean?" Paul left the hospital with Bud behind him.

"I have to tell Rachelle and Allan first thing tomorrow that we're going to speak to the makers of the mask."

It was 2:30 am when Paul rang the doorbell to Rachelle and Madison's home. Madison answered, and by the look on Paul's face, all she could say was, "What happened?"

"Please," Paul said, "get Rachelle."

Rachelle came out in her bathrobe and held on to Paul as Bud stood by. "Rachelle, Timothy has been killed," Paul said.

Rachelle covered her face with her hands and started crying. "What happened? Why?"

"He kept saying, 'Wrinkled Ghost Face, zombie, kidnapping' over and over."

"I don't understand," Rachelle replied as the tears flowed. Madison was holding her from behind.

"It's possible the kidnappers responded to the article and found him."

"I never used his name," Rachelle yelled, as tears flowed even more.

"All right," Madison said. "Please, let me take care of her."

Madison took Rachelle to bed and came back out to Paul. "anything else? Is my sister in danger?"

"I'm not sure yet," said Paul. "This is odd, but then this whole case has been odd from the beginning. She never mentioned his name in the article, yet the day the article is published he's killed. There has to be a connection somewhere. I'll be in touch. I'll pick Rachelle up in the morning for work."

"I don't think she'll be going to work tomorrow," Madison said. "She may have a few things on her mind."

"OK," Paul replied. "Call me if she decides to go out."

They left the house, and it was Bud's turn to vent. "Fucking almighty. Just what we need. This will be all over the country. Ghost Face returns to Port Jefferson. I can see it now!"

"Bud," Paul replied, "it's a mask connection."

Bud said, "Movies, TV, commercials. Why can't this be a normal case? That mask scares the hell out of me!"

Paul's cell phone rang. It was Detective Lieutenant Cronin. He said, "See me first thing in the morning. I want to know how you're going to handle this. You better have some answers because the FBI will be here in the morning." The phone went dead without even a goodbye.

Wednesday, June 15

Four Days Until Ransom Due

Jack O'Connor was at Detective Lieutenant Cronin's office at 9:00 am. "I see your men have bankers' hours," he said to Cronin.

Cronin knew that there were issues with Paul and Bud, but he wasn't going to take grief from an FBI agent. "They were on the job from 3:00 pm 'til 3:00 am yesterday, and quite frankly if you guys had solved this case sooner, we wouldn't be having this meeting this morning, would we?"

Although Cronin was in his late forties and had a decent-sized muffin top over his belt buckle, he was very intimidating at 6'4", with white hair, blue eyes, and the map of Ireland all over his face. He had been through so many close calls during his career that nothing really shook him up anymore. He still had a piece of a bullet in his face from a past assignment. Many famous killers over the past 20 years had been caught by him and his homicide squad, including the Long Island Sniper.

O'Connor took Cronin's remark as a cue to get some more coffee and wait for Powers and Johnson. At 11:00 Bud and Paul arrived in Cronin's office. O'Connor walked in without losing a beat.

"Well, congratulations! You had an article published and managed to get an innocent person killed," O'Connor sniped.

Bud replied, "Screw you, asswipe."

O'Connor looked at Johnson then at Cronin. "Very professional crew you have."

Then he turned his attention back to Bud and Paul. "Cut the shit, Detective. I don't want to hear it," he said. "You two clowns may have cost a life while we are getting ready to pay a ransom in four days to try to end this." He began to talk again when he saw Johnson silently mouthing the words "Fuck you, fuck." "Excuse me?" O'Connor yelled at Cronin. "Your detective is still unprofessional here, saying 'fuck you' to me."

"Sorry," Cronin said, "I didn't hear a thing. Continue, please."

O'Connor continued on with the plan for Sunday. "The drop is at the Cross Island Ferry, after a key is delivered to the Pink House in Belle Terre by FedEx from an office in Connecticut."

Paul sat silently as O'Connor continued to talk. "We will not have more than two agents on board. We cannot afford to be spotted, or we will lose Lance's daughter, if we haven't already. We will have agents in Connecticut on the other side watching to see where the car is driven to. I'm only telling you this out of courtesy and because it seems you can't stay out of this." He looked at Paul. "Nothing to say Detective?"

"You do what you have to do. We'll do what we have to do," Paul replied.

"And what is that?" O'Connor said, raising his voice. Paul stood up and looked at Cronin then at Agent O'Connor.

"We have a murder now. It's my case. You do what you have to do, and we'll try and stay out of your way. But please stay out of our way ." Paul walked out as O'Connor looked at Cronin.

"That's it. You guys have no idea what you're doing." Bud walked by O'Connor with a quick "Bite me" remark and walked out behind Paul. O'Connor stayed behind in Cronin's office.

"We're done here," Cronin said. "For now. You find the kidnappers, we'll find the killers. Hopefully they'll be the same people, and we can save some tax dollars for the public."

Paul got into the unmarked cruiser while Bud got in behind the wheel. "Where to, my partner?"

"Let's go to Fun World, Carle Place, Long Island," Paul said. On the way, he called Rachelle to see how she was holding up. She was home and thanked him for calling.

"Can I check on you later?" Paul asked.

"I hope you do," Rachelle replied.

Bud and Paul got on the Long Island Expressway, then took exit 42 and arrived at Fun World within 45 minutes. They walked into the vestibule, where they saw framed posters of the movies that had featured Ghost Face as well as television shows the mask appeared in.

"Ah!" Bud said. "The famous gold Ghost Face bust." He wanted to rub it to make a wish, but it was under glass. The receptionist called Albert and Steven Goldberg to tell them that Suffolk detectives were waiting for them. In five minutes both Goldbergs came down and invited the detectives to the conference room, where they could have some privacy. Paul explained they had a new murder on their hands and that the victim kept repeating "Ghost Face, wrinkled, zombie." Paul added that he was aware of a new zombie version from shopping in stores, that was released a couple years before, but would they know what he meant by "wrinkled"?

Albert and Steven looked at each other and called Roger Thompson, the licensing director, and told him to bring all the versions of the Ghost Face masks down to the conference room. Thompson came down and was introduced to the detectives; then he presented the versions of the mask to them. Zombie, Scarecrow, the original famous version, and a silver wrinkled version that was called Mummy Ghost Face.

Paul picked up the wrinkled one. "Tell me about this one," he said. Roger told him it was the newest version, currently only available at Spirit stores.

Paul said, "We have reason to believe that this version of the mask was involved in a murder last night as well as the Zombie and Scarecrow versions. It will be in the papers tomorrow. We asked them to hold off for 24 hours so we could get a head start on what's going on."

The Goldbergs were concerned over the information. Steven, the president, was an 86-year-old legend in the business. His son, Albert, was considered the future senior of the company and responsible for all of Halloween. Roger, as the licensing director, had been involved with the Goldbergs for the past 16 years in regard to the licensing and all the negotiations between the company and the studio responsible for the movies.

"Can we take these masks with us?" Paul asked.

"Certainly," the elder Goldberg replied.

The detectives got back in the car, this time with Paul behind the wheel. He threw the masks on Bud's lap as he turned the car on.

"Get the fuck away," Bud said as he threw the masks to the backseat. "I can't stand this shit. No one is wearing them, and they still make me drop a load in my pants."

"Why Timothy?" Paul spoke out loud. "Let's go to Timothy's Bar and Grill."

They got back on the expressway and were back in Port Jefferson in 45 minutes. They walked into Timothy's Bar and Grill, where it was very quiet out of respect for the loss. His silent partner, Ben Cooper, was behind the bar, and there were only four customers in the bar.

Paul flashed his badge at Ben and said, "Tell me what you know."

"I can't believe it. He's gone just like that."

"What was going on last night? Were you here?"

As Paul was talking to Cooper, Bud was looking around at 4 others in the bar. He wanted to see if anyone was interested in the conversation going on between Cooper and Paul.

Cooper was wiping down the bar in the same circle until Paul stopped him. Cooper said, "Tim was here last night working the bar. I stopped by to check in, and there was a crowd around him buying drinks like crazy. He was telling the story of the article and how he was one of the people Rachelle was writing about. He was telling people how well he knew her and that they would be dating."

Paul was taken aback by the remark. "Did he mention any other names?" Paul asked.

"Yes, he mentioned some other guy named Allan." Paul turned around quickly and started running for the door. Bud followed and got in the car as Paul drove up to Belle Terre while Bud tried to reach Allan on the phone. They drove up East Main Street to Belle Terre Road. They reached the security building, and Paul ran in to the building. There was Allan, eating a sandwich, startled by the entrance Paul and Bud made.

"What the hell?" Allan asked.

"Are you OK?" Paul replied.

"Just eating a sandwich, minding my own business, and you two cowboys come right in."

"Allan," Paul answered, "Timothy was killed late last night in the parking lot behind his bar." Allan dropped his sandwich. "He identified himself as the unknown local who went on the ferry trip to prove the theory as to what happened. He also mentioned your name. No last name, but he did say Allan. You have to be careful. Tim had no idea the level they would go to. Now we know." Allan was still stunned, shaking his head.

"Rachelle," Allan said. "Is she all right?"

"She's pretty upset," Bud replied. "We'll have to watch her."

"What about Saturday? Are we still on?"

"Yes," Paul replied, "but not you and Rachelle. The FBI will help us with this. The murder has convinced me they are here locally."

"What are you talking about?" Bud asked.

"It's all adding up," Paul said. "I'll show you Saturday. Let's go see Rachelle." They said their goodbyes and were over at Rachelle's in two minutes.

Rachelle answered the door in an oversized T-shirt, and she looked stunning to Paul. No makeup, no pants, no shoes, and to him she was the sexiest, most beautiful woman he had ever seen.

"How are you doing?" he asked as she walked away from the door, leaving it open to invite them in.

"I'm OK," she replied. She turned around with her arms folded. "What can I do for you?" she asked. Bud looked at Paul, surprised by the distance in her tone.

Paul paused to gather his thoughts and then said, "Listen, Rachelle, I don't think it's a good idea for you to come Saturday. It's apparent that whoever killed Tim believes you may know who they are, and I think it would be safer."

"Excuse me," Rachelle interrupted Paul before he could finish. "You listen. I'm not going to let this interfere with my responsibilities. This is a story. I feel terrible about Timothy, but I did not name him in my story."

Bud replied, "Tim spoke at the bar. He wanted his patrons to know it was him and Allan."

"See," Rachelle said.

Paul interjected, "The point is, whoever killed Tim knows you're the writer, Rachelle."

"Yes," Rachelle said, "and they know you and Bud are the cops, and if they followed you around now, they know where I live." Rachelle gave Paul an icy stare that even surprised him. It was clear that

Rachelle was confused over her feelings about Paul, the loss of Timothy and how this case would affect their relationship.

"I'm sorry," Paul said. "I came here because I'm concerned about you."

"Don't be," she replied. "Please leave me alone." They started to leave, and as Paul and Bud got to the door, she spoke again, saying, "I'll be there Saturday. You got me into this, and now I'm not quitting. I have a story to write for next week's paper, and I need to be better than *Newsday*. I'm writing this, not them."

"Rachelle," Paul said, but the door had already closed behind them. Paul looked back at Bud, who was shaking his head.

"Just thank your lucky stars you're not sleeping with her, my friend, because if you were, you would be hurting more than you already are."

"I am hurting," Paul replied. "and I wonder if I should order her as a cop not to show up" He sat down in the passenger seat instead of getting behind the wheel.

Bud put his hand through the window on Paul's shoulder and said, "That's the price you pay for having a good heart my friend," Bud looked back at the house before turning to Paul again. "remember, you are the one who wanted this, if you think you are going to tell a woman what to do then you still have much to learn when it comes to things like this. Besides, I think she wants to share this with you"

Paul nodded in appreciation to Bud as he walked around the car. Both of them were oblivious to Rachelle looking out the side of her window, behind the blinds. No one would ever know that she witnessed the hurt on Paul's face or see the tears streaming down her face.

Thursday, June 16

Three Days Until Ransom Due

The *Newsday* headline for Thursday read: Ghost Face Visits Port Jefferson Village with a Killing. The story detailed the killing of Timothy, Rachelle's article, and the flaws exposing the lack of security on the Cross Island Ferry. It even had the story of Paul and Bud getting involved and the relationship between the murder and the kidnapping of Deborah Lance and the fact that Rachelle's article was the "seed" of stirring things up. The article also went on to expose that there was a relationship between Robert Simpson, the butler, and Deborah Lance. "What the fuck?" Bud said as he read it over breakfast. He called Paul to come downstairs to Z Pita and, as if on cue, Paul sat down by the time his message machine had picked up.

Bud placed the paper down in front of Paul with his finger and said, "Read this shit."

Paul read it and said, "I think it's time we pay Mr. Simpson a visit."

"Agreed," Bud replied. "Let me get something first. I could eat a fucking horse!" Tina came by and took their order as they discussed the article. Even photos of the mummy, zombie and scarecrow masks were shown. Rachelle was also in the restaurant for the morning shift, but she did not come by the table. It was awkward for Paul and Bud, but they wanted to give her space. As they left, Paul said goodbye to Rachelle, and she gave a quick wave to them as if she was just too busy.

Paul was halfway out the door when he came back in and said, "See you tomorrow."

Rachelle returned a half-smile and replied, "OK."

"What's wrong?" Paul asked. "Why are you being like this?"

"I can't discuss it right now," she said.

"Are you going to speak to me?" he asked.

"I don't know," she replied. "Things are getting complicated for me."

Paul nodded in puzzlement and left. As he sat in the car, he said, "I don't understand women anymore. Maybe I don't need them."

Bud looked at him and said, "You into guys?"

"Are you nuts?"

"Sounds like a no to me. Then stop complaining and figure out how the fuck to handle this."

The car pulled out of the spot in front of Starbucks on East Main Street, took a right onto East Broadway as they headed to Belle Terre to the "Pink" mansion. As they passed Danford's on the way to the Pink Mansion, Paul received a call from the morgue that Tim's parents wanted to take his body to Florida, where they lived, so they could visit his grave at their convenience. There would be no funeral in New York or Long Island. His share of the business was also financed from his parents, and it was expected it would be sold to his partner.

They reached the gate to the Pink Mansion, identified themselves, and drove up to the front of the house.

"*She-Devil*," Bud said as they walked up to the front.

"OK," Paul said, "tell me."

Bud started showing his pride in his movie-trivia IQ. "This is the house that was in the 1989 movie *She-Devil*. Remember that, my partner. You'll win a million-dollar trivia question one day."

"OK," Paul said, "I'll try to remember."

The door swung open, and true to his job, it was Robert Simpson who opened it.

"May I help you?" he asked.

"Yes, Mr. Simpson, we need to speak with you."

Paul showed his badge, and as the detectives were about to walk in, the butler stopped them. "I'll be happy to speak to you outside for a few minutes, but not inside the home. I need to be respectful of the family."

"Oh," Bud said. "Respectful, which is why you were banging your boss's daughter."

"That's enough!" Simpson yelled. "There will be no discussion. Get a warrant or allow me to go to my attorney, but that's it."

"What do you need an attorney for?" Paul replied. Simpson stopped for a moment before continuing to the door.

Bud grabbed his arm and whispered in his ear, "Listen, fuckface, if I find out you're involved in this up to your ass, you won't be able to shit the regular way for a long time. You understand me?" Simpson pulled away and shut the door.

"What did you say to him?" Paul asked.

"I told him he smelled terrible."

"Yeah, right," Paul said as they walked away. Paul got on the phone and called Cronin to get Agent O'Connor's number.

"Boss, we need to get together with him again."

"You're seeing him tomorrow," Cronin replied. "Cover it all then."

Paul hung up the phone, and it rang again. This time it was his father asking what was going on and if Paul needed him to visit. He convinced him to stay away until the case was cleaned up, although he wasn't sure for how long.

"Where to Detective Powers?" Bud asked.

"Let's go back to Timothy's Bar and Grill and ask CSU if we got anything on Tim's Mustang. Maybe we got lucky since it happened next to the car. I also want to listen to the tape on the ransom call to the father." CSU was an acronym for Crime Scene Unit and it was common for the cops to use it.

It was what Bud liked a lot about Paul: he wanted to check everything out and rarely forgot anything. They balanced each other out well. Bud had a tendency to take the short cut, while Paul wanted to be certain everything was in order.

They spoke to everyone at the bar and recorded the names of the people there. Paul knew that Tim's murder was not about Rachelle's article. It was about Tim talking too much in reference to the article. He was more concerned about his possible 15 minutes of fame in the local Port Jefferson area than anything else. Paul also felt that the people involved in his murder were at the bar, and the only way they would want him quiet was if they were also involved in the Deborah Lance kidnapping. They left the bar with eight names.

Paul said, "Let's get these names run in the system. Call O'Connor. Let's listen to the tape and let's go back to the mansion to speak to the father. Tell O'Connor he can meet us there if he wants." They were halfway back to the mansion when they remembered Cronin hadn't given them O'Connor's number.

"OK, tomorrow then," Paul said.

As he drove up to the mansion, his thoughts were struggling with Rachelle's behavior and the amount of time that had gone by for the kidnapping. He was conflicted and didn't know what to do about it.

Friday, June 17

Two Days Until Ransom Due

Z Pita was very busy for a Friday business day, and it was insane for Rachelle. She loved staying busy and had the first smile of her day when Madison walked in with a hug. They sat and had coffee for 20 minutes and got caught up with girl talk. Madison was good at listening to Rachelle vent about everything, and she knew she was becoming overwhelmed with the job at the paper, Z Pita responsibilities, and the killing of Timothy.

"Tell me," she said to Rachelle, "what else?"

Rachelle just blurted out, "I don't want to be alone. I'm frightened of going through life and waking up one day and saying, 'Why didn't I take a chance at something'"

Madison looked at her, held her hands, and said, "Something or someone?"

Rachelle's eyes began tearing up again. "This damn period," she said. They both started laughing. It was quickly interrupted when Bobby came over to her to tell her that it looked like there was a water leak upstairs in Paul's apartment.

"Oh, shit," Rachelle said. "I've got to check it out. Oh, wait! Madison, come with me. I need a witness I didn't do anything other than check the problem."

Madison laughed and said, "OK, no worries."

They went upstairs, and Rachelle opened the door. The apartment was in good shape compared to other times she had been in there. Paul was a typical single male, not quite the slob she thought most guys were but still not to her liking, especially the pictures on the walls.

"OK," she said. "Bathroom time."

"That's your job," Madison said. "I'm your witness, but I draw the line going into a single guy's bathroom. It totally grosses me out."

Rachelle checked the tub, and there was no problem. She went back to the kitchen area and opened up the cabinet underneath the sink and found the pipes leaking. She called an emergency-service plumber and then called Paul's cell phone, which went straight to voice mail.

"Hi, Paul," Rachelle said. "You have a plumbing problem with your pipes. I called for service. Call me when you can." *Click.*

When Paul finally did pick it up, he thought, *OK, this is our relationship.* They had known each other for three years and had become close in every way except physically. Yet this murder was going to put distance between them.

Paul and Bud returned to the mansion, and when the butler Roger Simpson answered the door again, he had a smirk on his face. Paul showed his badge again and asked to see William Lance.

The voice behind Simpson said, "Let them in."

Simpson looked disappointed but replied, "Yes, sir."

Paul walked past Simpson, ignoring him. However, Bud did not do the same. "Asswipe," he said to Simpson as he walked by, then changed his whole facial expression as he greeted William Lance.

"Can we go somewhere private?" Paul asked. They went to Mr. Lance's private den, and Paul opened up a notebook. He rattled off question after question. Mr. Lance was very cooperative. Paul moved from questions about Debbie and started to dig into her relationship with Robert Simpson.

Lance said, "There was nothing I could do about the relationship. Robert has been invaluable to me since he was hired on 12 years ago. Deborah was 14 years old at the time, and he was 25. She went from loving him at age 12 to being in love with him by the time she was 16. Both of them promised me nothing would get intimate until she moved out of the house at 18 for college. It seems like an age gap, and it was at the time, but now she's 26 and he's 37. He is irreplaceable to me and to Deborah."

"Mr. Lance," Paul asked, "is there any chance in your mind that Robert is involved in her kidnapping to extort money from you?"

Lance shook his head. "No way. They've been in love for years; there's no advantage or motive for him to be involved."

"Did you speak with *Newsday*?"

"No," Lance replied.

Paul kept hitting him with question after question. He answered all his inquiries immediately until Paul asked about the tape of the ransom demand.

"Do you have a tape of the call?" he asked. Silence. "Mr. Lance," Paul pushed, "please answer the question."

"Agent O'Connor has it," Lance replied.

"I want to listen to the tape," Powers replied, with his voice stronger. Lance picked up his cell phone and started pushing buttons.

"Agent O'Connor, hold on please," he said, and handed his phone to Paul.

"OK," Paul said, "tomorrow then." He gave the phone back to William Lance. He looked over at Bud and explained they would listen to it the next day after the ferry trip.

As they got ready to leave and got close to the door, Bud turned back to Mr. Lance and said, "One last question. If your butler was not involved in any way, then why won't he talk to us?" Lance stood up and walked out with them to the vestibule.

"Robert," he called to him. "Please answer the detective's questions."

"Of course," he replied.

Paul said, "I would like you to tell us where you have been in the past week every night, plus give me your cell phone number."

"Give them what they want, Robert. I'll say my goodbyes now. Gentlemen, please help bring my daughter back to me." William Lance shook their hands and left, leaving Robert alone with the detectives. Once the father of Deborah Lance reached his office, his emotions took over and he began to cry for his daughter.

"Please," Paul said, "have a seat and give us the information." Robert sat down in the side room and started writing. Bud couldn't help but notice how Robert Simpson kept looking up at them while he was writing.

Bud looked over at Paul and, in a soft tone, said, "Looks like the butler is nervous."

Simpson overheard him and stood up yelling, "Personal assistant! I am his personal assistant! I am not a butler!"

Bud moved in closer until Paul stopped him. "Touchy," Bud said.

"Please finish the information requested, Mr. Simpson," Paul said.

"I will," came his reply, "but I want him outside," he said, pointing at Detective Johnson. Paul pointed for Bud to leave, and he did. Robert Simpson finished writing down his whereabouts for the past week and included his cell phone number.

As Paul walked out and Simpson went to close the door, Bud stopped it, saying, "I'll be watching you, shithead—count on it. Have a nice day." Then Bud smiled, put on his sunglasses, and walked toward the car.

As Robert walked toward the kitchen, William Lance was in the hallway waiting for him. He asked, "Robert is there anything I need to know that you haven't told me?"

"No, sir," Robert replied. "I want her back safe and sound as much as you do."

Lance walked away to his den, and once Robert reached the kitchen, he sat down at the table and covered his face with his hands.

Paul checked his voice mail and asked Bud to make a stop at his apartment. When he got there, there was a note from Rachelle:

Paul, your pipes were leaking water down to the restaurant. I had to have a plumbing service come right away. Any questions, ask Joey Z. I'm not at the restaurant 'til Saturday afternoon. Rachelle

He crumpled up the note and tried to throw it in his wastebasket. He rarely missed, but today he did. He ran back downstairs, ran around the front, and spoke to Joey Z for a few minutes. Within 10 minutes he was back in the car with Bud.

"We got a call from the boss," Bud said. "We have to get back to the precinct." Paul's thoughts were with the note Rachelle had left him. He was disappointed with what was happening.

Wayne Starfield opened up the refrigerator and looked for something to eat. Not because he was hungry but because he was bored. He shut the door and went into the bedroom. There she was, Debbie Lance, sitting in the corner of the room with her arm handcuffed to the bottom rail of the bed. The blindfold was on her, and even though she could free herself of the blindfold with her other arm, she was too frightened to do so. Wayne told her if she removed it he would have to kill her but not before he raped her for 24 hours. There was no way she would take the chance, so she listened to what she was told. Wayne was the caretaker of Debbie, and the four others involved were never in the house unless she was sleeping. There was no way they wanted their voices heard. Wayne was considered the crazy one of the bunch and was easily the best choice to keep an eye on Debbie. The leader, John Winters, also knew that Wayne was not attached to her, but he was definitely attracted to her.

As he approached Debbie, Wayne looked at her long, thin legs. "Hello, my pretty," he said, touching her breasts.

"Please," she whimpered. "I've done everything you asked me to. Please."

Wayne stopped but couldn't resist licking the side of her face. She was too frightened to wipe off his saliva while he was there.

"You know," he said to her, "there's a part of me that wishes you were not such a good girl. That way I could just eat you alive, if you know what I mean."

"Please," Debbie came back. "Don't hit me, I'll listen. I will always be good for you."

"Too bad," he shot back. "I really would enjoy punishing you, but then again maybe you would enjoy it too."

"You promised," Debbie said. "Please don't break your promise. I'll be good."

"Hmmmm," he replied with disappointment. "Well, we have a couple days. Let's see how you behave. Good night, my sweet!"

"Wait, please let me go to the bathroom."

"OK," he replied. "But the blindfold stays on, which means I have to help you," he said, as he let out a little laugh.

Wayne Starfield had a Napoleon complex. He could deal with most things except comments about how short he was. Any comment, whether serious or humorous, would change his attitude about anyone. His teeth were in terrible shape, for he was always afraid to go to the dentist. The condition of his teeth, his unruly hair, and his weight for his height made him look much older than his 40 years. Debbie had no choice but to lean on Wayne for help as he took her to the bathroom. He led her to the toilet, and she requested he leave, which he did, but he couldn't help but watch through the crack of the door. Debbie was not sure if he was completely gone or not, but she felt losing her dignity was better than risking losing her life by removing the blindfold. She flushed and heard his voice a few seconds later.

"Knock, knock, my pretty. Are you finished going tinkle?" he asked.

Debbie wanted to throw up at the sound of his voice and touch, but there was barely anything in her stomach to regurgitate. She had already lost four pounds on her thin 5'6," 110-pound frame. She had been sick a few years prior and had dropped her weight to 99 pounds, which made her look anorexic. It was a time when she had stomach problems, and Robert had helped her through it.

As Debbie left the bathroom, her thoughts went to her father. William Lance was always very protective of his daughter, who he called Deborah. He did not take chances while Deborah was growing up. Robert took her to and from school as well as maintained the house staff and was there at Mr. Lance's beck and call.

Deborah had a crush on Robert from the day he entered their lives. Robert thought she was adorable at 13, pretty at 15, and controlled his affection when she was 16. On her 17th birthday, she reminded Robert how much she wanted him to be the first. He reminded her he worked for her father and that she wasn't 18. She pursued him so aggressively that, during her 17th year, she would tell him repeatedly that New York state law recognized 17-year-olds as old enough to give consensual sex, but he held true.

When she turned 18 she wasted no time going to his bedroom. He could no longer hold back his love for her and promised her they would always be together. They shared the bond after she turned 18 but decided they would not tell her father until she moved to the dorm at Stony Brook University. She would stay on campus and come home for the weekends.

Although Stony Brook was only 25 minutes away from Belle Terre, Deborah wanted some freedom living at the school during the week. Her father was at first upset about the relationship with

Robert, but Deborah convinced him she was 18, and she thought he would be more comfortable with Robert in the family than someone else. He accepted the relationship as long as it did not interfere with Robert's responsibilities as his assistant. Robert never let him down. In fact, he excelled at his job and seemed content both professionally and personally.

William thought highly of Robert, but he wanted to be sure it wasn't his fortune that was the object of his affection. As the years passed, he felt comfortable that Robert loved his daughter for who she was. It was interesting to see the transition of the relationship from her protector to her loved one. Deborah was very popular through high school, but she never showed interest in the boys. It was Robert that she wanted. Her girlfriends would tease her about all the broken hearts there were because of Robert Simpson.

She had many girlfriends, but there was one who was her best friend, Patty Saunders. Patty met Deborah at Port Jefferson High School in the ninth grade, and they hit it off immediately because of their love of sports, good-looking guys, movies, and music. It seemed they had the same taste in everything. It was Patty who heard all Debbie's problems, as well as the good things, as they matured and entered the adult world.

William Lance sent Deborah to public school, even though he could have easily afforded private school. He felt it was overrated and wanted Deborah to be more down to earth as she grew up. He was very happy with how she had turned out. She excelled in all her classes except for mathematics and graduated from Stony Brook University with a 3.7 GPA. Her passion was to be an English teacher to young children, and Stony Brook had a terrific Education and Teacher Certification program accredited by the National Council for Accreditation of Teacher Education.

While William Lance spoiled his daughter almost to a fault, he felt she was entitled to it as long as she respected money and was good-natured to people, especially those less fortunate than her. During high school, Deborah volunteered at camps for the disabled with Patty and her friends. It was an experience that kept her well grounded. As Deborah fell in love with Robert, it was Patty who was with her, gave her support, and kept her secrets.

Patty herself was no plain Jane. At 5'4," with a well-toned body, she was what most men considered a petite bombshell. Patty always looked out for Deborah, but she had been boy hungry since she was 12 years old. It was anybody's guess when she lost her virginity, and Deborah took criticism for being her best friend, but she had fun times with Patty, with or without the boys. Her sense of humor about men/boys and sex made Debbie laugh so hard at times she could hardly contain herself. She knew Patty had issues, but her attitude was, "Don't we all?"

Double-dating with her was always an adventure. It was always Debbie and Robert, yet it was anybody's guess who Patty would be with. The pool parties were the best, and most guys couldn't keep their eyes off of Patty's small yet perfectly shaped frame. Debbie had no interest in the men Patty enjoyed. She was perfectly content with the man she literally grew up to love.

But now she was in a fight for her life, and as she lay on the bed with one arm shackled to the headboard, seeing only darkness because of the blindfold, all she could think about was her father, Robert, and how much she appreciated life. How much she appreciated her health, her friends, her work. All of this meant so much to her now. She started to pray,

"Dear Lord, I know I have been distant from you, and it seems when things are going well I have ignored you. Please Lord, help me. I will never take you for granted again. I ask of you to help me through this and to allow me to see my family again. I promise I will seek you to be in my life, but Lord I need your help. I know one day my journey will end, but I pray to you that it does not end this way. In the name of the Father, Son, Holy Spirit. Amen."

"Oh, isn't that sweet," Wayne said. He had been standing by, listening to her prayer. "Let me tell you, you pretty little bitch. You better start praying to me for your salvation, because it will be up to me if you are saved or not now!" he screamed. "Pray to me for your life!"

Deborah started shaking and tried to speak, but she was so terrified she wasn't making any sense. Wayne slapped her across the face as she started crying. "Pray to me!" He slapped her again. "Pray to me!" He slapped her again and finally said the magic words to her:

"Pray to me!"

"Please!" she yelped. "Please save me!"

Wayne moved in to slap her again, when his cell phone rang. It played a small Elvis recording that said, "Thank you, thank you very much." She had heard it before when his cell had a call. She could tell it was from someone who was giving him instructions. She didn't care at this point, as long as it stopped him from beating her. She began to pray again.

Paul and Bud arrived at headquarters to see Cronin, and they were met by an officer who told them no stops for anything, including the bathroom, to go straight to his office. They opened the door, and as Cronin looked up, he reached for his remote and turned on CNN and then Fox News. Both were televising the kidnapping and its possible connection to Timothy's murder.

"This is all over the country, detectives. Do you understand why?"

"Yes," Paul replied.

"Tell me," Cronin said.

"The media will use it for all it's worth with the Ghost Face masks involved."

"That's right."

"Um," Bud replied, "I said it first. Ghost Face, fuckface, what's the difference? But I knew this would go national." As Bud looked around at the silent stares he was getting from Cronin and Paul, he spoke again in an awkward tone. "Please, please, boss, continue," he said, as he moved his hand sideways in a friendly gesture.

After glaring at Bud for a few seconds, Cronin spoke again. "All the sickos of the world want to know more because these assholes used these particular masks. Now I have everyone but my mother asking me questions, and that's only because she doesn't like horror movies. Guys, listen to me. We have to push to get this solved. I will have the commissioner and district attorney on my ass within the next 24 hours as to the status. Do your thing on the ferry tomorrow. Let's work with the FBI, pay off the ransom, get Debbie Lance back, and let's get the killers involved with your friend's murder."

Bud just shook his head and replied, "Sounds so easy when you say it like that."

Cronin threw his pencil at Bud and said, "Detective, get it done, or I will find someone who will. You fuck this up, and I will have your badge and then I will beat the living shit out of you."

"Yes, boss," Bud replied as he walked out the door.

"Well?" Cronin said to Paul, who just stood there.

"This will end, boss, but there is more to this that we don't know. When we get back from my theory ride, we need to have Agent O'Connor and the executives of the Cross Island Ferry available. No one knows how to reach them. I suggest you have the district attorney help us with this. We're handling the murder. The FBI is handling the kidnapping, and the Coast Guard wants to know what's going on, since it most likely happened on the Sound."

"So you say," Cronin replied.

"I'll show everyone tomorrow," Paul replied.

"What makes you so sure?" Cronin asked.

"I've been riding the ferry since I was a boy. Tomorrow you'll see the only way they could have pulled this off."

"You're damn right," Cronin replied. "I'm going with you. By the way, we're moving to the sixth precinct to be closer to Port Jefferson Village. Dismissed." It was Paul's cue to leave.

Cronin was a no-nonsense guy with the most dry sense of humor Paul had ever encountered. He was also one of the bravest men he had ever seen. In the line of duty, Cronin was the one you wanted with you if your life was in danger. No one was better at backup or directing a group of fellow officers in an emergency situation. His temper was fierce. He excelled at his ability to get the bad guys.

Cronin was also Bud Johnson's first partner. He knew Bud could be a headcase who hid behind a clown's face at times, but his heart and loyalty to the force and to his partners was too much to ignore, which is why Cronin requested him for headquarters. He also thought Bud was a good match for Paul, a man a little too serious and afraid to bend the rules on occasion, and Bud was a maverick and needed someone to pull him in at times when getting too far outside the box.

Bud drove Paul back to his apartment around 5:30 pm, and Paul asked Bud if he wanted to have dinner with him.

"Sorry, my partner," Bud answered, "hot date tonight. I had

planned to get shitfaced tonight, but with our little trip tomorrow, and now that you've invited the boss, I don't even think I should get laid tonight."

Paul just shook his head with a grin and said goodbye as he got out, adding, "Don't forget to take what you need to work out of the sixth precinct for a while."

Paul went down to Z Pita about 6:30 and was greeted by Rachelle, who led him to table three but did not stay to speak to him. He didn't understand what was happening, but he didn't want to push it. Rebecca came over and took his order. Small talk ensued with people at the next table, and things were normal as Joey Z walked around both sides of the restaurant making sure things were running smoothly.

As he got up to leave the restaurant, Paul noticed Rachelle was in conversation with Rebecca, and he hesitated for a minute to say good night. But it was apparent she had no interest. As he opened the door to leave, he heard a good night from her. He came back in and said, "Thank you for taking care of the plumbing problem."

"No problem," she replied.

"OK," Paul said. "See you tomorrow."

"See you tomorrow," she replied.

He left with his thoughts going a mile a minute. *What, is she an echo tonight?* he thought. Paul walked around the building to his entrance in the back, walked upstairs, and dropped on his back on the bed. Everything in his mind was spinning with changing thoughts. From the kidnapper to the article to the murder to the use of the masks. He covered his face as he wondered if he was in over his head. Normally he would think not, but with all the publicity, he was having doubts about how all this was going to play out. He knew he felt differently because his friendship with Rachelle was changing and he wanted to speak to her about it, but again he held off. His thoughts rehearsed what he thought happened on the Cross Island Ferry over and over again until he drifted off to sleep.

Rachelle closed up Z Pita at 11:00 pm, and it was close to 11:30 pm by the time she locked up. She realized as she took the key out of the door that Paul wasn't there to walk her up the hill to her house. It felt strange, but she didn't want to bother him. Their relationship was changing, and she didn't even remember why anymore. She walked up Prospect Street and made it to her house in seven minutes. As she went to charge her cell phone, she realized she had received a text message. It was from Paul: "Call me if you need a friend to walk you home." She smiled and turned on the television and channel surfed until she saw Suze Orman.

Saturday, June 18

One Day Until Ransom Due

Paul had trouble getting more than a couple hours of sleep at one time throughout the night. His brain was so active rehearsing for the next day and dwelling on how the kidnapping had been pulled off that he could not fall into a deep sleep. He finally got up at 5:00 am to shower and check his emails on his BlackBerry. He was so used to having access to all his emails, it seemed hard to believe it was less than 15 years earlier that technology had been far less advanced and there was not such easy access to communication. He often wondered how the hell anyone got anything done.

He got dressed, sat down at his kitchen table, turned on his BlackBerry, got some paper and a pen, and began to write down everything he wanted to show and explain to Detective Lieutenant Cronin and Agent O'Connor as well as Bud and Rachelle. As his thoughts turned to Rachelle, he checked his BlackBerry. There was a text from her: "Thank you, but get some rest. We should talk." There was a sudden feeling of relief and calm within his body. He felt the difference just from those words. He made up his mind he would talk to her over the weekend. Maybe on Sunday, when hopefully all of this would be behind them.

He continued to write down thought-out bullet points of his theory and how the kidnapping had been pulled off. It crossed his mind that the killers might even be on the ferry to just check out what was going on. After all, Rachelle's article was very clear about when the reenactment would be happening. If only Tim had kept his mouth shut and let this play out, he would still be alive. The only one who gained from his death was his partner at Timothy's Bar and Grill, and there was little chance of his involvement. Ben Cooper already had 80 percent ownership in the bar and had given Timothy equity for his "sweat" in running the place and use of his name for the bar. The sweat equity, as well as Timothy's parents making an investment for their son, made it unlikely Ben Cooper was involved. It was the first time in years that a business survived in that location in the village.

Paul emailed Bud to be certain they had received all the names of those patrons in the bar Wednesday night when Timothy was killed. Credit card transactions and the memory of Ben Cooper was all they had for the time being. The only one Paul knew for sure who would know everyone that was at the Bar that night was Tim and he was gone. The detective shook his head as his thoughts went back to the 9:00 am ferry, and he began to write additional notes. One of his notes was to get the village of Port Jefferson to change their parking-meter program. As of now, the spaces were numbered, and you paid at a central meter by the number, which meant any vehicle could be in the space as long as it was paid for. Paul thought changing the meters to inputting license-plate numbers in the space would not only decrease crime but give the prior records of who was there during a crime, when one occurred. It was a long shot due to the low crime in the village, but he didn't see any negative to revising the meters.

He found himself scribbling the name Rachelle, writing it in different styles on his notepad. He laughed to himself and decided he needed to collect his thoughts and papers for the day ahead. He sent Bud a text to request Officer Davis, a female officer who was the officer who looked the most like Debbie Lance, to drive an additional vehicle onto the ferry behind Bud. He sent Rachelle a text to be sure she remembered she was a "walk-on" at the 9:30 am ferry. He too would be a walk-on with O'Connor and Cronin. He reminded all to pay cash. By paying cash the lack of security was going to be exposed on the ferry once and for all, and he was hoping Rachelle's article and this case would force the ferry to change and update their security procedures. While the ferry did have orange and black signs warning ferry riders of possible K-9 searches, no one that the detectives knew or friends had ever seen or heard that the dogs had been used.

He looked at the clock on the wall in his kitchen, and it was already 7:30. He dropped his pen and headed to the bathroom for his shaver. Bud was already at the precinct at 7:30, waiting for Officer Davis. Victoria Davis had been on the force for five years and was on her way up in the department. Not only was she an outstanding officer, she was well liked by both male and female officers at the precinct, which was a rarity in such a demanding and stressful job. Victoria drove up at 7:45 got out of her car in her civilian clothes and with her hair down.

Bud looked her over and said, "I won't ask where your gun is."

"Watch it," she replied with a smile.

"Let's get some breakfast before our field trip," Bud said. "I'm starving."

"You never change, do you?" laughed Victoria.

She followed him to Port Jefferson Village to the famous Toast breakfast/lunch café that resembled many small food restaurants in the Greenwich Village area of Manhattan. Usually if you got there before 8:00 am you didn't have to wait long for a table. They served alternative choices to the traditional fare, such as Cranberry and Pumpkin White Omelets. The coffee was served in many different kinds and styles of mugs, which gave the place a very different look. The walls were filled with local artists' paintings, which were sold on consignment. The only criticism anyone could think of was that it was a very tight squeeze because the tables were so close together, and it was difficult to have a personal conversation. Most patrons had been pleased when they expanded the space in early 2011.

Bud ordered a grilled turkey, grilled tomato, and spinach egg-white omelet, while Victoria ordered the mango pancakes. The servings hung over the plates, and the food was so good it was difficult not to finish every bite. It had been a while since Bud had talked with Victoria, and as his usual, he interrogated her on her life and work. Victoria liked Bud. If anything, he made her laugh, but she also respected the serious side that he had when it came to catching the bad guys. She had never worked with him on a case, but the stories other officers told her were enough to convince her that they had to be true.

Victoria insisted on paying for half of the meal, including tip. "This is not a date," she giggled.

Bud replied, "My favorite kind of woman; they pay their way."

"Yes, sir."

It was 8:40 am as Bud got in the Ford cruiser and Victoria sat down in her 2004 Sebring convertible. They drove up Prospect, bearing left at the fork, and drove to East Broadway, made the left, and within 300 yards were in the ferry parking lot. The attendant asked Bud if he had reservations. Both Bud and Victoria were told to say no. They were automatically put in a separate line of vehicles waiting. However, the important thing was, as expected, that they were not asked for names or identification. It looked as though there would be more than 65 cars on this ride to Bridgeport.

It was about 20 minutes, during which they sat parked in their cars, before Bud and Victoria spotted Paul, Cronin, O'Connor, and Rachelle walking into the ticket office to pay for walk-ons. It was only five minutes until they came out and began their walk down to the loading area to stand with about 50 other pedestrians waiting. They had paid cash, received their tickets, and Bud watched as they headed for the boat.

Bud called Victoria on her cell phone. "Ready, bitch?" he laughed.

"You are one crazy dude," Victoria replied and hung up. The boat, *John Adams*, pulled up to the dock, and within minutes cars were driving off the ferry. If there was one thing the ferry employees were good at it, was getting the cars off and on as well as positioning the cars on the boat to safely load them. The vehicles that had the reservations were loaded first. Then the other vehicles, including Bud's and Victoria's, were instructed to drive on, and within minutes they were on the top portion of the boat.

"OK," Cronin said to Paul. "The floor is yours."

Paul had rehearsed this with Bud and Victoria and had communicated with Rachelle through email about what would go down. He had wanted to speak to her about a review, but the distance over the past week was giving him pause. Today was different; Rachelle greeted him with a hug and a smile and seemed relieved herself they were going to talk later that day.

Cronin started walking away to view the show, and Agent O'Connor walked to the other side. Paul whispered in Rachelle's ear, and she started walking toward the vehicles on the top deck. O'Connor wouldn't take his eyes off the vehicles and Rachelle going toward them. Meanwhile, Cronin was scanning the people getting out of their cars. He kept asking himself whether there was anyone involved in the killing or kidnapping who would have the courage or dumbness to witness the reenactment based on what Rachelle wrote in the paper. Now that it was all over the news, he doubted it.

He was amazed at how no one paid any attention to anyone else. Someone could have had a bomb underneath their jacket, and no one would have known. He noticed that not one bag or person was searched, even though posted signs stated it was possible. Paul had told him he had been riding the ferry for more than 25 years and had never witnessed a search of any kind. In this day of airport security and talk of invasion of privacy, he was shocked how the Cross Island Ferry was completely the opposite. But then again, nothing had ever happened or at least was never reported to have happened.

Victoria got out of her car as Rachelle walked up to her.

"Excuse me, do you know anything about Bridgeport? I need directions."

Victoria laughed and said, "No GPS, lady?"

Rachelle, keeping in character, said, "No, I don't know how to use those things."

Paul scanned the crowd going into the doors to the main portion of the boat.

Bud came up behind Rachelle and Victoria and said, "Ma'am, you have a problem with your back right tire."

As Victoria went to look, he grabbed her keys and held her as Rachelle took the keys from him and pressed the trunk-release button. Within seconds, Victoria was in the trunk. Cronin continued to scan the crowd. No one was looking, and no one was paying attention. He noticed what looked like possible camera spots, which prompted him to make a note of them. O'Connor, on the other side of the boat, was taking all of this in.

Rachelle got into the backseat of Victoria's 2004 Sebring and asked, "Are you OK, Victoria? Do you have enough air?"

Victoria was calm. "I'm OK, let's play this out."

"OK," Rachelle said. "I'll be here if there are any problems."

Victoria started banging and yelling in the trunk to see if anyone would hear her or even care. Nothing. Bud went upstairs to the purser's office to pay for both cars. Meanwhile, Paul came over to the car, got the keys from Rachelle, and opened the trunk.

He had a squirt gun and put it to Victoria's face, staying in character. He said, "Continue to make noise and have people see or hear you, and I will be forced to put a bullet hole between your beautiful eyes."

Victoria reacted the way she thought Deborah would react, saying, "You're going to kill me anyway."

Paul got closer to her face and said, "All I want is a ransom." Victoria got quiet, and Paul shut the trunk.

"He's a good actor," Victoria said to Rachelle in the backseat. Paul went to find Bud as Agent O'Connor continued to watch them. Cronin watched on the other side but kept scanning the boat for anyone who would or could be possibly watching this unfold. Again, nothing.

Paul found Bud at the food stand and thought to himself, *Where else would he be?* As Bud was putting mustard on his hot pretzel, Paul asked him if any problems had occurred. Bud laughed. "Are you kidding? Now I know why they chose to do it this way."

They went downstairs to the vehicles. As Bud sat in the cruiser, Paul gave Rachelle the car keys and ticket as she got in the driver's seat.

Paul had a thought and went back to the rear of the car and spoke to Victoria through the trunk. "If you're thinking about pulling the emergency trunk release from the inside, I want you to know I'm a pedestrian on the boat. If you pull it and try to get away, I'll have nothing to lose, so I'll shoot you dead and throw your body in the water. Do you understand me?"

Victoria said, "Yes, dickhead, but a bullet makes a noise. I think you should threaten me with a knife."

Paul replied, "I'm sure she didn't say that."

"I know," she replied. "She was probably too terrified to even think about the release."

"OK," he said, as he walked away.

The boat docked into Bridgeport. The Cross Island Ferry workers grabbed the tickets from the windows without even looking at them. As the cars pulled off the boat, Rachelle and Bud were one of the last vehicles to come off. They drove about 200 yards away from the boat down the long straightaway toward downtown Bridgeport. Rachelle and Bud pulled over, and Victoria pulled the hatch to let herself out. They waited about 10 minutes before Paul, Cronin, and O'Connor walked up to them.

"OK," Paul said. "It was about a mile away from here that they found Debbie's Charger. They put her in the second vehicle and took her to the place they're holding her."

"And?" Cronin said.

Paul replied, "They took her back to Port Jefferson."

"I disagree," Agent O'Connor replied. "All the calls made are from Connecticut. They left her car here in Connecticut."

Looking at Cronin, Paul shot back, "You saw what happened and how easy this was. They put her in the trunk of the second car, got back on the ferry, and are holding her where they are comfortable. Besides, they reacted to Rachelle's article, which was in a local paper, and killed Timothy Mann when he opened his mouth about being one of the people involved in the reenactment."

"Speaking of which," Bud replied, "what happened to Allan?"

"I told him to sit this out," Paul replied. "We didn't know Detective Lieutenant Cronin and Agent O'Connor would be here, so I let him stay home with his family."

"Lucky ass," Bud replied.

Agent O'Connor still wasn't convinced but acknowledged Paul had a good theory. They got in their vehicles, turned around, and got in the non-reservation line for the next ferry back to Port Jefferson. They loaded onto the *George Washington* ferry and this time were on the lower level. Detective Lieutenant Cronin, O'Connor, Bud, and Paul were in one vehicle while Rachelle and Victoria were in the Sebring. In the cruiser, Paul started asking O'Connor questions from his list.

"What was Ms. Lance going to Connecticut for?"

O'Connor took out his notepad and answered, "She was going to the Harbor Field Arena to a Cobra Starship concert that evening."

"Who was she going to meet?" Paul asked.

"Her best friend, Patty Saunders," O'Connor shot back, proud that he knew the answer.

"Why meet her? She lives in Port Jefferson also," Paul came back quickly.

"She was visiting relatives in Connecticut and was stopping at the concert hall to meet Debbie."

"So Patty Saunders knows Debbie," Paul replied, "and has relatives in Connecticut? Have you spoken to her since the kidnapping?"

"Yes," O'Connor replied. "She was so shaken up about everything that it's unlikely she's involved. However, we do have an agent watching her house and keeping tabs on her cell phone use. So far, nothing."

"What is her relatives name?" Paul asked.

O'Connor looked at his notepad. "Tangretti, first name Linda."

"Who knew that Debbie Lance was going to be on that exact ferry other then Patty Saunders?" Cronin asked.

O'Connor looked at his notes and started flipping through his pages. He stopped and said, "The father, William Lance, and the butler, Robert Simpson."

Bud said quickly, "Don't call him a butler; he'll have an anxiety attack. He's the assistant."

Cronin got on his cell phone, but quickly found out it did not work on the ferry, and looked toward the backseat at O'Connor. He said, "You should have one of your agents dig into Lance's business affairs." Then, looking at Paul, he said, "Pay a visit to him again."

"By the way," Bud asked, "is Simpson living in the mansion also?"

"No," O'Connor replied, "he's staying in the guesthouse."

"What a sweet deal," Bud replied. "Good job, good security, banging the boss's daughter, who is worth millions. I don't like the guy, but he can't be involved. He's got too good of a thing going."

Cronin looked over at him and said, "I agree with you."

Behind them, in the other vehicle, Victoria and Rachelle were having a different kind of conversation.

"How long have you and Paul been sleeping together?" Victoria asked.

"Excuse me?" Rachelle responded. "We are not sleeping together. We've been friends for a few years, and…well…well, it's getting a little complicated."

"If you're not sleeping together yet, how is it complicated?" Victoria replied. "I see the way you both react to one another, even spending most of my time in the trunk," she laughed. She continued, "Honey, life is over in the blink of an eye. You need to work this out. See what happens, and if it doesn't work out, at least you won't have regrets. Don't be one of those people who will look back and wonder 'What if?'"

Rachelle looked at Victoria and smiled, saying, "You're sweet. Thank you. We're going to talk this afternoon to sort this out. I do care about him, but he's been so slow in everything, and I don't know how to interpret his actions and his lack of expressing himself."

Victoria replied, "Think about the things you've done, the time you've spent together. The phone calls, the dinners."

Rachelle interrupted her, saying, "And the walks."

Victoria just looked at her and said, "Girl, you better do more than just talk or you are going to bust."

As they both laughed, Bud got out of his vehicle and went up to the purser's office and paid cash for both vehicles and gave a ticket receipt to Victoria before settling back into his car.

As the Cross Island Ferry was 15 minutes away from docking in the village, Kyle Winters was standing on the corner of Main Street and East Broadway looking at the statue of the Golden Eagle and the block of granite underneath it that said, IN ALL OUR DAYS WE HAD NEVER SEEN A DAY LIKE THIS 9/11/01. IN MEMORY OF ALL THOSE WE LOST. Long Island was heavily hit with loss of life during 9/11, and memorials were placed throughout the island.

Kyle walked down East Broadway and stopped to look at the statue of the mother with two children on a park bench. It was inscribed, IN MEMORY OF DARLA WHO DIED GIVING LIFE AT THIRTY-SEVEN YEARS. Below the park bench was a quote from Shakespeare: DEATH LIES ON HER LIKE AN UNTIMELY FROST UPON THE SWEETEST FLOWER OF ALL THE FIELD. The statue in front of the Ocean City Bistro was very beautiful and often made people stop to read and wonder about the history behind it. Even people like Kyle Winters.

Kyle was carrying a long box with him as he started to walk behind the Ocean City Bistro building and the slightly taller building behind it with a flat roof. It was a building that looked like eight separate stores from the outside, due to the different signs over each window, but if you walked into one of the doors, you would find it was one store that carried all of the products that were displayed over their windows. They had a giant ice cream cone on the side of the building in front, but interestingly enough, the largest ice cream and confectionary shop on Long Island did not have the name of the store displayed. It was the Port Jefferson Dessert Factory. Apparently the sign had come down and had not been replaced. Kyle walked behind the back of the building into the area that was marked for employee and commercial vehicles. Calm, cool, and collected, he met Phil Smith, who was waiting for him.

Phil said, "Go up these stairs. Once you reach the top of the Ocean City Bistro, take the railing to the top of the Dessert Factory roof. You'll find the perfect spot to take care of Miss Rachelle Robinson."

"Come on up with me so you can hand the box up to me once I reach the top," Kyle said.

They went up the metal stairway, and at the top was an employee door, outside of which were two workers who could not speak English and who did not even seem concerned that there were two guys going onto the roof. They must have seen it quite a few times, with repairmen working on the air ducts. Kyle and Phil made it over to the top of the Ocean City Bistro, and sure enough there was a metal ladder to the top of the Dessert Factory building on the roof. Kyle climbed it, and once he reached the top, Phil pushed the box up to him.

"I'll be waiting in the car for you," Phil said. "Remember what John said—only the girl."

"Yeah, yeah, yeah," Kyle said.

Phil went down to the car and sat in the black Cadillac SRX to await the execution of Rachelle Robinson. John Winters, the leader of this group of thugs, had ordered the hit on her because he was tired of having her articles stir up all the national interest. He didn't like her theories and had hoped that killing Timothy Mann would scare her off, but he had learned that she was writing another article for next week's edition of the *Now* paper from her Twitter account. So he was about to give her something to really write home about, but only from within the gates of heaven.

Kyle lay flat on top of the famous ice cream shop and emptied his box. He pulled out a Browning A-Bolt stainless steel stalker. It was a beautiful weapon with a receiver of stainless steel matte finish, glass bedded with a barrel of stainless steel. John had supplied the rifle to him at Kyle's request, because the firearm was available in left-handed models as well. The rifle was worth more than $1,200, but Kyle didn't care. He was about to collect $20,000 for the takeout.

Kyle wanted to just break her neck one evening, but she was never alone and they could not find where she lived. They checked websites, and all they could come up with was her place of employment at the paper. If they had only known she was at Z Pita almost every night, it would have been more simple. Regardless, John Winters wanted to make a statement before the ransom was paid, and this was his chance.

Kyle lay there on the roof and thought about what he was going to do that night. Not one thought entered his mind that he was going to take a life and change lives forever. He didn't care.

The *George Washington* pulled up to the loading dock in Port Jefferson, and Allan was waiting for Paul and the rest to unload from the boat. Allan never got tired of watching the front of the boat open and seeing the cars unload.

As Kyle got comfortable on top of the roof across the street and adjusted the scope on his rifle, he started to get nervous when he didn't see Rachelle walk off the boat as a pedestrian. No Rachelle. As the cars pulled off the boat, he looked through his scope at the cars. He was lucky that only one car could drive off at a time. Eleven cars had driven off the dock—nothing. Then he spotted the Sebring with two young women inside. He wanted to ensure he didn't miss Rachelle, so he decided to shoot both of them. He fired at the windshield. Rachelle slumped over, and Victoria stopped the car and called for help. Kyle fired again and caught Victoria in the chest. True to her own words, her life was over in the blink of an eye.

Screams could be heard as cars drove away and people ran for cover. Without thinking, Paul ran to the convertible and jumped in, even as Detective Lieutenant Cronin tried to hold him back. Kyle fired shots toward Paul as Bud and Agent O'Connor tried to reach the vehicle.

Paul grabbed Rachelle and held her head with one hand while holding his gun with the other. Cronin spotted the shooter on top of the roof and started firing. Agent O'Connor also called for help as he returned fire. Cronin started giving Bud hand motions to try and work his way toward the roof. He finally yelled to him, "Get to the parking lot. He's going to try and make a run for it."

While the shooting continued, Bud made his move. Agent O'Connor also started to make a move toward the lot, but he caught a bullet in the leg and went down. "Stay put!" Cronin yelled to him.

Allan had been crouched on the side of his car but felt useless. He didn't know what to do. Kyle dropped his rifle and worked his way down the roof. By this time, Phil had heard so many shots that he drove away as calmly as he could. He felt it was unsafe to stay for Kyle, for it was clear that instead of a single shot, there had been at least 20 to 25 shots fired back and forth.

Kyle got off the roof and started working his way through the parking lot. Bud looked at Paul holding Rachelle and took off toward the lot. Detective Lieutenant Cronin followed Bud toward the lot after checking on Victoria, who was dead. Kyle ran through the metered parking lot, which was full. Saturday in Port Jefferson Village in June was always full, which is why the metered parking was put into effect. The town needed to control the vehicles whose owners used the lot as long-term parking.

Kyle worked his way through the lot as he headed to the stairway between the two main buildings that led to East Main Street. One building housed North Shore Interiors and the Red Sled, and on the other side of the stairway was the Port Jefferson Free Library, which was an added branch from the main library across the street.

As Kyle tried to catch his breath at the top of the stairs, he walked past the free library and opened the door to the Red Onion Café. As he stepped into the famous alternative food café, there was a line of six people in front of him, and he quickly got in line to try and hide in plain sight.

Bud was going through the parking lot looking at cars as he walked quickly toward the stairs. The people in the lot moved out of his way when they saw his gun. Cronin was right behind him and ordered Bud to go up to the stairs leading to East Main. By now, Cronin was in no mood for any games and had his 9mm Glock out. He checked the backseat of a car, and the driver said "Excuse me," to which Cronin shouted "Shut Up!"

Cronin continued walking through the lot with his gun out in the open as he eyed Bud going up the stairs. He could hear the screaming behind him at the dock. Allan ran over to Paul, who was holding Rachelle in the front seat. "Paul! Paul!" He was there still holding his gun in one hand. Allan reached for it. "Let me hold that for you before someone accidently gets killed." Allan quickly holstered Paul's gun for him as he held Rachelle.

"They killed them," Paul said, with tears in his eyes. "They killed them."

Allan checked Rachelle's pulse and said, "Paul, she's still alive."

The ambulances came, as did additional FBI, local sheriff's cars that had been in the area, and at least 10 Suffolk county police cruisers. The manhunt had begun. Victoria was pronounced dead at the scene, while Agent O'Connor and Rachelle were put into separate ambulances.

"Call Madison, Rachelle's sister," Paul said, as he got into the ambulance with Rachelle. "She works at Lasting Memories Dance studio next to Play 4 All."

"I'll pick her up and bring her to the hospital," Allan said. The door to the ambulance shut as it headed toward nearby Mather Hospital.

As Bud reached the top of the stairs, he went to the right and opened the door to the free library. People were startled when they saw his gun, so he identified himself. He shook his head and walked out and started scanning the street. He started checking the vehicles parked on the side of the road. He looked at the front of Beverly Frills clothing store and continued to walk toward the Red Onion Café. Bud put his gun away as he entered the café. He had been there many times for a hot green tea chai, which was the best, in his opinion. Most everything offered was organic and gluten free. The place was owned and run by young women who were always there, but this time Bud was scanning the men who seemed uncomfortable.

His thoughts were going a mile a minute. He walked toward the back of the deep and narrow café, where they had different types of colorful sofas and couches. There was a middle-aged woman in a track suit who looked up at him. A young couple on the sofa, alongside a man in his thirties, was staring into his tea. Bud started to walk away, took two steps, paused, and turned around to look at the man on the sofa. He kept his attention on his tea and would not look up. Bud stayed put and decided to play this out. He kept his eyes and attention on him. This went on for more than two minutes, and the longer it went on, the more Bud felt he might have the shooter in front of him. The man finally looked up and stared at Bud looking at him. As Bud made a step to walk forward, the man slowly got up and walked outside to the back deck of the café, which was called "Daniel's Deck," named after one of the owner's sons.

Bud took out his gun, and immediately people started to run. "Police!" Bud yelled. "Get everyone out of the building." The women in charge quickly ran around to the front of the booth to empty their café as Bud inched his way to the door of the deck. He peeked through the window of the door, and Kyle was just standing there. There was nowhere for him to go.

Bud opened the door with his gun pointed squarely at Kyle and told him to show him his hands. "Do it now," Bud said, cocking the hammer, and added, "I will blow your balls off," pointing the gun between Kyle's legs.

"I'm not armed," Kyle replied, "and you're a cop. You can't shoot me, my dear friend."

Bud replied calmly, "You killed two people, one being a cop. I'll shoot you in the leg and accidentally miss, splattering what small dick you have all over this deck."

Kyle gave a sarcastic smile and stepped toward Bud, who fired a shot into his groin. He did not know what this man would do but wanted Cronin to hear the shot from the parking lot.

Kyle went down to the floor of the deck, screaming, "You son of a bitch! I'm unarmed!"

Bud looked down on him, with his gun still out, and said, "I'm sorry I missed your leg and got the small leg." Bud kicked the man in the leg and said, "Now shut the fuck up!"

Kyle looked up at Bud, breathing hard, and said, "If you don't let me go, the bitch will never see the light of day." It was a confession and the first concrete evidence that the murders and kidnapping were linked.

Bud kicked him harder in the side and yelled, "I said to shut your motherfucking mouth up!"

A loud howl came from Kyle as he curled in pain. Cronin reached the deck from the outside and climbed up on it, thanks to the help of a table, to see blood coming from Kyle's groin.

Within seconds, police and FBI were all over the parking lot, as were half a dozen officers that stormed into the Red Onion Café to be sure no one else was hiding in any part of it. The two female owners of the cafe were already giving statements as to the events that took place. Cronin pulled the suspect up off the deck and asked him if anyone else was in the area. Kyle promptly spit in his face. Without missing a beat, Cronin ignored it and put the handcuffs on him, and they went through the door to get back into the enclosed part of the café. Bud gave Kyle another kick to his leg, and he went down. Cronin turned around and saw Bud picking up the suspected shooter.

"What's going on?" Cronin bellowed.

"Nothing , boss. Our man here is a little clumsy with a wounded groin and is having trouble standing up," Bud remarked.

"Then help him," Cronin yelled back as he directed the uniform cops to take the suspect to the hospital.

"Don't let him out of your sight," Cronin added. The detective lieutenant knew what was going on with Bud. He chose to ignore it and play dumb. Kyle Winters was in so much pain they had to take the handcuffs off so he could hold his groin. Whenever a fellow officer is shot down, the rules of the game are interpreted differently. He knew if they didn't get information from this man soon, another life would be lost. He also knew that if this crime was not solved, careers would be over, including his. Cronin scanned the surrounding streets and buildings: the main library across the street, the homes on the adjacent streets. He couldn't help but think about what had happened to this quiet little village. Other than the Belle Terre murder 20 years prior, there had been no problems. His office had set up meetings with William Lance and the Cross Island Ferry Company that owned the ferry service. Changes were going to happen, and they had to start immediately if people were going to feel like they were safe on the ferry and also in the village.

As Detective Lieutenant Cronin walked down East Main Street toward Arden Street, the officers were loading Kyle into the back of a squad car to bring him to Mather Hospital. He turned for a second and looked back down on the deserted street that only minutes earlier had hundreds of people bustling about. As his thoughts accumulated, Bud walked up behind him.

"Boss, I need to get to the hospital. Paul, Rachelle, and this asshole will all be there, as will Victoria's body." Cronin just stood there staring at the street, still thinking. "Boss," Bud said in a somber tone, interrupting Cronin's thoughts.

"Go," he replied. "I will notify Victoria's next of kin. See what you can come up with there and get back to the precinct in a couple of hours. I want you and Paul there for the meetings we have set up." As Bud took off, Cronin pulled aside Officers Lynagh and Franks and told them to get down to the Ocean City Bistro and the Dessert Factory to interview the manager and employees for information.

He walked back to the parking lot behind the Red Onion Café, where he met a couple FBI agents who were antsy to take control of everything. Cronin reminded them that this was a joint case with two murders that included a police officer. He wasn't sure if Rachelle was dead, so he did not include her in the count.

The ferry was shut down so the position of the cars was kept in place once the shooting took place. Cronin could see people from the lab already there going over the vehicles with a fine-tooth comb. He started climbing the metal stairway to the back of the Dessert Factory, proceeded to walk on the roof of the Ocean City Bistro, and climbed the metal ladder to the top of the ice-cream parlor. Laying there was the rifle that Kyle left. He instructed the lab people that were already there to be certain pictures at all angles were taken, including toward the ferry. He didn't expect to get fingerprints off the weapon, but he was hoping to get glove prints. Kyle still had the gloves in his pocket when they apprehended him. The detective lieutenant started thinking to himself again and believed Kyle had someone there waiting for him in the parking lot who must have taken off. There was no other explanation as to why the shooter ended up trying to become invisible inside the café.

Cronin worked his way down to the ground and went inside the parlor, where he spoke to the manager, Jay Rutherford, who had been there for more than 17 years. He did not offer any really helpful information about anything except that the two workers who spoke little English had seen the shooter go onto the Ocean City Bistro's roof and thought nothing of it. It was something that happened two to three times a week for various reasons.

It turned out that the same people owned both the Ocean City Bistro and the Dessert Factory, but Cronin did not think it meant much. He did, however, make a note of the names and contact numbers he received from Rutherford. Cronin went outside the parlor and walked across the street to the vehicles involved in the shooting. The windshields were cracked with bullet holes. The fact was that the glass had created a movement in the bullets' paths and may have saved Rachelle's life, and yet it may have cost Victoria her life.

The pieces of the puzzle were getting more difficult to put together the more he tried to make them fit: a kidnapping for money, and then an article in a small-town paper set off a killing spree. It was a jigsaw puzzle that somehow needed to be completed. Cronin called his office to be sure William Lance and the Port Jefferson people were on the way to his precinct. He walked over to Officer Lynagh and asked him to pick up Robert Simpson and take him to the precinct as well. He called back Gina, his assistant, to contact the Connecticut State Police to monitor the McDonald's stops along I-95. "I have a feeling we are going to hear from our friends who kidnapped Debbie Lance." he said.

He pushed the button to disconnect on his BlackBerry and pointed over to one of his uniformed officers. Cronin was showing his age by still using his first BlackBerry. "Give me a ride. It's time to do the worst part of this job," he said.

He looked back at the dead officer's vehicle, put his hand to his forehead, and said out loud, "I'm sorry, Victoria. We will have our justice." With that, he sat in the passenger side as the officer drove off to take Detective Lieutenant Cronin to Victoria's parents' house in Miller Place.

Officer George Lynagh drove up to the guesthouse and knocked on the door until Robert Simpson answered.

"You need to come down to the precinct with me now," Lynagh said.

"What for?" Simpson said, with a puzzled look on his face.

The officer replied, "There's been a shooting, and we need you."

"But..." Simpson replied.

Lynagh interrupted him. "Get in the car now, or I will bodily put you in there."

Officer Lynagh was a very direct, no-nonsense type of cop and rarely smiled. Whether you knew your rights or not, he was very rarely challenged when he made a request. A fellow cop was killed, and he was not in the mood to be polite. Simpson chose not to argue with him.

The ride in the ambulance took slightly more than five minutes to get to Mather Hospital, and Paul would not let go of Rachelle's hand. She had a pulse, but he thought she wouldn't last long, and he wanted to be the last one she felt. The medic in the ambulance looked carefully at her head where she was hit and realized she had been grazed by the bullet, which had caused a concussion. He believed she was going to make it unless something internally had been damaged by the bullet nicking the side of her forehead. He couldn't tell if the bullet had entered anywhere else until she was examined.

They unloaded her and brought her into the triage first and left Paul outside to wait. It was only a matter of minutes before Allan and Madison came rushing in. Madison hugged Paul and started crying.

"I can't lose her. I can't lose her. She is all I have left," she said.

Paul held on to her tight and said, "Listen, Madison, the bullet did not enter her head. We have a very good chance here."

Madison stared back at Paul and began to hug him again. Madison was still in her aerobic outfit but didn't care. The way that Allan barged into the dance studio, everyone thought they were under attack. As soon as he saw Madison, he knew she was Rachelle's sister. "Come with me," he said, as he grabbed her hand. "Your sister has been shot and is with Paul at the hospital."

Madison had never met Allan before but had heard of him through conversation with Rachelle. Besides, she could read his eyes, which were full of fear and truth. Without hesitation, she left her students and got in the car with him.

Bud came into the hospital about 10 minutes later and pulled Paul aside. He said, "Listen, we have to get back to the precinct. We have officers with O'Connor and Kyle Winters."

"Where's his room?" Paul said.

"No fucking way," Bud said, "he has officers at his door. He's our ticket to finding out who else is involved. Besides, they are in triage now. The officers are guarding empty rooms at the moment."

Madison stood up and said, "I don't want the man who did this in a room near my sister."

Paul realized that their conversation had been overheard by both Allan and Madison. "We need him alive to see where this will lead us. We have to do that, Madison. Understand?" he asked. He looked over at Allan and said, "I have to get back to the precinct and work this while it's fresh. Can you stay here with Madison and Rachelle 'til I get back?" Allan nodded as he put his hand on Paul.

"Paul, I will be here and send you updates by text." Paul left with a hug, and he kissed Madison before he left.

As he approached the door, Madison asked, "Paul, why is this happening, and why Rachelle?" Paul paused and turned around to face Madison.

"I blame myself Madison. I wanted Rachelle to be involved with what I thought was a kidnapping case, and I thought we could flush a bunch of amateurs out by Rachelle writing an article. I wanted her to be with me because I care about her, plus I thought she could help at the same time. I'm sorry; this is my fault, and if we lose her, I will not forgive myself, and I wouldn't expect you to forgive me either. I'm so sorry."

Madison was surprised by Paul's confession but replied, "Rachelle is a big girl. She would never do what she didn't want to do. If she wrote and got involved with this for you, it's because the feeling was mutual. Find these people, Paul, and keep me informed." He nodded as he left the hospital, but he couldn't hide his feeling of depression. His world was crashing down all around him. The case, and now this.

As he reached outside the hospital entrance, he realized he didn't have a car, and he wondered if it was symbolic of what was happening with his life. Things were falling apart all around him, and the simple thing of not having a vehicle to get to the precinct was about to be the final straw.

As the hair on the back of his neck was starting to get wet from stress, he felt a hand on his shoulder. It was Allan, who gave him the keys to his car. "Don't worry about us. I'm sure you will be back here later, and if Madison or I need to leave, it's a short cab ride to the village," he said.

Paul nodded in appreciation and, without saying a word, took the keys and got into Allan's 2006 Cadillac and drove to the precinct.

When he walked in, Bud was already there with Detective Lieutenant Cronin, Agent Sherman from the FBI, assistant district attorney, John Ashley, as well as Commander Jason Williams from the Coast Guard. John Ashley was quick point out the political fallout from this mess and that it needed to be cleaned up. As the banter continued between Ashley and Agent Sherman, Detective Lieutenant Cronin motioned to Bud and Paul to get closer, so they could have a private conversation about everything that had just taken place.

Cronin looked at Bud and asked, "Was it necessary to shoot him?"

"He came forward, boss," Bud replied. "I told him to stay still with his hands out. I had no choice. I had no way of knowing if that was a gun or knife in his pants or if he was just happy to see me." He said it with such a serious face that it even caught Cronin off guard.

"You're a real comedian, aren't you? Listen, get yourself to the hospital; you are under stress. PBA will assign a lawyer to you. And leave your gun here."

Bud looked puzzled and said, "Boss, I know they need my gun to check ballistics, but a hospital? Is that necessary?"

Cronin looked at him with those steely Irish eyes. "Yes, the good guys need representation, just like the bad guys. He was a cop killer, so I think this will be cleared up fast, but you need to protect yourself. Now go to the hospital, and I will call you later. Keep your backup piece."

A sudden loud voice from ADA Ashley was heard. "Are we interrupting anything, gentlemen? There should be no secrets; we are all on the same side on this one." Cronin motioned for Paul and Bud to stay silent.

"I'm just making sure, John," Cronin replied. "We all fired weapons, except for Paul, at a cop killer, and Bud shot him in the groin. I don't want my men going through this thing to where the investigation is hampered or delayed because Internal Affairs is looking to nail someone."

Ashley responded quickly, "We are talking about a cop killer; they will do the routine investigation. However, this guy was unarmed when Detective Johnson shot him."

"He had just killed one of us!" Cronin bellowed. "He wouldn't show his hands! He wouldn't stand down and moved toward Johnson after what happened. Any cop would have fired, maybe killed him. Bud intended to shoot him in the leg and hit him in the groin."

Cronin motioned for Bud to leave, and he did. Commander Williams and Agent Sherman were enjoying the show and stood there silently watching. Then Cronin got a call from the chief of police, wanting to know what Cronin was going to say at the press conference. "I haven't rehearsed it yet, Chief, but I will give one within the hour," Cronin answered.

He put the phone down and looked at Paul. "Where the hell are William Lance and Simpson? Get their asses in here, or we will show up at their house," he said. As fate would have it, Officer Dugan knocked and opened the door to Cronin's office and told the group both men were at the precinct. They came in, and by William Lance's face, Paul knew something else was wrong.

"What now?" he asked.

Lance looked at Detective Lieutenant Cronin and said, "They called. The ransom drop is canceled for tomorrow. The new demand is $5 million and the release of Kyle Winters without questioning, or they will send parts of her body to me in the mail."

Agent Sherman finally spoke up, saying, "They won't harm her. They want the money too much."

Cronin turned around and looked out his window in the parking lot. "Yes, they will," he replied. The room grew silent, waiting for his follow-up. "They shot up the Cross Island Ferry, killed an officer, and put hundreds of people in harm's way. They value their freedom more than the money. They want Winters freed so he won't talk, or they will try and kill him, and if Deborah Lance has seen her kidnappers, they will kill her also."

As he turned around, he looked at Lance and Simpson. "I'm sorry, Mr. Lance, but these are the cold, hard facts. If there is anything that has happened today that shakes your memory, anything that seems like a coincidence or reminds you of anything, now is the time."

Lance sat down in one of the chairs as another officer came in with the list of license-plate numbers that Cronin asked for that were on the streets and metered parking lots of Port Jefferson Village. He gave a list of names to Paul, Lance, and Simpson. "Any names familiar on the list? Take a good look."

There were more than 350 names on the list. While they were studying the list, Cronin looked at Ashley. "John, I have a press conference in 20 minutes, and I don't even know what I'm going to say yet. This is such a fucking mess because we are not coming up with why this happened in the first place."

Paul interrupted, "Well, well, well, looky here. Roger Thompson from Fun World was parked on East Main."

William Lance interjected, "Patty's car was in the village lot behind Pasta Pasta restaurant."

Cronin looked at Paul and said, "Bring them both in here." He then looked at Lance and Simpson and said, "Patty Saunders, your daughter's best friend, correct?" William Lance nodded. "Anything else we need to know about her?" Cronin asked.

"They went to high school together and have stayed close," Lance answered.

"That means you know her?" Cronin said, as he looked at Simpson.

"Yes, I know her," he replied.

"Where has she been all this time since her best friend was kidnapped?" Cronin shot back.

"She's been in touch with the family. She's upset; she was supposed to be with her the night of the concert, as you know," replied Simpson.

Paul interjected, "Why wasn't she with Debbie on the boat? Why was she already in Connecticut?"

"Ask her yourself," Cronin said to him. "Get her ass in here quick."

Agent Sherman, who had been very patient during this conversation, finally spoke up. "Detective Lieutenant, I'm sorry about your police officer, but we have an agent shot and injured as well as the kidnapping. This will continue to be a joint investigation, especially now that Internal Affairs is involved with all the shots fired from your gun today. We were also aware of Patty Saunders from O'Connor's input of the investigation. The FBI will be with you at the press conference."

Usually Cronin would have fought this, but he decided that misery loves company.

"Yes, Agent Sherman, I agree we need to work together on this. I would suggest we listen to the taped call before the press conference." He looked at Commander Williams, who was taking notes and using his tape recorder during this meeting, and said, "And you, sir? What are you going to be working on?"

Commander Williams was quick to respond, "The Coast Guard is going to find out why executives of the Cross Island Company didn't show up today at the meeting and we are going to draw up a suggested outline of what they should be doing from a security standpoint from now on. If they don't comply, we will work hard to shut the operation down until our waters are safe between New York and Connecticut."

Cronin nodded and looked back at Lance. "Did the agents at your house say where the call came from?" he asked.

"It was Connecticut," Lance said, with no surprise in his voice.

The Detective Lieutenant looked back at Paul and said, "Well, that's a bunch of horseshit. Detective Powers here was right all along.

There are too many things happening here in Port Jefferson Village. The comfort feeling is just too—well—comfortable. The calls may come from there, the car may have been abandoned there, but they are here, hiding in plain sight, and now we have one of them." He called for Officer Lynagh to come into the office.

"Sir," Officer Lynagh replied.

"Make sure Rachelle Robinson has two officers outside her door at the hospital. No one enters other than her doctor, her nurse, me, Detective Powers, Detective Johnson, and immediate family. The same goes for O'Connor's room door. Add Agent Sherman to the list on the rooms. Anybody else that requests entry, call me for authorization." He looked back at Agent Sherman and asked, "Can we get the recording of the call relayed here?"

The tape was played in Cronin's office. In a disguised voice, the caller said, "The ransom has been increased to $5 million, and Deborah Lance will only be returned alive if Kyle Winters is returned without questioning. We are watching. Release Kyle Winters from the hospital, or any possibility of her return is eliminated."

Cronin looked at everyone in the room and said, "Mr. Lance, I will see you in a couple hours, and Mr. Simpson, stay close by. I still have questions for you." He pushed his intercom and reminded Gina to send some officers to pick up Patty Saunders and Roger Thompson. He looked at Paul and said, "Meet back here in a few hours. Go to the hospital and check on everyone and keep Bud in 'low mode' 'til we get a clear on this from Internal Affairs. I don't expect a big problem."

Paul left the precinct and got into his car and drove over to Z Pita to speak with Joey Z about Rachelle and then drove to Mather Hospital. He met Allan with his car keys, thanked him, and told him to get home to his family. As he approached Rachelle's room, the two officers were already at her door and nodded to Paul as he showed his badge and they checked his name on the list. He walked in, and Madison was there at her bedside.

She looked up and smiled at Paul, saying, "She's going to be OK. The bullet grazed her head, and the glass from the windshield created the other cuts, but she's going to be fine," as they hugged.

Paul looked back at Rachelle and said, "I'm going to sit with her for a bit before I go back to the precinct. Why don't you take a break for a couple hours? I'll be here 'til you get back. Give yourself a chance to get out of that dancing suit and clean up. Shit," he added, "I sent Allan home; he could have given you a ride."

Just then one of the officers opened the door and said that a gentleman named Allan wanted to know if Madison needed a ride. They looked at each other and laughed as Madison said goodbye.

Paul looked at Rachelle laying there, taking a nap. He sat down where Madison had been and started looking at all the papers that Madison had spread out. They were articles all written by Rachelle. He had only half-read most of her work because of time constraints, but now he wanted to read them. The article that captured his attention was the piece he had heard about on and off for a year: the history of Port Jefferson Village.

Rachelle was such a history buff that it was why she had first applied at Z Pita years before. She knew it was Port Jefferson's first firehouse building and fell in love with the historical pictures that hung on its wall, such as the original bank of Port Jefferson that had a view of Z Pita as the firehouse with the bell tower as well as the New York Bakery and many others. It planted the seed for her to write about Port Jefferson, originally called "Drowned Meadow," because the present business district had been a marshland that flooded with every high tide. Her article contained information about the first resident of Port Jefferson, John Roe, who built his home in 1682, which was still standing today. John Roe's descendants lived in the area into the 19th century, and although there were only five houses in 1797, Port Jefferson was a prominent commercial center by the 1850s. Her article was so well written that Paul couldn't stop reading.

As he sat there, he came to appreciate Port Jefferson even more because of the simple facts and details she had written. Things such as a quote from Captain James McAllister in 1912 saying that "Port Jefferson harbor was the most beautiful he had ever sailed into." The town was renamed Port Jefferson in honor of the third president, Thomas Jefferson, in March 1836, and became a bustling port.

Rachelle's choice of living on Prospect Street was because of all the historical homes, such as the Capt. C.E. Tooker home, the R.H. Wilson home, and the John Mather home. Her article went into detail about the Mather home and Mather, who had left money for the hospital that she was in at this moment. She studied the history of the village so much that she grew to love it with a passion.

Paul looked at her and held her hand. As he held her hand, Rachelle awoke but was too tired to speak. She laid quietly as Paul began to speak to her aloud, not knowing she could hear him. "Rachelle, there are many things I don't understand right now, but I want you to know how much you mean to me. We have been friends for years, but when I'm not with you, I miss you, and when I'm with you, I feel whole. I need to be whole and be me, and I can't do that without you. I have been stubborn and shy in wanting to talk to you about my feelings, but my insecurity has stopped me from telling you these things. When all of this is over, I will speak to you and tell you all of this, but it's important for you to get well." He kissed her hand and continued as Rachelle listened. "I will not take you for granted anymore, as I sit here and think about our past, our talks, our laughs, and your incredible work and success at the restaurant and the paper. I wonder if this is my fault, but I want you to know I will do everything to protect you—not because it's my job but because I need you in my life. If that sounds selfish, I'm sorry. I guess it's good you are not hearing this because I'm probably screwing this up!"

Paul leaned in and bent down closer to Rachelle's face as he moved strands of her hair. "I would kiss you now, but I don't want the first time I touch your lips to be like this. I need you to want it too." He moved up her face and kissed her forehead. He went to the door of her room to look for Bud and to check out a television to see if Detective Lieutenant Cronin was having the press conference. He went to the lobby of the hospital as Rachelle opened her eyes with a half smile on her face and a tear in her eye.

The lobby had Fox News on, and there was Detective Lieutenant Cronin in a recorded conference that had been shown live 30 minutes prior. It was short and to the point, and he took no questions. He said, "This has been the longest day of my career as a police officer. Today we lost one of our own, Officer Victoria Davis. An outstanding officer, a better person, and a friend to all of those who worked with her. We have been investigating the kidnapping of Deborah Lance and the murder of Timothy Mann, which are proving to be connected. And now we have the death of Officer Davis and injuries to FBI agent Jack O'Connor, *Now* reporter Rachelle Robinson, and the suspect himself, who was shot by one of our detectives. There is a list of demands by the kidnappers/murderers, which we are evaluating now. We will act accordingly to bring this to a close in the best possible way to resolve this case without any more injuries and death. Thank you."

As he started to walk away, a reporter shouted, "That's it! Just walk away. No questions, no answers!"

Cronin stepped back to the microphone and said, "I had to go inform the parents of Victoria Davis that their daughter died today in the line of duty while trying to save the life of Rachelle Robinson. We are not going to jeopardize any more lives at this juncture of the investigation. I don't want to visit any more parents. Please respect that for now, and be patient with us."

The silence from the reporters was a perfect time for Detective Lieutenant Cronin to walk away.

Paul went back to check on Bud, and a PBA delegate had just left the room when he got there.

"Paul," Bud said, "I really don't want this. We have work to do."

"Listen," Paul said, "it's for your own good. This will be over soon, but we have to be certain Internal Affairs is not looking for a badge to take in all this, especially yours."

Bud sat back, shaking his head, and said, "OK, OK, I can't wait to get home.

"You'll be out of here in another hour. Go home, and we will talk tomorrow. Better yet, come over to Z Pita for breakfast, and we can talk. I'm going back to Rachelle's room until Madison gets back, then going down to the station to interview Patty Saunders and Roger Thompson."

Paul gave Bud a big bear hug, left the room, and visited Agent O'Connor for a few minutes before going back to Rachelle's room. It was past 8:00 pm when he got a text from Cronin that Thompson and Saunders were being brought in for the morning. Paul was happy about it and squeezed Rachelle's hand. She opened her eyes and smiled. He looked at her and put his hand on top of hers. She turned her hand to intertwine her fingers with his.

"When you are out of here, we can have our own chat," he said.

"OK," she said.

Within minutes Madison was back to relieve Paul, and she wouldn't let go of Rachelle.

"I'm fine," Rachelle said, giggling. Paul said good night to both of them and checked in again with Agent O'Connor's room and Kyle Winters' room.

"Sorry, sir," an officer said to Paul, "no admittance to Kyle Winters' room without Detective Lieutenant Cronin's authorization. Do you want me to call him?"

"No, no," Paul replied. "It can wait."

As Paul walked down the hall, the officer called Cronin anyway to tell him Detective Powers had come to the room. As Paul went outside the hospital, he had déjà vu. Again, no car to get home. He decided to take a walk to his apartment from the hospital. He needed the fresh air and time to think. The walk took him about 20 minutes. He was looking forward to the next day. Although it would be Sunday, he knew there would be no days off until this was resolved. The national spotlight on the case gave no options. This was going to be the rule until this was over.

He arrived at his apartment and turned on his answering machine to hear messages from Allan, his father, Joey Z, and Bud. He turned on the television to Fox News and what they were calling the Port Jefferson murders—"The Face of Fear"—under the "breaking news" bar. Apparently the media was linking the murder of Timothy Mann and Officer Davis with the kidnapping. Paul shut off the television and started returning phone calls. The first one was to his father. He listened to the concern and worry of his father for almost an hour before hanging up. He decided to take a shower before making the other calls.

John Winters picked up his knife and held it in his hand as he watched the news about his brother. Sitting next to him were Phil and his younger brother, Mason.

He looked at Phil and said, "You bastard. If you had gotten Kyle out of there instead of driving off, we wouldn't be in this mess."

Phil shook his head and replied, "John, he fired six to eight times, and at least 20 to 25 shots were fired back. It was a war zone."

John grabbed his neck and shouted, "And now they will be all over us if Kyle talks! I know he hasn't yet or they would be raiding next door. If we go down, I want people to suffer. I want the reporter dead, I want the cop who shot Kyle dead, and I want Wayne to torture and kill the pretty little thing before it's over."

He picked up his cell phone and called Wayne to check on how their hostage was doing. He was yelling at Wayne because he seemed as if he had a few drinks in him. He hung up and threw his glass of Jack Daniel's at the television screen. His patience was wearing thin. "I will have to move to Wayne's house in the early morning. I expect the cops to be at my brother's house by morning and figure out I'm next door. Kyle doesn't know your real names except for Mason, so you and Wayne don't have anything to worry about."

He picked up his cell phone again and called another number. At the other end was a female voice. John spoke very slowly to her. "Listen to me, you bitch. Keep your mouth shut, or I will cut you up into little pieces and feed you to the sharks in the Riverhead Aquarium."

The voice on the other end bellowed back, "There was a deal that no one would be killed. What are you doing, you crazy fuck?"

John answered calmly, "Just drop out of sight. We don't need you around for a while."

"And what about my cut of the ransom?" the female said.

"We have bigger problems to think about, you dumb bitch. If we get out of this, I will contact you."

John Winters hung up the phone and looked at Phil. "You are going to have to eliminate her before she speaks a word to anyone."

Phil got up and started heading for the door. He said, "John, as much as I don't want to, I'm afraid your own brother is going to have to be eliminated as well."

Mason stood up at this statement to argue, but John cut him off, saying, "We have no choice, Mason. If we don't, he will give all of us up. He got himself shot after killing a police officer. No way will they let him go. Trial or no trial, they want me, and he is their only ticket."

Mason sat down as Phil went out the door. Phil got in his black SRX and drove away from the Thompson Street house wondering if it would be the last time he would be there. He stopped at the end of the driveway and looked back at the house next door on Thompson Street, the home of Kyle Winters. Phil knew if the cops got to Kyle, he may give them up, plus once they got his home address and realized John Winters was next door, all hell would break loose. He slammed the steering wheel hard with his open hand as he realized it was over for all of them unless the three Winters brothers were wasted. There would be no connection to Phil or to Wayne or even to the girl who they had met online if the brothers were gone. Phil made the left on Thompson Street to drive the five minutes to Mather Hospital. He knew what he had to do.

The two officers were getting tired, for they had not been relieved since they started guarding the door at 3:00 pm. It was now midnight, and a relief team was more than an hour late. Officers Barry Smith and Alex Walker now had chairs in the hallway. Walker decided to get some coffee and stretch his legs. "Bring me back some, black," Smith called out to him.

Smith was alone for two minutes when a hard crack against his head knocked him to the floor. The intruder walked into the room where Kyle Winters was and walked up to his bedside as Kyle opened his eyes to see the famous white mask with peanut-shaped eyes. The person behind the mask whispered to Kyle, who answered her and begged for his life.

Before he could let out a cry for help, his mouth was covered and the face whispered in his ear, "No more killing for you" and, with a sudden thrust, put a knife through his heart. The blood started gushing out almost immediately. The intruder left the room and ran down the hallway, leaving Officer Smith on the floor.

As Walker came around the corner, he dropped the coffees on the floor as he radioed for backup and checked on the condition of Smith. Bud, who was still in the hospital on the advice of his attorney, heard the call and came running to the room, only to find Kyle Winters dead. He took Officer Walker's club from his belt to check the floor of the hospital, including the rooms. Even though it was past midnight, two doctors and three nurses were on the scene rather quickly.

As Bud checked the rooms, he went over to the nurses' station to shaken nurses who had just witnessed the attack on the monitors. "Play it back!" Bud started yelling, almost making one nurse jump out of her seat. She was nervous and crying but managed to move the recording back 10 minutes. As Bud watched, he couldn't believe his eyes. Moving quickly, the intruder—wearing tight black pants, black sneakers, tight black shirt, black gloves, and the famous white Ghost Face mask—knocked out Officer Smith, went into the room, and within 35 seconds was out the door and running down the hallway. The detective couldn't help but notice the blood splatter under the eye and along the right side of the eye of the mask.

"Where's the rest of the video?" Bud screamed.

The nurse replied the videos were for rooms and small portions of hallway to watch patients. Bud thought it had to be one of the kidnappers to keep Winters from talking. Suddenly he thought of Rachelle and started running to her room. The two officers were missing from the door as Bud rushed in to see Rachelle sleeping and Madison's head on her.

"What's going on?" Madison asked, annoyed at being awoken.

"Where are the officers that are supposed to be at this door," Bud replied in a statement, instead of in the form of a question.

"Bud, I've been here sleeping with Rachelle. I haven't been checking the doors." By then there were three police cars on the grounds. Bud went back to the nurses' station and called Paul on his cell phone. Paul told Bud he would be right there. Detective Lieutenant Cronin was notified as well and said he would be there within minutes. As Bud hung up the phone he looked at the nurse and said, "And I wanted to be a cop in a quiet town. Play the video from room 209."

She played it back over and over, and there were two officers on film until 11:30 pm, then they were gone.

"What the fuck?" Bud kept saying. "They left? No relief, nothing?"

Bud returned to room 209 to see two new officers there. "Don't leave this area until you are relieved in person by two other officers," he said.

Detective Lieutenant Cronin arrived at the hospital as calls were being made to the officers who had left the room. It turned out they never left the hospital. They were hospitalized themselves with food poisoning, and no one had the smarts to call it in for replacements for room 209.

It was apparent to everyone as Paul arrived back at the hospital that the people involved in the kidnapping and murder were cleaning up house to avoid getting caught. It was going to be a very long weekend.

Cronin grabbed a radio from one of the uniformed officers and said, "Send officers to Patty Saunders' and Roger Thompson's homes now. I want to know what they have been up to tonight."

Detective Lieutenant Cronin and Bud walked to Agent O'Connor's room, flashed identification, and walked in to a sleeping O'Connor. "Don't wake him," Cronin said, "as long as things here haven't been disrupted."

They walked back out to the hallway, where Cronin spoke almost in a whisper to Bud. "I can understand why they wanted Winters dead, but poisoning two officers at Rachelle's door and she's OK? This is not making sense, unless they just wanted the officers out of the way."

Cronin went back to the nurses' station to view the video and found Special Agent Sherman already there. They both viewed the tapes and were impressed by the quickness of the masked intruder.

"He could have killed the officers," Sherman said, "but he only wanted Winters. I have a team at this moment tearing the house apart on Thompson Street."

A piece of paper was handed to Cronin as they were talking. He read it and said, "He has a brother next door on Thompson Street."

"Let me go," Bud said.

"You can go," Cronin said, "but remember you only have your backup piece, and check with your attorney."

"Sure, sure," Bud replied.

He ran to his room to get his belongings and called his attorney, who flat-out said, "No, not under any circumstances. You'll have to wait."

Bud was so disappointed that he insisted, and his attorney said he would no longer represent him if he went to the house. It simply was not in his best interest. Paul came into the room and told Bud to stay in the hospital that he would go to the house with Officers Lynagh and Healey.

"Look after Rachelle and Madison," Paul said.

Bud shook his head in minor protest. He knew this was the way things happened when you fired your weapon and struck someone.

Paul left the hospital but not before checking in on Rachelle and Madison. He kissed Rachelle's forehead and the back of Madison's head as she slept with her head on Rachelle's leg.

He left the hospital in the police cruiser with Lynagh and Healey as they drove to Thompson Street. When they got there, they saw that agents were walking through Kyle Winters' house. Paul walked up the stoop next door and starting ringing the doorbell.

John Winters answered the door with the greeting, "It's 2:00 am in the fucking morning; what is this about?"

Paul identified himself and requested to come in. John let them in, and as they stood by the door, Paul asked, "Do you mind if we search the house, sir?"

"Yes, I do mind. Do you have a search warrant?"

"No," Paul said. "Do you have something to hide?"

"No," John said, "but I am a very private person with my things, and it's 2:00 am. What is all this about?"

Paul walked closer to John as the two officers scanned the room to be certain there would be no surprises coming out from any of the doors or hallways. Both Lynagh and Healey were the most serious and hard-nosed cops, which is why Paul preferred their company on inquiries such as this. Paul peppered John with many questions, such as the last time he had seen Kyle. Apparently they were close, since he lived at the next house.

"We were always in close proximity," John replied, "but not always emotionally. It's the same with Mason, my younger brother, who lives here with me. He is sleeping upstairs." Paul nodded to Lynagh to check it out.

As Lynagh started to move toward the steps, John protested.

"Listen," Paul said, "I'm sorry to tell you this way, but your brother was involved in a cop killing yesterday afternoon. He was shot, captured, and was murdered over an hour ago in his hospital room after two officers were poisoned and one seriously injured. All this, and he lives next door to his brother. It may be debated in court, but I think I have probable cause to check this house to be sure there is no kidnap victim by the name of Deborah Lance here."

"I'm puzzled," John said. "What does a kidnapping victim have to do with someone killing my brother?"

Paul walked closer to John and said, "That is what I'm going to find out. Now, are you going to let this officer check upstairs voluntarily, or are you going to force me to make a decision for probable cause?"

John sat down in his chair and looked up at Paul and smiled. "I think I like the latter," he said. There was silence in the room.

"Sir," Lynagh said to Paul.

"Shhh," Paul said. "Hear that? Coming from upstairs."

"Sounds female to me, Detective," Lynagh said.

"Check it out," Paul replied. "Officer Healey, check the rest of the house."

The smile on John Winters' face disappeared as he stood up.

"There it is again," Paul said. "Officer, check that noise coming from upstairs. Let's make sure there is nothing going on up there. I'll stay here and keep Mr. Winters company."

Lynagh went up the stairs with his gun drawn and was up there for about four minutes. The entire time was a complete stare-down between Paul and John Winters. No words were spoken, but if eyes could talk, there would have been another person going to Mather Hospital. The officer came down to inform the detective one male was sleeping in a bed in one of the bedrooms. "Search the rest of the house," Paul told the two officers as he stared John Winters down.

Upstairs, Mason Winters rolled to his side and pulled out a shotgun from under the covers. The officer escaped with his life by not tearing off the covers to his bed while he was upstairs. John Winters stayed in his living room without saying a word as both Paul and he eyeballed each other while the two officers searched the house.

"Nothing, Detective," the two reported as they came back into the living room.

"Sorry to have disturbed you, Mr. Winters," Paul said. As they reached the door, Paul turned around again to say, "Sorry about the loss of your brother also."

"I'm sure you are," John said, moving forward to shut the door behind them.

"You're right," the detective replied, "I'm not sorry, and I won't stop until I find out who was behind all of this, which includes the shooting of Rachelle Robinson and the killing of Officer Davis."

John Winters moved closer to Detective Powers, but Officer Lynagh stepped in between them as he stared him down with his head cocked in such a way as if he was challenging John Winters, until he backed away from the detective. Paul went next door and spoke with a couple of agents to see if anything was found in Kyle Winters' home, and the answer was nothing of significant importance. Paul had the officers drop him off at his apartment above Z Pita. It was past 3:00 am, and there was more work to be done the next day.

Sunday Morning, June 19

Paul got up at 8:00 am, took a shower, and started thinking about so many things that he looked for a pen and paper while soaking wet. He wanted the tape from the hospital looked at to see if weight and size could be determined for the masked intruder who had killed Kyle Winters. He finally got dressed and called his father, who said he was coming up from Florida because he was getting too nervous watching all of this on the news. "No, Dad," Paul begged. "There is too much going on here. Give me a week or so."

He hung up, dialed Allan, and told him to meet him downstairs at Z Pita for breakfast. He had thoughts and wanted to run them by him. It just seemed there were so few he could trust these days. He made calls to Bud and Rachelle at the hospital to check in. Bud was going home and was already told to report to desk duty Monday. Detective Lieutenant Cronin told him, based on everything that had happened, he felt Bud would be reinstated quickly. Internal Affairs had already warranted Cronin's use of discharging his weapon at the now-deceased suspect during the gunfire at the ferry. Rachelle told him that the doctors were going to release her Monday morning, and she was already writing her article for the *Now* paper and *Newsday*, who had offered her a fee for a freelance story on everything that was going on. Paul was not happy about it but did not want to upset her while she was still in the hospital. He went downstairs at 8:45, and Allan was already sipping a cup of coffee, waiting for him.

Paul arrived at the precinct at 10:00 am, and Roger Thompson and Patty Saunders were both waiting for him without attorneys. He sat with Roger Thompson for one hour asking questions, from why his car was parked on East Main Street during the shooting to how much he had to gain by the Ghost Face mask getting national attention again. Detective Lieutenant Cronin was behind the glass with the assistant district attorney to listen to Thompson's alibi and reasons for not being a part of this. He lived only 10 minutes away, he was off Saturday, and he frequented Port Jefferson Village many times during the month. Cronin and the assistant district attorney, as well as Paul, ruled him out for now.

When it was Patty Saunders' turn, as soon as Paul started questioning her, the tears started to flow down her face. She believed it was her fault because she wanted Debbie to meet her in Bridgeport instead of going together.

"If," Paul replied, "you were meeting her in Bridgeport, what was your car doing in the Village?"

"I went to Bridgeport earlier without the car," she answered. "The Arena is close enough to where the boat docks in Bridgeport are, and I walked to the arena and planned to go back with Debbie. I went earlier to visit relatives in Connecticut."

Patty was let go with the department's thanks for her cooperation. Paul came back to where Cronin and ADA Ashley were, and they all decided that both of them were not involved at this time. All three went to the back of the precinct, where the crime-scene unit had a copy of the video tape from the hospital. They reviewed it about 10 times in regular and slow motion to see if they could catch a glimpse of anything that would help indicate who the masked killer was. The agility and quickness was what struck them the most. The tape was already on the Internet and in papers, with headlines reading, GHOST FACE STRIKES MATHER HOSPITAL. The *Post*, famous for its headlines, had, THE FACE OF FEAR STRIKES TERROR IN QUIET TOWN.

As they walked back to the Cronin's office, Cronin stopped and said, "Don't you find it odd that there has been no communication on Debbie Lance? They kill one of their own, and now the FBI has heard nothing." He looked at Paul. "Get me the files on all the Winters brothers. Get a court order for their cell-phone records and all the credit-card charges they have made over the last 30 days. Special Agent Sherman will help while O'Connor is in the hospital. Have a couple of the guys look over them in detail and have them get back to us with anything that doesn't look kosher."

Cronin walked over to the television set and looked at the "breaking news" bar. Port Jefferson Village was now on the map across America. He turned away, walked to his office, and closed the door.

Paul gave instructions to officers to contact the Winters brothers to allow cell-phone records to be checked. He expected them to say no, so he left a message with the assistant district attorney to get court orders for their records. He drove over to the hospital to find out Bud was already home, and when he walked into Rachelle's room, she was laughing with Madison, who had gone home and come back twice that day to be with her sister. Rachelle smiled at Paul and waved. Madison took her cue and left to get a cup of coffee.

Paul went over to Rachelle, looked down at her, and said, "I thought I lost you."

"Never," she said, "not a chance."

He kissed her forehead and began to tell her he was worried about her writing her newest story. "Do you think it's needed, Rachelle? It's all over the news."

"Yes," she said. "I'm living this and telling it."

"OK, OK," he replied. "I'm just worried about you."

"The shooter is dead," she replied. "Plus I have you to protect me," she said as she grabbed his hand. Paul moved in again, but Madison walked in, and he was uncomfortable kissing Rachelle in front of her.

Paul looked at Madison and asked, "You are picking her up to bring her home tomorrow?" She nodded back.

"Look," Rachelle interrupted, "look at what I've written so far." Paul picked up the papers and began to read. It was the previous week in detail, from the plans to the meetings to the theory of how this was done to Rachelle's conversations with Paul before the shooting to the reenactment on the ferry. Although it gave Paul great pause, he was proud of Rachelle and how talented she was as a writer.

Rachelle told Paul the article would be released within five days for the *Now* paper and would be released to *Newsday* on the sixth day. "Maybe all of this will be resolved by then, and you'll have an even better story if you hold off," he said.

Paul truly thought it was the better way to go, but he also had Rachelle's safety on his mind. She nodded her head with body language that expressed she would consider it as he kissed her forehead before leaving.

"Call me when Maddie gets you home," Paul said.

She smiled as he left the room, and she gazed around her environment, talking to herself. "Time to get the hell out of here," she said, even able to let out a giggle as she looked at something humorous on the television in the silent room.

Monday, June 20

Monday morning arrived, and as usual Bud knocked on Paul's door and ran up the stairs, only to find Paul in the shower.

"Always late," Bud said to himself.

Paul came out, only to be startled. He said, "One day, you son of a bitch, you are going to be shot."

"Yeah," Bud replied. "Then you have to go through what I'm going through. Only a backup and Internal Affairs on my ass." He raised his hands up with his forefinger and middle finger to make quotation marks in the air. "OIS, my ass. He's lucky he didn't go to his grave with no balls. Whoever did him in may have done me a favor." OIS is short for Officer Involved Shooting, and Bud was not happy about only using his backup piece.

"I think so," Paul said, as he grabbed a shirt already lying on his bed. "Rachelle comes home today, and she wants to come back to work at the restaurant and paper right away. Thank God Joey Z told her to take a few more days."

"Don't forget, dress blues for the funeral Wednesday," Bud mentioned. "I still can't believe she's gone, just like that." Paul nodded in agreement.

"I know Deborah Lance is here somewhere. The fact that they were comfortable having her in the area is now a detriment to them. We need to get those phone records checked," Paul said as they ran down the stairs.

In the car, Paul called Agent O'Connor, who would be released Tuesday, and inquired if the FBI could push along the court order for cell-phone records. He would see what they could do. This was more than just a competition between the FBI and local law enforcement. It seemed they were now working together on the same team. They all knew the national media was watching almost to a fault, not because of the killing of a police officer or the complex case it was becoming but because it involved the famous Ghost Face mask. "What a crazy world we live in," Bud said as they drove to the precinct.

It was during the day Monday that Rachelle called Paul to tell him she thought about what he had said in regard to holding off on releasing the article until it was played out and that she agreed.

With a sigh of relief, Paul said, "Good choice. Listen, Danford's is having a banquet on the upstairs level on Wednesday; Victoria wanted this after her funeral. Please join Bud and I and a few of the guys and friends. We need this for a couple hours. Bring Maddie if you'd like."

"Sure. I'll meet you there," Rachelle replied.

"8:30," Paul said. "See you there, and I'm glad you are home."

Monday was a day filled with paperwork and phone calls. Paul could see the tension building on Cronin's face, as the case was not progressing well. He expected the phone records to be a big help once the court order was received. Agent Sherman, as well as O'Connor from his hospital room, were making calls to contacts to get it done.

Back at Prospect Street, Rachelle was working on what she was calling, "The Status Report." It was an outline summary of what had happened and what was being investigated, with all the details left blank. She wrote it with cryptic messages, creating a "puzzle" of the crimes and what she expected would happen next. You could say it was a big tease before the real story was released and finalized. She had fun with it, and even her boss, Steven Anderson, thought it was creative when he received it through email. He gave it to a couple of interns after he checked it for proper grammar and spelling and instructed them to get it ready for print for the Tuesday edition of *Now*.

Rachelle left her house to walk down to Z Pita to see her colleagues and her partner Joey Z, who greeted her with open arms. They had a chance to talk for a bit and catch up, and she told him she would be back Thursday after the funeral of Victoria Davis on Wednesday. As she left Z Pita, instead of normally turning left to go home up Prospect Street, she took a right turn to go to the Starbucks on the corner of Main Street and Arden Place. They say that life and death depends on the choices we make. Sometimes those choices are made within seconds.

Rachelle walked into Starbucks to get herself an iced coffee that she had a craving for and did not notice the man sitting in the corner chair contemplating his next move. He noticed who she was from the photo accompanying her articles in the newspaper in regard to the shooting. "My lucky day," he said to himself as he watched her smiling face get her iced coffee and leave.

Mason Winters was right behind her and followed behind her about 20 to 30 yards, all the way until he witnessed her walk in the front door of the house at the top of Prospect Street. "You're mine now," Mason said aloud as he walked to High Street and took a quick right up to Thompson Street.

As he opened the door with a big smile on his face, John greeted him with, "What are you so happy about? We have to bury our brother tomorrow."

Without missing a beat, Mason replied, "That bitch that Kyle couldn't kill, the reporter, she lives two minutes from us! You can walk there! What a great town this is!"

John looked out the window and said, "Well, well, well, my little honey. My brother may have failed, but we will not." He turned around to Mason and asked, "Have you heard from Phil?"

"No," Mason replied.

John slammed the wall he was standing next to and said, "He's not answering his phone. He was successful killing Kyle in the hospital, and I'm sure he now wants us out of the way. He feels this is his only way of getting out of this. So we are going to have to get rid of him after the girl. We can't have anymore stories being circulated. Get some rest, Mason. This is going to be a busy week."

Mason went upstairs to bed early as John turned on the television. He knew they were in a mess and wasn't sure how they were going to get out of it. He was determined to bring as many people down with him as he could. The saying was true—misery loves company.

As he sat in his chair and lowered the television sound, he picked up his cell phone and dialed. Wayne's phone rang in the basement room where Debbie was being held. On the other end, Debbie knew it was Wayne's boss because she heard the famous Elvis quote, *"Thank you, thank you very much."*

Wayne got off the phone and walked over to Debbie as she curled up on the bed. He moved in up to her face and started licking the side of it.

"I bet you are quite a ride in the sack, aren't you?" he asked.

"Please don't hurt me," she spoke back, with her hands tied to the bedpost.

"Well, my sweet one," Wayne said, "I believe we are coming to the end of our relationship. The boss says you gotta go soon. Looks like no ransom, because it's just too crazy."

She looked back at Wayne with her eyes closed and said, "Forget him, my father is rich. I will take care of you. Let me go, and I will give you money to live on the rest of your life."

Wayne looked intrigued. "Tell me more, my chickadee."

"Listen," the young woman went on in a desperate plea, "they won't need you once I'm gone. You are a witness to everything. In fact, you are the only one that has spent time with me. If you are out of the way as well, then there is no connection to my kidnapping. Think about it. Have you made demands? I've been here over a week. What is going on?"

It was interesting to Wayne how Debbie Lance was getting more brazen as the days went by. Either that, or she thought it was her only chance of survival. He moved in closer to her as she kept her eyes shut. "How about a fuck here and there, and maybe you will live longer because of the enjoyment you bring me?" he asked.

Debbie wanted to regurgitate at his words, but she managed to keep it together and said, "Well, let me think about it. It would be easier for me knowing what is going on. I would consider it if you could get a message to my father."

"What kind of message?" Wayne said.

"Just a message so he knows I'm alive and well."

"What do you want me to do?" Wayne said.

"Tell him I love him and please pay anything to get me home."

"You know, I just thought of something," Wayne said. "I could do whatever I wanted to you now, and no one would know a thing, no?"

Deborah yelled, and Wayne grabbed and ripped her shirt almost entirely off in one quick rip.

"No! No!" she screamed.

"Shut up!" he yelled back. "You've been needing this."

He grabbed her pants and started pulling them off as she fought, moving her legs. "No!" she cried. She fought hard, but he got her pants off and went right to her panties, which came right off with the strength of his hand. "No!" she cried louder.

He slapped her hard across the face and held her head tight as he got close to her ear and said, "You need this, you bitch! Play nice, or I will tear you apart." He slapped her again as Deborah resigned herself that she was going to be raped and killed. She no longer had the energy to fight him off.

When Wayne's pants were halfway down, he heard a smash in the next room. He opened the door, and as soon as he did, there was a large deer-hunting knife that went through his navel. He looked down at his wound in disbelief and looked back up again to stare at the white mask with blood splatter and those eyes at a tilted angle. As Wayne started to reach toward the mask with his hand, the knife was twisted in his stomach. Wayne went down to the floor and died with a look of puzzlement on his face. The masked intruder looked at Deborah curled up with her hands tied to the bedpost doing her best to hide her naked body.

"Please, no!" Deborah cried softly in a voice of resignation. She looked at him—black tight pants, black shirt, black gloves, the mask with a big hood. As he walked to the bed, Deborah began saying, "No! Please, no!" The figure raised his knife to Deborah. "God! No!" she screamed, as the knife came down on the ropes holding her, cutting her loose. She sat there not knowing what to say as she stared at the masked stranger, who had most likely saved her life. He reached for Wayne's cell phone and threw it on the bed at Deborah. She glanced at it, and when she looked up, he was gone.

She called her father, who in turn called 911. Within 10 minutes there was a circus of emergency vehicles at the house on Pine Hill Road. Bud was the third officer on the scene, and all were waiting until female officers and the FBI and Agent Sherman arrived. Bud called Paul a few times but could not reach him. When he walked into the room where Debbie was, he could see why they were waiting for female officers to get to the house. However, he couldn't help himself. He walked over to Deborah, who had a blanket over her and was shaking. Bud was aching to put his arm around her but knew the rules on sexual assault victims.

"It's going to be all right now," he kept saying. "We are not going to stop until all of this is resolved. It's OK now." He had never met her before this moment, but his heart was breaking knowing what she must have gone through. "Listen," he said, "let's go to the other room and get away from this bad guy here laying on the floor. He is a bad guy, right?" Bud said with a half-assuring smile but in the form of a question.

Deborah smiled at the way Bud asked her and confirmed, "Yes, he is a bad guy."

"Tell me what happened," Bud replied. He turned on his tape recorder, and Deborah told Bud about what was going down when the masked intruder met her kidnapper at the door then cut her loose and suddenly disappeared. Bud's face got a little more serious when she told him what mask he was wearing. Bud had been carrying photos of the wrinkled version, scarecrow, zombie, and the white version, which is what the killer was wearing.

Bud asked, "Was there a blood splatter on the mask?"

"Yes," she answered. "When he leaned over to cut my ropes, I could smell a vanilla scent."

Bud made a note of it and questioned her more about the agility of the masked intruder and if she knew more about whom else was involved in her kidnapping. His interrogation stopped once the FBI entered the house as well as the medical examiner and the medical team from Mather Hospital. Bud thanked Deborah and touched her hand before saying goodbye. He managed to ask her before he left if she was raped, and she told him she had managed to avoid it. The medical team put her in the ambulance, where they informed her that both her father and boyfriend, Robert Simpson, would see her at the hospital.

Bud picked up his call from Paul and informed both him and Detective Lieutenant Cronin on his speakerphone as to the information he got from Debbie before taking her away under the protection of the FBI.

"Bud," Cronin said, "go to the body, get his cell phone, and check the calls that came in. Do it quick, and get back to us."

Bud went inside the house and found Wayne Starfield's phone had slipped halfway under the bed. He wrote down all the numbers received on the phone before leaving. Agent Sherman caught Bud on the way out.

"Detective Johnson, what are you doing out here by yourself without your partner? And you haven't even got your gun back from Internal Affairs yet, have you?"

"Agent Sherman," Bud replied, turning around to see eye to eye, "normally those would be good questions that should be answered, but I'm asking for understanding here. We have a joint investigation with you guys because of two people being murdered. One of them a police officer who we are burying tomorrow."

Agent Sherman nodded in silence and replied, "We are getting phone records from John Winters' phone tomorrow. We will bring them over after the funeral. We will see you there."

Bud thanked him and got into his cruiser and drove down to the precinct. He walked in to see Paul at his desk looking over newspaper articles from the past week.

"Where have you been?" Bud asked. "I called you four to five times during all of this."

"Sorry," Paul replied, "I was here but had to take care of some personal business for a bit." Bud got up to take a look at the numbers written down.

"When are we getting answers?"

"Soon, my friend," was Paul's answer.

Detective Lieutenant Cronin was at his desk when an officer from the crime-scene unit came and gave him the list of names and numbers that had been received on Wayne Starfield's cell-phone number. One name was not a surprise. John Winters had called at least twice a day for the past week. The second name was a surprise. He got up and walked out to Bud and Paul.

"Bring in Patty Saunders now! I want her here before the FBI gets ahold of her. She called Starfield's cell phone four times since this mess started.

Bud and Paul got up to leave as Cronin bellowed, "Dress blues tomorrow for the funeral, but get this woman in here now!"

Bud and Paul arrived at Patty Saunders' apartment complex at Knolls Apartments on Belle Terre Road. There was no answer at the door, but they heard a cell phone ring inside.

Bud finally yelled, "Open the door, or I will huff and puff and blow this motherfucking door down." Paul looked at him like he had lost his mind.

"What the fuck," Bud said, "I don't have my main piece."

The door slowly opened, and Patty was already dressed to go down to the station. "You're in a bit of trouble, missy," Bud said.

"Ma'am," Paul said, "I'm going to read you your rights, but we have questions for you at the precinct, and I'm sure the FBI will also."

They brought her in to the precinct, where they questioned her for more than two hours. It was at this interrogation where pieces of the puzzle started coming together. She admitted to being involved in the kidnapping of Debbie Lance. Debbie had everything most people wanted in life—a big mansion, a rich daddy, money, a good job—and Patty couldn't have any of it, so she went after Robert Simpson. Patty felt empowered when she seduced him a few times when Debbie was out of town. He stopped it out of emotional guilt after a few months, so she had gone after Daddy, the ultimate conquest, but he would have nothing of it. He was such a good dad he never told his daughter, for fear it would hurt her too much.

Patty had been promised Debbie would never be physically hurt during the ordeal, but $5 million was too tempting. Patty got the ball rolling from meeting the Winters brothers online through Facebook. They met a few times in Port Jefferson at Pasta Pasta over dinner to discuss their plans. During the interview, Patty broke down in tears that Bud felt were of the crocodile nature.

Paul moved in on Patty to remind her that because of her actions, two innocent people, one of them a cop, was killed and three others were seriously injured. "You're going away for a long time, because of jealousy." Patty nodded in agreement, with tears in her eyes. She continued her story and the involvement of Kyle and Phil Smith, who she believed was behind the killing of Kyle, and now Wayne.

"I guess he wants me dead now," Patty cried.

Bud looked at her from the wall he was leaning against and said, "Honey, I think more than a few people are going to want you dead when this all comes out."

Detective Lieutenant Cronin, who was looking through the one-way mirror with the assistant district attorney said, "We should bring in William Lance and Robert Simpson to be sure they're not involved. The butler at the very least had an affair with Patty, so he may have had cause to be involved with this." ADA Ashley agreed.

"Send two officers to pick them up," Cronin replied quickly.

"I think I'm going to let Paul and Bud do it," Cronin said. "When this thing goes to court, I would like to have them involved in most of this since they are knee-deep already."

ADA Ashley replied, "OK, but the way this is going, there won't be anybody on trial the way the body count is going."

John Ashley was a slim man of 38 who had been with the Suffolk Police Department since graduating from Columbia University in New York City 12 years prior. His dark hair and brown eyes were a hit with the ladies, but his job and passion kept him a bachelor. He walked out the door as Cronin pushed the intercom button and told Paul and Bud to leave the interrogation room.

"What's up, boss?" Bud remarked as they came through the door to the viewing room.

"Have one of the officers book Saunders, you two go pick up William Lance and Simpson, now. The FBI may have already beat us to it."

"Boss, my gun?" Bud replied.

"Not yet," Cronin replied. "If you don't want to go with Paul, then sit this out."

"I'm going," Bud replied.

Bud and Paul arrived back at the end of Cliff Street in Belle Terre to learn that the FBI had already picked up William Lance while he was visiting Deborah at the hospital. Robert Simpson did not go to the hospital, so Paul and Bud turned their attention to the guesthouse. As they knocked on the door, they heard a crash. Paul kicked in the door as Bud ran around the back and collided with Robert.

"What are you, some kind of dumbass?" Bud said, as he held on to Robert. Bud put Simpson to the ground and started talking into his ear. "Where you going? What are you running from? Why are you banging Patty at the same time as pretty Debbie? You must be a dumbass."

Simpson started to talk. "Shut up!" Bud interrupted. "You have the right to remain silent. If not, I may put a bullet up your ass." He stopped as Paul came around the corner and told him his accurate rights.

As they put Simpson in the car and closed the door, Paul turned to Bud and said, "The next time you want to put a bullet up someone's ass, make sure no one can hear you, but more important, you better have a bigger gun to do it with."

"Sorry about that, my partner," Bud replied.

As they drove to the precinct, Bud picked up the paper lying on the seat. It was the Tuesday edition of the *Port Jefferson Now*. He read the article written by Rachelle that included insightful detail yet cryptic messages as to what had been going on and what was yet to come.

"She's very talented," Bud said as he looked at Paul driving.

"Yes," Paul replied.

"She's very smart," Bud said.

"Yes."

"She's very pretty."

"Yes," Paul replied.

Bud paused for a moment and said, "Is she good in bed?"

Paul looked at Bud and said, "Read the article."

"I can't read anymore," he replied. "It gives me a headache. I know you don't know if she's good in bed because you barely have kissed her. I was just checking to see if you were listening to me. Life is going to end, my friend. One day you are going to look back and say, 'I blew it.' At the very least know what it was like to be alone with her. You almost lost her forever a couple days ago. If you have feelings and care about her, stop the being shy shit and make a move when this thing is over, or you will regret it the rest of your life… however long that may be. No one has been murdered here for 20 years, and now we have four people in the last week. Yes, sir, we are the hot spot among killings, and we even got a Ghost Face running around."

Paul turned on to Route 83 South to Coram as he glanced at Bud and said, "Are you going to talk the whole way to the station, or can I listen to music?"

In the backseat, Simpson started to talk and Bud cut him off. "Shut up, dickhead," Bud said. "Just keep yourself in the back with your mouth shut, and I might not make good on my promise." He was, of course, referring to his bullet-up-the-ass remark back at the guesthouse, but he did not want to say it again in front of Paul.

Bud put the radio on and started surfing the channels. As he did, there was a quick bite of *Twist of Fate* from Olivia Newton-John. "Stay on that," Paul yelled.

"Stop, will you," Bud replied as he switched the channel. "That shit's old. How old are you? Twenty-nine? Thirty? What's with this Olivia thing?"

Paul replied back quickly, "Come on, no one was better than her in the '80s, and she's still selling concert tickets in her sixties."

"I know, you already told me that. It's the 21st century, man. What the fuck?" Bud replied.

Paul smiled and said, "I was seven years old and my parents took me to one of her concerts. My dad loved her music, looks, and personality, and I loved her in *Grease*. I was trying to enjoy watching her from the good seats that we had, but it was difficult until my dad put me on his shoulders so I could see her better. Watching her on stage was so incredible, especially when she did songs from *Grease*. Finally, during the show she started to sing 'Magic.' There was a musical interlude at the beginning of the song, and at the first lyrics—'Come take my hand'—she reached out her hand to me and kept it there 'til my dad got me to the stage so I could touch her. She held it tight while she sang a few more lyrics and kissed me when she had a pause from singing the lyrics. It was something that always stayed with me. I guess you could say I was a fan for life because of the attention she gave to a little boy. I grew up buying her CDs as well as others, but there has always been a place in my heart for her. The cancer ordeal she went through, her boyfriend disappearing…but it was the music, her voice, and her sincere appreciation and kindness to her fans that kept me in her corner. Don't forget, the results are there: seven number one songs in a row. The 'Physical' video was so far ahead of its time."

Bud just sat there in the passenger seat with a puzzled look on his face and finally replied, "Man, you are fucked up. This is the most I have ever heard you talk at one time since I have known you, and it's about Olivia Newton-John. I can't even leave. I'm trapped in the car with you listening to this. And I'll tell you something else, give me an Olivia Newton-John song that you can really dance to on a dance floor in a club setting. Tell me that. Tomorrow night, when we get to Danford's, I will show you what entertainment music is all about." Bud looked out the window then back at Paul and said, "Olivia Newton-John?"

From the backseat Simpson barked, "Can you guys talk about something else besides Olivia Newton-John?"

Bud turned around quickly and said, "Shut your fucking ass up or I'll put you in a cell and play nothing but Olivia Newton-John songs. How's that, shithead?"

"I wouldn't mind that," Paul replied with a giggle.

Bud just gave Paul a blank stare and replied, "I want you to know that I will never forget this ride with you. Of all the times we have been together, I can tell this is the one I will always remember. Riding to the precinct with the butler listening to you go on, about Olivia Newton-John."

"I'm not a butler," Simpson replied, "I'm William Lance's executive assistant."

"Oh," Bud shot back. "You're now the horse's ass, and if you are involved in your girlfriend's kidnapping, I will save that bullet for you."

"I would never be involved in that. I love Debbie," was his reply.

"Well, you have a funny way of showing it, shit for brains," Bud replied. "Quiet 'til we get back to the station." He looked at Paul and asked, "Is there anything else we should talk about before we get to the station?"

"No," Paul said, "I think we have bonded enough for now." He glanced at Bud with a smile, and his partner laughed as he gazed out the window. Paul pushed the radio button and stopped it on Katy Perry's "California Girls" with Snoop Dogg. "Is there any song you don't know the lyrics to?" he asked as he watched Bud mouth the lyrics.

"Yeah," he replied, "Olivia Newton-John songs."

"Oh, brother," Simpson said in the back.

"Shut the fuck up," Bud yelled back. Then he looked back at Paul and asked, "You're not stuck in the '80s or some weird shit, are you?" Paul just laughed as Bud continued, "You're not going to tell me you loved the show *Life Goes On* or anything, are you, because that would really freak me out."

Paul shook his head with a smile and replied, "That show was from 1989–1993, so it was a '90s thing."

Simpson shook his head in the backseat as Bud just stared at him. Then Bud spoke again, asking Paul, "And you watched every episode, right, and loved Kellie Martin?"

Paul laughed and answered, "All 83 episodes, and no, I loved Corky, played by Chris Burke."

"OK," his partner answered, "let's go back to Olivia Newton-John."

"Oh, shit," Simpson said, as Bud grabbed a paper and swatted him.

"I said for the last time shut the fuck up!" Bud said.

As Paul laughed, Simpson kept talking, saying, "I think I'd rather be in jail than listening to this."

Paul pulled into the sixth precinct on Route 25 Middle Country Road, Coram, where they handed Simpson over to officers to allow him to get an attorney before questioning. He would be held overnight as a suspect in the kidnapping, plus they knew the FBI would be interested.

As Simpson was locked up, Paul walked up to the bars with Simpson behind them and said, "Your girlfriend was kidnapped. Her girlfriend, Patty Saunders, who you were banging, is involved. And yet what I find most mysterious is that you didn't go to the hospital to see Debbie after going through all of this." Paul walked away, leaving Bud there to take over.

"You really are a dumbass, aren't you?" Bud said and then walked back to Paul to call it a night. They had a funeral to attend to in the morning.

Paul got in the car to drive to the village and called to check on Rachelle. Madison picked up the phone, and they spoke for a few minutes.

Madison said, "Rachelle is sleeping, Paul; she's doing great. She is resting for tomorrow. She wants to be at the funeral."

"OK," Paul replied. "You're a good sister, Maddie."

"No," she replied, "Rachelle is a good sister."

Paul hung up from Madison and called Cronin to give him the latest updates on Simpson. Cronin informed him of the statements being gathered by the FBI at the hospital. Cronin also told Paul there was a dress rehearsal during the day for the funeral in the morning. Paul wasn't surprised, due to the tremendous number of people who attend a fellow officer's funeral, in addition to the need to coordinate traffic, parking, and seating. Cronin had set it up with the FBI and sheriff's office to help out with controlling the traffic and getting help with traffic cones, water, signs, and portable restrooms. The planning and execution of a police officer's funeral was quite a task, especially in the middle of a national case. Detective Lieutenant Cronin was expected not only to speak at Officer Victoria Davis' funeral but also to the media outlets afterward.

The dress rehearsal went well, but that does not always equate to things going perfectly the day of the funeral. Many things need to be coordinated, and all on a strict time limit. Planning such as this requires personnel trained for such unexpected occurrences during the day. Cronin welcomed the services of the New York City agency to help with the planning and burial services at Mt. Sinai Cemetery. Without their help and experience in planning and rehearsing a funeral such as this during the investigation, the Suffolk County Police Department would have been under tremendous stress to send off Victoria Davis in the proper manner. The agency had worked with the New York Police Department in the city for years planning funeral processions.

Paul hung up the phone, ready to get back to his apartment. He knew it would be a long day tomorrow. A funeral for Victoria, interrogation of Robert Simpson, and Internal Affairs was scheduled to meet with Bud about the shooting. As Paul drove home he wished there was more time in the day.

As he drove to Main Street to turn right on Arden place, he decided to keep going straight, which led him directly to the Cross Island Ferry. He made a right turn on East Broadway and a quick left into the parking and loading dock area of the ferry. He got out of the car and stood in the spot where they were when the shots were fired. He kept going over and over in his mind as to how and why it had gotten this far.

He started at the beginning, the kidnapping on the ferry, which they now understood. A jealous girlfriend who wanted Debbie Lance's life and felt empowered by seducing her boyfriend and who had even tried to bang her old man. Timothy was killed because he was overheard talking about himself being the person with Rachelle reenacting a theory on the ferry through her article. Attempts on Rachelle and the rest of the people who were on the ferry, again as a result of the article. Kyle got killed in the hospital, yet the cops were not. Debbie Lance got saved while Wayne Starfield got killed. Patty Saunders admitted to being involved and implicated Kyle, Wayne, and Phil. The evidence said Phil was the one knocking off his ex-partners, which Paul liked. He nodded his head and said "Yes" with a slight grin.

He walked over to the dock at Danford's and walked all the way to the end of the pier. Along the way, he paused to check out the names on the back of the boats. He loved what people would name them. He had many friends who told them the happiest day of their lives was when they got their boat and when they sold the boat. As he walked along the pier, he looked at the names: *Prince Charming, Who's Sorry Now, New York State of Mind, Blessed Event, Aunt Mary, My Rosie, It's About Time*. He laughed as he read a few more.

Anthony Powers, his father, had always wanted to get his own boat and call it *The Wonder of You*. His father always thought it was the most romantic song he had ever heard and wanted to christen his boat with that name. It never happened, but Paul made a mental note that if he ever won the lotto, he would get that boat for his dad. His father had to sell his house on Long Island because the property and school taxes were just too high for him to afford. One of the biggest complaints about beautiful Long Island was that people worked hard all their lives to pay off their mortgages, then they were forced to move when they retired from their jobs because the taxes were too high. Paul walked back to his car, got in, and drove back to Z Pita. He knew he would have a deep sleep that night.

It was getting late, and Cronin was sitting at his desk looking at all the emails from his superiors, journalists, and peers regarding the publicity of the case. He covered his face with his hands, hoping it would make his thoughts become a bit clearer. *I'm getting too old for this bullshit,* he thought. It was a fleeting thought, and as he turned on the TV to see Fox News covering the story, he was reenergized to think, *I'm not going away just yet; we will play this through.* His thoughts changed again when he played his voice mails on his speakerphone. It was the commissioner barking, asking what was going on. He covered his face again, but this time his head was nodding sideways.

Tuesday, June 21

Paul heard the knocks at the bottom of the stairway, then the running up the stairs. It could only be Bud, judging by the intermittent steps. In he walked, in full dress blues, and Paul could tell the gravity of the situation had hit Bud now that they were putting Victoria to rest. It was surreal to Paul also. He buttoned up the top portion of his uniform, put on his white gloves, and both he and Bud walked down the stairs and got into their cruiser to drive to the United Methodist Church in Patchogue. Victoria's family lived on the South Shore while Victoria was growing up, and she stayed loyal to the church when they moved to the North Shore in Miller Place.

The beautiful church was filled to capacity with friends, family, and uniformed police officers. The casket, draped with the American Flag, was brought down the center aisle to the front. Pastor Tom came out and gave a stirring memorial service for Victoria. It lasted more than an hour, with her brother, niece, and Detective Lieutenant Cronin giving memorial speeches about Victoria.

The police then emptied the church in an orderly fashion, and as the casket was carried out from the front of the building, the officers were lined up on both sides as it was brought through. Bud and Paul had requested to be in the line, and it was approved, although Bud still did not have his gun returned to him. The officers stood at attention and saluted as the flag-draped casket was slowly walked through the line.

In the crowd were Rachelle and Madison. Madison could not talk Rachelle out of being there, but the protective side of her was clearly evident, as she would not leave her side. Nearby, Agent O'Connor, on crutches, was with Agent Sherman. Debbie Lance had wanted to be there, but the doctors were not ready to release her until possibly later in the week. The FBI as well as the police were happy with the decision to keep her in the hospital. There was no way to know for certain if her life was still in danger until the case was closed. To be sure, Detective Lieutenant Cronin had officers checking identification on patients and family who were entering the hospital, in addition to the FBI having standing escorts in the hallway near her door. Cronin also assigned Officer Lynagh to Rachelle, whose only assignment was to keep an eye on her during the funeral.

He, like Paul, was concerned about the articles being released and what was to come out later when this was closed. Rachelle wanted to be a writer as well as run a business, and it was noticed that Rachelle had started to carry a small cassette recorder with her to remember her notes. He just hoped it didn't get her killed in the end. She was lucky to be alive now, and Cronin knew that sometimes when luck ran out for the perpetrators—or perps, as cops often referred to them—and they felt they had nothing to lose, all bets were off.

This particular morning, Rachelle had on a gray-and-black matching skirt and top. Her hair was pulled back to help with the already hot morning, and there was still a small bandage on the side of her forehead—a reminder of what had happened only four days before. Paul gave her a quick glance while he was in the line for the casket and thought to himself that even here, even in this circumstance, she was as beautiful as he had ever seen her.

The casket was loaded into the hearse as the parents of Victoria Davis put their hands on the back of the car. Victoria's father held her mother steady as the tears came down her face. Paul could only imagine what the wake had been like the night before. Her mother had insisted on a private wake for close friends and family and would have had a private funeral had it not been for her daughter telling them six months prior that she wanted a police funeral if anything happened to her. She was proud to be a cop and loved her brothers-in-arms. After the funeral, she told them she wanted her fellow officers to have a party in her honor. Her request was going to be honored, and Bud had already made arrangements at Danford's, upstairs, to celebrate her life.

The funeral procession to Mt. Sinai Cemetery, which took about 30 minutes, went without a hitch. The dress rehearsal to figure out the logistics of what needed to be done paid off with dividends. Most do not know the amount of time and effort it takes to coordinate a police funeral. However, Victoria received a meaningful, dignified memorial worthy of her.

When her casket arrived at her final resting place, the pastor spoke for a few minutes about her life, hopes, and desires and finished with, "I knew Victoria from the time she was a young teenager to being a proud member of the Suffolk County Police Department. We spoke many times about her beliefs, likes, and dislikes. During one of our conversations, Victoria told me that she believed that when someone died, there was a reason in how and why and when they died. No life lost is wasted if a lesson was learned. As for the funerals, she told me that they are for the living, for the memories from a funeral will last the rest of us for our lifetime. For that reason, she wants you not to grieve her loss of life but to celebrate her life by remembering her and by not letting her death be in vain." As the pastor spoke these words, Bud considered how he thought he had known Victoria, and yet it appeared he hadn't taken the time to know her enough. Her thoughts, beliefs, and spirit touched him through the voice of the pastor.

The most emotional part of the funeral started as the flag that draped the casket was being folded by members of the American Association of Police Officers. The flag was given to Detective Lieutenant Cronin, who slowly and in a military fashion brought it over to Victoria's mother, thanking her for her daughter's service, and presented the flag to her. In an unusual move, Cronin leaned over and whispered in her ear for about 10 seconds then stepped to the side and leaned over and whispered into Victoria's father's ear for the same length of time. He stepped back, shook his head, and saluted the flag her mother was holding a final time and marched away.

There were more than 400 people at the funeral, more than 300 of whom were officers who paid their respects to Victoria Davis' short life. As the funeral ended, Paul thought that Victoria would have been proud of the way everything went. Yes, it was a funeral, but it was more like a memorial. One that was perfect for her. He walked by the casket, touched it, and said goodbye to her. As he walked away, he saw Rachelle and Madison walking to their cars. He tried to catch up to them but was slowed down with the crowd and the need to exchange cordial hellos and greetings with his fellow officers. He took his cell from his pocket and sent Rachelle a text message: "Sorry we couldn't talk today, but you looked beautiful." He put it back in his pocket when Detective Lieutenant Cronin walked up to him.

Cronin said, "Paul, you need to get back to the precinct to question Simpson. The phone records came in for Winters, and Internal Affairs wants to talk to Bud. Get your asses moving."

Bud met Paul back at the car, and it took them almost an hour just to get themselves on the road to the sixth precinct. On the way, Paul pulled out his phone to find a message from Rachelle. It said, "Thank you, I thought you looked very handsome in your uniform."

Paul smiled as Bud looked over at him and said, "If you don't start taking care of business with her, I'm going to introduce someone to her."

Paul just looked at Bud and then stared out the window. Bud started talking again anyway, saying, "Make sure she comes tonight. I've got something very special planned, my friend."

"I'm sure you do," Paul replied. He sent Rachelle a text to remind her to come. He offered to pick her up at her house, but she texted back that she would meet him there. Madison would be going with her but would be leaving the club early on a date. Rachelle sent a text to Paul that he could walk her home from Danford's when the evening was over.

Bud and Paul walked in to the precinct to find out that Cronin was in a meeting with Internal Affairs in his office. If only they could be a fly on the wall now. Paul told Bud he would meet him later and wished him well with his meeting with Internal Affairs. Still in his dress blues, Paul met Assistant District Attorney Ashley for a brief meeting before going in to speak with Simpson. Patty Saunders was still being held without bail in lockup in the back of the precinct. Robert Simpson was sitting in the room, clearly upset and nervous, but he had waived his right to an attorney because he claimed he had nothing to do with the money or the kidnappings.

As Paul walked into the room, Simpson started yelling, "How long do I have to be here! I haven't seen Debbie yet!"

Paul sat down in a chair and said, "I wouldn't worry about that right now. I don't think she will be in too much of a hurry to see you by the time the FBI is finished with her."

"No!" Simpson started yelling.

"Calm down," Paul said, "or I'll leave and have Detective Johnson come in and question you. Right now he's trying to get his gun back from Internal Affairs. Sometimes he fires his gun a little too much."

"Keep that psycho away from me!" Simpson yelled.

"Listen," Paul said, "just answer my questions. Calm down."

Robert finally settled down and started answering Paul's questions. For two hours, Robert discussed his life with Debbie, his work with William Lance, and even his intimate encounters with Patty for a few months. His indiscretions during these months were the genesis of all that was to follow.

Paul stood up to stretch his legs and looked down at Simpson. He said, "You may have had nothing to do with kidnapping Debbie Lance or the killings that followed, but by letting your dick do the talking for you—yeah that's right, by not keeping it in your pants because you had to have another piece of ass—it was the root of all this evil. As of now, we are not going to charge you, but quite frankly I think your punishment is going to be worse because I have no idea how you are going to explain yourself to Debbie and her father. And if you are still with her and working for the old man after all this, I may just want your autograph because it would be the greatest magic trick of all time. Hold on a second," he said as he left Simpson there and entered the viewing room with the assistant district attorney.

"Let him go," Ashley said. "We have nothing on him for now, but I want to hear the tape again anyway."

Meanwhile, Bud had his own interrogation to be concerned about. Officer Steve Rubelli was going through the motions, questioning Bud about the shooting at the Red Onion Café, and for one of the few times in his career, Bud took and followed the advice of both Paul and Detective Lieutenant Cronin. His answers were straight and to the point.

It had been Cronin's statement before he walked into the room that made an impression on Bud. As Bud was walking to the room, Cronin had grabbed his arm and said, "No hiding behind a clown face today. There are people here who care and are concerned about you. I let you go out on calls with just a backup gun because I want you involved in the trial. Don't prove to them that I misjudged you. Don't prove to them I don't know what I am doing by making poor decisions when it comes to you. But most of all show them how intelligent and how good of a cop you are without sidestepping stress with the humor. This is serious. Make sure you project the attitude that you know how serious it is."

Bud had gotten to the door, turned around, and said, "I won't let you down, boss." Cronin nodded as Bud stepped inside.

Detective Lieutenant Cronin had also spoken to Rubelli in his office before his meeting with Bud and told Rubelli just how he felt and what he would do if Bud didn't get his gun back. When Rubelli asked Cronin if he was threatening Internal Affairs, the detective lieutenant answered back quickly, "No, I'm protecting you. I'm telling you that you have a good cop here who witnessed a fellow officer shot and killed, who is knee-deep in the middle of this case, which is the biggest case in this town for the past 20 years and for certain the rest of our careers. He finds himself alone in the back of a restaurant with a cop killer. He did what every one of us would do, and quite frankly many cops would have done in the shooter. Detective Johnson had the frame of mind to shoot when he felt threatened. So what I'm saying, Officer Rubelli, is that I'm letting you know if he doesn't get his gun back from the review board, I'm going to fight it aggressively. And quite frankly, I don't think public opinion on this one would be too interested in your side of things. So go do what you have to do, but keep things in perspective. We are talking about a gunshot to someone who was murdered at the hospital by someone who was involved in the killing of a cop. Thanks for your time and for listening."

Officer Rubelli left the office knowing that Cronin had a point, and unless Bud surprised them with answers completely out of the ordinary for this type of case, Johnson would get his firearm back. Bud did not let anyone down. He sat in the meeting before the Internal Affairs review board and convinced them he attempted to avoid the discharge of his firearm. He ended the interview by saying, "I love being a cop. I love my brothers-in-arms family and I'm proud to be here and I understand why you need to do this, but I need you to understand that we officers who have gone through something like this need the support from all our brothers. A good cop was killed because she happened to be in the same car as the target. It's more important to me that we lost Victoria Davis than it is about me shooting a cop killer in the groin."

Bud was excused and went back to Detective Lieutenant Cronin's office to give him the details of the meeting. Phone records came in of John Winters' calls to Patty Saunders, seven times; Phil Smith, eight times; his brother Mason, four times; Kyle Winters, five times; and Wayne Starfield, 14 times during Deborah's kidnapping.

"I guess we have enough for a warrant," Cronin said as he picked up his phone and called Agent Sherman and informed him they had pretty good evidence to pick up John and Mason Winters. As soon as he hung up the phone, it rang again. This time it was Rubelli on the other end. "Thank you," Cronin said as he hung up the phone. He opened his draw and pulled out Bud's Glock 9mm gun, an Austrian-made pistol that was a favorite of cops and standard issue to FBI agents. Cronin amused himself by thinking it was also a favorite of rap stars. After putting it back in its holster, he gave it to Bud.

"Congratulations, Detective Johnson, you are now a brother *with* arms again. Rubelli was impressed with your statements."

"Yeah," Bud said as he got up to leave. "Thank goodness I didn't tell him I had to take the biggest crap of my life while I was in there."

The door shut as Cronin shook his head and said, "The Comedian."

Bud met Paul to drive over to Mather Hospital to visit with Deborah Lance to try and get some information while it was still fresh on her mind. They met with her doctor, who told them she was severely beaten and barely escaped being raped when Starfield was killed. Physically, she would eventually be OK; however, emotionally would be a different story. He said she would need intense therapy to get through this. Also at the hospital was Agent O'Connor, who had come in for some follow-up questions while still on his crutches from the gunshot wound. They had seen him at the funeral earlier, but it was not appropriate to speak with him there. He told Bud and Paul that Debbie's face was pretty bruised but that she was holding up well until they broke the news to her about Patty's involvement with the kidnapping and her involvement with Simpson the prior year.

"She took it pretty hard," O'Connor explained. "She loved him. The old man took it hard too but told him he had three days to get out of the guesthouse. He wants him gone before Debbie gets back. She wouldn't even see him. We told her we didn't think he was involved in her kidnapping, but she's done with him, I think."

"Thanks," Paul said, "we are going to speak with her for a few minutes. Can you just make sure your guards let us in?" O'Connor nodded and waved to the agents at the door to let the two detectives in the room.

They walked in to see Debbie Lance sleeping and her dad sitting at her bedside holding her hand. He looked up at Bud and Paul and acknowledged to them to come over. Paul stood by her bedside looking at the young woman sleeping and could not hear Bud talking to the father regarding the events over the past week. Paul was in one of his trances where he blanked everything out except what he was looking at and thinking. He looked at her pretty face with bruises on her cheek and her left eye. Starfield walloped her so hard he had fractured her nose and made her eye swell up as well as giving her rib cage a fracture. To think what he would have done if he had not been stopped by the masked intruder.

Paul was very touched by watching her father stroke her hair as she lay there. His thoughts went to Rachelle and how she could have been lost. Officer Davis, Timothy, Kyle Winters, Wayne Starfield. All dead, with Debbie, Rachelle, and Agent O'Connor injured seriously because of a jealous girlfriend who wanted money and power from the Lance family. Paul's head was spinning with all the possible angles. His thoughts had taken over so much that he didn't even hear Bud call his name to see if he had any more questions for William Lance. Finally, Bud touched Paul on the arm to get his attention and said, "Paul, any questions for Mr. Lance?"

"Yes," Paul said. "Mr. Lance, is there anything you are not telling us out of embarrassment to you, your daughter, or your business about all of this?"

William Lance seemed stunned by the question and sat back in his chair and started to stare in the air to gather time and his thoughts.

"Why do you have to think so hard and so long?" Paul went on. "Your daughter was beaten and almost raped. People are dead, and our case is saying that Patty Saunders instigated all of this out of jealousy. Is this what this case is about? And, by the way, you never told us about Ms. Saunders trying to get you into bed. Mr. Lance, did you have a life-insurance policy out on Debbie?"

"Not here," Lance replied.

"Yes or no, Mr. Lance? Was there a policy on her?"

"Yes," he replied.

"How much?" Paul asked. "How much?" Paul said again in a much stronger voice.

"Five million dollars," Lance answered.

"Five million dollars for a 26-year-old woman?" Paul replied. Bud was just standing there silently watching Paul ask the questions. There was no one better in Bud's eyes than Paul, when he got on a roll with questions.

Paul moved a little closer to William Lance and said, "Mr. Lance, tell me why you had a $5 million policy on your daughter." William Lance stared back at Debbie sleeping.

"Not here," he said.

"Then let's go get a cup of coffee," Paul said. Bud looked at them and said he was going to stay with Debbie in case she woke up.

As William Lance and Paul walked down the hallway to the coffee shop, Agent O'Connor informed Paul that the FBI had raided both Thompson Street homes for the Winters brothers, and they were not surprised they were not there. A manhunt was now under way, but quite frankly these were not the type of guys to skip from their comfort zone, so it was just a matter of time. O'Connor accepted Paul's offer to witness the questioning as they headed toward the café. In Debbie Lance's room, Bud was looking at her when she opened her eyes.

She smiled and said, "You again?"

"Hi there, Ms. Lance," Bud said as he smiled back.

"You are the detective that was there at the house."

"Yes," he said. "Call me Bud."

"This time I have clothes on," she replied with a half-hearted laugh. "What a way to meet someone for the first time."

"Don't worry about that," Bud said. "The important thing is that you are going to be fine and this thing is almost over." She turned her head, and Bud could see the tear tickle down her cheek.

"My best friend seduced the man I have loved since I was 13 or 14 years old. They both betrayed me, and now innocent people were killed by trying to help find me." As the young woman started to let out a burst of tears, Bud sat by her.

"Listen," he said. "We are going to figure this out, I promise. The important thing is you are going to be OK physically; emotionally, there are going to be people to help you. This is my card, call me any time. I was there when your clothes were off, I am here with your clothes on, and I will be there no matter what."

The young woman looked at Bud in amazement that a cop would speak to her like that, but he started laughing and told her, "That means no matter what, I will be there for you if you need me. By the way," he added, "you look like a Deborah to me." She started laughing for the first time in a while. "Listen," Bud said, "can I ask you some questions?"

"Sure," Debbie replied. "If I can ask you a few."

"OK," Bud said. "Let's take turns."

"Deal," she replied. Bud asked her questions about the five days she was held hostage. He wanted anything that would help with evidence during a trial once charges were filed against Patty Saunders and the Winters Brothers. In turn, Debbie asked questions about what they knew about Patty and Robert. One of them being if there was evidence that her boyfriend was responsible for her going through this.

Bud answered as honestly as he could to her, saying, "Right now, the only evidence we have is that he used poor judgment in getting involved intimately with Patty. He ended the relationship over his guilt of betraying you, but a woman scorned is a very dangerous thing."

"How would you know?" Debbie asked.

"I grew up with three sisters and my mom. So I know these things. That's a question, so it's my turn again."

She laughed and said, "Are you a comedian or a cop?"

"That's two questions in a row, so I get two."

"OK, OK," Deborah said, smiling.

Bud's face turned serious again as he asked, "Deborah, tell me why your dad would have a $5 million insurance policy out on you."

"I asked my dad that question about three years ago. He looked at me and just said, 'Because you are everything to me.' That's all he told me. I just figured when we lost our mom, he reacted a bit by insuring me."

"Did you see anyone else the whole time you were held hostage, besides Starfield?"

"No," she replied.

"What about on the ferry? Can you tell me how they did it? We had our own theory, which was put in an article in the paper. We believe the article was so close to the truth it prompted the shootings to eliminate the reporter who wrote the article."

Deborah told him everything that had happened on the boat, and Paul's theory was almost dead-on. The only difference was that once they had her in the trunk of one of the cars, they didn't want to take a chance of anything happening on the ferry, so the car that held Deborah drove around back to Long Island on the Connecticut Turnpike then most likely on the Cross Island Parkway back to the Long Island Expressway back to Port Jefferson. No tolls involved, except for the Throgs Neck Bridge. The second car simply turned around and went back on the ferry after they dropped off Deborah's burnt-orange Charger.

"How do you know that?" Bud asked.

"I heard them talking through the trunk," she replied.

"This is good," Bud said. "How do you think or who do you think made the calls from a payphone at McDonald's rest stop?"

"I don't know," Deborah said.

"Look at me," Bud said. "Does Patty or Robert have relatives in Connecticut that you know they have kept in touch with?"

Deborah looked at Bud with her glassy eyes and said Patty had a cousin in Milford, Connecticut.

Bud nodded his head in acknowledgement and said, "You're doing great."

"I'm kind of tired," Deborah replied.

"I know," Bud replied. "Thank you, Deborah."

"You know my dad is the only one who calls me Deborah; everyone else calls me Deb or Debbie."

"I'm sorry," Bud replied. "I'm partial to formal names."

"It's OK," the young patient replied. "You can call me Deborah." With that she closed her eyes and drifted off. Bud smiled, looking at her, and realized how lucky she was to be alive.

He wrote a note on his writing pad that said, *Thursday; watch interrogation video of Robert Simpson with Paul.* He left the room and walked down to the café and sat down at the table where Agent O'Connor and Paul were with William Lance.

"Mr. Lance, excuse me if this is a repeat question that Agent O'Connor and Detective Powers have already asked, but I would appreciate knowing why there is a $5 million policy out on Deborah Lance?"

"As I mentioned earlier in the conversation, I insured Deborah because when I bought the policy I had not sold the 8:15 office business yet. My plan was to have Deborah run the business; therefore, the large policy was not unusual."

"Who else knew about the policy amount?" Agent O'Connor interjected.

As Lance hesitated, Paul chimed in, "Let's make it easy for you. Did Robert Simpson and Patty Saunders know about it?"

As Lance put his head down, he said, "Yes."

"So we have motive on both of them," Paul said. He called Detective Lieutenant Cronin, who in turn sent officers to pick up Simpson again.

"Mr. Lance," Bud went on. "Why would Patty Saunders know about something like this? Simpson was your assistant and almost family. Why and how did Patty know about this?"

Lance shook his head as he answered, "They were so close, it just came up during a conversation one day. We were talking about the business, how Deborah would eventually have it. She promised Patty there would be a place for her."

Paul looked at Agent O'Connor and Bud, then turned to Lance. "So when you sold the business last year, Patty lost her career job, lost her best friend to Simpson with a possible marriage, and she would be left out in the cold. Tell us about the relationship with you."

William Lance looked directly at Paul, making eye contact, and said, "I'm a 60-year-old man. What normal guy my age would not be tempted to have a 23-year-old at the time and a very beautiful girl in my bed? It was hard to not fall victim to her."

"It was hard, all right," Bud interjected. Paul gave Bud a whack on his arm.

"Continue," Paul said to Lance.

He leaned forward to speak again, saying, "As hard—or should I say difficult—as it was not to fall prey to her, I would not betray my daughter. In addition, my reputation as former Suffolk County executive, my business, there was no way I would ruin my life, which would have affected my girl too much." Paul believed him.

Bud couldn't stay silent any longer and said, "What did Patty do to attempt to get involved?"

"One night," Lance started, "I went upstairs to leave the kids at the pool and Patty came in my room about 10 minutes later to talk to me. She got close, and I couldn't help it. We kissed, and within seconds she grabbed my crotch and wanted to, quote, 'See my Lance,' so to speak. She had her top off when I pulled her off me and told her I couldn't go through with it. She told me not to worry about it. No strings attached, she said, but I knew there were always strings attached when it came to young women and older men with sex."

"When exactly was this?" O'Connor chimed in.

"Last summer," Lance answered.

"Same time as Simpson," O'Connor replied.

Bud looked at Lance and added, "So when she couldn't tame you, she went after Deborah's boyfriend, and he couldn't hold his load, which is the root of all this evil."

Paul just gazed over at Bud, thinking, *Wow, what a way with words.*

"How much did you get for the business?" Paul asked.

"Forty-seven million, plus 5 percent of the profits for Deborah's lifetime."

"So, Deborah is a millionaire for her entire life," Bud added.

"Anything else, Mr. Lance? Do you know the Winters brothers?

John, Mason, Kyle? Have you ever heard or seen them before?" Paul asked.

"No," Lance replied. "I would have preferred Patty blackmailed me instead of this happening to Deborah. Listen, I need to get back to her. We can talk as much as you want later, but no one has been in her room for almost an hour."

"No problem," Paul said. "We will talk later. Thank you for your cooperation."

William Lance left the room, leaving the two detectives and the FBI agent to discuss their notes.

"He's not involved," O'Connor started off the conversation. "In fact, he's a little boring. This thing with Patty was the most exciting thing that happened to him in years, yet he didn't go through with it because he was afraid of losing his daughter's love and respect."

Bud looked at O'Connor and said, "I'd say that's a pretty good fucking reason not to bang her. You got to have a lot of love and discipline not to follow through on the one-yard line. Fucking guy was that close to a touchdown and extra point, instead, he went back 10 yards and punted."

Bud got up to take a call from Detective Lieutenant Cronin and stepped away from the table. O'Connor looked at Paul and asked him, "Listen, your partner, is he still on medication?"

Paul laughed and said, "No, he's not. He may seem like a clown, but he chooses to be this way to see reactions from people. He reads people very well. He's a good cop and has solved many cases with me, and quite frankly he likes to take the stress out of situations with his words."

"You mean like telling Simpson he would put a bullet up his ass?" O'Connor replied.

"Yeah, like that," Paul answered. "How did you know about that?"

"Simpson told Agent Sherman this morning when the FBI questioned him. I asked him not to put it in his report." Paul thanked O'Connor.

"I guess we need to help him a little on his people skills, Agent O'Connor."

"Call me Jack," he said, as he put out his right hand to shake. Paul shook it as Bud came back to tell him the Detective Lieutenant wanted them back at the precinct.

"We'll catch up later, Jack," Paul said, getting up.

"Later, Jack," Bud said as he shook hands with the agent and walked away. O'Connor just shook his head as he gathered up his crutches to leave.

When Bud and Paul arrived at the precinct, Cronin quizzed them about their interview with both Deborah and her father. He was satisfied William Lance was not involved at this time.

"Why would these guys go to all this trouble to kidnap her on the ferry? Why not just take her in Port Jefferson?"

Paul looked at the chalkboard of notes in his office and said, "Boss, I think they wanted the question mark of the possibility of being in Connecticut and not under our noses in Port Jefferson."

"Maybe," Cronin replied. "Do we think that anyone else is in danger besides Debbie Lance 'til this case is closed?"

"Rachelle," Paul replied. "Her articles about all of this, and the repercussions as a result of this, would piss me off if I were them. They have nothing to lose now by killing her. At the very least Phil Smith, who we think has turned on them, would want her dead if the Winters brothers didn't."

Bud interjected, "Maybe if we didn't look for Phil, he would kill the remaining Winters brothers and save the tax payers quite a lot of money." Cronin and Paul continued as if they didn't hear Bud.

"Let's get a female officer over to Rachelle's house," Cronin said. "You know her well. Convince her to have an officer with her until this thing is over."

"Right," Paul said. "I will be seeing her tonight at Danford's for the celebration for Victoria. I will convince her."

"Go over there now and talk to her," Cronin said. "Let's make it happen now. Bud, get a female officer assigned over there within the next couple hours. I have a meeting with the district attorney and the chief in an hour. Both of you, get lost. Tomorrow, Paul, work with Agents Sherman and O'Connor to tie up loose ends, and let's find those two assholes. Bud, what's on your agenda?"

"My plans are to watch Paul's interrogation of Simpson and question both of them based on my notes from it," Bud replied.

"Good, good," Cronin replied. "Now get out of here."

"Drop me off at Rachelle's, Bud. I want to speak to her about a few things," Paul said.

As Detective Powers went to the parking lot to wait, Bud got ahold of the desk sergeant to look at what officers were on duty for the next 24 hours. His finger stopped at Officer Sherry Walker, a young African American officer who Bud had met a few months prior. Nice, but a tough cop. He had the desk sergeant get ahold of her to have him patch her through to him in the car as he was driving to Port Jefferson.

He was in the car with Paul for five minutes when the call was put through. "Officer Walker," Bud said, "you have just been assigned to protective custody. Meet us at the house at the top of Prospect Street, Port Jefferson. You are one lucky cop. Who knows, maybe you will be on the news when this is over."

She answered back, "Is it you I have to protect?"

"Ah, a smartass," Bud replied, "Very nice. OK. Just meet us there." It took Bud about 12 minutes to reach Rachelle's house. It was about 5:00 pm, and they were all meeting at Danford's at 7:30 pm.

The door was answered by Madison, who greeted both detectives warmly. They stepped in, and within a minute, Rachelle was walking into the foyer to greet them both with a hug and a kiss. They were now more than cops to Rachelle; they were not only friends but were bonded together by this chain of events that would forever link them together. Paul looked at Rachelle and wanted to stroke her hair but got control of himself. He wanted to ask her about protective custody but decided to take a more firm approach.

"Rachelle, we have assigned an officer to stay with you 'til this case is over. She starts in an hour and will be with you until the morning, to be relieved by another female officer."

Rachelle just looked at him and Madison and said, "Do I have a say in this?"

"Rachelle," Paul replied, "you have a say, but if you said no I would assign her outside on the street, and I think she would be more comfortable just being in here with you than out there on your front porch. It would also be less stressful on me."

"Why is that?" Rachelle asked.

Madison could tell from Rachelle's facial expression that she was looking for Paul to express feelings for her, but he kept it as professional as he could. The detective stuttered for a few seconds but managed to explain the job itself would be easier knowing someone was with her.

Rachelle looked at Madison and said, "What do you think, Maddie? You live here also."

Madison was quick to answer, "I say yes, do it. Besides, I can go on my date tonight and have less stress also." She winked at Paul.

Rachelle looked at Bud and said, "You're very quiet through all of this."

"I just don't want to be an influence one way or the other, but I will tell you this now that you asked. There is no downside to having an officer here, and speaking of stress, quite frankly, I think it will relieve you of some, and you might like Sherry."

"OK," Rachelle said. As if there was such a thing as perfect timing, the doorbell rang. Madison answered the door, and it was Sherry with a piece of luggage.

"Hi there," she said. Bud introduced Sherry to everyone, and Madison showed her the pull-out sofa in the den.

"No worries," Sherry said. "I'm all set."

"Paul," Rachelle remarked, "follow me; I want to show you something." He followed her to her side office next to her bedroom. While they were still in the hallway, they could hear Bud singing "Sherry Baby," by the Four Seasons, to her.

As soon as they got to Rachelle's office, she turned around and looked at Paul. "Do you really want this for me?"

"Yes."

"Why can't you tell me why?"

"Because I'm a cop trying to solve this thing first, and truth be known, you know why."

Rachelle stared at Paul, still wanting to hear why from him, but understood. She asked, "Do you want to look at what I'm writing for the *Newsday* and *Now* papers? As soon as this thing is over, all this will be published. I'm so excited about it."

"Well, I'm glad you are waiting a bit. Thank you," Paul remarked.

They started to walk back to the foyer, when Paul suddenly turned around and hugged Rachelle. He held on to her and Rachelle closed her eyes, with a sigh of relief on her face. As they reached the foyer, Rachelle thanked Sherry for coming.

"Are you going with us to Danford's tonight?" she asked.

Sherry looked at Paul and Bud and said, "Not if these two are going to be there. I think I will wait for you here, as long as they bring you home."

"No problem at all," Paul said. "OK, we shall see you at the upstairs club in a couple hours."

As they left the house, Bud was singing again, and Sherry answered the call. "Bud, you're a cop ruining a perfectly good song to the status of shit. I should arrest you for it." Bud waved his hand up, acknowledging her as he walked away.

"Seems like you met your match," Paul said, laughing at Bud.

"Yeah, yeah, kiss my ass," Bud replied with a smile.

"I'll meet you at the club," Paul answered. "I'm going to walk down the hill to my place."

"Later, my friend," Bud replied as he got in the car. As Paul walked down the hill, passing the museum shop and the Port Jefferson Historical Society house, his thoughts turned to John Winters.

John Winters slammed his hand down against the desk. The vibration was so hard that the objects on the desk popped up for a millisecond. "I should have never gotten involved with amateurs," he said.

Mason walked over to him and said, "If we are going down, the least we can do is take as many as we can with us." John looked out of the abandoned window they were at.

Mason continued, "Starting with that bitch that wrote and started this. Take her out, then we go after Phil before he gets us. After we finish off the girl, maybe we need to lay low for a few days. We might get lucky and Phil will get captured or killed by the cops."

John nodded and said, "It's going to be him or us, but it's the girl that forced all of this."

Mason smiled and replied, "She will die, John."

"We can't stay here too long," John replied. "We have every FBI agent and cop looking for us. Make sure no cell phone use. We need to make sure we finalize all plans before we separate. We'll stay here a couple nights then move to a motel until we are finished. Pay for everything by cash. I put aside about 20 grand the past few years in envelopes just in case something like this happened."

"John," Mason replied, "that's good, but 20 grand is good for a couple of months, maybe a little more. What's next?"

"After we take care of business, we leave and start a new life with a different look. Our life is over here, including the equity on the homes. This is why people are going to pay for my inconvenience." As he slammed the desk again, he said, "You get ahold of that pretty little thing, and you tear her apart from limb to limb. Then we get Mr. Phil Smith and we will remind him who the boss is. You know where she lives, but don't forget they may have someone watching the house. Most likely they are keeping an eye on pretty Miss Debbie-two-shoes at the hospital as well. We may not get out of this, but I want a few people before I go." He sat down on the chair, took a piece of paper, and started writing names down in order: Rachelle Robinson, Phil Smith, Debbie Lance, Bud Johnson. He started scribbling all over the names once he was satisfied that this was the list of names he wanted before his own life was over or taken.

Paul decided to stop at the restaurant before going upstairs. He asked for Joey Z, who sat down with Paul.

"Has Rachelle told you when she will be back at work?" Paul asked.

"She told me Friday," Joey answered, "but I have extra help scheduled with Tina and Emily in case there's a problem."

"OK, good," Paul answered. "I'm concerned about her, but there's only so much you can say to her. Listen, if she does come to work, there will be a female police officer outside just in case. She will be looking at who's coming in or out, and if you see a complete stranger and want to bring it to her attention, let her know."

Joey Z hesitated for a bit then replied, "Listen, I love Rachelle, she belongs here, but we have a business to run here. If you think there is a possibility someone will try to harm her while she's working in here, it's not good for her and it is not good for the business."

Paul digested what Joey Z said and replied, "I know where you are coming from. I will talk to her tomorrow."

"Listen, Paul," Joey added, "I will speak to her also. This is hers also, and we need her, but I can't risk the business being harmed and would never forgive myself if someone harmed her here."

Paul nodded and said, "I understand, Joey. Hearing it from you, I have to agree. You have to forgive us cops; we are not the best when it comes to running a business."

Joey Z grabbed Paul's hand and said, "You got to solve this thing. We want her back, and this town needs to go back to the way it was."

"I hear you," Paul said as he put his free hand on top of Joey's.

"How about dinner?" Joey said.

"No, not tonight. Thanks. Going to Danford's for a party Officer Davis wanted us to throw for her."

"Nice," Joey said. "Me, well, I don't have a life. This is my life, but I wouldn't trade with you right now."

Paul laughed as he left the restaurant to go around the back and up to his apartment. His voice mail was full of messages, mostly from his father, who threatened to come up to New York again because he had not heard from Paul. There was a Woolworth reunion coming up in a week, and his father was attending anyway, so it really didn't matter, but he was hoping this would be over by the time he came up. The reunion was in the city, so he wouldn't even see his dad for at least a couple days after, so he figured he had about 10 days for him and Bud to get this case finished.

One of the messages was from Cronin, whose voice boomed out of the machine: "Don't answer your cell phone calls and texts? Give me a call before I drive over there and ruin your party tonight."

Paul called Detective Lieutenant Cronin, knowing his bark was worse than his bite, at least with the good guys. The bad guys, well, his bite had rabies. No one wanted to be around him when he was foaming at the mouth. A figure of speech, sure, amongst the officers at the department, but as the saying goes, "There's a bit of truth in everything said in jest." Detective Lieutenant Cronin wanted to know what Paul thought of Sherry.

"She seems good," Paul replied. "A little small but good."

"Don't worry about the small part, she would kick your ass, and she scored higher than you in marksmanship."

"Thanks, boss. Is that all?" Paul replied.

"That's it. Enjoy your evening." The phone went *click,* and Cronin was smiling that he had pushed Paul's button as he got his coat to go home.

Paul took his clothes off while watching Fox News and jumped in the shower to get ready for the evening. While he was under the water, his thoughts went to Rachelle. He thought tonight he would have had an opportunity to be alone with her. Yet again, another circumstance with a guard at the house, it just was not going to happen. He'd known her for more than three years and they had never had a chance to be more than friends. His job, her job, his friends, her friends, his father, her sister, now a murder making national headlines, not to mention almost losing her forever to a bullet that grazed her head. He made up his mind he would speak to Rachelle Thursday about holding off on returning to Z Pita. He wanted her to have a good time tonight, and Paul knew that Thursday was going to be a long day.

When he stepped out of the bathroom he heard Shepard Smith on Fox News, signing off, which meant it was 8:00 pm. He had gotten into the habit of keeping his television on the Fox channel because of his dad. His father loved Bill O'Reilly, Sean Hannity, and Shepard Smith, and Paul found that by watching the Fox channel he got closer to his dad. They did not always agree on the subjects, but he loved the debates they had. Anthony Powers considered himself a Reagan conservative, while Paul thought of himself as a Giuliani moderate. The debates were fun, challenging, and only got heated a couple of times. Paul learned never to bring up politics with anyone else. People he considered close friends became acquaintances after conversations that involved opinions on the status of the current administration.

He picked up the phone to dial his dad's cell phone and got his voice mail. When he heard the beep, he said "Hi, Dad, this is Paul. I was watching Fox News and was thinking about you. I love you, Dad; just wanted you to know. See you soon. This case has got us all a little busy, but like you always said, it's not about being busy, it's about the priorities in your life. You were right, Dad." He hung up the phone.

Rachelle finished brushing her hair and walked into the kitchen, where Sherry was pouring herself some water. They engaged in conversation about being a cop and how Rachelle ended up having two jobs. They took an immediate liking to each other and shared a few laughs. The conversation eventually turned to Bud and Paul.

"Are they good cops?" Rachelle asked. Sherry seemed surprised by the question.

"You know them, right?" Sherry asked.

"Yes, I know them," Rachelle answered. "Paul has been a tenant of the restaurant for five years, and I know Bud through Paul. They are good people, but I asked if they were good cops."

"Both of them are very different from each other but none more loyal to each other. I know Bud better than Paul, but he has said he wouldn't have any other partner in a time of need. They close more cases than most. Why do you ask?"

Rachelle replied, "Just curious."

"OK, girl," Sherry replied, "you're going to have to elaborate when you get back tonight. Do you hear me, girl?"

"Yes, I do," Rachelle said as she laughed, going into the bathroom.

Sherry looked at the door close but still said out loud, "I smell trouble, girl." She walked back to the den to pull out the sofa to get sheets on it. She would lie down, read a bit, and watch television until Rachelle got back from the celebration. She was happy that Paul and Bud were with Rachelle tonight. She would much rather lie down in peace and quiet. Madison came out of her room looking like a million bucks.

"Whew! Look at you!" Sherry exclaimed. Madison laughed. At 5'9", Madison's long, slim, and toned legs were featured in her short skirt and top. With the heels she was wearing, she was close to six feet tall, yet she looked even taller with her slim body. "Somebody's got a hot date tonight!"

"You are funny," Madison laughed out loud. "And yes, he is hot. The problem is, so am I, and I don't mean in the vain sense."

"Oh, man!" Sherry yelled. "To be single again in this day and age."

Madison stopped in at the foyer, turned around, and asked, "You are married?"

Sherry nodded and said, "For about two years now. You would think once we are married no more protective custody?"

"I guess I never thought about it, but it must be difficult to be married with a job like this."

Sherry just waved back and said, "Honey, let me tell you. A gig like this is very rare, and you will learn once you're married, you need a break once in a while. Trust me."

"OK, I'll trust you," Madison replied, "but I don't know if I could ever marry at this point. It seems like every man I meet, whether they are good in bed or not, they are a slob when it comes to the house, especially the kitchen and the bathroom!"

"Well," Sherry answered, "if you think you're going to marry them, you better start training them early, but you may be right about the slob part."

Madison and Sherry continued their conversation as Rachelle put the finishing touches on getting ready for the "Life Celebration" at Danford's. They talked about everything from world events to one day having children. Sherry was very easy to talk to about anything. She grew up in the Central Islip area as a kid, which was and still is considered not to be the safest of areas on Long Island. The schools are not considered to be among the best, and the rate of crime is high relative to the surrounding areas on the Island. Sherry recognized this as a teenager, and it was all these factors that made her driven to make something of herself. At 5'5", she was about the same height as Rachelle with the same tone and muscles of Madison. She worked out three to four times weekly and took a self-defense class.

The process of going through the steps to become a detective is filled with an examination. Once you take the exam you are placed on a list to fill in openings in the detective department. To get on the actual placement can sometimes be a matter of who you know and not what you know. Even though the political process was a part of it, Sherry had a positive attitude that with her record, education, and the support of Detective Lieutenant Cronin, it was just a matter of time before she wore civilian clothes for work.

After she graduated from the police academy at 29, she expected to be a detective within a year. In many departments going from patrol division to detective division was a lateral transfer, but not in Suffolk County, Long Island. You had to go through the process of being promoted to sergeant, then lieutenant, and so on. Sherry loved to read, and going through 10 to 14 books a year was no problem for her. Books about the courtroom were her favorite, which is why she loved most of what John Grisham wrote. Her taste in music was Rihanna, Beyonce, and Usher, and she was fully aware the music tonight was not going to have very much of that. Regardless, she would have attended the affair if she had known Victoria Davis. She was at the funeral in the morning and respected her fellow officers regardless of their personal choices.

Tonight's book would be *The Confession* by John Grisham. She had read every book he had written, with her favorites being *A Time to Kill* and *The Pelican Brief*. She even wrote John Grisham a letter encouraging him to write a sequel to *The Pelican Brief* and wanting to know whatever happened to Darby Shaw after she went into seclusion. She even liked the movie with Denzel Washington and Julia Roberts, which was a rare thing for her after reading a book she enjoyed.

Rachelle and Madison came into the foyer to say goodbye to Sherry. However, Sherry had other plans. "No, no, no. I will walk you over there, and only when you are with other cops will I leave you. Then I will see you back at the house. If none of the officers are gentlemen, then call me and I will come and meet you. OK?"

"Yes," Madison replied.

Rachelle saluted Sherry and said, "Yes, Mom."

"Ha ha," Sherry replied.

The officer asked for Rachelle and Madison's cell-phone numbers and began to walk them down the hill toward Danford's. One of the things that most found attractive about Port Jefferson Village was how close together everything was. Within a three-minute walking distance from the ferry you could have your choice of more than 24 restaurants, two hotels, a couple of bed & breakfasts, inns, and more than 100 independent and franchise stores. In the summer, so many tourists from across New York and the rest of the country jammed into the village that it took an extra 15 minutes just to get into the area due to traffic, and once you made it into the Village, getting a parking spot was even more of a challenge. It was for this reason the town installed metered parking. This would help control the flow of traffic, but even more important, it eliminated the overnight parking due to cars being left for ferry passengers.

The heavy motorcycle clubs also had to be reined in. The bikers used to take so many spots in the ferry parking lot that it was one of the deciding factors in creating the metered parking spots. When it was first instituted, the bikers protested the change by taking all of the parking spots with only one motorcycle per spot, creating no parking spots for any vehicles that needed to make a quick stop into one of the stores. The town responded by installing signs that parking on the side of the road would only be for 30 minutes. The biker protest lasted for about two weeks and eventually died out. Paul had the conversation with Joey Z about the change in parking rules, and he got the impression it was favored amongst the business owners for the most part. The locals who initially disliked paying for parking and then paying for a meal were appeased by most of the restaurants paying for the parking. Joey Z had a meter station installed outside of his building so all a customer had to do was give him their parking-spot number, and Joey Z would insert the coins himself and pay for two-hour parking.

Rachelle, Madison, and Sherry reached Danford's within five minutes, and Sherry was impressed with the beautiful harbor. She walked the two women into Danford's, and they were escorted upstairs by the host. When they reached the top, there was a beautiful large banner that read, WE CELEBRATE YOU, VICTORIA.

Upstairs at Danford's is known as the Brookhaven Room. It had a dance floor about 100 feet by 50 feet, with a bar and an atrium that held more tables and a room at the far end of the dance floor that held seating for more than 100 people. While beautiful, it made Rachelle emotional, and Madison had to give her a supportive hug for a few seconds. Sherry looked around the room for a bit and found Bud.

She walked the women over to him and said, "I'm going to leave her with you and Paul now. Give me a call if you need anything, and give me a call when you are bringing her home so I know what's going on. I don't want to end up shooting your ass." Bud acknowledged her by singing "Sherry Baby" to her. She shook her head and said her goodbyes to Rachelle and Madison.

"Don't forget," Madison remarked, "I'm leaving here about nine and won't be back at the house 'til about 1:00 am."

"No worries," Sherry said. She left the club and ran into Paul as she exited.

"Take a walk on the dock," he told her. "It's beautiful, and the boats are pretty awesome."

"I'll do that," she answered.

As Paul went upstairs, Sherry did just that. She took a walk on the dock, and during this stroll she was impressed at how beautiful this harbor was, from the mansions up on the cliffs to the boats in the water to the surrounding buildings. She thought it was only about 30 minutes from Central Islip, yet it seemed a world apart.

Instead of cutting through the parking lot known as Trader's Cove, Sherry walked on East Broadway from Danford's to Main Street to take a look at the stores and restaurants. Everything was there in this beautiful little town. She had read the reports on the case before going to the house and watched the news on the case, so she couldn't help but stop and pause at the area where the shooting took place. She walked over to the Ocean City Bistro and the Dessert Factory building behind which Kyle Winters had changed this town forever. The interesting thing is it had not appeared to hurt business too much. Although traffic was down in the village, the spots involved in the shootings and the capture seemed to have the interest of the people.

Sherry decided to cut through Trader's Cove and look for the Red Onion Café on East Main Street where Bud had shot and apprehended Kyle Winters. As soon as she entered the parking area, the sign for the Red Onion Café was on the back of the restaurant, so it was very easy for her to find. As she approached the front door, she noticed the café usually closed at 6:00 pm based on the sign. It was now 8:20 pm, and it was still open with people inside. It was apparent that this alternative food café was now also a point of interest among the locals and tourists.

Sherry walked inside to find an attractive cozy spot with chalkboards full of healthy menu choices. Her cell phone buzzed, indicating a text, and as she looked at it, she saw it was from Bud. It said, "What are you doing, Sherry Baby?" She wrote back, "You are one crazy psychic cop. I happen to be in the Red Onion Café, where you shot up Kyle Winters' balls." He texted back, "Have the peanut butter and banana wrap. My favorite there." She laughed and did just that.

While she was waiting, she walked out to Daniel's Deck on the outside. She could just visualize how everything happened from the time he stepped into the café just from the way he wrote it in the report. As she was going back inside, a young couple came out to the back deck, and Sherry giggled as she heard the young man explain to his date, "This is where the cop shot one of the killers." *Yes, sir*, she thought. The Red Onion Café was now on the map. The young officer was intrigued by the name Red Onion and scanned the walls of the café until she found her answer. The owners had placed a sign on the wall with the explanation due to all the questions. Sherry read with great interest.

When we decided to open a café filled with healthy food choices for our customers we looked for names that would best symbolize our goal. We ultimately decided on the Red Onion because of all their health benefits. They are packed with one of the best natural sources of antioxidant properties and possess the cancer-fighting Quercetin. Red onions also provide Allkin, which is a health-promoting compound. They are a rich source of chromium as well. We knew that by taking the name Red Onion Café we had high standards to live up to in providing a healthy alternative and philosophy in eating. Besides, we thought it was a catchy name!

Sherry smiled at the last sentence and felt she had learned something interesting about red onions.

She picked up her wrap and walked over to Prospect and turned up the hill to Rachelle and Madison's house. When she got to the house she settled in at the kitchen table and ate her wrap. It was the best peanut butter and banana sandwich she had ever had. She was conflicted as to whether she should tell Bud, though. His head was big enough. Her thoughts amused her so much she started laughing out loud. She decided to text Bud and tell him he was right. She never got an answer, because Bud was having a grand old time doing one of his favorite things: listening, dancing, and singing to songs of the "Master DJ from PJ from Rantin' Ravin' Entertainment," a local celebrity on the dance scene who canceled a gig just to be at this memorial celebration. The party sounded so good that many of the local young women could not resist going upstairs to check it out to crash the party.

Bud did not even realize that Paul was over in the corner talking to Allan, Rachelle, and Madison. He managed to catch a glimpse of Madison leaving for her date about 8:30 and caught her eye for a second to wave goodbye to her. The Master DJ from PJ then put on the song that raised the party to a new level. The beginning riffs of Lady Gaga's "Bad Romance" started, and it was all Bud needed to be the main attraction. He started lip-syncing the song like he rehearsed it a few times. Everyone stopped what they were doing to watch, some with their mouths open, some moving their hips watching Bud, and some smiling. Everyone stopped to watch Bud take center stage. By the time the second verse started, Bud had everyone captivated. He moved his arms and legs perfectly to the music while he lip-synched the lyrics. All were in shock as the crowd watched as the verse from the song repeated again and went into the fourth verse. Bud didn't miss a word as everyone stopped talking and socializing to watch him. There was heavy sweat coming off his forehead, but he carried on without missing a beat. Paul watched without missing anything, but Rachelle did hear him say, "You are one sick, crazy bastard!"

She swatted him on the chest. "Hey," she said laughing.

Paul just shook his head, smiling as Bud continued. He was determined to do the whole song without missing a beat or a word. Even the DJ was having a great time watching. It had been a very long time since Rachelle had laughed, smiled, giggled, and danced at the same time. She cheered Bud on to finish the song. "Keep going, Bud, don't stop. Love it!"

Paul glanced around and noticed how some of the women seemed to be getting turned on watching Bud do his thing. As the four-minute song came to an end, Bud received a rousing ovation. He high-fived as he left the dance floor and went through the young women who wanted to meet him.

"What are you doing, you sick puppy?" Allan said to him.

Bud replied, "I gotta take a piss. Don't let anyone leave." All they could do was laugh and be impressed with Bud's talent.

Rachelle leaned over to Paul and said, "I wish Madison had seen this. If you were not here to see it, it's kind of tough to appreciate it."

"I know," Paul agreed. The party continued to be strong until about 11:00 pm, but there was no doubt the peak was Bud's dance to "Bad Romance."

At 11:00 pm, John Blanchard, Victoria's partner for the past three years, asked for quiet so he could make a toast to say goodbye to Victoria Davis. "Victoria, I hope we did you proud tonight. You wanted your friends and coworkers to have fun in your name, and we did. But not as much fun as if you were here with us. Thank you, Victoria, for being a part of my life and everyone's here. We will miss you." With that, the glasses that were raised went to the mouths of the crowd. The party was a little more low-key after the toast, and Paul could see Rachelle was visibly upset again. It was difficult for her to get over the shooting and being in the same car. It was still less than a week ago, and Paul thought she was doing amazingly well.

He grabbed her hand and said, "How about a walk on the pier before I drop you home?"

"Let's do it," she smiled. Paul waved goodbye to a few people as they left. One of them was Bud, who acknowledged Paul leaving with Rachelle with a thumbs-up.

Paul couldn't believe that it appeared he was going to be alone with her as they walked the pier. No Bud, no Madison, no Joey Z. Paul grabbed her hand, and she intertwined her fingers with his to get a firm grip.

"You never told me how you ended up with such a beautiful name," Paul said.

Rachelle laughed and told him the story of her name. "My father wanted to name me Michelle after the Beatles song, and my mother was adamant not to give me a common name, even if the song was such a big hit. Mom wanted Rachael, so the names were so different from the other that they ended up in this big fight and didn't talk to each other for a couple days. When calmness finally arrived between the two of them, they compromised on combining the two names together, Rachelle. There you have it!"

Paul replied, "I would expect no less." He laughed, "I'm glad they had that fight because the name is so perfect for you. It's beautiful, different, and the essence of being feminine. It's you!"

"You're making me blush," Rachelle replied, laughing in a nervous way.

"Tell me, how did Madison get her name?" Paul asked.

"Oh, now that's easy," she answered. "Mom wanted to name her after Madison Avenue because it was her favorite place to shop. Dad said, 'You are right, it is,' and that was it."

As he smiled at the story, Paul received a text from Bud. It said, "Did you kiss her yet?"

Paul was quick with his typed reply: "No, leave me alone."

Before he could put the phone in his pocket, he got an answer: "I'm going to come out and check your pulse in a minute." Paul wanted to shut the phone off, but he thought better of it.

"Come on," he said, "I'll start walking you home." Rachelle seemed disappointed and almost suggested going to his place, but she resisted. The conversation during the seven-minute walk consisted of Rachelle's article to come out after this case was over, but she explained that starting the next day, cryptic messages with a puzzle would appear in both the *Now* paper and the Long Island edition of *Newsday*.

Paul was concerned about it, but Rachelle assured him nothing would be given away. It was simply a tease to keep readers on the edge and hungry for the story that was about to be published. As they reached the doorstep to say goodbye, Rachelle faced Paul and decided to stop the tension between them.

"I would ask you to come in and stay, but as you know, I have a bodyguard now."

"I know," he said, "but I want to kiss you before handing you over."

"What are you waiting for?" she replied.

As Paul started to kiss her, the door opened and Sherry said, "Did you have a good time?"

Paul looked at Sherry with a look of disappointment. Rachelle laughed as she invited Paul in.

As they went in, Mason was in a parked car four cars down on Prospect on the phone with John Winters to tell them they were in the house. Both were now using disposable prepaid phones. From his angle, he did not see Sherry answer the door. Madison's car was gone, and now all he needed was for Paul to leave. "Come on," he said out loud, "no sex tonight, boys and girls."

Inside, Paul greeted Sherry and officially handed Rachelle's safety over to her. With an awkward goodbye to Rachelle, Paul waved goodbye to Sherry and left to walk down the hill to his apartment. Mason looked at his watch; it was 12:20 am. He decided he would wait 30 minutes before going in for Rachelle. At 1:00 am, the lights went off in the house, so Mason waited another 10 minutes before he left the car to approach the home.

He walked around the home checking out the windows, the sliding door in the back, and walked back around the front to check out the lock on the front door. There was also a door facing High Street on the side of the house. It was so quiet you could hear a car that drove by at the bottom of the hill on Main Street. Mason went back to the side of the house facing High Street and found a window half-open next to the door to let the air in through the screen, but he felt it would make too much noise trying to get in. Mason went to the back a second time and attempted to open the sliding door. He gently pushed the door back, and it barely moved. He pulled back harder the second time, and the door opened. He was lucky; he thought he would have to go through a window.

He entered the back of the den and, to his surprise, heard Rachelle in the bathroom. He waited at the corner of the den and the kitchen, waiting for her to come out of the bathroom into the hallway. He pulled out his knife and waited. As he stood there, he noticed the blankets and sheets on the pulled-out sofa. He had a look of puzzlement on his face as he heard the bathroom door open. It was Sherry. She had waited until Rachelle went to bed before washing up for the night. It was the only time she didn't have her gun, and she was about to pay the price.

She went past Mason, heard him, and turned around, but it was too late. He cut through her and watched her go down. He looked at her and enjoyed the started look on her face as she was about to die. As he watched her in the dim light, he realized she was black. He turned on the light and knew he had just killed the wrong person.

He headed down to the bedroom and opened the door that was closed. He approached the bed as Rachelle opened her eyes to see a figure with a knife walking toward her. As Mason thrust his arm up for power and came down, Rachelle rolled to the floor with the covers. Mason tried to pull the covers from her, but Rachelle was screaming while holding on to the throw blanket for dear life. Her screams were piercing as Mason pulled with all his might, but Rachelle was so tangled in the sheets and blanket, he began to blindly stab her. He stopped and again tried to pull off the sheets. It was his sick need to see Rachelle's face as he stabbed her that caused the delay from killing her with alacrity. He managed to get the sheets away from her and then heard shots being fired in the house. It startled him enough to stop his rampage at Rachelle to go back to the hallway to see Sherry lying on the floor with her weapon in her hand.

Officer Sherry Walker had crawled to her pillow, got her cell phone, dialed 911, and began firing her gun in hopes it wasn't too late to save Rachelle. "Don't move," she said to Mason.

He moved quickly between the rooms, closer to her, and Sherry fired, just missing him. He came closer and could hear the *click* that she was out of bullets. He ran up to her and kicked her so hard in the face the gun flew out of her hand and flew to the other side of the room. The gunfire had been so loud he felt he had run out of time as he ran for the front door. Rachelle, who was in the corner shaking and terrified, managed to get herself to the window to look and saw a figure dressed in black tight clothes with a white mask on grab Mason by his collar, throw him down, and lean into his face, pause, and then stabbed him multiple times. Rachelle fell back into the corner of her room screaming, with the throw blanket on her. Bud was still at Danford's with four other officers, including Lynagh and Healey, talking stories, when he got the text, "Shots fired, Prospect Street."

Bud jumped up, telling his fellow officers, and they followed behind him. He ran down the stairs and out the door, crossed East Broadway, crossed the back parking lot behind Z Pita, and raced up the hill to Prospect Street he called Paul who was already running down the stairs. Bud arrived with four other officers to find two police cruisers, which had arrived three minutes earlier.

As Bud went into the house, two officers were trying to get the blood under control with Sherry until the ambulance came. "Rachelle! Rachelle!" he yelled.

"She's back here," an officer yelled.

Bud ran to the room, and the young officer already there told Bud, "She won't let anyone touch her."

Bud went toward her, and she covered herself up more. She was shaking so hard he wanted to hold her but didn't want to take any chances. Officers Lynagh and Healey started looking around the outside of the house for clues other than the body of Mason Winters lying on the front lawn. A second later, Paul ran into the room and moved toward her. She pushed herself back harder to the corner and squeezed the throw blanket so hard her fingers and arms were becoming cramped.

"Rachelle," Paul said. "Rachelle, let me make sure you are OK, please."

"Paul," Bud said.

Ignoring Bud, Paul said again, "Rachelle." As he moved his hand gently toward her, she spoke her first words since the attack.

"Where were you? Why did it take you so long to be here?"

"Rachelle," Paul answered, "I was here within minutes, please." He moved closer.

"Don't touch me," she said. She started to cry again, asking for her sister.

The ambulance arrived quickly for Officer Walker. With Mather Hospital only being a two-minute drive from Rachelle's house, Sherry was in surgery within 18 minutes of the attack. Madison was driving home when she got the call from Paul to get home. She was there within 10 minutes. The second ambulance was there, but no one could get near Rachelle. Madison ran to the room and ran to Rachelle, who did not resist her.

"Shh! Shh!" Madison said gently as she held her head. "I'm here now, Shh! It's OK, sister is here." Within minutes, Madison had Rachelle calm enough to go in the ambulance to be medically checked out.

"Don't leave me!" she said to her sister.

"I'm here, honey," Madison said. "I'm here."

"Rachelle," Paul said.

"No," Rachelle replied. "No."

Paul tried to go with them to the ambulance, but Madison gave him a stop signal with her hand. Paul was confused by all of this, but Bud went up to him.

"Come on, let's take a look around," he said.

As they searched the house, the crime unit was marking the floors and the bullet holes, which, for the most part, were in the ceiling except for the two in the hallway. There was blood, most likely Sherry's, smeared on the floor and carpet. As they were checking the back sliding door, Detective Lieutenant Cronin had arrived and was on the front corner lawn looking at the body of Mason Winters. With multiple stab wounds, it was evident he was taken by surprise.

As Cronin entered the house, everyone could hear him say in a low voice, "Son of a bitch." He looked at Bud and Paul and asked, "Do we know what happened yet?"

Bud answered him, "Paul dropped Rachelle off at 12:20 am. It's pretty clear that Winters entered the house about 1:15 am. Officer Walker dialed 911 from her cell phone at 1:21 am, and shots were fired at approximately 1:22 am. We received texts at 1:24 am. I arrived on the scene at 1:28 am, Paul at 1:30 am. Uniform officers were on the scene about a minute before me and attending to Sherry and trying to attend to Rachelle. However, no one could touch her 'til her sister arrived from her date at 1:35 am."

Cronin then asked, "Was it a coincidence the sister got home at 1:35 am?"

"No, sir," Bud replied. "Paul called her as he was running up to the house. She was already driving home. She just stepped on the gas when she got the message."

"And the body outside?"

Bud again replied, "He was the intruder, most likely. We are not sure yet because Sherry was unconscious with a knife wound when officers got here and put her in the ambulance."

Cronin looked outside at the body of Winters and noticed Bud was the only one doing the talking. He said, "So everyone is getting killed who was involved in this mess. You two get to the hospital, try to get statements from Sherry Walker if she makes it out of surgery, and now Rachelle is most likely the only one that can tell us what happened to our friend on the lawn." As they left the house, Cronin followed them.

"Paul!" he yelled. "Detective Powers, I would suggest you get your head out of your ass." Paul acknowledged him and got in the car with Bud as they drove over to Mather.

Cronin stayed at the house to look around a bit, both inside and outside the home. He had Lynagh and Healey check the vehicles to identify Mason Winters' car to have it brought in for evidence. "Well, well, well," he said as he stood on the front porch. "Mr. Phil Smith, you are doing such a good job of eliminating everyone."

He called Bud's cell phone and told Bud, who had just arrived at the hospital, "Bud, try to get someone to talk tonight. I want to know if the mask that was at the hospital and the killing of Starfield was here tonight."

As Cronin turned around to go back in the house, he said to himself, "Mr. Phil, why are you not killing Deborah, why are you not killing Rachelle? Who are you, Mr. Phil? Who are you this time, Ghost Face? Hmm, I will find out, I promise."

As he entered the house, he looked at the den where Sherry was to sleep. He went into every room of the house hoping to find one detail that would help with the case. He found nothing until he went into Rachelle's office, where he found pages of written notes on the back of desk calendar pages. There were hundreds of pages with handwritten notes on them. It looked to him like she was writing a book. He flipped through the pages, going over her notes. Some of the desk calendars had the format of a story, and others were of outlines—character summary, chapter summary with a brief outline for each chapter. Rachelle was writing a book called *Vanished—The Port Jefferson Murders*. He found her cryptic messages that were going to be in *Newsday* for the next seven days.

On her desk, stuck against the back shelf, between the crack of the shelving, were photos. There were Rachelle with Madison, younger photos of her with her parents, a photo of Paul at the restaurant standing alongside Rachelle and Joey Z. He opened the drawers to her desk and found more photos. They consisted of the Cross Island Ferry, outside and inside. There were signs that photos were not allowed, but somehow she got them. Based on the events that happened, the detective lieutenant really wasn't surprised she had gotten away with it.

In the bottom drawer were papers, what seemed liked notes. It looked as though Rachelle saved every note that was given to her. Many of them were from Paul, written on the back of business cards and napkins, and it was clear there was an emotional attachment for Paul and apparently for Rachelle, if she was saving everything he wrote to her. There was nothing in the notes that was inappropriate for a police officer, but it was clear there was some kind of relationship. It was more clear to Cronin as to why Paul seemed so out of it, and he began to question himself having the detective stay on the case.

He put his attention on the other side of desk drawers. They were filled with the articles she had written for the *Port Jefferson Now* newspaper. Award certificates, correspondence, and columns on letters written to the paper from the local community and fans. Cronin began to walk away from the desk when, hiding in plain sight, was new mail lying on her bureau. He picked up the short stack of mail, which he thought was interesting because it was all addressed to Z Pita or the paper's address. He sorted through Cablevision bills, Verizon cell phone, bank statements, and stopped at the envelope that had the return address of Phil Smith. He had used the address from his home, but since the house had been under 24-hour surveillance, the return address was just a formality. It had not been opened, but he didn't wait or care.

With the amount of bloodshed and the possibility of another cop being killed he opened the letter and read, "*Dear Ms. Rachelle Robinson, I hope this letter finds you alive. I say this because I really don't know how much longer you can survive this. You put yourself into something that is way over your pretty little head. Even so, I can say the same thing* for me. The important thing is that I want you to know that the person going around killing my former partners is not me. True, by wearing a mask it would leave room for doubt. However, that is the point. Someone is wearing the mask and killing because they want to frame me for this. Someone wants a freebie. I expect you to print this in your next article if you are alive. If you don't, I will make sure you won't be alive for the following week. If I am going to be framed and if it appears there is no way in proving it, then I have nothing to lose, right, Ms. Robinson? Our only intent was for the $5 million to return Debbie Lance. If I have to, I will come for you, and I won't be wearing the mask. I will want you to know it's me. With anticipation of your cooperation. Phillippe Smith. P.S. Have a nice day.

2:00 AM Wednesday Morning, June 22

Cronin picked his cell phone from his pocket, forgetting it was 2:30 am, and called FBI Special Agent O'Connor. He said, "Jack, meet me at 9:30 am if you can at *Port Jefferson Now* editorial offices. It's in regard to the case. Oh, sorry, it's 2:30 am. Having another one of my cops likely murdered will do that to you." O'Connor volunteered to meet Cronin at the hospital, but the detective lieutenant declined. He said, "Get some sleep. See you in the morning."

He walked back out to the kitchen, where there was an answering machine. He pushed the button and played back all the messages. Nothing out of the ordinary. Maybe one. It was Bud singing to Sherry, checking up on her at 11:30 pm. It seemed ordinary for Bud, though. As Detective Lieutenant Cronin left the house, he instructed two uniformed officers not to leave the house until they were relieved. There would be uniformed officers assigned at the house until the case was finished or, as he thought when he walked away, *till no one was left alive*. A morbid thought, but he was beginning to think it was a realistic possibility.

He got in his car and drove the short distance to Mather Hospital. He was sure that Suffolk County executive Marshall Collins would be there for another cop fallen in the line of duty. Even the chief of police might be there or on the way. Cronin walked in to the hospital and told some of the officers to make sure the press was controlled outside as word of the events spread. He was met in the hallway by Agent Sherman, who decided to stay up when he heard about the shooting.

"It's pretty clear the murders and the kidnapping are all tied together," Cronin said as he greeted the FBI agent.

"What about John Winters?" Sherman asked.

"What about him?" Cronin replied. "If we don't find him soon, he will probably show up dead. Someone wearing the mask doesn't want a trial; they want this to be over."

Sherman responded, "The letter doesn't mean Smith is not the killer. This could be his way of trying to frame others."

"True," Cronin replied, "but if he had killed Deborah Lance and Rachelle Robinson while he was killing his former partners, he wouldn't have a hell of a lot of witnesses to worry about."

Sherman continued the debate, saying, "Debbie Lance and Robinson never saw him anyway."

Cronin came back at Sherman again. "He has done everything to show us he is a lowlife; he hasn't done anything to show us he's a killer except this letter on his intentions. It raises the question, doesn't it? Which is what he wants anyway. We have to find John Winters before we find him in the gutter. One more thing," he said to Sherman. "No one, and I mean no one, other than you is to know about this letter, understood?"

Sherman paused then replied, "Understood."

Cronin found Bud and Paul outside of the surgery room and inquired as to her chances.

"We don't know anything yet," Bud replied.

Cronin looked over at Paul and asked, "Are you going to talk tonight?" His voice was heard throughout the wing.

"Yes," Paul replied.

Cronin stepped in front of him and said, "I don't have to remind you that you are involved in this up to your ass. The events that kicked this off were based on your theory."

Paul shot back at the detective lieutenant, which he had never done before, saying, "Are you blaming me for this, or are you saying I kidnapped Deborah Lance and wanted all this to happen?"

Without missing a beat, Cronin came back, "I'm saying the turn of events after the kidnapping is based on your gut to figure this out. I'm also blaming myself. I let you run with this."

"It was the right thing to do," Paul interrupted him.

"Tell me, why?" Cronin questioned.

"If we had not drawn these assholes out they would have gotten the money and moved on to someone else after they killed the girl."

"Yes!" Cronin yelled. "But we would not have had a dead cop and another one likely on her way."

"No," Paul yelled back, "this case most likely has stopped what would have gone on! The FBI had no leads that they told us about. This would not have been solved."

"Paul," Cronin replied, "our main witnesses are here in the hospital, and the killers are being eliminated by one of their own or someone else with a vengeance."

"Someone else?" Bud finally spoke. Cronin pulled out the letter and let Paul and Bud read it.

"Do you believe it?" Cronin said to Paul. "Look at me, Detective. Do you believe after reading this letter that it's bullshit or there is someone else playing vigilante behind the mask?"

"It's one of two things," Paul answered. "It's Phil Smith trying to throw us off, or he doesn't want to be framed for it. Whoever is doing it, it is clear they want us to believe it's Phil."

"Or," Bud said, "whoever is doing it doesn't really give a shit what we think and is just taking care of business."

"Why?" Cronin remarked.

"We are going to find out," Paul answered.

"Listen to me," the detective lieutenant remarked. "I have a press conference in the morning, which is about five hours from now. I really don't give a shit if you two never get shut-eye again. I want a report on the status of this given to me 45 minutes before I go on national television as to why this is happening. Have you spoken with Rachelle yet?"

"No," Paul answered.

"If you find out anything, I want to know if she saw how Mason was killed and if the killer was wearing the mask. The same one, or a different one, and if the body type is the same that we saw on the hospital video and was described by Deborah Lance."

"I know what to do," Paul replied sarcastically. It was not in his nature, and Cronin was caught by surprise by his defensiveness.

"Paul, are you too close to this case? Is there something I need to know about your relationship with Rachelle? If you lie to me, I will make sure you're suspended for 90 days. Tell me the truth, now."

Paul looked at him straight in the eye and said, "The truth is we are friends, but I was and have been hoping for more. I care about her. That is the truth."

Cronin paused and asked, "Can you handle this case?"

"Yes," Paul replied.

"Listen," Cronin said as he looked at both Bud and Paul. "I know this is different than anything we have ever worked on and maybe different than most cops have had to deal with, but if we don't come through this and end this soon, it will be something that we regret forever, not to mention the disappointment we will carry with us. Now I need both of you to do what you have to do within the law to get this case over and out. Get with O'Connor and Sherman, and let's put our heads together to find John Winters and Phil Smith. I need you guys to step up and be with me on this."

As he started to walk away, Paul yelled, "Boss, can we make a copy of the letter? I think we should each have it on us."

Cronin shook his head and gave it to Bud, saying, "Keep the letter to just the three of us right now, understood?" Cronin didn't mention that Sherman knew about it and didn't feel the need to tell them at that point.

As they waited in the hallway, Cronin asked one of the doctors if they had information on Officer Walker. He replied that they had given information to her husband about five minutes prior and that he was in a room set aside for immediate family in surgery.

"We are family also," Cronin remarked.

The doctor simply replied, "Let me speak to her husband to see if he will come out and talk to you."

Bud came back with the copy of the letter and gave the original back to Detective Lieutenant Cronin. Sherry Walker's husband, Gabe, came out to greet the three cops. They all stood there waiting for him to speak, afraid to ask if she was going to make it.

Gabe took the cue and said, "She was lucky. The doctor told me many factors are going to save her life. The hospital being so close, her physical conditioning, and most important, the stab wound in the abdomen missed the abdominal artery. The fact that medical assistance came quickly to control bleeding is another factor." A sigh of relief came over the detectives.

"Mr. Walker," Cronin replied, "we are so pleased to hear this. We don't know everything yet, but by the evidence, it's likely she saved the life of Rachelle Robinson during the attack and intrusion of the house."

Gabe shook his head and said, "Well, that's Sherry. She's always been a hero to me, and now she is to someone else."

"Mr. Walker," Cronin said as he turned to walk away, "I'm sure the mayor of Port Jefferson and the chief of police as well as fellow officers will be paying their respects to Officer Walker throughout the day. They won't expect to be allowed to see her, but they will want be in the hospital to show support. I just wanted you to know, so you don't feel bad about obligation to them. They understand, but a brother or sister in uniform in the hospital, they will want to be here to show support and respect."

Gabe Walker shook his head and thanked Detective Lieutenant Cronin. He then said, "Maybe in a couple days, you can tell her yourself."

"Count on it," Cronin replied. "I'm going to get a couple hours sleep. See if you guys can find out anything here. Maybe take a nap for an hour or two while you're waiting here."

As he walked down the hall, Paul said he was going to Rachelle's room. Bud decided to tag along before he went to see how Deborah Lance was coming along. They were told she would be released on Thursday, and Bud wanted to see the list of names who visited her while she was in the hospital. Paul and Bud flashed their badges at the two cops standing guard at the room. They nodded as they entered to see Rachelle sleeping, with Madison holding her hand, also asleep.

"We should wait," Paul said. "We are going to be here all night anyway."

As they turned around to walk out, Madison's voice was heard saying, "It's 3:00 in the morning."

Paul and Bud turned around, and Paul said, "Sorry, Madison, we were just checking in on her."

"You know," Madison replied, "my sister's life was a good one until the two of you got close."

"Wait a minute," Bud replied.

"No," Paul said, "let her get it out of her system," as he held up his hand to Bud.

Madison continued, "It's one thing to be friends, but you got her involved in this, she was shot in the head, which could have killed her, and now she's right back here again, scared out of her wits to even open her eyes. She's going to need therapy, she's so messed up right now. You know, Paul, I really don't think you are healthy for my sister, and as you cops say, I have the evidence to back me up. My sister is everything to me, and I'm not going to let her get killed simply because she cares about you."

"Madison," Paul said gently.

"Don't Madison me," she replied. "Now I'm asking you to do your job, but I don't want you hurting my sister anymore, and I'm not talking about emotional issues. You are not safe to be involved with." She looked at Bud and said, "And that goes for you too; let my sister live a normal life."

Paul answered her, "So this means you are going to ask her to stop writing articles that bring attention to herself?"

"You! You!" she pointed back. "You had her write the articles to begin with! I will speak to her, but please stay away from her unless you have a job to do."

"We will need to speak with her as soon as she wakes up," Bud replied. Madison started to walk back to Rachelle's bedside.

"Let us do our job," Bud said.

"You do your job," Madison replied, "but stay away from her when this is over. I don't want you around her, and if you want her safe, you will understand what I'm saying."

She turned her head to look at Rachelle sleeping and brushed her hair off her forehead. Paul walked out the door and headed down to the café, which was not serving anything at 4:00 am, but he went there anyway. Bud gave him some space for a couple minutes and thought better of it and went to check on him. He walked in and saw something he never even thought would happen. It was Paul sitting at the table with his hands over his face. He could tell by the sounds coming through his hands that Paul was shedding tears. Bud was torn up seeing his partner in a state of tears, and he sat down across from him and just sat there. No words, no talk, but he was there for Paul if he wanted to talk. Bud let Paul have the next 20 minutes to shed tears and think about everything that had happened in the past week.

Finally he spoke, saying, "She's right. I almost lost Rachelle twice in the past week because she has been with me."

"Yes," Bud said, "because she wanted to be with you. She wants to be a part of what you are and what you do because it's what she has wanted to do. Don't you get it? This is her choice. You didn't force her to do anything. Everybody is a little emotional right now, but I will tell you this: you let Rachelle make the decision on her life. Not Madison, not you. She is going to do what she wants."

Paul replied, "When I saw her frightened to death sitting in the corner of her room, my heart broke in two, which tells me that maybe Cronin is right, that my head is not clear on this. All I cared about was trying to hold her and protect her, and she wouldn't let me touch her."

Bud put his hand on Paul's arm and said, "She wouldn't let anyone touch her."

"Yes," Paul said, "but she looked at me and said, 'Where were you?' like I let her down. I want to just jump off a bridge somewhere, watching her eyes look at me and saying, 'What took you so long to be here?' I felt my heart being stabbed."

He went on for another hour, talking to Bud about his life, his father, his years knowing Rachelle, his relationship with Cronin. For once, Bud was a rock. He was supportive and he was serious. The conversation changed subjects as Bud spoke about his childhood. Paul learned so much about his partner and why he, as they would say, "hides behind a clown's face."

"I needed humor to save myself," Bud said. "My dad was an alcoholic; he would beat my mom when he had too much to drink. I tried to stop him a few times, but he would pummel me. One night, when I was 12 years old, I went into my parents' bedroom with a baseball bat, and I swung as hard as I could. I hurt his arm, and he grabbed the bat from me and was ready to swing back when my mom started screaming while covering me. I pushed her away and said it was OK, that I was no longer afraid of him. He was a coward in my eyes. I knew I wanted to be a cop to put people like him away. I suppose he could have killed me if he wanted to, but he stopped. I guess when he realized I was no longer intimidated by him, he simply packed up and left. We never saw him again. I was close with my mom, and it was devastating to me when I lost her to cancer when I was 25. Not a day goes by that I don't think about her. Anyway, humor has helped me get through school and my life after losing her. One thing I did get from my mom besides her fun approach to life was learning. We read so many crazy things. Not books like normal people, but things like, hmmmm, things you didn't know about Long Island."

Paul was captivated listening to Bud. It was the first time he had seen Bud in such a serious mode. It was the closest to normal he had ever seen him. "Tell me about some of those details," Paul said. After all, they had time to kill. Deborah, Rachelle, and Sherry were all in the hospital, and they were waiting until they were awake to speak.

"Well," Bud said, "did you know that 'God Bless America,' written by Irving Berlin, was penned while he was stationed on Long Island? One that I found amusing was that the fictional sleuths the Hardy Boys are from Bayport, Long Island."

"What else?" Paul said.

"Did you know that Huntington, Long Island, native Mariah Carey's nickname in high school was 'Mirage' because it seemed like she was never in class?"

"You are just full of information," Paul said. "Now I understand why you know so much about dates, music, and trivia."

"We never really sat like this, my partner," Bud replied.

"You're right," Paul agreed.

Bud put his arm on Paul's shoulder and said, "I know this is difficult, and I know I have kidded you about going too slow with Rachelle, but things are different now. The last thing we need is emotional attachment. Do you know what I'm trying to say?"

"Yes," Paul replied. "It's too late on the emotional attachment, but there has been no intimacy, and I know it probably never will be, but she's important to me and I want to be important to her."

"You are!" Bud said. "It's obvious! I'm your friend and your partner. I will be here or there if you need me." Paul shook his head.

"Now," Bud said, "enough bonding for now. It's 6:00 am; let's go have breakfast at Maureen's Kitchen. They have the best fucking baked oatmeal you ever had. We'll get back by 7:30 am, and maybe we can talk to Sherry or one of our girls by then."

As they got up, Paul put his arm around his partner and said, "Thanks, Bud."

"Don't get mushy on me," Bud said.

They got into the car and drove to Maureen's Kitchen in Smithtown on Terry Road and Paul reconfirmed that Bud was the expert in food. He was right. The baked oatmeal was the best he had ever had. It was ordered as an appetizer, while Bud had the Dinosaur Egg, which was three egg whites and one yolk while Paul had the pistachio pancakes. The coffee alone, in nice-sized mugs, was better than Starbucks. The only drawback to this famous institution on Terry Road was if you came after 8:00 am, you would be waiting for a while for a table. Once you got your table, it was a little loud, but the experience of home-cooked and unique offerings from the chalkboard and the friendly staff made it a favorite of Bud's. He not only considered himself an expert of trivia but also of food, and that was something Paul would never dispute. A couple mugs of strong coffee would help Paul and Bud get through the day after being up all night.

Bud tried to keep things moving a bit, and he was used to Paul taking the lead on cases, but he realized if they were going to get through this for everyone's best interest and safety, he was going to have to step up in the lead. Particularly if it involved Rachelle. The bill came to $40.00 with tip, and it was worth every penny.

The ride to and from Maureen's Kitchen was 20 minutes each way, and counting the 40 minutes they were there, they arrived back at the hospital at 8:30 am. Both Deborah and Rachelle were awake, and while Bud went to question Deborah, Paul wanted to see Rachelle. He entered her room and saw her talking with Madison.

"Hi," Paul said in an awkward tone.

"Hello," she said.

"How are you feeling?"

"I'm doing OK," she replied, "considering everything, but forget about me. How is Sherry doing?"

"She's going to be fine. She was lucky," Paul answered.

"She saved my life." Rachelle said it again. "She saved my life, I owe her my life."

"I'm grateful that she did," Paul said.

Rachelle looked back at Paul with a tear in her eye and spoke with her voice cracking, saying, "You, me, it's too complicated."

"I know," he answered. "I know. The important thing is for you to get right emotionally, physically. You are what is important. Everything else is secondary. OK? Just get well." She looked at her sister, who gave her a look of agreement on her face.

"Rachelle, as a cop I need to ask you some questions about what happened," Paul said. He asked her a few questions about the attack in the house and soon realized it was Sherry who would have to fill in the missing pieces. When he moved to the outside of the house, Rachelle told Paul she looked outside her window and saw the masked killer stab Mason.

"Anything unusual other than the stabbing?" Paul thought it was a dumb question; however, it had become routine. As it turned out, it was a good question.

"The killer bent down after he knocked Mason down and went into his face almost like he was saying something to him. It was about five to ten seconds. Then he started stabbing him. I screamed and fell back to the corner. I thought he was coming in for us, but apparently he ran away, having heard Sherry's gun."

"No," Paul said. "Apparently the person wearing the mask is after those involved in the kidnapping."

"If that's so," Madison asked, "how did he know to be where Deborah was held or be at our house?"

"Well," Paul said, "if it's Phil Smith, he knew where Deborah was being held. Knowing where you lived is another story that we have to find out, but one thing is clear, it's either Smith trying to frame someone else, which is why he didn't kill Deborah and why he didn't go in your house at all, or we have someone involved that we don't know yet. We are going to figure it out. In the meantime, cryptic messages started coming out, starting today in *Newsday*, about this story, so it's not going to help."

Rachelle looked at Paul and said, "Call me dumb or irresponsible, but I'm not going to stop my job or my life."

Paul replied, "Rachelle, is it the same mask? The Ghost Face mask?"

"God, yes," she answered. "The same as what hangs on your coat rack."

"OK," Paul said. "Get some rest. Thank you." He grabbed her hand and touched her finger before he thought better of it and pulled away. He nodded to Madison and walked out of the room. He didn't see the tears come down Rachelle's face or her lips tighten as her eyes followed him out the door.

Bud was sitting in a chair next to Deborah Lance when she opened her eyes.

"Hey, sleepyhead, today is the big day, going home."

"Yes," she smiled at Bud. "What are you doing here?"

"Well," he answered, "we are here visiting our special girls," a term he emphasized with finger quotation marks, "and since you were still here, I thought I would speak to you a bit and see if there was anything you may have remembered that would help us."

"I really don't want to talk about it," she said as she brushed her hair back with her left hand.

"Are you left-handed?" Bud asked.

Deborah looked at him suspiciously and said, "Yes, I am."

"Me too," Bud said. "Did you know that left-handed people use the right side of their brain, unlike right-handed people who use their left, which means that only left-handed people are in their right mind."

She laughed, "You are a funny guy."

"That's what they tell me," Bud replied. "They claim everyone is born right-handed but only the greatest overcome it."

She laughed again and asked, "What's your real name, Bud?"

He leaned back in his chair, surprised by her question. "My real name is Donald. They nicknamed me 'Bud' because Irish American families…"

Deborah interrupted Bud and finished his sentence, "Bud comes from the Irish nickname 'Brud,' which is short for 'brother,' so I assume you have an older brother."

The Detective was impressed and said, "Yes, I have an older brother, Sean. He's always been a pain in the ass, but he's my brother. So why would you know about the name Bud?"

"I love to read," she said. "I love trivia."

Bud's eyes lit up as he said, "Really? We have a few things in common."

"Maybe," she said. "But I'm not as funny as you." Bud smiled back at her, and then Paul walked into the room.

"How's it going?" Paul asked.

"I was just finishing," Bud replied as he got up.

"Wait," Deborah said. "Is everything true about Robert? They told me he had an affair with Patty. Did he have me kidnapped? The FBI said no, but I would like to know what you think, Bud."

Bud looked at Paul then back at Deborah and said, "He did have an affair with her, but as of now, there is no evidence he was involved in your kidnapping. As of now, it looks like Patty was behind this." Debbie's eyes became glazed.

"We are going to get all of this resolved, Ms. Lance," Paul said. "This will be over soon."

"It may be over," she answered, "but I have lost my two closest friends. One betrayed me with my other friend, and the other betrayed me for money when she couldn't get the man I loved for most of my life. This will never be over for me."

"I'm sorry," Paul replied. "More than ever, you should want to help get who is responsible for all of this. We lost a cop, almost lost a second cop, we lost a friend, and we came close to losing Rachelle Robinson, a reporter who has been writing about the case. It was her articles that drew out your kidnappers. People have died during all of this, and I believe it was all of this dying that in reality has been a part of saving your life."

There was silence in the room for a few seconds, which for Bud was rare. Paul continued, "Ms. Lance, if there is anything you know that can help us find John Winters and Phil Smith, I believe we can close this case."

The young woman recalled and spoke to them about everything that happened to her from day one, from the ordeal she went through during her captivity to the phone calls between Wayne Starfield and John Winters. Bud and Paul were not surprised by anything until she remembered hearing Wayne on the phone discussing the $3 million in cash at the house.

Bud looked at Paul and changed the subject, asking, "Deborah, when you leave here, what are your plans?"

"My dad wants me to come home for a while," she answered. "I could use some private time at the old Pink Mansion," she smiled.

"Deborah," Bud leaned forward, "how did you feel about your dad selling the business? After all, you were going to run it."

"I didn't care," she said. "It's so difficult these days to run your own business. He got over $45 million for the chain plus 5 percent on profit for the franchise. I'd rather have the time to enjoy my life than work too hard to maintain the lifestyle. I don't want to sound like a snob, but I grew up watching how hard my dad worked and how much time he was away from me. As much as I would have worked hard to respect my dad's business and make him proud, I'm not upset about the business being sold."

Paul asked, "What about Patty Saunders and Robert Simpson? It appears they were upset about the business being sold."

Debbie looked away and was clearly upset. She looked down at her hands and said, "I loved Patty, and I've been in love with Robert since I was a teenager. I don't understand why they thought I would ever hurt them in any way."

Paul spoke softer, saying, "Money can create evil things, Ms. Lance. I'm sorry. Listen, you are going home today, you are going to spend some time with your father. I'm sure the two of you have much to talk about."

As they prepared to leave, Bud turned around and said, "Listen, when all of this is over, I would like to take you to lunch and have a little trivia challenge with you. You seem to be a threat to my throne, so I have to check this out."

"You are a funny guy," Deborah said, and smiled.

"Sounds like a yes to me," Bud answered as he waved goodbye. The smile was still on her face when the door shut.

While they were walking down the hallway to Sherry's room, Bud mentioned, "Interesting about the original $3 million ransom. Only the father, Deborah, and the butler knew it was $3 million exactly stashed at the house."

"Keep it alive in your brain, my friend," Paul answered.

As Bud shook his head, he said, "We are going to come to the conclusion that I should have put that bullet up his ass."

"Now to the next patient," Paul answered.

Bud replied quickly, "If I spend any more time in this fucking hospital, I'm going to get sick, have to stay here, and then I'll really be fucked."

They showed their badges and entered the room. Sherry's husband and her parents were in the room giving support. Sherry raised her finger to the detectives, indicating she wanted a few minutes with her family before the questions came. Paul and Bud started a small conversation between themselves in the corner of the room to allow Sherry to have privacy with her loved ones. Within five minutes, Sherry's parents were introduced to them and they left the room.

As Paul and Bud came closer to the bed, Sherry asked her husband to leave so she could speak freely as a police officer and not as a victim. Gabe understood, kissed her forehead, and left the room. As Paul turned his attention to Sherry, he could see the damage Mason had done by kicking her in the head. Her face was swollen with bruises and she had suffered a concussion. Bud turned on his pocket recorder. Sherry told the whole story of what happened in the house, from her walk from the bathroom to the attack in Rachelle's room.

"I thought I failed in my duty when I heard Rachelle screaming. All I could do was fire my gun, hoping it would make him rush out and not finish her. I don't know how he didn't have the time to kill her."

Paul responded, "It's apparently in her hysterical state it might have given her enough time for you to get your gun and fire. She would be dead if not for you, Officer Walker. You're a hero." She looked back at Paul and appreciated the smile on his face as he said it.

Bud concurred, "You're a hero, all right—the call to 911, shooting your firearm like you're at some circus!"

"Oh, here we go," Sherry laughed.

Bud grabbed her hand and said, "Seriously, you're a hero, and if you were not so banged up right now, I'd give you a hug."

"Last question," Paul said. "The masked killer outside on the front lawn, did you see or hear anything?"

"No," Sherry answered. "I was out like a light after that son of a bitch kicked me. By the way, you guys look terrible."

"We really have had no sleep since this happened. We have to close this case. There have been only 22 officers in Suffolk County who died in the line of duty since formation of the Suffolk County Police Department. Victoria was the 23rd, you were almost the 24th. The pressure is on."

"Well, you look like shit," Sherry answered.

"OK," Paul said, "time for some rest for you."

Bud smiled at Sherry and started singing "Sherry Baby."

Sherry put her hand up to Bud as Paul reached the door and said, "It's a good thing I understand it's your way of showing affection or I'd shoot your ass too!"

"Oh, come on," Bud replied, "let me finish."

"No, get out of here. It's white men like you that make me angry at my mom for giving me that damn name."

They closed the door, and Sherry had on her face what most people had when Bud left the room—a smile. Sherry's parents and husband were in the hallway as the two detectives walked up to them. They brought Gabe up to date with as much information as they could and Sherry's mom even asked a few questions about what was going on. The verbal exchange lasted for about five minutes while Sherry's father remained silent throughout. As they said their goodbyes, Mr. Jonathan Angall, Sherry's father gently grabbed Bud's arm and spoke for the first time.

He said, "There are many things I can accept and understand because my daughter, my only daughter and child, is a cop. And I really don't know everything that is going on here, but what I do know is that people are losing their lives and keep coming back to this hospital. I also know that my only child had a knife stuck through her and was kicked in the head like she was some kind of animal and left to die. You find whoever it is behind all of this, and before you put them behind bars or in the ground, my request is that you make them aware of all the pain and suffering they have caused us."

Bud looked at Mr. Angall with almost an intimidated look on his face. He couldn't even think of anything to say except, "Yes, sir."

Jonathan Angall held on to Bud's arm and said, "I have your word then," as he looked in Bud's eyes.

"You have my word," Bud answered as Mr. Angall let go of his arm.

As they walked away, Paul asked Bud, "Are you OK?"

"Yes," he replied. "A quiet man, yet he knows how to get his point across."

"This is it, my friend," Paul replied.

"There will be little sleep now; we have to end it. Let me stop in and say hello to Rachelle," Bud said. "Wanna come back in?"

"No, I don't think I should," Paul answered. "Meet you in the lobby in 10 minutes." As Paul walked to the lobby, he felt his heart beating through his temples. This was a warning sign to him through experience that if he didn't calm down, he would be having an anxiety attack. He sat down in the lobby and tried to think of other things before the back of his head became soaked. If his hair got wet, he knew he would be in trouble. He went outside the hospital to call his father to take things off his mind.

"Rachelle, my belle," Bud started singing to the tune of "Michelle." Both Madison and Rachelle clapped their hands after he finished.

"How are you doing this morning?"

"Well," she replied, "I think I'm doing better than you. You look like shit!"

Bud interrupted, "I know, I know, that's what they tell me." He looked up at the television and saw Suze Orman giving someone an approval for a vacation. "You like her?" he asked.

"Yes, yes, yes," Rachelle said, clapping her hands. "One day I will get to see the whole program to the end."

"Well," Madison said, "I think you need some time away from here for a bit, so you will have some time."

"My younger sister looking out for me," Rachelle said as she looked at Bud.

Bud nodded as he smiled at Rachelle and said, "OK, we gotta go catch some bad guys. Paul is waiting for me outside."

"Oh," Rachelle answered. He gave her a kiss at the top of her head and walked out with Madison to the hallway.

He told her, "The house will have a 24-hour car outside until the case is over."

"OK," Madison replied.

"One more thing," Bud asked, poking his head back in the room to speak to Rachelle. "Did you notice if the white mask being worn during the stabbing had a blood splatter on it?"

Rachelle squinted her eyes as she thought. She said, "I saw red, but I was so scared I really didn't think about it."

"Thank you," Bud said as he left the room again.

When Paul reached his father, he was surprised when his dad said he had flown up to New York and was now on his way to Long Island to see him.

"Dad, what are you doing?"

"Paul," his dad answered, "I have the Woolworth Reunion in a few days anyway, so I needed to spend time with you."

"Dad, we have a case that is all over the national media."

"Listen, Paul. I want to have dinner with you a couple nights. No big deal, but one day you are going to be a father, and when I see you, I'm going to play back the message you left me on my voice mail, and then I want you to tell me if you would not have done the same thing if your son left a message like that to you."

"OK, Dad," Paul said. "I guess I was feeling a little down." Bud heard the last part of this conversation as he walked up behind Paul. Paul finished with, "OK, you will be at the apartment in a couple hours? I'll see what I can do. OK, see you then."

"Listen," Bud said, "I have to get back to the precinct, then I need to get some shuteye before Cronin starts looking for us. See your dad, get a couple hours shuteye too. Maybe we need some rest. It's been forever since I shut my eyes."

"I agree," Paul said. "Give me a call at 4:00 pm, five hours from now."

Bud dropped Paul off at the front of Z Pita, and Paul went in to talk to Joey Z about Rachelle. After 10 minutes with the owner, he left and made his usual cut through the alley between the buildings to get to the back of his apartment. The alley always gave him the creeps, but the 10 seconds it took to walk through the alley saved him 10 minutes of walking around the buildings.

Paul went upstairs, played his messages, and got to the one from his Dad: "Son, it's your father. I got your message. I love you too. I know things are challenging right now, but you will get through this. You are a good cop, a better person, and a great son. I'm proud of you." *Click.* Paul played it three times before he leaned over on his bed and fell asleep.

Even though Bud had very little sleep, he pulled the interrogation that Paul had with Simpson for two hours. He went to the vending machines, selected the microwave popcorn, heated it up, got a soda, and started viewing the interrogation while having his popcorn. He made notes while watching and eating, played back a few segments, and started playing it again. He then requested the tech manager to play the hospital video of the masked killer going in and out of the hospital room to kill Kyle Winters. He scratched his head a few times and started writing additional notes. He went back to the Simpson interrogation again and viewed the last five minutes of it again. The tape finished, and there was silence. Exhaustion had caught up with Bud, who had fallen asleep in the video room—popcorn, soda, notepad, and pen all beside him.

Agent O'Connor, limping and with a cane, met Cronin at the *Port Jefferson Now* offices to meet with Steven Anderson, who showed them Rachelle's desk and computer. As Cronin poked around, he kept one ear open to listen to O'Connor's questions to Steven Anderson. Her work habits, good, bad, problems, past assignments, future assignments, the book she was writing, the letter that came to her from Phil Smith.

Yes, Cronin thought to himself, *he's very thorough.* The detective lieutenant did not find anything else unusual or any unexpected surprise at her desk. It appeared that Rachelle was ambitious and a hardworking woman who did not want to be intimidated or forced not to have the life she wanted to lead. Cronin asked Steven Anderson questions about himself, such as his years at the paper and the places he enjoyed spending time while he was in the village.

"Thank you for your cooperation," Cronin said. "All I ask right now is that no one, including Rachelle, use the computer on her desk 'til we have someone look at it."

"Fine," Steven Anderson said. "No one has been on it except for

Rachelle and the other cop." Cronin and O'Connor stopped in their tracks.

"Other cop?" Cronin said. "Do you have a name?"

"Yes, hold on a second. Detective Paul Powers."

"Did he show you his badge?" Cronin asked.

"Yes, of course." Anderson replied.

"When?" the detective lieutenant asked.

"Two days ago," Anderson replied.

"How long did he spend on the computer?" O'Connor asked.

"About 30 minutes," the editor replied.

"Thank you," Cronin answered. "No one goes on the computer 'til I give you a call with who is coming. OK?"

"No problem," Anderson replied.

As they left the building, O'Connor asked, "What do you think?"

Cronin looked at the agent and said, "I think it's strange he didn't ask us about how Rachelle was doing."

"Maybe he was nervous," the agent replied.

Cronin looked at him and replied, "Or maybe he's just an asshole who doesn't know any better. I've got to go to the precinct. I will catch you later."

"OK, I've got to check in myself with Sherman and get the leg checked out."

As Cronin got in the car he got a text message from the chief of the department wanting a review and update as to what was going on. Cronin arrived at the precinct and had his assistant, Gina, notify the chief that he was in the building. He was called into a conference room, and sitting there was deputy chief commissioner Ken McGuire and the chief of the department, Bob Jameson. The detective lieutenant sat down in front of them.

"I'm impressed. Where is the police commissioner?"

"Are you being sarcastic to your superior officers, Detective Lieutenant?" Chief Jameson asked.

"No," Cronin answered. "I guess you could call it trying to get through the day. It's been a long week."

"Tell us about it, Detective Lieutenant. We are all over the news, and we are anxious for this to go away."

"And I'm not?" Cronin answered. "We are working day and night to resolve it. The good guys and the bad guys are getting killed. It's going down to the final piece of the puzzle."

"Review the summary with us."

"Why?" Cronin answered.

"Because we want to know what is going on, that's why," Chief Jameson answered.

"I'll give you the facts of the case to date."

"Then do it," McGuire bellowed.

Cronin looked at McGuire and thought better of what he wanted to say. He reviewed the case from the beginning, from the ferry to the present day. The two chiefs only looked at each other when the detective lieutenant got to the parts when the masked killer was involved. The summary took more than an hour, and when he finished he was asked if he needed additional detectives on the case.

Cronin answered, "Thank you, but at this point, they would only be in the way. I will need additional uniform officers to guard the house, the hospital, and to insure no one speaks to Patty Saunders, including her attorney, without me knowing about it. I would also like a car watching the *Port Jefferson Now* editorial offices and the Lance Mansion on Cliff Road. There will be overtime on this one, but as you said, we need to end it as quickly as possible."

"When will you have a suspect or who else is behind this besides Winters and Smith?" Jameson asked.

"Why do you think anyone else is involved?" Cronin asked.

"Don't you?" Jameson asked.

"Yes, I do," the detective replied.

"Who?" both chiefs asked.

"Sorry," Cronin said. "Can't divulge at this time."

"Hold on," Jameson said.

"No," Cronin answered, as he got up to leave. "I'm not going to get into that right now. Besides," he said as he looked at them, "I really don't know who to trust right now."

Chief Jameson stood up and yelled, "What are you implying?"

"It's not me," Cronin said as he opened the door to leave. "It's just your interpretation of what I'm saying. Now, I have a job to do. If you want to chat again when this is over, I'll be happy to do that." Cronin looked at Chief Jameson and said, "Have a good day, sir. I won't let you down."

The door shut while McGuire started to speak, but Jameson cut him off when he said, "Sit your ass down, Ken."

Cronin walked into his office and was told Bud was sleeping in the video room. "Let him have another hour, then wake him up," he said. he then followed that with, "Get Lynagh to bring in Robert Simpson again. I would like to speak to him. And get Agent Sherman on the line for me."

Cronin sat back in his chair and turned on the television, and the national news already had the latest continuing saga of what was going on. From Rachelle's cryptic message on what was apparently going to end up as a book to the latest attempt on her life and the heroism of Sherry Walker in saving her life. Of course the media knew how to get the public's interest going. They played up the masked killer for all they could. Headlines were all over the papers, from THE REAL THING, NOT A MOVIE to GHOST FACE ARRIVES IN PORT JEFFERSON. His favorite was Rachelle's headline, THE FACE OF FEAR IS HERE. Her cryptic messages from her Twitter account also had poems that hinted at what she thought was going on. There was no doubt that between her rhymes on Twitter and headlines in the papers, she antagonized the kidnappers to draw them out.

The real mystery was why the killings continued, and whoever was behind the mask was causing confusion. The confusion and mystery was that only the bad guys were being killed by whoever was wearing the Ghost Face mask with the blood splatter. Was it Phil Smith eliminating his partners and witnesses, or was it someone else trying to make it look like it was Phil Smith so they could get away with murder? But why? It wasn't clear to Cronin; not yet, anyway.

He picked up the phone and said, "Get Patty Saunders into the interrogation room. I have some questions." He shut off the television and looked over his paperwork for an hour before he was told Robert Simpson had arrived.

"Have him come to my office," Cronin said.

Officer Lynagh seemed stunned by the request and said, "Sir?"

"It's OK. Have him come to my office."

The officer escorted Simpson to Cronin's office, and Cronin told him it was OK to leave. He shut the door, and Simpson asked if he needed an attorney.

"You're not under arrest," Cronin answered. "You came here on your own free will."

"Oh, really?" Simpson said. "This is the fourth time Officer Lynagh has brought me here, and if he ever cracks a smile, his face might fall off. What choice do I have? Especially with threats of being shot in the ass! In case you haven't noticed, he's not the most pleasant person to be around. Your crazy-ass Detective Johnson threatens me every time I see him."

"I apologize," Detective Lieutenant Cronin said. "Have you told anybody else about that silly comment?"

"No, because he threatened me again if I said anything."

"Then why are you telling me?" Cronin said.

"Because I'm no longer a suspect in this, right? And you're his boss, so I'm just letting you know, you have a whack job for a detective."

"Listen," Cronin said, "I'd like to get off your ass for a moment and talk seriously with you."

"What about?" Simpson answered.

Bud came out of the video room and was met by Officer Lynagh, who told him to look in Cronin's office through the window. He walked toward the large window and could see Cronin and Simpson talking. "What the fuck?" Bud kept saying to himself. He started looking at his watch to time how long the conversation continued. Bud was surprised no one else was in on the conversation.

John Winters looked at his cheap watch, and it was 3:00 pm. The abandoned building with the big crayons in front serving as columns had served him well for the past 36 hours, but he knew it was time to move on. It would be difficult for him to get out of Port Jefferson unless he was able to get to a house and clean up and change his appearance. He had lost both brothers in the past week, lost his homes, lost the ransom money, and it seemed that the person who started all of this was sitting in a comfortable jail cell. He wondered if her empty apartment was being watched. He didn't want to sleep on the floor of this old building that was once a school for the physically challenged. It had been closed for at least five years, and it appeared that St. Charles Hospital, which owned the building, did not know what to do with it.

One of his favorite things about Port Jefferson was that it had two hospitals within five minutes. Most people liked all the restaurants, but John Winters amused himself by thinking the hospitals would be getting the attention now.

As he looked out the window into the empty parking lot, he heard a crackle noise. He stopped breathing just to see if he could hear it again. He heard a soft footstep. He started sweating and pulled out his gun and aimed it at the door. He froze while waiting. Nothing. He started to breathe a little and heard it again. He held his breath. A cat came to the front of the door and stared at him. *Just my luck*, he thought. *A black cat.* "Scram, fella," he said. "My luck can't get any worse."

He approached the door as he put his gun away, and into the entrance stepped the masked figure. John caught the hand holding the knife by the intruder's wrist, but a swift kick to his stomach sent him reeling back into the room and onto the furniture. The figure came at him again, and he pulled out his gun. Another kick to his ribs made him drop the firearm but not before it fired. The Ghost Face attempted to strike again as John moved quickly to get to his gun. He reached it and started firing into the dark shadows of the room. He was on his back. Quiet, waiting, he did not move for 60 seconds, but it seemed like an eternity. He had to get out of the building as quickly as possible because of the noise from the shots being fired.

He got up, looked out the window to see if he could see anything, and as he started to turn around, the knife went through him. As the blood came out of his mouth, he raised his hand to take the mask off of his killer. There was no attempt to stop John Winters. The person holding the knife in his body stood there as John tore the mask off. It was pure enjoyment to see his puzzled look before the knife was turned and twisted to tear up his organs. The mask was put back on, and the killer left with lightning speed. Before doing so, a chair was thrown through the front window. The killer wanted to be certain the body was found, just in case the sound of the gunfire was not heard.

The sixth precinct got the call, and a young officer answered the inquiry as to the building and possible gunfire. He called it in as Cronin was about to question Patty Saunders.

Albert Simmons identified himself to Cronin at the wrong time, saying, "You, Detective, were you going to question my client without her attorney? Answer the question!"

Cronin turned around and said, "Have you met with your client yet?"

"No," Albert Simmons answered loudly.

"Go talk to her, I'll be back."

"You didn't answer my question," Simmons roared back.

Cronin turned around again and told officer Rand, "Search Mr. Simmons carefully, Officer Rand, and wear your gloves."

"What the hell are you doing!" Simmons yelled.

Cronin stopped again and said, "I don't have time for this. She is under arrest for kidnapping and murder. You told me you had not met with her yet. How do I know you don't have anything on you that won't help her escape?"

"Why, you bastard," Simmons bellowed.

Bud could not help but overhear as he walked down the hallway. "Let's go, you're with me!" Cronin said as he walked away.

Bud looked back at Officer Rand and said, "And don't forget to check his fat ass, it looks suspicious to me."

"Fuck you," Simmons yelled back as Rand put on the gloves. Bud jumped in the car with Cronin and brought a muffin and a coffee with him. They were discussing the case when Cronin asked Bud to give Paul a call. As he turned the corner, Bud's muffin broke apart and went all over Cronin.

Cronin shouted, "In my 25 years of driving, never has anyone had a muffin break and spill all over my car like you. Son of a bitch!" he said, scraping the muffin crumbs off with one hand and driving with the other. "you and your food" he said in a sarcastic voice he shook his head.

"Sorry, boss." Bud said.

Cronin looked back at him and asked, "Did you really save my life four years ago?"

Bud smiled and nodded. The answer was yes. They had been in a car chase on Nesconset Highway in Smithtown when a teenager who was not paying attention to the sirens and the emergency vehicles continued through a green traffic light and slammed into their vehicle. Bud and Cronin were in an upside-down cruiser with gas leaking. Bud was able to get out of the car, but Cronin was pinned. He ordered Bud to leave in case the vehicle blew, but Bud went around to the driver's side and freed Cronin's legs and cut the seat belt off him. He stayed to pop the upside-down trunk to get the fire extinguisher out and used it to keep the fire from burning him alive until the fire department arrived with the jaws of life. Cronin spent 10 days in the hospital and three weeks on disability, but it was clear he was working again because the man who hid behind the face of a clown was also a good cop and a hero as well.

They arrived at the abandoned building that was once the St. Charles Hospital Educational and Therapeutic Center. Detective Lieutenant Cronin and Bud walked into the old classroom to see John Winters sitting on the floor with his back to the wall. His eyes were open wide, his mouth was open, and his hands were on his fatal wound. Cronin looked around the room as Bud kneeled at John Winters' body.

"Was it worth it?" Bud asked, as he moved his eyes to the blank stare coming from Winters' face. "I hope it hurt."

As he stood up and moved away from the body, he looked at Cronin and said, "He looks like he saw a ghost."

"Maybe a Ghost Face?" Cronin replied. They worked the room until the crime lab came, at which point Cronin ordered the abandoned building sealed off. When they left the building, there were four police cruisers and the ambulance from St. Charles Hospital across the street. Bud mentioned that during the past week, it was a good thing there were two hospitals in the town or it would be getting pretty crowded.

Cronin looked at Bud, shaking his head, and said, "You are a piece of work, you know that?" Bud smiled as they drove back to the precinct to talk to Patty Saunders.

Paul woke up from someone touching the hair on his forehead. It was his father.

"Dad..."

His father interrupted him, saying, "Paul, listen to the message you left me on my phone." He put the cell phone up to Paul's ear, and the young detective was silent as he listened.

"OK, Dad, I was a little down, and I wanted to speak to you."

"What's up, son?" His father replied.

"I've made my life complicated by falling for the girl in the middle of a case, and there's no happy ending. I have to fight my emotions and solve this case and move on. I know how difficult it's going to be because I won't be able to turn it off. She works downstairs. She owns a part of the restaurant. We have been friends for years, and if I want more, we won't be friends. I'm screwed either way."

"OK," his father replied. "I get it. Listen, you have a job to do, and if you let it conflict you, it may cost a life, maybe your own. What's more important to you, being her friend, her boyfriend, or none of the above?"

"Her friendship is the most important," Paul replied.

"Then be her friend," his father answered. "Because if there is one thing I learned about women, it is that they have a way of letting you know when they want to be more than just your friend."

"Thanks, Dad," Paul said.

"Now tell me about what's going on with this case."

"Can't do it, Dad. We got a live one here."

"Then let me buy you dinner tonight."

"Sure, Dad, maybe Bud can join us. I've got to get back to the precinct before Cronin kills me. See you later."

When he reached the bottom of the stairs he yelled, "Dad, where are you staying 'til you go to the city?"

"I'm staying at Danford's for a couple nights," he yelled down.

"See you at 8:00 pm. I'll call Joey Z to hold a table for us. Later ,Dad," Paul said, closing the door behind him.

Paul got down to the precinct in time for the start of questioning of Patty Saunders. Her attorney was still angry over Cronin having him practically strip-searched and wanted the police to wait. Albert

Simmons had made calls to the district attorney's office, which had not been returned. The district attorney, Barry Steinberg, knew of Albert Simmons and knew Detective Lieutenant Cronin. He delayed calling back Simmons to let Cronin have some space to see how this played out for a bit. Paul walked into the viewing room behind the mirror to see Bud and Cronin sit down across from Patty and her attorney.

"Enjoying your stay, Ms. Saunders?" Cronin asked.

"Don't answer that," Simmons interrupted.

"I'm sorry," Cronin said, "I just wanted to know, since I think you are going to be a guest with us for the rest of your life."

"OK, we are leaving," Simmons said as he stood up.

"Go ahead, but if you do, any possible deal we were going to make goes out the door with you." Cronin looked at Patty to see her reaction. She looked up at Simmons with a facial expression that said she wanted to hear what he had to say.

Simmons then looked at Cronin and said, "With all due respect, Mr. Cronin…"

"Detective Lieutenant to you," interrupted Cronin.

Simmons took a deep breathe and repeated himself, saying, "With all due respect, Detective Lieutenant Cronin, if we are going to talk about a deal, where is the assistant district attorney?"

The detective smiled back and said, "I have much influence, so I would suggest you sit down."

Patty grabbed his hand to sit down. The attorney sat down. Cronin continued to speak, while Bud gave him a note that said Paul was in the viewing room. Paul had sent him a text. He was actually enjoying watching Bud be so quiet, but that's the way it usually was when Cronin was in the room.

"Ms. Saunders, we seem to be losing everyone who can explain what is going on. First, Deborah Lance is kidnapped. Things don't go the way they were planned, and the killing starts. First, Timothy Mann, then our own Officer Victoria Davis, attempted murder of Rachelle Robinson, and then the tables turned. Kyle Winters is killed in the hospital, Wayne Starfield is killed, and then Mason Winters, and today John Winters is killed. We have six murders in a week, and

I'm not even counting the attempted murder of Officer Sherry Walker and the second attempt of Rachelle Robinson."

Albert Simmons was getting annoyed again and said, "So you get an A for history. What do you want from us?"

As much as Cronin was agitated with Simmons, he was right; he hadn't asked a question to her yet. Cronin said, "Ms. Saunders, I do have some questions for you, and if you cooperate, I will speak to the assistant district attorney about handing you over to the FBI on the kidnapping charge, which means we would consider not pursuing the murder charges against you. However, the offer only stands if we find out the rest of the story."

Simmons whispered in Patty's ear, and she replied she would cooperate. The questions began.

"Have you been in contact with anyone since your arrest?"

"No."

"Have you been in contact with the outside world in any form?"

"No."

"Were you involved with anyone else other than John Winters, Mason Winters, Phil Smith, Wayne Starfield, and Kyle Winters?"

"No."

"Feel free to speak a bit. You are not in a courtroom; you don't have to just answer yes or no. OK?" Bud said.

"Yes."

"Who's paying for Albert Simmons here?"

"Don't answer that," Simmons said, putting his hand on her arm.

"Do you know why Phil Smith is dressing up killing the rest of his ex-partners?"

"You know why, Detective, and besides, do you know for sure that it's Mr. Smith?" Simmons replied.

"Do we, Patty Saunders?" Cronin asked.

"No, I don't know, but I think it is. I can't think of anyone else who would be doing it," Patty Saunders replied.

"Someone who wants us to think it's Phil Smith. Someone who wants to get away with killing the bad guys, but quite frankly, I don't think he's smart enough to pull this off. I don't think Phil Smith has the courage to kill in hospitals, break into homes and abandoned buildings and kill. I think he was brought in to mastermind the kidnapping of Deborah Lance and get the ransom," Cronin stated.

"Yes, he was brought in for that specific reason," Patty Saunders answered.

"Did you know they were planning to kill Rachelle Robinson and kill Deborah Lance after the ransom was paid?" Cronin asked.

"Don't answer that," Simmons growled.

"Do you have any idea how Phil Smith or anyone knew where to find John Winters in the abandoned building to kill him?"

"No, I really don't," Patty stated.

Paul walked into the room and, with Cronin's approving gaze, pulled up a chair across from Simmons as he looked at Patty.

"Patty, if you have had no contact with anyone since you have been arrested, then why is Robert Simpson living in your apartment since he was kicked out of the Lances' Pink Mansion?" Paul asked.

"Well, I…" she began to stutter, looking at Simmons.

"If you want consideration on the deal, answer the question and follow-ups or everything is off the table," Cronin said.

"He contacted a relative of mine in Connecticut to ask me to stay. I didn't want the apartment to be unattended while I was here, so I said OK."

"Why did you not indicate that in the initial question regarding contacts being made?" Paul asked.

"Because I didn't want anyone bothering him. I got him involved in something he knew nothing about. He has lost everything because of me. Please don't bother him."

"You have a Twitter account?" Paul asked. Bud's eyes lit up at this statement, as he loved it when Paul got going with a suspect.

"Yes," Patty said.

"When was the last time you used it?"

"I've been locked up for almost a week. So about five days."

"Your last entry showed four hours ago. Who has your Twitter name and password?"

Patty looked at Simmons, and he encouraged her to answer. "Phil has it," she said.

"Why would he have it?"

"Because he wanted to follow Rachelle's tweets. She has been sending out cryptic messages about all of this, and he wanted access without identification."

"Ms. Saunders, why would a kidnapper/murderer want to use your Twitter account?"

"I just told you," Patty exclaimed.

"Who else?" Paul asked. "He would not use your account knowing you are in jail for murder unless he is a dumbass. Who else?"

Patty looked at her attorney then back at Paul and said, "I don't know, but there is someone else."

"How do you know?" Paul asked.

"Phil told me someone else was in charge of things and the only way for us to get out of this was to follow his directions," Patty said as her voice started cracking.

"Did Phil say if the person was a he or a she?" Paul asked.

The young woman was getting nervous but answered, "All he told me was it was a he. I didn't care, I just wanted all of this to go away." She covered her face with her hands.

"Look at me, Ms. Saunders," the Detective pushed harder.

"Did Phil Smith indicate to you there would be more killing or just that people involved in the kidnapping would be eliminated?" Paul asked.

"I don't want to die," Patty said.

"Look at me," Paul said, his voice getting stronger. "Other than the Winters brothers and Starfield, who else was scheduled to be taken out?"

"Debbie Lance," she said as she began to cry. "Rachelle Robinson and...and Bud Johnson."

"Did he tell you why Bud Johnson was on the list? We know why the girls were on the list."

Patty was crying a little more now, and Simmons wanted to take a break, but Paul insisted, saying, "Ms. Saunders, did he tell you why Detective Johnson was on the hit list?"

"Whoever was calling the shots didn't like him," she answered.

"So he met Detective Johnson?"

"He didn't say," Patty said through her tears.

"Listen carefully. When he talked about taking out Detective Johnson, did he only say he didn't like him, or did he mention anything about Detective Johnson putting a bullet in Kyle Winters?"

"No, no, no, nothing like that. He didn't like him, he didn't like his attitude."

Cronin was so impressed with Paul's questioning that he hadn't spoken a word in almost 15 minutes.

"Ms. Saunders, who else in the group had Twitter accounts?" Paul asked.

"Just myself."

"How did Phil follow what was going on, on Twitter, before you were arrested?"

"You can follow someone by just signing up with a name. You go to their profile and read their tweets, but you don't have to write anything yourself."

"Did you follow Rachelle?"

"Yes."

"Deborah?"

"Yes."

"Simpson?"

"Yes."

"William Lance?"

"No, he's not on Twitter."

Paul asked firmly, "Who else?"

"No one of importance."

"Were you communicating with Simpson after the affair was over?"

"Yes, of course. I was best friends with Debbie."

"Did you communicate with him through direct message?"

"On occasion."

"Who is 'Fun Mom' and 'Stay Tuned' on Twitter?"

Her mouth opened, and she said, "What?"

"Who are they?" Paul asked.

"They are relatives of mine from Connecticut."

"Did any of your so-called group meet them, such as Phil?"

"No one."

"Did they help you pull off the kidnapping by giving assistance for shelter or food during this period of time?"

"No, no, no, and if they did, I would never give them up."

"Oh, I think you would, because if they were involved, I have a feeling a certain masked killer is making the rounds on all the bad guys. Someone doesn't like that Deborah Lance and Rachelle Robinson have been through hell. If you want to keep them alive, tell us now about them."

Patty put her head down on the table and then lifted it. Her leg started trembling under the table as she said, "Fun Mom is my cousin Linda in Connecticut. She was worried about me and followed me."

"And Stay Tuned? Who is it?"

"Listen, I don't know if it means anything, but..."

"Who is it?"

"It's Steven Anderson of the *Port Jefferson Now* paper."

Cronin looked over at Simmons, and they both had a look of surprise on their faces.

"Did you ever meet Mr. Anderson?" Paul asked.

"No."

"Did you ever communicate with him on a direct message on Twitter? And remember, everything is recorded on Twitter and documented."

"Yes."

"What were the direct messages about?"

"Mostly questions about the Lance family. He said it was research for a story."

"How did he know about you, that you were in the middle of this?"

"I don't know," Patty said, getting restless.

"Have you heard from him since your arrest?"

"No."

"Your Twitter name, 'BFFRSDL.' Did anyone ask you what it meant?"

"No."

"What does it mean?"

"Oh, come on," she answered.

"How about, *Best Friends Forever, Robert Simpson, Deborah Lance?*" Paul said.

Bud took a deep breath and couldn't believe what he was hearing.

Paul continued, "You updated that Twitter nickname about a month ago. You changed it from Port Jeff Lady. Why did you change it?"

"I just felt like changing it."

"Was the kidnapping only your idea, Ms. Saunders, or was Deborah Lance involved in her own kidnapping?"

Bud's mouth dropped at the question.

"Wait! I would like to speak to my client alone and have some privacy before we continue this," Simmons said.

"OK," Cronin said. "I could use a breath of fresh air right now. Guys, let's take a break and get a cup of coffee." They left the room and walked down the hallway.

"Holy shit!" Bud was saying. "This can't be."

"Wait!" Cronin said, "till we get out of the hallway. Get a coffee and get back to my office so we can discuss this in private."

Paul opened up his cell phone and called Joey Z for a table of four at Z Pita. He looked at Bud and asked, "You're having dinner with me, Dad, and Allan tonight, right?"

"Are you kidding?" Bud answered. "I'm not letting you out of my sight."

They went into Cronin's office and shut the door. As they sat down, Cronin spoke. He said, "Pretty impressive, Paul."

"Well," the young detective answered, "I guess the sleep helped."

Bud sipped on his coffee and interjected, "We don't really think Deborah is involved in this?"

Cronin spoke, saying, "Bud, there's a difference of not being involved and not wanting someone to be involved."

Detective Powers replied, "The truth is, I'm not sure yet, but it's a definite possibility."

Bud answered, "This woman was thrown in a trunk, beaten, sexually assaulted, and almost killed."

"True," Paul said.

"But if all of this doesn't go to plan, and Daddy's money doesn't happen because cops like us spoil the fun by changing the plans and even shooting one of them, you get yourself on the hit list as well."

"How did you find out about Twitter?" Cronin asked.

Paul answered, "I've been on Twitter for a couple of years and have had fun with it communicating with Rachelle. I started poking around a bit yesterday after visiting the hospital."

"OK," Cronin said. "We are working this case overtime 'til it's over. *Newsday* is working on a story that Suffolk County homicides are the highest in the past 20 years, with more than half unsolved. In 2010 alone there were 50 murders, and only 22 were solved. This is not going to be one of the unsolved."

Bud, the trivia king, chimed in, saying, "Our department has a 74 percent solve rate."

"Yes," Cronin said. "I said Suffolk County rate was below half." Cronin picked up the phone and ordered a watch team to keep an eye on Steven Anderson.

"Listen," the detective lieutenant said as he looked at Paul, "I asked *Newsday* to stop the daily cryptic messages coming out from Rachelle's name, but they refused. Can we get her to stop? I'm being told they have another five days of cryptic messages coming out, not to mention her tweets."

"I will speak to her," Paul answered.

"As a cop," Cronin answered.

"Yes," Paul answered.

"Just remember," Cronin answered, "a personal connection gets in the way. It blurs your judgment."

"What is her Twitter name?" Bud asked.

"BF_TJ_GW," Paul replied. "Her heroes. Ben Franklin, Thomas Jefferson, and George Washington."

"I like it," Bud answered.

"OK," Cronin said, "I think they have had enough time." They re-entered the room and were greeted with a half-smile from Simmons and a nod from Patty.

"Now that you have had time with your attorney, we left off with the question about whether Deborah was involved with her own kidnapping," Paul said.

"Yes."

Cronin and Bud turned their heads to Paul, who said, "Yes to where we were at? Or yes that Deborah was involved in her own kidnapping? And if we find out your attorney encouraged you to lie and say she was so your sentence will be lighter, we will find out, and both of you will be in a jail cell next to each other for a long time."

"She wasn't happy about her dad selling the business. She knew she had money coming to her, but she wanted a lump sum for her and Robert."

"What does that have to do with her being involved in her own kidnapping?"

"I told her I had an idea and that she would have to trust me."

"And?" Paul asked.

"I came up with the kidnapping plan, made my contacts, and made the arrangements. Once she was kidnapped, I was going to tell her to relax, but it got out of hand so fast," Patty answered.

"So she did not know about it?"

"She knew something was going to happen, but I guess she didn't know what or when."

"You're reaching a bit, aren't you, Ms. Saunders? Is there anyone else we haven't talked about that we should be talking about?"

"I guess not. What's going to happen to me?"

"Well, one thing is for sure, you are protected here, so you won't have a knife go through your body like your friends. The odds are good that you will at least be alive. OK, last question, why did you inform *Newsday* of Deborah Lance's relationship with Simpson?"

Everyone in the room was stunned by the question.

Patty began to stutter, "I…I was told to."

"By who?" Paul pressed on, repeating himself. "By who?"

"I…I don't know…it was over the phone."

"Give us a name," Paul said, getting louder.

Patty looked at her attorney for his blessing, then turned back to Paul, saying, "I only know of his voice, not his name."

Paul continued, "Was it someone other than the Winters brothers, Wayne Starfield, or Phil Smith?"

Patty was starting to shake, and Simmons put his arm around her.

She answered, "I'm not sure. I think it was Phil Smith, but I'm not sure. The voice was disguised."

Paul looked over at Cronin before he spoke again, asking, "Ms. Saunders, did you know that Deborah Lance had a life insurance-policy on her for $5 million?"

Simmons stood up with his hand on Patty Saunders and told her to be quiet. He said, "This interview is over for now, 'til I have a chance to be with her privately."

Paul looked over at Cronin, who spoke up, saying, "I guess we struck a raw nerve."

The attorney pulled Patty up and replied, "We can continue at another time. Thank you, gentlemen. Are there any other questions before we leave?" he asked just for formality.

"Just one," Bud answered. "Did you ever communicate with Rachelle Robinson on Twitter?"

"I sent her a couple of tweets, but she never replied."

"What did the tweets say?"

"They were questions about how she was feeling after the shooting."

"That's all for now," Cronin said.

As Patty was taken away, Simmons looked at Cronin and said, "A productive day."

"Yes," Cronin answered back. "Thank you, and I'm sure we will be seeing you soon."

Cronin then turned to Paul and Bud and said, "OK guys, it's been a long 24 hours. Give me a call tomorrow and let me know what you're working on."

When Paul and Bud got to Z Pita, Paul's dad and Allan were catching up on old times. Before Paul could sit down, Joey Z came up to him and showed him the Twitter column from Rachelle that was in *Newsday*. The message of the day read, "You didn't have your way, it may have been yesterday, not counting the cop there have been five, but I'm still alive." Paul couldn't believe what he was reading. Joey Z was clearly upset.

"Listen, I don't know what's going on, but we can't let her back here while she is antagonizing the crazies. Is she going to see someone for help?"

Paul dropped the paper and said, "I will be speaking to her about this." He sat down at the table and greeted his dad with a kiss on the top of his head. For one hour they were able to forget about the magnitude of the case. Brie cheese fondue at Z Pita with Joey's famous Greek salad and eggplant skordalia had a way of helping you forget about world events for a while.

The elder Powers mentioned that he noticed, on the way into the restaurant, a car completely in the design of the Yankees uniform. Paul explained to him it was owned by Barry Dubin and was a common sight in the Village. He rode around often in it with his father, George Dubin, who was well known in the Village for wearing his World War II Veteran hat.

"In fact," Paul said, "the Yankees would have used it for promotional purposes if it had been a Toyota or Ford instead of a Hyundai."

Deborah was released earlier in the day, but she hung around for a while because she wanted to meet Rachelle in her room. She had fallen asleep, and Deborah wanted to wait until she awoke. When she entered the room, it was as if they had a bond that would never be broken. Deborah's eyes met Rachelle's, and she leaned over the bed so they could hug before they even said a word to each other. She looked over at Madison, and they greeted each other with a tear in their eyes.

"Have a seat," Rachelle said. "We may have much to talk about."

Madison got up to excuse herself for a bit to give them privacy. "I'll be back in a couple hours to make sure you get some sleep," she said as she kissed Rachelle.

Deborah and Rachelle talked about everything they could think of and how their lives had become intertwined. Deborah expressed appreciation that she believed it was Rachelle's articles and tweets that brought out the kidnappers and delayed her execution. Rachelle agreed modestly with her but wondered if she was responsible for the death of Officer Davis and of course the attempts on her own life. Regardless, Deborah expressed appreciation. The conversation even turned to the men in their lives. The betrayal of Robert and Patty was too much for Deborah to comprehend.

When Madison walked back into the room two hours later, they couldn't believe the time had gone by so quickly.

"Where is Robert staying now that he's not at the mansion?" Rachelle asked.

"I don't know," Deborah said. "Probably at Patty's while she's in jail. Where else would he go? It's almost deserved, from the Pink Mansion to the Fairfield Apartments. It really doesn't matter anymore. I need to go home and clear my head on this. Here is my number. I would like to get together when this is over, if you're interested."

"Yes," Rachelle answered. "I think it would be nice." They exchanged numbers before saying goodbye.

Thursday, June 23

Deborah woke up at 8:07 am and yelled, "Dad! I'm hungry!" He could hear her from his office, and it made him laugh for the first time in about 10 days. Deborah used to yell from bed when she woke up when she was a child growing up. It was really sweet to hear her say it again after all these years.

William Lance walked into her room and sat beside his daughter with her head on her pillow and arms tucked underneath on her side. He could tell by her staring into space that the chain of events was a bit much for her to take in a week. "Talk to me, my sweet daughter," he said to her.

Deborah rolled over on her back and expressed herself as she stared up at the ceiling. "Dad, I've had such a great life. I could not have asked for more growing up. We didn't have Mom, but you took such good care of me. I tried to be a good person. You taught me well. I know I was young when I fell for Robert, but it was like he was family. He took care of me, and he respected you and me 'til I expressed my desires to him at 18. We had everything. I mean, I tried to give him everything. We were so happy."

William Lance listened intently as she continued to talk to him as her eyes looked at the ceiling as if she was watching a movie. "I loved him, and I loved Patty. When you sold the business, I had mixed feelings. Part of me wanted to have the challenge and another part of me wanted the freedom to do what I wanted to do. I let Patty vent about how she was betrayed by it. I had a few drinks one night, and she asked me to trust her. I didn't know what she was going to do. If she told me she would break the law or hurt someone, let alone have me kidnapped, I would have never let this happen."

There was silence from her father, and Deborah turned her head to look at him, saying, "Dad, never ever. I love you too much and would have never hurt you this way."

"I know, baby," William Lance replied as he pulled her toward him and held her tight.

Paul woke up with a *bang* at his back entrance and ran down to open the door. It was Thursday's paper with the cryptic message for the day taken from Rachelle's Twitter account at 2:20 am, just in time for *Newsday* to print it. Attached to the highlighted column was a note from Joey Z that said, "I'm scared for her."

The tweet for the day said, "Listen to what I say. It may be Thursday, but if I had my way, I will make you pay." Paul got up and rushed into the bathroom to wash up. He was on his way to the hospital to visit Rachelle. On the way to Mather, he called Bud and asked him to meet him there. Bud declined and said he would meet him back at the precinct. Paul arrived at the hospital at 9:10 am only to find out Rachelle had checked out 10 minutes earlier. He went to see Sherry in her room to say hello and check in with her. He was surprised to find out that Detective Lieutenant Cronin had been there earlier. As he left the hospital, he asked the nurse for the list of visitors Rachelle had had since he left her. Deborah and Madison the previous night and Detective Lieutenant Cronin was with her this morning when she checked out.

Paul was scratching his head as he left the hospital to drive to Prospect Street to speak to her. Rachelle answered the door and walked away, yet she left the door open to allow Paul to walk in the house. He noticed when he drove up that there was an unmarked car parked in front of the Mather Museum two houses down.

He walked in and broke the silence, saying, "Rachelle, I'm very worried about the tweets you are sending out that are being published in *Newsday*."

"Don't be!" she answered without turning around to look at him.

"Why?" he answered. "You have been a victim twice, and now this, antagonizing animals to come after you. Why?"

"I'd really rather not talk about it. I'm sorry."

"Rachelle, did you leave the hospital with Detective Lieutenant Cronin today?"

"Yes," she answered.

"Did he ask you questions?"

"Yes."

"What questions?" he replied.

"Maybe you should ask him," she answered as she looked at him. There was silence as they looked at each other, and he could see the pain in her face.

"OK, OK," he answered. "I will leave you alone. You don't need me to give you more stress."

He left her, and for the first time in years, it was without at least a hug. Paul walked toward the unmarked car.

Before driving to the precinct, Bud decided to drive to the Lance Mansion to check on and speak to Deborah Lance. As he drove all the way to the end of Cliff Road, he noticed a 1999 Honda parked outside the gates on the side of the road. He parked alongside it and noticed it was Robert Simpson. He got out to walk over to him as Robert was shaking his head.

"What brings you here?" Bud said as he looked in the driver's window.

"Listen," Simpson replied, "I haven't had a chance to speak to Deborah. I need to speak to her. I know she loves me, and I need her to know I had nothing to do with this."

"Blah, blah, blah," Bud replied. "Did you know that I checked last week on you, and you have failed to pay a parking ticket you had with full payment?"

"What?" Robert answered.

"Yes, it's true," Bud answered. As he raised his forefinger to point at Robert, he spoke again, saying, "I could arrest you for a misdemeanor, and not too long ago I could strip-search you for it."

"Oh, for God's sake!" Robert answered.

"Listen," Bud said, "I want you to leave."

As he spoke those words, Allan, who was on his shift for security in Belle Terre, pulled up to see what was going on.

"Allan," Bud yelled, "would you please escort Mr. Simpson off of these premises?"

"Follow me, Mr. Simpson," Allan said.

"Before you go," Bud said, sticking his head in the window, "as for your involvement in all of this, it's not over yet, so I just want to let you know that you don't want me to find out that the butler did it. You know what I mean? Because it will not only disappoint me in this little adventure, it will piss me off. OK, now you can go," he said as he patted Simpson on the shoulder.

Simpson turned on the ignition and followed Allan down Cliff Road toward the front entrance. Bud got back in the unmarked cruiser and drove up to the gates and pushed the buzzer. They opened after he identified himself.

When Bud was let inside the mansion, Deborah fixed her hair and put some makeup on before she went downstairs to greet him. He watched her come down the stairs. He was so enthralled in how good she looked that he was ashamed of himself for thinking, *Please don't fall, I might have to come to your rescue.* He snapped out of it when she stuck her hand out to greet him.

"Can we talk somewhere private?" he asked.

"Sure, let's go outside on the back deck. We can look at the harbor as we speak. The view is breathtaking."

"Deborah, I need to ask you a difficult question. Did you know of Patty's plan to have you kidnapped?"

Deborah looked toward the harbor then back at Bud before saying, "No, I did not. I just told my father everything this morning. She said she had a plan, but I thought it was some way to convince Dad not to sell the business, but it never happened."

"What do you mean?" he asked.

"Well, he went through with selling the business and nothing happened, so I never thought about it again. This happened after he sold it, so I would have never thought Patty was involved."

"OK," Bud answered. "Did you know Robert Simpson has been trying to reach you?"

"Yes," she answered. "I have not been able to bring myself to speak to him yet."

"I noticed you have three or four pictures of the Statue of Liberty in the foyer. What's that about?"

Debbie was surprised by the question but answered it, saying, "I've always loved the history of it. It's so beautiful and represents so much. It's such a beautiful piece of history. Maybe someday when we have time, I can give you a history lesson on it."

"Sounds good," Bud replied.

"Did you know what anagram you get from Statue of Liberty?" he asked.

"No, but I bet you are going to tell me," she replied.

He took out a piece of paper from his notebook and wrote as he spoke the words, "Built to stay free."

She looked at him and said, "You're a funny guy, Bud Johnson."

"I know," he answered. "That's what they tell me. I'll be in touch, but I don't want you leaving the house without a police escort until this is over. Understood?"

"You don't have to worry about me," she said. "The way I feel right now, I won't ever leave."

"Things will be fine. I promise you," he said as he left the deck. She followed him to the front and thanked him.

"Here's my number, Deborah," he said. "Call me anytime if you need anything."

"Thank you," she replied.

She put her hand out, but when he took it, she gave him a hug.

As he left the house, her father said, "I saw that hug."

Deborah laughed, saying, "Can't help it; he's like a cuddly koala bear."

They both laughed as Deborah went back upstairs to her room. When she reached her bedroom, she pulled out a sheet of paper and wrote *Statue of Liberty*. She slowly wrote the letters of "built to stay free" underneath the words of her favorite historical symbol, crossing out each letter of "Statue of Liberty" as she wrote down the letters. It worked, Bud was right.

When Bud got to his car, he sent Deborah a text that said, "See, I told you." He smiled and drove down to the security office to speak to Allan. He didn't see the amazed look he put on Deborah's face when she read his text, but he imagined it and enjoyed the thought of it, from the way he was smiling as he got behind the wheel and drove over to the Belle Terre security building.

As Cronin sat in his office, he played out the sequence of events over the past week in his mind. The only thing he was having trouble understanding was why Bud was on the hit list. The scenario wasn't clear to him, unless it was to cause confusion in the first place. He called Gina to find out the locations of both Bud and Paul.

His thoughts turned to all the different versions of the mask being used. He blinked his eyes a few times, thinking maybe he was hyperanalyzing the meaning of it. He sipped his coffee and wrote down a list of people that Bud has had contact with during the past seven days when all of this started. After he wrote down the list, he made column headings that read *good/bad/maybe*. It took him about 15 minutes to write the list. He had only two people under the *bad* heading and one person under the *maybe* heading. He folded up the paper and put it in his wallet. His office phone buzzed, and Gina said that Bud was in Belle Terre and Paul was on his way to the precinct. Cronin pulled out the paper again and circled three names on the list. He tapped the paper a few times with his pen as he thought again about the names.

"What's going on, Allan?" Bud said as he walked into Allan's office.

"All's quiet, Officer," Allan said with a laugh.

"Did he give you any trouble leaving?" Bud replied.

"Not one peep," Allan replied. "What do you expect him to do? Shoot the place up with guards at the gate, you poking around, security driving the premises? I guess you take him for a real dumbass." Bud helped himself to a cup of coffee as Allan looked at him for a response.

"Well," Bud replied between sips, "he's either a dumbass or a ruthless killer playing a hell of a game for the moment. We have no evidence on him other than that he had an affair with Patty Saunders, who was behind the kidnapping."

"So she says," Allan replied.

"What? What?" Bud replied. "What are you thinking?"

Allan got up to refill his cup and said, "How do you know she is not taking the fall for someone?"

Bud shook his head, saying, "Don't say Deborah Lance. Please don't say it."

"OK," Allan replied, "I won't say it. But how do you know she's not protecting this asshole Simpson?"

"I don't," Bud replied. "The whole mystery is the killings of the Winters brothers and Starfield. It only makes sense that it's Phil Smith." As Bud made the statement, he wanted to mention the letter addressed to Rachelle from Phil Smith but kept it to himself as Cronin wanted. Not even Rachelle knew about it. She evidently had been handed a stack of mail at the *Now* newspaper and hadn't looked through the pile before the attempt on her life.

"Bud," Allan replied, "whatever happens, keep an eye out for Paul. I've known him since high school. He's going to need your support and trust on this one. I'm worried about him on this one. He won't admit it, but his heart is conflicting with his head. Just be there. I'm restricted to Belle Terre while I'm on duty. He's going to need you."

"Don't worry," Bud replied, "I will be there for him." Allan held up his coffee cup as if to say cheers to Bud. "As for Deborah Lance," the detective continued, "I know she has protective detail, but I want to know when she leaves the house and where she is going. It's OK. Just tell her I requested it."

"No problem," Allan answered.

"OK, my friend, *you were always on my mind.*"

"Oh, shit!" Allan laughed. "Don't start singing that shit to me."

Bud giggled and said, "I'm off, my friend. Later. I'm sure we will have dinner soon."

They hugged each other as they said their goodbyes, and Bud drove to Prospect Street to speak with Rachelle. He radioed in to his partner, who was almost at the precinct to check in, and Paul brought Bud up to date, including Rachelle leaving the hospital with Cronin.

"Paul, when you get to the precinct, check on why we didn't bring in Simpson on the misdemeanors for the parking ticket. Someone squashed it."

"Will do," Paul replied. "I hope you have better luck with Rachelle. She won't really speak to me anymore."

"You are too close, my friend," Bud laughed.

"I wish," Paul replied as the transmission ended.

Bud knocked on the door, which Rachelle answered. He looked around to be sure there was security as he entered.

"Where's Madison?" he asked.

"She does have a job, you know," Rachelle answered. "Would you like something to drink, Bud?"

"No, no thank you. Rachelle, as a cop we are concerned and need to know everything to protect you. As a friend, we are worried, and whether you want it or not, Paul is sick over this."

"Talk to Detective Lieutenant Cronin," she answered.

"About the tweets or about everything when it comes to you?" he shot back firmly.

"Maybe about everything," she answered, moving her eyes away from Bud.

"OK, I will," he said, as he started to walk away. He then turned to get closer to Rachelle, saying, "Just know one thing. Paul will do everything and anything to protect you, and it's the *anything* part that has me worried. Would you be able to live with yourself if he destroyed his life or even died for you because he doesn't know everything?"

"No," she said. "I could not live with myself, but you need to speak to Detective Lieutenant Cronin."

"I am," Bud replied. "You see, Rachelle, I may be this guy that makes people laugh and smile, but I can turn on a dime when people I care about are hurt or going to be hurt. I will do what I have to do. Kyle Winters found out until someone slit his throat. Let us help and protect you. Tell me why you insist on sending messages out on Twitter and *Newsday*. And don't you dare tell me it's because their circulation has increased 20 percent since this started."

Rachelle folded her arms and looked at Bud before saying, "I'm not going to let these people stop me from what I want to do. You know, Paul asked me to write about this, and I agreed. Now that we are involved in one of the biggest murder cases ever on Long Island and I've been a target twice, it won't change anything if I stop. I'm doing what I think is right for me and for this case."

Bud shrugged and asked, "Even if it gets more people killed? Because you know Paul won't stop; he will die for you. And not because he's a cop; it's because he loves you."

"Oh, come on," Rachelle answered.

"Stop!" Bud yelled. "You're a smart girl. I'm a smart guy. He may not have said anything like it to you but only because he's afraid of losing you as a friend. Sad in a way, to be afraid to tell someone you love them for fear you will lose them in your life. He's my partner, and I will be one unbearable cop if his life changes for the worse because we don't know everything."

"I understand," she replied.

"Do you?" Bud shot back. He repeated himself, saying, "Do you? I don't want any more killing for anyone. This town has suffered enough, you have suffered enough. Sherry, Victoria's family, Timothy, enough. One thing is clear. I will protect my partner, but when it comes to you, I won't be able to protect him. So think about what I'm saying. I'll see you later." He gave her a hug and she grabbed him and held on for a few seconds before letting him go.

"Are you OK?" he asked.

"No, I'm not. Go, go. You have a job to do."

"OK, see you later." He left her walkway and waved to the unmarked vehicle about 50 yards down Prospect Street. When he got in the car, he was receiving a transmission from Paul.

"What's up, my partner?"

"It seems Simpson was not arrested because of Detective Lieutenant Cronin's directive. I think we need to talk to him about a few things."

"OK," Bud replied. "I'll be there in 15 minutes."

When Bud arrived at his desk, Paul was anxious to go to Cronin's office. They arrived at his door, and he waved them in as he spoke on the phone. They stood by silently as he finished his conversation, placed the receiver down, and looked at the two young detectives.

"What can I do for you?" he asked.

"Boss," Paul spoke, "you had Simpson excused on a misdemeanor?"

"So?" Cronin replied.

"So he could be in jail and off the streets."

"He's not our vigilante killer or responsible for any of the killings or the kidnapping. I want him out and about, and it's my feeling whoever else is responsible will want to contact him. Any more questions?" the detective lieutenant asked.

"This morning, you met with Rachelle and left with her from the hospital?" Paul asked.

"Yes," Cronin said. "I had more questions to ask her," he replied.

Paul said, "She won't stop the tweets on Twitter."

"I know," Cronin said.

Bud spoke up, asking, "Boss, why is Rachelle telling us to speak with you when we ask her certain questions?"

"Because she doesn't want to lie to you."

"Lie about what?" Paul said forcibly.

"We will discuss it later," Cronin answered. "In the meantime, I need you guys to spend the rest of the day with Agent Sherman and gimpy O'Connor. They have some information and a theory on Phil Smith. I'm beginning to wonder if he is even in this town."

"The postmark on the letter has Port Jefferson," Bud said.

"Yes, it does," Cronin said. "I will see you guys tomorrow. In the meantime, I want you to see what our good friends at the FBI are doing."

They left the detective lieutenant's office and passed the precinct commander on the way out. "What's happening, boys?" he asked.

"Detective Lieutenant Cronin," Paul answered.

The remark surprised the commander, and he made a mental note to mention it to Cronin when he saw him.

As Bud and Paul drove in the car, it was clear that Paul was visibly upset. He said, "It's days like these I just want to pack up and move away."

"Hang in there, partner. Who knows, maybe we'll get shot and get disability," Bud replied.

Paul looked over at Bud and started laughing. Then he said, "You're a funny guy, Detective Johnson."

"That's what they tell me," he answered.

Friday, June 24

Paul got himself up at 8:00 am, took his shower, and was downstairs at Z Pita to meet his dad for breakfast before he headed into the city for his reunion. He sat down after giving his father a kiss on the top of his head and was served his coffee by Rebecca before he even said good morning. He asked to see a copy of the morning *Newsday*, and because of the popularity of Rachelle's tweets, there was a subheading at the bottom of the page for BF_TJ_GW's daily tweet. Her messages had become so popular that the Internet searches for the three founding fathers had increased by more than 14 percent in the past week. He turned to page four. There was her miniature picture with the daily tweet: "I know what you want, it's the MONEY, which makes it very FUNNY." Paul covered his eyes in disbelief as he handed the paper over to his dad to read.

His father put the paper down and said, "You have really gotten yourself in a situation."

Paul looked at his Dad and replied, "You're right. If I didn't ask her in the first place to write the articles, she would not be in this thing so deep, but I have tried to get her to stop. She's making herself a target, and I don't know why."

"Well, you just have to see how this thing plays out now," his dad replied. "Come on, let's talk about something else before your old man heads into the city."

Joey Z stopped by to say hello and sat down at the table, which was very rare for him.

"Have you spoken to Rachelle?" Paul asked him.

"Yes," the restaurant owner replied. "She told me she will be back within a week, that all this will be over. However, I have concerns even when this is over."

"What's that?" Paul asked.

Joey Z looked around to make sure things were running smoothly, as he always did, before he looked at Paul again and said, "She is a celebrity, she's in *Newsday* every day. The *Port Jefferson Now* has her tweets in order in the weekly paper. The whole damn town is on the national news, and it's not just about the killing. They're giving Rachelle so much attention. Between the articles, the shootings, I'm really thinking hard, but Paul, I'm not sure I want this attention at the restaurant. If cameras and news reporters are going to be in here covering her, my business will be hurt badly. I love Rachelle, but life changes as we get older, and right now I have doubts about all this."

There was silence at the table, and then Paul's dad chimed in with, "I think that's the longest amount of time I ever heard you talk."

Joey Z smirked for a few seconds before he looked at Paul as the detective spoke. Paul said, "I know and understand what you are saying, Joey, but all of this will pass. It's true what you say, everything you say, but Rachelle wants to be a part of this restaurant. She loves being here, loves the staff and you; maybe one day she will love your tenant also." The last statement appeared to go right over Joey Z's head as Paul continued, "Keep your mind open, Joey. Don't make any final decisions 'til you sit with her for an hour when this is over."

"I agree," Joey Z responded. "I will hold on. We want her here, but I need to think about my customers and my staff. The attention needs to be on the customers, not the owners or the managers."

"I agree," the elder Powers said. "How about a refill on the coffee?" Rebecca was over in seconds to fill his cup.

"I understand you are off to the city," Joey Z said to Mr. Powers.

"Yes," he answered. "I can't take all this excitement. It's time to see old friends and talk about the memories of what was a great company that was destroyed by outsiders."

"Oh, here we go," Paul said. "See what you started?" he said to Joey Z. "OK, I have to run, I've got to get to the gym for an hour. Dad, I love you and will speak to you tonight." He kissed him on the head and winked at Joey Z as he left. He could tell by the look on Joey Z's face that he was expressing a sarcastic thanks for leaving his dad with him to talk history.

It took Paul 15 minutes to get upstairs to retrieve his gym bag and get to the Planet Fitness in Rocky Point, which was about five miles east of Port Jefferson. The treadmill for an hour did his body and mind good. He always had trouble keeping from being bored on the treadmill until he joined the Planet Fitness club. They had 12 televisions, all in a row, showing different channels, so he could switch to any channel while he was working up a sweat. He didn't hear his cell phone ring because it was in his locker. Bud was on his way to the precinct when his cell rang. It was Allan at the security building in Belle Terre.

"What's up, my partner's high school friend?"

"Bud," Allan replied quickly, "Deborah and her father are leaving town. They have a home in Marco Island, Florida. I've asked them to wait, but they are going bye-bye."

Bud turned the car around and said, "Tell them to wait. I will be there in 10 minutes." He hung up as he sped up the engine.

Allan went out to the car and told Deborah that Bud wanted to say goodbye. While she waited for Bud, she called Rachelle to say hello and goodbye and told her they needed to get together when all of this was over. She hung up the phone as Bud's unmarked cruiser drove to the security building. He greeted William Lance and then gently touched Deborah's arm to pull her aside for some privacy.

"What's going on? You shouldn't be leaving the house."

"Um!" she said. "We were told it would be best to leave town for a week."

"Who told you that?" he asked.

"Detective Lieutenant Cronin," she said. "He suggested it to us, and we decided it would be good to be away."

Bud was puzzled and exclaimed, "What the fuck?"

"Hey!" she said, "no *F* words," and hit his shoulder.

"OK, OK," he said. "Listen, keep in touch with me, please, while you're in Florida."

"OK," she said.

"Promise me!" he said again.

"I promise, I promise." She leaned her head in and kissed the side of his cheek. The look on his face told the story of his disappointment as William Lance drove away.

Bud turned to Allan and said, "I don't know what the fuck. I mean, shit is going on, but it's clear Cronin knows something we don't."

"Take it easy," Allan said to him. "Just go talk to him."

"Listen," Bud said to Allan, "keep an eye on the house."

"Don't worry," Allan replied, "the electronic security there is pretty tight."

"All right, see you later," Bud said. "I've got to get to the precinct. Did you call Paul?"

"Yes," Allan replied, "no answer on his cell." Bud got in his car and drove to the precinct. He entered Detective Lieutenant Cronin's office and shut the door, a sign that Cronin knew would not be good.

Rachelle and Madison were in the kitchen talking over a cup of coffee when Rachelle's cell rang. "Hello," Rachelle answered.

The voice on the other end was disguised and said, "Just who the fuck do you think you are?"

"Oh, hi! How are you?" Rachelle answered.

"Don't ask me how I am, you little bitch."

"What do you want? Oh," she replied, "you read my tweet today. I'm glad you enjoyed it. Listen, my sister is here now. Can you call me back in 20 minutes?" *Click*, dead silence.

"Who was that?" Madison asked.

"Someone from *Newsday* asking about the article I promised I would submit, but I said I would hold off until the investigation was finished. I've always wanted to write a book, and I think it's my destiny with everything happening the way it's going."

Madison finished her coffee and got up to leave.

"Half a cup today?" Rachelle asked.

"Yes, ma'am," Madison answered. "I have dance classes to worry about."

"You have a perfect body," Rachelle said to Madison as she was going out the door in her leggings and body suit.

"I'm younger than you," she grinned as she kissed her goodbye.

"Ha, ha, very funny," Rachelle said, closing the door. She sat down in the kitchen, and within 10 minutes her phone rang again.

"Yes," Rachelle answered.

"What do you want before I kill you once and for all?"

"You can't kill me," she replied. "You've tried twice, and now I have everyone watching me, so good luck with that one."

"What do you want?" the eerie voice said. "Don't make me ask again, you snub little shit." There was silence for a few seconds.

Rachelle took a deep breath and came out with it. "I want some of the money," she said.

"There is only three million!" the voice yelled.

"Tax-free three million," Rachelle replied, "and I can find out exactly where it is in the mansion, plus the family is on their way out of town as we speak. I want half a million. I will have my contact get the money, take my 500,000, and give you the two and a half million."

"How do you know I won't kill you?" the voice on the other end said.

"You won't because I have tweets locked away that will be published if something happens to me. They're in good hands. So think about it, and let me know, because, you see, I know who you are." *Click.* She covered her face with her hands as they shook uncontrollably. "What am I doing?" she said to herself.

Paul left the gym and called Allan back after hearing his voice mail. Allan brought him up to date on everything as Paul drove to the precinct. His thoughts were frustrating him. He had gone to the gym for 90 minutes and the Lances left town on the advice of Detective Lieutenant Cronin.

When he arrived, Bud was already in the office with the boss. He knocked and opened the door to repeat the question that Bud had asked regarding Debbie Lance leaving town with her father.

Cronin picked up some papers to look busy and raised his eyes at them to say, "Because she will be safe, she's not involved with any of this except that she was kidnapped and beaten and would be dead if not for our hero friend in the mask, as well as Sherry."

Bud and Paul looked at each other as Agents Sherman and O'Connor came in to the precinct with a vengeance. They opened the door as Cronin expected.

"Just who the hell do you think you are?" O'Connor yelled as Cronin just looked at his papers, ignoring them.

"Cronin!" Sherman spoke. Cronin began writing scribble on a piece of paper, but they didn't know.

In a calm voice Cronin said, "You didn't knock first."

"What!" O'Connor yelled.

Bud interjected. He said, "You didn't knock first, numb nuts!" He looked back at Cronin to see his displeasure and said, "OK, he didn't say the numb nuts part, that was me."

Sherman pulled O'Connor, closed the door behind them, knocked, and came in.

"How can I help you?" Cronin said. This whole play put a smile on Bud's face.

"You sent Debbie Lance and William Lance out of town, therefore possibly jeopardizing the investigation."

Cronin stood up and sat on his desk before saying, "First of all, I didn't force them to go anywhere. I suggested it. They have a home in Marco Island, Florida. If the FBI wants to speak to them, I will give you the address."

Bud added, "You guys do have an office down there, right?"

"Bud!" Cronin yelled.

"Sorry, boss," Bud replied.

Cronin looked back at Agents Sherman and O'Connor and said, "Look, we want them safe. Plus someone is killing the suspects. How do we know it's going to stop there? If Phil Smith is doing the killing with the mask on, we don't know for sure he would stop. And by the way, if it wasn't Smith, then he should be coming up dead shortly. Come on, guys, we don't need Deborah Lance here on protective detail."

Sherman replied, "Don't you think you should have said something to us? It's just not about the police in the handling of this."

Cronin answered back, "If it makes you feel any better, I didn't tell my team either. I just didn't think about it when I offered my opinion to them. That's it, fellas, that's all it is."

O'Connor replied, "You will keep us informed on the information you received?"

Cronin looked at Paul, who in turn answered, "Yes, of course."

As the FBI agents turned to walk out, Bud asked, "How's the leg feeling?" to O'Connor.

"It's feeling OK, no thanks to you. People get shot when they are around you."

"Not me," Bud answered as they closed the door. Paul was laughing at Bud's remark as he looked at Cronin's serious face.

"You two clowns ready to get to work today?" Cronin asked.

"On it, boss," Bud said as they left.

"Wait!" Cronin yelled. He handed a piece of paper to Bud, saying, "This is the Lances' address in Marco Island. Get with the local authorities and have them keep in touch with us."

Bud took the paper and said, "I noticed you didn't give the address to the FBI."

"They didn't ask me, Bud," he replied. "Pay attention to the details."

Bud looked at the address on Collier Boulevard. He had stayed at the Marriott on Marco Island a few years before and had fallen in love with the little town near Naples. He smiled and sent Deborah a text. She was on the Expressway, exit 49, westbound in the stretch limousine when she saw it. It said, "Enjoy Marco, maybe I'll visit Marco after we catch the bad guys." He got a text back that said, "If anyone can, it's you." He got in the car with Paul behind the wheel.

"Where to, my partner?" Bud said.

Paul replied, "Let's go see how Officer Walker is doing first." They turned on to Middle Country Road as Bud began singing "Sherry Baby."

Rachelle got out of the shower with a towel wrapped around her as she looked out her front window. The unmarked cruiser with two officers was now a little closer to the house but still off to the right about 30 yards away. She turned on the television and surfed the channels until she saw the marathon of *NCIS* on the USA network. She loved the character of Ziva David, pronounced *Daveed*. She was beautiful, smart, but a trained killer who over the years grew a heart. It was her favorite character of all time. The only thing she couldn't figure out was why Ziva and DiNozzo never got it on. *No way*, she thought. *If it was real life, they would have at least relieved the sexual tension between them.* Same thing between Benson and Stabler on *Law & Order: Special Victims Unit*, but Stabler was married. She had stopped watching when his character left the show.

Then Rachelle started laughing to herself because she thought,

Look who is calling the kettle black. She had been the same exact way with Paul over the previous three years. Maybe *NCIS* was more real than she thought. She finished getting dressed, left the house, and started walking down Prospect. She turned right on to East Main Street and within five minutes walked into the Red Onion Café. She ordered herself a smoked turkey wrap on whole wheat with a skinny green tea chai. She waited a few minutes, got her food from the young woman who co-owned the establishment, and sat down at one of the tables in back. She was there for about seven minutes when a man walked in, got himself a coffee, paid for it, and walked over to Rachelle's table and sat down.

"Hello," Rachelle said.

"Hello. So?" he said. "Looks like fate has brought us together." Rachelle sipped her green tea as she looked at Robert Simpson sitting across from her.

Bud and Paul walked into Sherry's room and visited with her for about an hour. Sherry was more alert and awake and was able to give extraordinary details about everything that had happened three nights earlier. She expressed that she failed her job by getting herself stabbed; however, both detectives praised her as the hero she was. It was her shots and call to 911 that stopped Mason from finishing off Rachelle, not to mention the masked killer did not have time to kill anyone else. Sherry mentioned that she even wondered if the masked killer would have killed Rachelle if he had the time. Even Sherry realized that if the masked man was Phil Smith, why didn't he kill Deborah? Paul and Bud agreed, but Paul added it would be a great cover and alibi for Smith to just knock off his partners, then possibly disappear himself with the chance that everyone else thought he was eliminated. Only difference was that his body would never be found. One thing they all agreed on was that the case needed to get closed and not be another cold case for Long Island, with all the media attention.

Sherry told them the doctors gave her another week in the hospital before they let her go but that she would be on disability for a few weeks. She told them her husband had asked her to leave the force and think about having children. Her decision would be made after she healed from her wounds and she had a chance to speak at length with her entire family. Bud asked her how her parents were doing, and she told them it was difficult for them, especially for her dad. "Yeah," Bud said, "I got that impression."

Paul asked Sherry if she had heard anything said during the whole episode. Paul looked at Sherry and said, "Sherry, I need to ask a question, and I want you to answer yes or no as fast as you can. It is really important to tell me your first instinct when I ask the question. Are you ready?"

"Yes," Sherry answered.

Paul moved in to take a close look at Sherry's eyes and said, "The screams you heard, were they real, or was it an act?"

Sherry returned Paul's eye contact and said, "Yes, they were real."

Paul looked at her and said, "OK, thank you."

"Wait," Sherry said, "you are going to have to do better than that."

"Yes," Bud said, "enlighten us."

Paul sat down on the chair next to Sherry's bed as he spoke. "It's a question that had to be asked, and I wanted to see your face when you had time to think about it when I asked you."

Bud looked at Paul and asked, "Are you having any doubts about her?"

"Not anymore," Paul said. "If I'm wrong, I won't be around much longer."

"Cut this shit out right now!" Bud yelled. "Why are you talking like this?"

Paul stood up again and said, "This thing has been like some mystery puzzle from the beginning. If you look at this piece by piece, day by day, we found out who the bad guys were, yet we have a mystery that keeps getting more mysterious every day." Sherry tried to sit up a bit as she listened to Bud and Paul exchange theories on the case and the chain of events that happened late Wednesday night.

Finally she added, "Who would benefit by having Rachelle dead other than the people who kidnapped Debbie and killed Timothy?"

"Why would they even care?" Paul added.

"So she wrote articles and tweets?" Bud added. "Why is this bothering you now, Paul?"

Paul wiped his forehead and pulled out his phone. He showed Bud the text on his phone and then to Sherry. It was from the watch detail on Rachelle. It read, "Rachelle is having lunch with Robert Simpson right now at the Red Onion." Bud couldn't believe his eyes, so he pulled Paul's BlackBerry closer to him.

"Now you know why this is becoming more of a puzzle every day," Paul said as he sat down. "I don't know whether to go over there and ask her straight out what's going on or bring her in as a suspect to question her."

"Hold on a second," Bud said with both his hands out in the air as if it was going to help him figure out this latest piece of the puzzle. "Rachelle knows she's being watched, even if she wanted to do anything, she knows that she could not get away with anything."

Sherry sat up even more and said, "Not unless she had lunch with someone that we have no evidence against, and that's Simpson, right?"

"Other than being an asshole, no, there's no evidence against him," Bud replied.

"Regardless," Paul said, "we don't have evidence of any kind on him, so why is she having lunch with him?"

"Maybe we need to ask her," Bud replied.

"Maybe," Paul said. "I have a feeling we better speak to Cronin first, but somehow I have a feeling he already knows."

Paul called Cronin's phone and, as he suspected, he was already aware of the lunch. He hung up and said angrily, "Great, it seems we all know about the lunch. The whole damn world will know tomorrow!"

"Why didn't you ask him about questioning her?" Sherry asked.

Paul looked at her and replied, "I didn't have to. He told me to let it play out."

Bud threw his hands up and said, "That's great. What the fuck?"

Sherry spoke up, saying, "We could talk about this all night, but maybe Cronin is right, let it play out. If Rachelle knows she is being watched, then maybe she knows what she's doing."

Paul stood up and said, "You mean like her desire to get herself killed because she's looking to establish herself as a serious writer?"

Paul sent a text back to the watch detail and asked if they were still together and how long it had been. He received his answer within minutes that they were still together talking, drinking, and eating and that it had been for one hour and fifteen minutes so far. Paul shook his head as he told Bud and Sherry.

Sherry had a look of disappointment on her face as she spoke up to say, "Well, I have to tell you, if I took a knife to the abdomen for nothing, I may just shoot the girl myself."

"No," Paul said, "there is more to this. Let's go over everything."

Paul, Bud, and Sherry went over the entire case again, step by step.

"It's clear the masked killer is Phil Smith," Sherry said.

"I don't know," Bud said. "What do you say, Paul?" he asked.

"I'm still stuck on Rachelle's involvement," Paul said.

Paul called Rachelle's number.

"What are you doing?" Bud asked.

"I'm calling her," he replied.

"No," Bud said. "You heard the boss."

"Doesn't matter," Paul replied. He put his BlackBerry on speakerphone to allow Bud and Sherry to hear the recording.

"The number you have called has been disconnected. Please check the number and try again."

He dialed again, and the same recording came on.

"She changed her number," Paul said. "I don't want to believe it, but we may have to bring her in."

"No," Sherry said. "If you bring her in, we may not find out the whole story. Listen to Cronin and leave her alone. She knows she is being watched."

"Sherry Walker," Bud added, "maybe we should call you 'Detective Walker.'"

"You will," she replied, "or you will be calling me civilian Sherry Walker."

Bud smiled and asked, "How much longer are you going to be here?"

"Another week, guys," she replied. "What can I say, the price you pay for being a hero is high." They laughed for the first time since they had arrived in the room. It was perfect timing, for Sherry's husband came into the room as they were leaving.

When they got to the parking lot of Mather Hospital, Bud told Paul he hadn't been able to reach him in the morning.

"At the gym, my friend," Paul said. "It wouldn't hurt you to get in a workout here and there."

"Hey," Bud replied, "I'm very deceiving looking. I can do miles and miles on the treadmill."

"Show me," Paul said. "Tomorrow morning, 8:00 am, pick me up, and I'll give you a workout."

"You got it," Bud answered.

While they were driving to the precinct to get some paperwork done, which never seemed to go away, Bud sent Deborah a text that said, "When you get this you will have arrived in Florida, so welcome to the sunshine state." Then he sent her another one that said, "Text me back to let me know you got this." He then called the local authorities in Florida to make arrangements for them to keep an eye on the house and Deborah while she was down there. As they drove to the precinct, Bud's thoughts were on the events of the day. His doubts about who the masked killer was were starting to concern him. They were thoughts he wanted to keep to himself for now.

Rachelle got up from the table at the Red Onion after an hour and 45 minutes conversing with Robert Simpson. When she got up to leave, she did not even turn around to look at him. When Rachelle left the café, she made a left, then crossed the street to Thompson Street and went into the Port Jefferson Free Library. She went right into the computer room, signed in with her library card, and signed on to Twitter. She wrote an update: "Thanks for the meeting TODAY. JUST REMEMBER IT DOESN'T MATTER WHAT YOU SAY. I'm not going AWAY." When she finished the tweet, she started Googling for information, not noticing or caring that one of the watch detail had entered the library to be certain nothing happened to her or anyone else in the library while she was there.

She got up and walked downstairs to the adult book section. She was there for 15 minutes before she left the library. Instead of walking on East Main Street toward Prospect, she walked down Arden Place to go to Z Pita on Main Street. As she walked to Z Pita, Paul's Black-Berry buzzed as it always did when one of Rachelle's tweets was published. He showed it to Bud and said, "Forget the paperwork. Let's go see Madison and then Rachelle. If we are going to solve this thing, we sure as hell need to know what the hell is going on."

Rachelle greeted everyone at Z Pita with a warm hug. Joey Z let her get through all of the formalities so he could greet her and then speak to her. He brought her to table three in the back of the establishment on the other side so they could have as much privacy as possible. They sat and talked for almost an hour about the past and the memories built while she was at the restaurant.

Finally, Joey Z broke the ice and asked, "Are you coming back, Rachelle?"

She looked at him with a tear in her eye and said, "Yes, I will, if you want me."

Joey was very quick with his answer. "I want you. We all want you. But I don't want this case unsolved, and I want to be certain you, yourself, are OK. You have gone through more in the last week than most experience in a lifetime. I want you back, I want you right, and I want you feeling well—physically, emotionally, and mentally. Take a month, two months, and then you will need to tell me you are ready for this. My feelings for you cannot overshadow the business, the staff, and of course the customers. I know you understand that."

Rachelle replied, "Yes, of course I do."

Madison greeted Paul and Bud with a hug at her dance studio, where she gave her kids a break.

"Just a couple of quick questions, Maddie," Paul said. "Did you know that Rachelle changed her cell phone number?" Maddie walked over to her desk and called Rachelle, and it went straight to voice mail.

"She has the phone off, but she didn't change the number I use."

"She had two phones?" Bud said.

"Yes, one for business-related and one for personal."

"Oh," Bud said, looking at Paul.

"How has she been, Maddie, other than what we would expect?" Paul asked.

Madison answered as she wiped the sweat from her neck, saying, "She seems OK. She's going to need therapy so she can talk about it to someone, but I think she will be OK. I'm not worried to death about it. I'm concerned as a sister, but she's a strong woman."

Bud spoke up, saying, "Do you know of any reason why Rachelle would have lunch with Robert Simpson today?"

"What?" she replied. "Is this a joke?" When she looked at Paul's face she knew it was not a joke and said, "No, I don't know what is going on."

"Welcome to the club," Bud said.

"You will need to see what you can find out, Madison," Paul added, "before more lives are lost."

"I'll see what I can do," Madison replied.

The two detectives got in the car, and Paul called Joey Z about his meeting with Rachelle. The watch detail was certainly doing their job as far as watching her. Joey Z excused himself while talking to Rachelle and mentioned to Paul discreetly she was still sitting with him at the table.

"Good," he said, "keep her there."

Paul and Bud walked in the front door within minutes and saw Rachelle and Joey Z in the back.

"Let me have this, Bud. I'll call you. Have a drink with Joey Z." He walked up to the table to greet Rachelle and the owner.

"Hi," Rachelle said, "I was just leaving."

"OK," Paul said, "can I walk you home?"

"Sure," she said with a smile. She said her goodbye to Joey and hugged Bud before she left the restaurant with Paul.

When they turned on to East Main and reached Prospect, Paul started talking. "104 Prospect, R.H. Wilson house, built in 1840. This is the house where he made the sails for the *America*, the vessel that won the first America's Cup in 1843. The bird's-wing-shaped sail revolutionized sail making for all time. 105 Prospect, the Edwin Tooker home, built in 1875. 108 Prospect, the Hamilton Tooker home ,built in 1854."

As they walked up the hill, Paul continued, saying, "114 Prospect, Capt. C.E. Tooker home, built 1852, one of the founders along with P.T. Barnum and others who founded the Steamboat company in 1883. He was a captain on the first ferries. They must be turning over in their graves now," Paul added.

Rachelle was enjoying listening to Paul talk history, so she let him continue. "116 Prospect, built in 1850, bought by Billy Brown in 1869. He ran a horse-drawn stage service to the train station and to Patchogue. 115 Prospect, John Mather built this house after the street was laid out in 1840. At that time, it was called North Street. The Mather family built approximately 54 vessels in the Mather shipyard, and it was their fortune that left money to build the Mather Memorial Hospital built in 1929, and thank goodness for that! And who lives at the top at Prospect? Rachelle Robinson, who I assume will make history of her own and will have this house in the brochures of Port Jefferson."

Rachelle stopped at the doorstep of her house and said, "I'm impressed. You know more about history here than I ever thought."

"I read your articles," Paul answered as he looked at her.

"Thank you," she replied.

"Is there anything you want to tell me, Rachelle?"

She looked down, then up at him, and said, "Yes, but not now." She put her hand up to the side of his face, gently touching him before entering her house and shutting the door.

Paul phoned Bud to meet him at the Red Onion Café.

"Yeah, OK," Bud answered, "I'm sure they are all anxious to see me there."

Paul waited for Bud to arrive, and they both walked in together. The place was fairly busy. It was apparent the notoriety was not a negative for the establishment. Bud approached the young woman who was behind the counter and identified himself and Paul and asked to speak to the owner.

"I'm one of the owners," the young woman said as she smiled.

"Anything unusual happen in the café today?" Paul asked.

The woman looked at Bud and asked, "You mean like someone getting shot," as she tilted her head in a sarcastic look.

"Anything you would consider unusual," Paul replied.

"No, I'm sorry, nothing unusual today," she answered.

"Thank you," Bud replied. "Could I have a hot chocolate with soy milk to go?"

"Bud!" Paul replied.

"I'll be right there. Please," he said, looking at the amused owner behind the bar.

Paul waited for Bud on the sidewalk, and when he came out, they walked across the street to the library.

Paul looked at Bud as he sipped his soy milk hot chocolate and asked, "Do they serve normal food in there?"

"No" Bud replied, "if they did they would be like any other café."

Once in the library, they identified themselves and asked if they could request to search the sites that Rachelle Robinson had visited while signed in on her library card. The answer was quick, Twitter and Google. They left the library and decided to walk up Thompson Street to the two homes owned by the Winters brothers. The homes were being guarded by FBI agents, and no one was allowed in them without approval of Agents Sherman or O'Connor.

The agents at the house were able to reach O'Connor, and access was denied. "Isn't that interesting?" Bud said as they started walking back down Thompson Street. They turned right on East Main Street to the corner and turned left on East Broadway and walked down to the ferry next to Danford's. They stopped to look around at the beautiful village and commented how surreal everything seemed. It had only been one week since the shooting, yet it seemed like a dream long ago, or a nightmare.

Rachelle greeted Madison with a hug and a kiss as she entered the house. Madison wanted to talk to her about her conversation with Bud and Paul but decided to wait until the next day. It seemed as though everyday had been filled with stress for her, and she didn't want to add to it. Those were her thoughts, yet her curiosity got the best of her.

"Rachelle, did you change your business cell number?"

"Yes," Rachelle answered. "I felt safe doing it. I really don't want to talk about it, please."

"OK," Madison replied. "Let me know when you want to talk about it."

"I will," Rachelle answered.

"Thank you. Do you have any appointments set up with the doctor?" Madison didn't want to say "psychiatrist."

"Yes" her older sister replied. "Next week."

"Anything happen today?"

"No," Rachelle said.

"No?" Madison replied.

Rachelle looked at her younger sister and said, "Just ask me, Maddie."

"OK," her younger sister replied. "Why were you having lunch with Robert Simpson?"

"Oh, God," Rachelle answered as she went to her room.

Madison followed her to her room and said, "Rachelle, I'm scared for you. You're my sister. Please tell me what is going on."

"I don't know," Rachelle replied. "I'm just trying to find answers. I had lunch with Simpson hoping he could shed some light on what's going on. I'm writing about this. It's who I am. It calms me. That's all."

"You won't be writing if this ends up getting you killed! Rachelle! Please! Please let us help you."

"You are," Rachelle said as she put her hand to Madison's face. "Just love me," she said, kissing the side of her face. "I need to write a bit," she said, as she sat down in her room, which had space for a little office.

Madison walked back to the kitchen and leaned her head against the refrigerator as many thoughts spun around inside it.

Paul and Bud finally made it back to the precinct, where they tried to catch up on paperwork. They had always been behind, but the shooting and the demand to close this case had made the paperwork assignments more challenging. Bud would normally get bored after just a couple hours at his desk and say something like, "I feel the need," and then add to it with whatever he was feeling he wanted to do to get away.

Paul was moving along at a good pace at his own desk when his father called from the city. He had just had a late lunch at the Evergreen Diner on 47th Street and was pleasantly surprised to see Sean

Hannity from Fox News come in for a bite to eat. The little hole-in-the-wall diner had pictures of most of the Fox News personalities, including Bill O'Reilly and Shepard Smith. Paul's dad was excited to tell him of his little surprise. The server had told the elder Powers that it was a common occurrence to see them, since their headquarters was just around the corner on Avenue of the Americas.

Usually Paul rushed his father off the phone, but not today. He enjoyed listening to his dad's enthusiasm about saying hello to the Reagan conservative host of his own program. Paul was laughing when his dad mentioned he wanted to tell Mr. Hannity his thoughts on the Great American Panel and some of his guests, particularly Dick Morris and Don Imus' wife, Deirdre, but he thought better of it because he was there for a lunch and not a debate.

"Good choice, Dad." Paul said.

As Paul spoke to his father, Bud got up and made a phone call of his own. Instead of a normal hello, Deborah Lance answered with, "Hello, funny guy. How are you?"

"Thanks for the text," Bud replied. "We have to keep an eye on you."

"Oh, well, thank you, but I'm safe and sound, and we are going to take a walk to Starbucks in a few minutes. I'm not a security expert, but it looks like we are being watched down here."

"I assume whoever is watching you has a real face," Bud said.

"Ha, Ha," Deborah replied.

"OK," the detective said. "Just checking in."

"Well, thank you, sir, speak to you later."

"Why don't you give me a call tomorrow if you have the time?" he replied.

"Well, I may have to do that to make sure you are staying out of trouble."

"OK, speak to you then. Bye," Bud said as he hung up.

When Bud got back to the desk to dig in again and attack the paperwork, Paul was still speaking with his dad. Paul said, "Dad, you just let me know if you ever see Monica Crowley. Then I will be really jealous." He was laughing as he hung up.

Paul was a fan of the "conservative warrior princess." He admired her strong views and her challenges to the good-ol'-boy network. She wasn't afraid to attack the media when she felt they had double standards, especially when it came to a female candidate being considered for president. He had always enjoyed her on *O'Reilly Factor*, but he didn't become a true fan until he found her on her three-hour radio program on 77ABC while he was on the treadmill at the gym on a Saturday morning.

"How's he doing?" Bud asked.

"He's great," Paul replied. "I'm shocked he didn't find a way to inform Sean Hannity his son was investigating the biggest case to hit in Long Island history, but he's doing fine. He hated the interview with Hasselbeck, and he expressed it. Not too many people made mention of it, but April 4 was also the anniversary of the shooting and assassination of Martin Luther King. A date my dad never forgot. He was in eighth grade when he was sent down to the principal's office for talking too much in class. My grandfather was stationed at Ramstein Air Force Base in Germany at the time. Anyway, when he got to the principal's office, they had the television on about the assassination in Memphis. The principal spoke to him and made him sit for 30 minutes before sending him back to class. When he walked in, the teacher said to him in front of everyone, 'Well, did you learn anything?' My dad said, 'Yes, I did. Martin Luther King was assassinated!' The teacher was so upset with his answer she practically dragged him by his collar back to the principal's office and, upon their arrival, learned that my dad was indeed correct and promptly apologized to the eighth-grader. The experience made my dad learn more about Martin Luther King, and he grew to respect the man and what he stood for. His favorite song to this day is Elvis' tribute song to him, 'If I Can Dream.' It brings tears to his eyes every time he hears it."

Bud leaned back in his chair as he said, "You remember many details with your dad."

"Yeah," Paul replied. "This case seems to be changing all of us. I want to remember more details. This case has made me appreciate many things."

The remark made a mental impression on Bud, and he wanted

to ask Paul why they never discussed the letter from Phil Smith to Rachelle. He knew why the letter was not mentioned in the hospital room with Sherry, for only he, Paul, and Cronin knew about it. But the subject never came up between them, and it was bothering Bud. He noticed Gina, Cronin's assistant, going toward the coffee café and asked where the boss was.

She answered, "He told me to take messages, that's it." Bud and Paul looked at each other.

"OK," Bud said, "tell him we said hello and we will see him Monday unless he needs us tomorrow."

"I will tell him," Gina said as they got up to leave.

"By the way," she said, "Detective Lieutenant Cronin wants a report on your progress on his desk in regards to the case and today's findings."

"Thanks for telling us now," Bud said. They both sat down for another two hours before heading home, not aware that as they were writing their reports, Cronin visited Sherry at the hospital, spoke to William Lance on the phone in Florida, and stopped by to speak to Rachelle outside of her home away from all ears.

Saturday, June 25

Bud knocked on the door and, as usual, ran up the stairs at 8:00 am sharp.

"Rise and shine! Time to go to the gym, time for this chubby guy to show off on the treadmill!" he yelled.

Paul was just putting his gym shorts in his bag when Bud greeted him. "Let's go," Paul said. "We will see what kind of shape you are in. Did you bring a headset for the televisions?"

"Nah," Bud replied. "I have my Katy Perry on my iPod; that's all I need."

They got to Planet Fitness in Rocky Point by 8:30 am and changed their clothes in the locker room. They got to the treadmills, and Paul put on Level 6, Random 4.5 speed to start for 60 minutes. Bud started at 3.5 speed on Level 6, determined to show he was in better shape than it appeared.

Paul watched his television program and was 20 minutes into it when he noticed both girls and guys would walk by he and Bud with unusual smiles on their faces. He thought nothing of it until a couple of girls were laughing while looking at them. He glanced over at Bud to see if he noticed anything funny, when he saw that Bud did not have his gym shorts on. Instead he was wearing his boxer underwear with a large Superman logo shield on the front and back. He tapped Bud to remove the earplugs from his ear.

"Bud! You forgot to put your gym shorts on! You have everyone laughing looking at your Superman shorts underwear! Go change!"

"No," Bud said, "I'm just breaking a sweat. Can't stop now."

"Oh my God!" Paul said. "You are out of your mind!"

"What can I say?" Bud replied. "I forgot the shorts. I was wondering why it felt like I had nothing on."

Bud finished his workout on the treadmill and walked to the locker room to the amusement of the other patrons and finally met

Paul to work out on the universal equipment for 40 minutes. They showered and were out of Planet Fitness by 10:30 am.

They returned to Z Pita for a Sunday breakfast, where Paul saw Joey Z's parents for the first time in more than a year. George and Marguerite were both in their late eighties and a delight to catch up with. Paul would often think how lucky Joey Z was that he still had both his parents.

While Paul spoke with the elder Z family, Bud sent Deborah Lance a text, and they exchanged messages for 10 minutes. Their breakfast was served while they read the Sunday newspaper. Paul turned the page and saw the column featuring Rachelle's tweet for the day: "I know it's you, you know it's true, I even know your car is blue." Paul was shaking his head.

"Holy shit! Look at this," he said to Bud. Bud read it.

"Who has a blue car?" Paul put his fork down and got up to go to the men's room. Bud cut out the tweet and put it in his wallet. He had a fleeting thought that Paul had a dark-blue Honda Accord. Timothy had a Kona blue Mustang. Allan had a blue BMW. Madison had a red Kia. Bud had a gray Hyundai when not driving the unmarked cruiser, which was blue. Bud decided that Rachelle's clue was not specific enough, but it was good enough to cause controversy.

Paul came back to the table and told Bud he was going upstairs to relax and then go over his notes on the case the rest of the day. Bud needed some time also and said he would see Paul Monday morning. As Bud got in the car, he had about 20 subjects on his mind, from Deborah Lance to Rachelle to the masked killer to Sherry Walker to Detective Lieutenant Cronin and Paul Powers. It was the first time in his career where he felt overwhelmed with what was going on. Instead of getting in his car, he walked to the Starbucks on the corner of Main and Arden Place, walked in, and got a Cinnamon Spice tea. He sat down and started putting a list together of everyone that had a blue car or that had anything to do with a blue car.

Maybe it was a waste of time, but he had peace and quiet as he sat on a stool facing the window toward Main Street. Timothy, dead, blue. Bud, good guy, blue. Paul, cop, partner, blue. Allan, blue-and-white, two-tone. Vicky, dead, not blue. Agent O'Connor, ass, FBI agent, blue. John Winters, registered red car. Madison, red car. Cronin, gray. Patty Saunders, yellow car. Robert Simpson, another ass, gray car. Deborah Lance, pretty, burnt-orange. William Lance, black limo and white corvette. He called Paul on his cell and read him the list of names he had written down.

"Who did I leave out?"

Paul answered, "Phil Smith."

"Duh," Bud said.

Paul continued, "Sherry Walker, Kyle Winters, Steven Anderson, and Agent Sherman."

Bud hung up and called the precinct with these names and asked what color cars were registered to them. He waited about 10 minutes until he got his information. Sherry Walker, green. Mason Winters, green mint. *Figures,* Bud thought. Kyle Winters, dark blue, but very dead. Steven Anderson, light beige. Agent Sherman, red. This was going nowhere, and Bud even thought about asking Rachelle what the hell was going on.

It was a beautiful Sunday outside, and since Bud had never spoken to Steven Anderson at the *Now* paper, he decided to see if he was in to talk to him about Rachelle and the tweets that were causing a stir, and quite frankly a problem, for the cops. He knew that Cronin was getting heavily pressured and the Twitter adventures in cryptic messages were not helping. He turned left outside the Starbucks and walked toward the *Port Jefferson Now* offices. He walked past Theatre 3 and the CVS store and finally reached the little strip mall behind the parking lot available for customers.

He opened the door to the office, surprised it was unlocked. He saw a figure sitting on a chair, not moving, as he called out, "Hello!" As he approached the figure not answering him, Bud pulled out his weapon.

"Hello? Please answer me." He reached the chair, turned it around, and woke up Steven Anderson and scared the hell out of him as he saw Bud's gun pointing at him.

"Are you all right?" Bud asked.

"I would be better if I didn't wake up with a gun in my face."

"Sorry about that," Bud replied.

"What are you doing sleeping here?"

"I have to work Sundays especially with what is going on. Circulation for our paper has gone up 20 percent in the last week, and I know *Newsday* purchases are up 7 percent with Rachelle's tweets and promise of an article."

"Why do you think Rachelle is tweeting about a blue car. Does it mean anything?" Bud asked.

Steven shook his head and said, "I'm not sure. She could be just doing it to shake things up, but I will tell you it's working."

"Yeah," Bud said. "When is the last time you heard from Rachelle?"

"I get an email from her every day," Steven replied.

"OK," Bud said. "Keep me informed of anything unusual."

"Sure thing," the editor replied.

Bud walked out the front door of the *Now* offices as the shots rang out, one after the other. The detective went down and didn't move. The front windows were shattered with bullets, as was the door. Silence. Everything stopped as Bud quickly got up and dove behind a car as more shots were fired. His cell phone fell out on the ground, but he wasn't about to try and get it. Steven Anderson had crawled under his desk and managed to call 911. Two minutes had gone by, which seemed like 10 minutes, and the firing had stopped. Bud decided not to be a hero and waited behind the car until squad cars pulled up. Paul was there within three minutes of the officers on the scene and began checking Bud out. He wasn't hit at all. "Terrible shots," he said to his partner.

Paul looked at Bud and said, "Maybe it was a warning, Bud. Maybe missing you was no accident."

"Thanks for making me feel good," Bud replied.

"Let's question Anderson while they collect the bullets," Paul answered.

"So much for a relaxing Sunday." Anderson had his face in his hands and appeared to be shaken up. He explained why he was in the office and heard the shots. He was sure Bud was hit and ducked under the desk while dialing 911.

"Show me what you're working on," Paul said. Steven pulled

out updates from Rachelle that were to be released in Wednesday's *Now* edition. Since *Newsday* was daily, Anderson was compiling the past five days for one big article for Tuesday. Anderson's hands were shaking as he showed Paul the work and the articles. Paul looked at the papers for a few minutes and handed them back to Anderson. The crime lab was on the scene, and Paul was surprised to see Agents Sherman and O'Connor pull up.

"Sorry, guys, we are investigating an attempted murder of a police officer."

"Can we take a look around?" Sherman asked. "We all believe this is related to the original kidnapping."

"Sorry," Paul said.

Sherman seemed confused and spoke again. "What's with the attitude, Detective? I thought we were working this case together."

"Me too," Paul replied, "but you made it clear we weren't when you denied access to us on the two Winters' homes." Paul started walking toward Bud and put on his sunglasses.

"I don't know anything about you guys being denied access to the homes."

"Ask your partner in crime here," Paul replied, pointing to O'Connor. O'Connor turned his back on Paul, facing Sherman, and told him he had denied access until the FBI was finished with the house.

Agent Sherman pushed O'Connor aside and told Paul, "Let me know when you want access to the homes."

"Today," Paul said. "Right now."

"How about a compromise," Sherman said. "You let us take a look around and question Bud and Anderson, and we will go with you to the Winters' homes, and you can look around to your heart's content."

"OK," Paul said. "Let them in, Officer Dugan." Dugan was a very intimidating figure that looked like the younger brother of the Rock or Dwayne Johnson, depending on your age and whether you're a movie or wrestling fan, but in a cop uniform.

As the two detectives and two FBI agents were going in, O'Connor couldn't help himself and said to Bud, "Seems like people are still getting shot around you."

"Yes," Bud replied, "so watch your back."

O'Connor turned around quickly and asked, "Are you threatening me?"

Bud kept on walking into the offices as he replied, "You want to play the game, you better know how to play it well."

"OK, boys," Paul said, "we have to play nice."

The FBI agents looked around the offices as O'Connor and Anderson greeted each other with a "hello again" greeting. As the lawmen were walking through the shooting, Paul got a call from Detective Lieutenant Cronin, who was relieved to find out Bud was OK.

Paul's end of the conversation went thusly: "Looks like eight shots fired, boss. No, Bud did not return fire. No one else is injured. Crime lab is here, FBI is here. Sherman and O'Connor."

Bud always liked to guess what the voice on the other end was saying while he listened to Paul's side of the conversation. Paul continued, "Anderson is pretty shook up, but it appears it was meant for Bud." Paul walked away from Bud while listening to Cronin's message on the other end.

He continued speaking, saying, "I wasn't here, boss, but from the looks of things, Bud is either the luckiest guy in the world or someone didn't want him dead. No, we don't need you down here; we are going to take a look at the Winters' homes after we leave here. Right, boss, talk to you tomorrow."

Paul walked back and asked the crime lab if they had an idea of where the shots were fired from. The technician felt the shots had come from behind one of the homes in the wooded area up on the hill across the street, but he told Paul he would need more time before being able to determine for sure. The FBI agents spent another 30 minutes inside the *Now* offices before being satisfied and leaving the building.

They drove up to the top of the hill by way of Spring Street. At the top, they all got out and saw the view the shooter had. Paul walked the wooded area looking for any kind of evidence. There were no shells, boot prints, torn clothing…nothing. He picked up a rock and threw it toward one of the trees in his frustration. Bud and the agents walked through, and nothing was found.

"The guy is a professional," O'Connor said.

"Unless," Paul added.

"Unless what?" Bud asked.

"Unless he didn't shoot from here. That would explain why nothing is here. Wouldn't it?" They walked about 25 yards to the right. Tacked to one of the trees was a note spelled out in magazine print. As soon as they came upon it, Paul's head was ready to explode. The note said: DETECTIVE POWERS...STOP THE KILLING...OR NEXT TIME I WON'T MISS YOUR PARTNER. They all looked at the note in silence.

Finally Bud spoke up and said, "Just wonderful. Tell me what this means, Paul."

Paul turned around and said, "It means we have to get this case solved or whoever wrote this note will punish me by trying to eliminate you."

"Well," Bud said, "if that's not an incentive, I don't know what is."

Paul called the technician down at the building and ordered the wooded area blocked off and for the note to be examined. They waited until a couple of squad cars came to the area to be sure no one else walked through the area while the four of them drove to Thompson Street to take a look at the homes. During the drive, Bud got a call from Sherry, checking in to be certain he was OK. To prove it to her, he started singing, and she hung up on him.

When they reached Thompson Street, Paul's phone buzzed. It was another tweet from Rachelle, and it said, "Without justice, courage is weak. —Benjamin Franklin." He showed it to Bud as they walked into the home on Thompson Street. They went through the house top to bottom in about two hours and found articles that Rachelle had written. Finally, Paul asked both agents what had been taken out of the house that they didn't know about.

"Only handwritten scribble on paper, newspaper articles, and magazines that John and Mason piled up in their rooms," O'Connor replied.

"What's going to happen to the homes? They have other family?"

Sherman hesitated then answered, "There are still loans out on the homes. The banks will take over, and I'm sure the state will look to take the difference if there is asset forfeiture with no family claim."

Paul looked over at Bud and asked, "Ready for next door?"

"Yeah, I guess," his partner replied.

As they left the front door and walked over to the next house, Bud remarked that it had certainly turned out to be a nice day off.

Paul, serious as ever, kept walking past Bud up the steps but replied, "Doesn't it make you wonder how the shooter knew where you were going to be? It wasn't on your schedule. It's a Sunday. You walked up there, right?" Bud nodded as Paul continued, "So whoever it was waited until you were at the *Now* offices and decided to fire warning shots near you and toward the offices. To warn you, to warn me, and to warn Anderson possibly about what was going to be published in Tuesday's edition. Regardless of whom they were trying to warn, they had a good idea where you were going to be."

They four men stepped into the house of Kyle Winters, and it smelled like a home with cats that had not been kept clean. O'Connor stepped in with Sherman and told them there had been 10 cats in the house and it was apparent he did not keep them or the kitty-litter boxes clean. Bud and Paul did a thorough search up and down. Bud even checked a piece of crinkled paper in the trashcan beneath the sink. On it was a group of numbers—*6423999*. He gave the paper to Paul, who opened up his cell and dialed. It was a number that had been disconnected.

"We will need to check and see who this belongs to," Paul said.

O'Connor asked for the number too and said the agency would also check. When the two detectives were satisfied, Paul asked for access to the home on Pine Tree where Debbie Lance had been held hostage by Wayne Starfield.

"No problem," was O'Connor's answer.

"Gee," Bud said to Paul, "he's starting to be nice now that he knows someone wants to blow me away."

"Yeah, I can understand that," Paul replied.

Bud took a quick glance at his partner, and Paul was smiling. Bud said, "Oh, I see. Now you have developed a sense of humor over all of this. Great, just great."

The two detectives got in their car. As they were driving over to Starfield's house, Bud's cell started playing "California Girls" by Katy Perry, which meant he had a phone call.

"You got to be kidding me," Paul yelled.

"Hey," Bud replied, "I wanted 'I Kissed a Girl,' but it wasn't available."

"No wonder someone wants to shoot you," Paul remarked.

It was Debbie Lance, who had heard from her father that Bud was involved in another shooting. Paul was listening to Bud's side of the conversation, and he could tell what Debbie was saying just from Bud's remarks. "Yes, a nice relaxing day off. They missed, I'm OK. No, I hurt my shoulder diving to the ground and hit my head behind the car, but I'm fine. Sure, no problem. Thanks for the concern. I will speak to you later. Bye, Deborah."

"Oh, man," Paul said. "I hurt my shoulder diving to the ground and hit my head behind the car. Why didn't you just tell her you were a klutz trying to get the hell out of the way?"

"My version is more exciting," Bud replied as he looked at Paul.

"Maybe I should shoot you myself," Paul said as he started to laugh.

They pulled into Starfield's driveway, which also had two FBI agents in front.

"I guess the taxpayers are going to love the cost of this case," Bud remarked as they walked right in with no problem from the agents. They were unaware that Sherman and O'Connor had motioned to the agents that it was OK for them to pass through. Unlike Kyle Winters' house, it was immaculate. Every room, including the bathroom and kitchen, was spotless, which was unusual for a man. When they reached the basement, it was a different story. There were still parts of Deborah's clothes that had been ripped from her body and bloodstains on the carpet. The basement looked like a large room filled with enough food, water, and toilet paper to last the next six months. The bed to which Debbie had been handcuffed had not been touched since the Crime Scene Unit examined it.

"This is really sick," Bud remarked.

"I know what you mean, but it's not about them. It's about someone else," Paul said. "Phil Smith can't be doing this by himself. If he is, he deserves to get some kind of award before he is sent away for life."

Bud looked around to see if O'Connor or Sherman were around then walked up to Paul and said, "If it goes that far, it's going to take everything in my power not to do him in if I find him."

"I didn't hear that," Paul replied.

"Good," Bud said as he walked back to the room where Debbie was held. He felt compelled to send her an email from his BlackBerry at that moment. He wrote, *"Deborah, I want you to know that I'm sorry for everything you have experienced this past week. I am sorry for the things done to you, said to you, and for the things we have found out. I'm sorry, and I will be here if you need me."* He put his BlackBerry in his pocket as he walked around and examined every space of the room, hoping for any clue.

Paul went upstairs and looked in Wayne's bedroom. He approached O'Connor and Sherman and asked what had been taken from the house. They answered nothing except for the photos in the house and the masks believed to have been involved in the killing of Timothy Mann. Paul requested to see the photos and masks, and O'Connor said they would bring them to the precinct first thing Monday morning. Paul pressed for them later in the day Sunday, but it was impossible, according to the agents. Paul pushed harder and asked why the photos were taken from the premises. It was a simple answer. The FBI was checking everyone that was in them.

"Were there photographs taken from the Winters' homes?" Paul asked.

"They had no photos in the homes," O'Connor replied.

Paul went back downstairs to the basement to see what his partner was up to. He walked up to Bud as he was checking behind the bedpost.

"You OK?" he asked.

Bud took a deep breath before answering, "I can't imagine what she went though. She must have been so scared. It's a miracle she didn't have a stroke during this."

"It's a miracle she wasn't raped," Paul replied.

"She would have been," Bud answered, "but our hero, killer, masked man, vigilante, whoever it is, prevented it."

"Why would Phil Smith care about preventing a rape after she was beaten?"

"He wouldn't," Paul replied, "unless he wanted you to think it was someone else wearing the mask."

"Or," Bud said, "someone else wanting us to think it's Phil Smith."

"Are you confused yet?" Paul laughed.

Bud's thoughts again went to the letter that had been sent to Rachelle. There had still been no mention of it to her.

"This is pissing me off," Bud replied. He looked over at the two agents who were talking amongst themselves and said, "I would like to go to Patty's apartment and take a look around."

"Let's go," O'Connor said.

As they were walking up the stairs, Bud asked O'Connor, "Jack is a nickname, right? What is your real name? John?"

"No," the agent said, "it's Jason."

Bud replied in a surprised tone, "How did you get from Jason to Jack?"

As they left the house, O'Connor told him that his father was Jason senior and that he didn't like to be called "Junior" so they started calling him Jack.

"Interesting," Bud replied.

As Paul and Bud got in the car, Bud said aloud, "And to think all this time I though Jack was short for jackass."

"Very funny," Paul said as they backed out of the driveway.

They reached Patty Saunders' apartment within six minutes from Starfield's house. Her place was more interesting because nothing had been taken from the house. Paul went straight for all the framed photos in the house. There were many photos of her and Deborah Lance, as well as group photos of their circle of friends.

"Have all the people in the photos been identified yet?" Paul asked.

"Not yet," Sherman replied.

"OK," Paul said. "I would like to take the photos to Patty."

"I would hold off," Agent Sherman said. "We have a search warrant, but legally I'm not sure if it means we can take photos out of the house."

"Agreed," Paul answered. "Let's find out," he said, and asked Bud to make a phone call.

"Where are you going with this investigation?" O'Connor asked.

Paul continued to look at the photos but answered the agent, "In this particular case, I'm going where the investigation will lead us. You know as well as I do this case is unlike any we've ever worked on, and if we do not handle it this way, it will never get solved. And I plan on it getting solved, don't you, Agent O'Connor?"

"It will get solved with or without the Suffolk County Police Department," O'Conner answered.

"I doubt it," Bud interjected.

"Oh, shut the fuck up," O'Connor yelled back.

"What are you so touchy about?" Bud remarked. "I'm the one that's been shot at twice in the past eight days."

"Give me a break," O'Connor answered loudly.

"Hey!" Agent Sherman yelled as he walked in. "Come on! We have to work together on this. Let's solve it and go our separate ways."

Bud started singing the lyrics to "Separate Ways" in tune as he held up his fist to be a microphone. It was a song by Elvis from 1972 that was written when he and Priscilla were divorcing. Somehow, Bud remembered reading about it and didn't know why, but he was glad he could antagonize O'Connor in this particular instance.

"I think we are done here for now," Paul remarked.

As they were leaving, Robert Simpson came into the apartment.

"What's going on?" Paul asked.

"Nothing much," Simpson replied.

"Really? What did you have for lunch today?" Paul asked.

"I don't have to answer that," the ex-assistant to the most powerful man in town said.

Bud walked by Simpson and in a low voice said, "Bullet up the ass," and walked out.

O'Connor and Sherman acted like they didn't hear the remark as well and left the apartment to Paul and Simpson.

"I guess Ms. Saunders is OK with you being here," Paul stated.

"Yes, she is."

"Maybe she thinks she will get laid again, but I don't know what the attraction would be."

"That's your opinion," Simpson remarked. The two didn't know Bud was standing on the other side of the door listening, just in case there was a problem.

"What were you doing with Rachelle at lunch yesterday at Red Onion?" Paul asked.

Simpson answered in a very slow, cocky voice, "Maybe she finds me cute."

Paul rushed at him and slammed him against the wall and locked the door all in the same motion. Bud tried to get in but realized the door had been locked.

"Paul! Open the door! Now!" Bud screamed.

Paul had his arm in Simpson's throat and went into his face. "You listen, this is not a game to me. I'm not sure what you are up to, but my partner has been shot at twice, and Rachelle has been through hell. If anything happens to them, whether it's your fault or not, I will kill you. Do you understand me?" Paul said and then repeated himself, holding Simpson's throat.

"Yes," Simpson answered, barely audible, as Paul let go, turned, and walked out.

The two agents stared at Bud as the detective starting waving his arms. He said, "Everything's cool. Just awesome. No problems."

Simpson finally got his voice back and yelled, "He threatened me!"

"Sorry," Bud said, "didn't hear a thing." Looking at Sherman and O'Connor, Bud spoke again, saying, "I know you guys didn't hear anything because you were behind me and the door was jammed, so there was a lot of noise out here." The two agents just stood there. Bud kept talking. "You two look like *Men in Black*. Come on, take those shades off."

"You!" he said, pointing at Simpson. "You get that fucking door fixed. Since you been living here, you fucked up that door."

He walked out to the car, where Paul was waiting for him, and said, "Are you calmed down now? If you want to hurt the dumbass, at least wait 'til here is a good reason and you're not going to jam up your career."

He walked around the other side of the car and waved to the agents, saying, "See you guys. Thanks for the tour. We will be in touch."

He got in the car and told Paul he had had enough for the day. He didn't plan on working for five hours and getting shot at during his time off. Paul took Bud back to his car on Main Street. As Bud got out, he looked at Paul and said, "We don't know how this is going to turn out, but don't regret anything. Give her a call and talk to her as a woman friend you care about. Don't talk about all this bullshit. Talk about her and you. Even if it's this one time. Learn about her and let her see you, Paul. This whole thing has fucked so many things up, but it's worth a shot."

Paul smiled at Bud and said, "Since when are you the expert on relationships?"

"Hey," his partner answered, "just remember the women love the Budster. Did you see them at Danford's Wednesday? I had them in the palm of my hand."

"Yeah, yeah," Paul replied. He saw Bud get in his car and drive off. Paul turned right onto Arden Place and went into the parking lot behind Z Pita. He went to his door, opened his mailbox, got his mail, and went upstairs and plopped on his bed. He fell asleep for 35 minutes and jumped in the shower when he woke up.

As Bud drove home, his head was throbbing. He didn't know what to think or what to do, for he had heard his partner tell Simpson he would kill him.

Agent Jason "Jack" O'Connor was still going on about what had happened, as Sherman drove. "Do you believe these two? They're going to screw up this case or get someone else killed," O'Connor ranted.

"Give the guy a break," Sherman replied. "His partner is on a hit list and some asshole is running around in a mask killing people involved in the kidnapping."

"Don't forget I was shot too," O'Connor remarked.

"No, you are not going to let me forget that, are you?"

"No, I'm not," O'Connor replied. "It's what got you on this case to begin with."

Paul picked up his phone and started to push Rachelle's home number, hoping that hadn't changed also, but he got nervous and hung up. He called again and hung up again. He sat there thinking how ridiculous he was and called again…and hung up again.

"Shit!" he said to himself. The phone rang, and it was Rachelle.

"Hi," she said, "did you call here?"

"Hi, Rachelle. Yes, I did. I thought I called the wrong number, so I hung up and was going to try again."

"No, you had me," she laughed.

"How are you doing?" he asked.

"I'm OK," she said. "It will take time."

"You know," Paul interrupted her, "you mentioned to me that you might be going to Philadelphia during July 4th. You should still plan to go; you will really love it."

"You think so?" she remarked. "Tell me why," she said, laughing.

"Well…" Paul said.

"Wait!" Rachelle interrupted. "You seem very relaxed. Are you having a glass of wine right now?"

"Yes," he answered. "A glass of white Vinetara wine."

"OK, just checking," she replied.

"Anyway," Paul continued, "it's one of my favorite places to be. Old City Philadelphia is the most historic square mile in the United States. When you go there, Rachelle, it will be difficult for you to leave, the way you love history and the Founding Fathers. You should stay at the Morris House Hotel. It was the home of Robert Morris, who I'm sure you know was one of the signers of the Declaration of Independence. Well, he basically financed the war during that time, but they turned this landmark building into a hotel, and you feel like you've gone back in time. It's walking distance to my favorite building, Independence Hall. You step inside, and you try to imagine the actual words and actions that took place when it was the Pennsylvania State House. To think about Ben Franklin, Thomas Jefferson, and George Washington walking around knowing they would be the architects, along with John Adams, of America, it's just amazing to see."

Rachelle was so enthralled with Paul's description, there was a few seconds of silence before she asked him to go on. Paul continued, "Across the street from the hall is what they call Independence Mall. A huge lawn for people to mingle or sit and have lunch or watch an event in front of the building that was 'the Birthplace of Freedom.' Also across the street at a 45-degree angle is where the Liberty Bell is kept. You can see it through glass windows when you are on Chestnut Street in front of the hall. If you want to get close to it, you can go through security at the other end of the building and get within a few feet of it. My favorites, though, are the National Constitution Center on Arch Street and Christ Church Burial Ground, where Benjamin Franklin is buried. People throw pennies on his grave every day, and the groundskeeper told me they get about two to three thousand dollars a year, which is enough for upkeep to his final resting place."

"I hope that one day America and the schools realize how much more Ben Franklin did for this country than fly a kite to prove the existence of electricity from lightening," Rachelle said.

"One day," Paul added, "they will realize all the documents he was involved in signing and the influence he had with the French coming to the rescue to defeat the British in the Revolutionary War."

"You continue to surprise me," Rachelle replied. "I never knew you had so much knowledge about history and places like Philadelphia."

"I guess we never really had much of a chance to talk about things like this," he remarked. "What about you, Rachelle? Tell me the places you've been."

"Well, when I was little, we would go to Great Britain. My dad had relatives there, which meant that I had and still have cousins over there. My mom was an O'Neill, which meant I had family in Ireland, so we would go there until Mom got sick and passed."

"Well, I bet you didn't know," Paul remarked, "that I'm an expert on Irish trivia. When I was growing up, my dad would quiz me all the time about it. Everyone thinks that Bud is the trivia king, but when it comes to Irish questions, I'm rarely stumped."

"Come on," Rachelle laughed.

"Go ahead," Paul said. "Give me a try."

"Hmmmm," she remarked. "OK, well, first tell me a famous Irish saying."

"That's easy," Paul remarked. "'Life's too short not to be Irish.'"

"Very good," Rachelle giggled. "OK, how about what's the real name of U2's lead singer Bono?"

"Paul Henson," Paul replied.

"What a great real name he has! Wait," she said, "how do I know that's right? I just made the question up.," she laughed.

"You can look it up," he replied.

"OK, Mr. Powers, I'm not fooling around anymore. Now for a really tough one. OK, tell me what days Irish Pubs are closed?"

Paul answered back right away, "Good Friday and Christmas Day are the only days they are closed."

"Gotcha!" Rachelle answered. "I don't think they ever close!"

"Well, my dear friend, you will have to look it up," Paul said, "and you will have to let me know what you find out."

"I will do that," she answered.

"What else do you like to do, Rachelle?" he asked. "I know you like to write."

"Well, believe it or not, I love to watch television. It relaxes me. I love the reality shows, I love advice shows, such as Suze Orman, but it seems I never have time to watch them 'til the end. I love the USA channel reruns of *NCIS* and *Law & Order*. If I had the time, I would love to sit in the house and just watch a marathon all day. I love the cooking shows. I enjoy Cat Cora. In fact I met her in New York City at the Bon Appétit Studios a couple years ago. Madison treated me to a birthday surprise with her making me dinner. It was so great, and she was so nice to me and kept saying happy birthday to me. Even when I had a few glasses of wine in me and was, I'm told, getting overly affectionate with her, she was very patient with me and gave me a memory I will have forever. I couldn't believe how pretty she was in person. Such a small little thing, but she was so good to me on my day."

"That was nice of Madison," Paul said.

"Yes, she's very good to her older sister."

"It's so quiet here," Paul said. "Is she out?"

"Yes," Rachelle said. "She had a few errands to run—grocery store, Walmart—thank goodness the stores stay open late on Sundays on Long Island in the summer. So, tell me, how is your dad doing?"

"He's doing great," Paul answered. "He called me yesterday. He ran into Sean Hannity at a diner on 47th Street, and you would have thought his life was complete," he said as he laughed. "They had the Woolworth reunion last night, so I'm sure I will be hearing from him soon. He has told me on more than one occasion that he wants you to do a story on the downfall of Woolworth. It's a historical company, and he says the truth has never come out."

"Interesting," Rachelle replied.

Paul continued, "He believes that the outsiders they brought in were the reason for the eventual downfall of the company. I don't know if it's true, but he told me the top peak of the building was cut off to present as a gift, which is a no-no for a landmark building. At the very top was a penny with the year 1912."

"Well, I think I will have to check on that and put it down on my list," she replied. "Tell your dad we will have to make a date to discuss, quote, 'The Truth of the Rise and Fall of Woolworth.'"

"I like that title," Paul said.

"Well, maybe it's a deserving title," She answered. "Talk to him," she continued. "I will probably be able to do some research in a few months, so next time he comes up from Florida, I can ask him some questions."

"He will love that," Paul replied.

"Where does he stay when he sees you?"

"He's a big shot," Paul laughed. "He stays at Danford's."

"Oh," she laughed.

"Well, when you were writing about the restaurants in Port Jefferson, he loved it. He said you were right most of the time between Billie's Saloon to Salsa Salsa, Toast, and even Z Pita. He said you were on the mark."

"Ahhh," she said, "that's sweet of him."

Paul wanted to mention Timothy's Bar and Grill and the Red Onion Café also but thought better of it.

"Well, if there is one thing about Port Jefferson, besides the harbor and the different types of homes and colors, it's the restaurants," Paul said.

"Yes, true," Rachelle confirmed. "East Hampton is a gorgeous village also. When you consider the restaurants, the beaches, and the shops, no wonder they call it 'Hollywood East.'"

There was a pause before Rachelle said, "OK, I have a question for you." Paul could see her old self was coming back. "What was East Hampton part of before the Revolutionary War?"

Paul was stumped and said, "I have no idea."

"OK, then I know something you don't know. The answer is Connecticut!"

"No," Paul said. "Really?"

"Yes! Really!" she replied.

"You got me on that one. I'm going to use that one on Mr. Trivia King, Bud, and I'm sure I will get him on that one."

"So, how was your day today?" Rachelle asked him.

Paul was afraid to bring up the case or what had happened to Bud, so he totally left it out. Instead he said, "Not much, usual things. Personal things to catch up on. Just trying to keep active, but it's funny you should ask because I took Bud to the gym today." As Paul continued to tell Rachelle in detail, step by step, of Bud wearing his Superman shorts on the treadmill at the gym, he had never heard Rachelle laugh so hard and for so long at one time. It was so great to hear that beautiful laugh of hers again. He even stretched the story out and exaggerated a tiny bit just to get a few more laughs from her. She couldn't believe Bud stayed on the treadmill to finish the workout.

"He's lucky to have you for a friend and partner," she laughed.

"No," he answered, "I'm the lucky one."

"That's so sweet," she answered.

There were a few seconds of silence, and Paul wanted to continue the conversation before the awkward stage set in. He said, "You should come to the gym with us sometime. I think you would enjoy the workout. If you got up early enough, you might even be able to join us at Bud's favorite breakfast place, Maureen's Kitchen."

"Oh, I love Maureen's Kitchen," Rachelle yelled with excitement. "They have the best baked oatmeal!"

"Oh, you too," Paul laughed. "Bud will be happy, you both have something in common."

"Oh, we have more than that in common!" Rachelle replied.

"OK, really? Well, you want to tell me?"

"Yes, I will," she answered. "One day. But tell me where you like to go for breakfast."

"Oh, I'm easy, but I enjoy the Station Coffee Restaurant at the Port Jefferson Plaza, and Joey Z has a good breakfast downstairs."

"Yes, he does," she added. "I miss being there."

"You will be back," Paul said, trying to steer away from the problem subject. "You know it's Bud's birthday on July 9th, and it falls on a Saturday. I'm going to give him a little surprise by bringing him to Danford's. I'm going to tell him a group of us want to take him to dinner, but I'm really going to have some extra people there and give him a good time."

"That's nice," she answered. "I have to say, watching him dance and lip-sync to 'Bad Romance' was one of the funniest things I ever saw."

"I know what you mean," Paul replied.

The conversation between them continued for another 35 minutes. The subjects ranged from school to family and back to their childhood dreams. In total, it was almost 90 minutes of talk that made Paul remember why Rachelle was important to him.

"Rachelle," Paul said, "I've never told you, but I always thought you were attractive, but getting to know you these past few years, well, it convinced me you are beautiful."

There was silence on the other end until she finally spoke, saying, "That's so sweet, Paul; thank you so much."

He followed Bud's advice, with nothing about the case mentioned at all. His partner was right. It was great. By the time they hung up the phone, they had shared so many memories with each other. Paul put his cell phone in his battery charger and went outside for a walk in the beautiful little harbor village. He was feeling good about himself again.

Bud got home to his house on Parkside Drive in Miller Place. He had grown up in the home and bought his brothers share of the home when their parents died. He added a couple of extensions since then, but with the taxes on Long Island, it was challenging to hold on to a house as a single guy. If it was not for his overtime pay, it would have been impossible for him to do it.

He picked up the phone and dialed the hospital and was connected to Sherry Walker's room within a minute. She seemed in good spirits and was happy to hear from him. He was surprised how much information Sherry knew, being in the hospital, but he figured courtesy was the very least that could be given to her, considering she did save Rachelle's life and took a knife to the body and a kick to the head.

Sherry told him she was getting the itch to get out, but she was told no way for at least another five days. Bud told her the case would be over by then, but he did not want to take a bet with her when she said no way! Bud told Sherry about the shooting again in more detail and told her about the note to Paul that was pinned to the tree. Sherry urged Bud to be overly cautious about things until Phil Smith was captured. Bud questioned if it would be over even if Phil was captured, but because of Cronin's orders, no one knew about the letter other than himself, Paul, and of course, Cronin. It was challenging for Bud to explain his feelings to Sherry when she asked him to elaborate about why he felt the way he did. He explained it away as a gut feeling and that it just seemed like it was too easy for the masked killer to be Smith trying to eliminate witnesses and having to share the money, if any.

"What about the money?" she pressed. "There's no money now?"

"We don't know that for sure," Bud replied. "Besides, what's keeping this guy here, if he is here, and what is keeping the asshole butler here?"

"That's easy," Sherry said. "He's here because of Cronin. Plus, he won't give up on Debbie."

"There's nothing against Simpson," Bud remarked. "How can Cronin keep him here, and how do you know that?"

"He told me," Sherry replied. "He told Simpson not to leave town."

"Odd," Bud said. "He also pulled all the security away from the Lance Mansion today and asked the FBI to do the same. They will probably pull away tomorrow. William Lance sent all the staff away on vacation."

"Cronin told you all this?" Sherry replied.

"It came up during our conversation."

"And you?" Bud asked "What about someone at your door?"

She laughed and said, "No, he still has fellow officers at my door here."

Bud seemed puzzled. "You just can't make this shit up," he said. "I guess I'm going to have another busy day tomorrow."

Sherry remarked, "Bud, I have a feeling there will be no days off for anyone 'til this thing is over with."

Bud sat down at his computer desk as he was talking to Sherry and signed on to Twitter. Rachelle had posted another tweet. It said, "Inactivity is the sign of the clouded mind." He read it to Sherry.

"That's deep," she answered. He read her the other tweets Rachelle had posted during the past 24 hours.

"My opinion?" Sherry said. "She either knows something she hasn't told us, or she has lost all reasonable thought process with all of this."

"Or…" Bud said.

"Don't go there!" Sherry got louder on the phone. "She's not part of this, Bud."

"Maybe not," Bud said, "but she's involved in this much more than being the victim."

"You don't have to be a genius to know that, Bud," she answered. "Look at the articles, look at the tweets, she is, in reality, the star of all of this. If they made a movie of this, she would be the star."

"That's interesting," Bud replied. "Maybe it's time to join the game."

"What are you thinking?" Sherry asked.

"Just thinking," he answered.

"Oh, Lord," she replied. "Time to say some prayers."

"Just get well," Bud said. "I will speak to you tomorrow."

They hung up as Bud looked at his computer screen. He wrote,

"You may know who you are. You may know the color of the car. But I won't let you become the star." He didn't have many followers, so he put BF_TJ_GW @NEWSDAYLI in the message.

Steven Anderson went back to his offices to finish up. It was already 9:00 pm, but he had lost about four hours during the afternoon shooting. He had a deadline, and he never missed one and wasn't about to start now. He worked at his desk for a few minutes when he heard a slight noise, almost like a creaking sound. He stopped what he was doing and there was silence. He went back to his computer, finished his spreadsheet and his emails and printed them out by 10:30 pm. He left notes for his staff because he would be in late Monday. He had already had the windows boarded up from the shooting and the glass company would be there by 11:00 am and claimed they would be finished by 3:00 pm.

He wanted to write down what had happened during the afternoon while it was still fresh in his mind. The *Now* edition coming out on Tuesday, between the status of Rachelle and now this, had businesses across Long Island begging to have the paper on their premises. Instead of driving away tourists, the town of Port Jefferson was overflowing with the traffic, especially on the weekends.

Steven finished up and sent a text from his phone as he went toward the door. As he put his hand on the handle, he was slammed into the door by a human body who ran into him. He fell to the floor and looked up in time to see the knife come down into his body. The sleek figure in tight black pants and shirt stared at him behind what his paper called "the Face of Fear." As he looked at the blood pouring out of his body, he touched the blood with his hands to see if what was happening was real. He looked up at his killer as the assailant took the mask off. Steven shook his head with a "No!" as he saw the real face of the person who cut into him. He tried to speak, but it was too late. The knife came down hard again to finish him. The killer stood there as the last seconds of life left Steven Anderson. As the killer witnessed the last movements of the editor, he looked at the papers the editor had in his hand. He took one and left the rest with the body that would be discovered the following morning when the staff came in to work. The mask was put back on as the disguised killer left the building and disappeared into the night.

Deborah was out all day at the Marriott Hotel in Marco, swimming, and forgot to check her emails all day at the encouragement of her father and friendly acquaintances down in Marco. She had been so distracted by all the relaxation and the massages she had received that it was already 10:00 pm when she finally did check her emails.

She saw the email from Bud in bold black and began to smile before she even opened it. Her smile turned to tears as she read the message filled with kind words that apologized for the things that had happened to her. She covered her mouth, then picked up a tissue to wipe the tears from her eyes. She hadn't had much time to really even think about Bud as a person during all of this, but at that moment, she missed him.

She wanted to call him and thank him for the beautiful message but decided it was too late. Instead she wrote him back. *"Dear Bud, thank you for sending me such a beautiful note. It brought tears to me. Tears of happiness that you took the time to be so sensitive toward me and that I was in your thoughts. You are a very sweet man. I'm sure we will speak in the next couple of days. Deborah."*

She had always signed her name Deb or Debbie, but now since her father and now Bud were calling her by her formal name, she decided to start using it. She checked the rest of her emails and saw a couple from Robert. She opened the first one. It read, *"Don't let this change things. I love you. You know I would never do anything to hurt you."* As Deborah deleted the message, she thought, *Except fuck my best friend behind my back.* She opened the second email, and it read, *"Debbie, I love you, please talk to me. I miss my Deb."* As she deleted the message, she said aloud, "I'm glad you never called me Deborah." She checked the other emails and eliminated about 30 junk emails before she crawled on the couch next to her dad to watch some television before turning in for the night.

Paul came back from his walk about 11:00 pm and had actually worked up a sweat from the steep hills of Port Jefferson. He took a shower, laid down in bed, and turned on the television to see what was going on in the world besides the now famous village of Port Jefferson. He was in a good mood from his talk with Rachelle, so he called Bud.

Bud picked up the phone with, "What the hell, you miss me already?"

"Hey, Bud, trivia king, before the Revolutionary War, what was East Hampton a part of?"

Bud replied, "Connecticut. Any asshole would know that."

"I didn't know that," Paul answered.

"Then you're not just any asshole," Bud remarked. "You're a different kind of asshole."

"Good night, you bastard," Paul said, laughing as the phone went *click*.

Bud smiled as he hung up and opened Deborah's note to him on his BlackBerry. He was so happy he caught himself opening the refrigerator, which was a habit he had when he was happy. Suddenly, he had an urge to take better care of himself. He closed the refrigerator and poured himself a glass of water as he lay down in bed.

Sunday, June 26

The body of Steven Anderson lay in the *Now* offices all day. There were no calls he was missing from anyone, not even his family. He had made the mistake of telling his wife not to worry about him, that he would be traveling most of the day. He had a special meeting with a major newspaper in the San Francisco area for a job opportunity, and Sunday was the only day that both could accommodate each other. She thought nothing about his not calling, for it was something she had gotten used to over the years. The truth is that Steven Anderson had a meeting Sunday with someone that was a secret, and he didn't want the pressure of family obligations Sunday. It was apparent he got his wish.

The man sitting at Danford's downstairs restaurant waiting for him was not happy with waiting for him for more than an hour before leaving at 3:00 pm. He dialed his cell number three times, and all he got was his voice mail. As he got up from the table, he spoke to himself, "You're a dead man, Steven Anderson." Little did he know, someone had saved him the trouble.

Monday, June 27

It was 8:34 am when Paul's phone rang and he was told to get to the *Now* offices. He checked his text, and Bud said he would pick him up by 9:00 am so they could both go in one car. He met Bud downstairs at 9:03 am and was told by Bud they found the body of Steven Anderson sitting up against the wall near the front door. A young intern who had come in at 8:00 am to get things ready for the day found the body and screamed bloody murder as she ran out to the parking lot, startling morning commuters who also worked in the small strip center.

Paul checked his Twitter to see if Rachelle had released a tweet, and she had about 10 minutes earlier. "It was you from the start. You broke my heart. Now we need your friend so this can end." He read it to Bud, who just shook his head as they pulled in to the lot.

Detective Lieutenant Cronin was already there and greeted both of them with a grumpy hello. They walked and examined the crime scene, and it was determined the *Now* offices would be closed until further notice. Between the shooting and the murder, the police and the FBI didn't need additional people around.

Cronin yelled at both detectives, "When you guys are finished here, I need you both at the precinct!" He drove off as they checked out the hallway and the body. They checked out the papers he had, and Bud requested them to be checked for fingerprints. Agents Sherman and O'Connor drove up and got out of the car with a *Newsday* in their hand.

"Guess who's getting their tweets in the paper now?" O'Connor said as he flashed the paper to Paul.

"What's going on, Bud" Paul asked, as he read it.

"Just a hunch, go with me on it," his partner replied.

O'Connor spoke, saying, "Are you sure you're not trying to get yourself killed?"

"Just think," Bud replied, "with me out of the way, your odds on getting shot again go way down."

"Well, that's true," the agent replied.

"What brings you back here?" Paul said to Sherman.

"Come on," the FBI agent said. "This is all related, you have to know that. It's another piece of the puzzle to what started out as a kidnapping across state lines. Now another killing, and I would think it's fair to say your partner is in danger based on the note from yesterday. Instead of having a low profile, he's here and now writing tweets that are bound to piss someone off."

Paul replied, "Or draw the killer out."

"You already drew the killer, duh!" O'Connor answered. "What I'm having a hard time understanding is the original victim in all of this is down in Florida basking in the sun, getting a tan, and everyone else on Long Island is either getting injured or killed. For Christ's sake, even her boyfriend is free with no charges!"

"And why is that?" Paul asked.

"You tell me," Agent Sherman spoke up.

"Because someone we don't know is calling the shots," Paul answered.

"Well," Sherman replied, "your boss, Cronin, pulled the security detail off the Lance Mansion, and I really don't see why we should be watching it either. I'm pulling them off today. Hell, there's no one even there, and they have an alarm system."

"Be my guest," Paul said. "Do you guys want to take a look at the body?"

They went in to look at Steven Anderson before they moved him, and O'Connor remarked, "Another visit by Bud, another person shot or killed."

"You're with me right now," Bud replied, "so be careful."

As they were getting ready to leave, the medical examiner also stated that the way the wounds were inflicted suggested the killer was left-handed. Anderson was stabbed six times, all on the right side of his body. That suggested the stabbing was done by a left-handed person. Anderson had no defensive wounds on his hands and none on his feet, which indicated he was totally surprised."

Medical examiner Lawrence Sun summed it up in a sentence, saying, "Whoever did this was filled with hatred and wanted him to know he was going to die."

Bud couldn't help himself and said, "So in other words, Doctor, the attacker was pissed off."

Ignoring Bud's attempt at humor, the medical examiner continued, "This was consistent with the other wounds of the other victims. I will know more once we test for prints either from the hands or gloves, but I believe it was probably the work of the same masked killer who has been wearing the Ghost Face mask. Also, this man was killed over 36 hours ago, judging by temperature and stiffness of his body."

"Great," Bud said, "something else for national news."

As they got in the car, Bud said, "Speaking of national news, is it me or does it seem almost every woman on Fox News is a blonde?"

"Let's go," Paul remarked, ignoring his quip.

"OK," Bud said. "It's either that, or I go insane."

As Paul drove on Route 112 and went past Jefferson Plaza, Bud asked if there was time for breakfast at the Station Coffee Restaurant. Paul reminded him they just had the seventh murder in eight days and that breakfast might not be a good thing at the moment.

They arrived at the precinct about 15 minutes later, got themselves some coffee, and planned to be at their desks most of the day while the FBI was still searching for Phil Smith. They had his photo at all the train stations on Long Island plus Islip MacArthur, Newark Liberty, John F. Kennedy, and LaGuardia Airports, and they even had the Cross Island Ferry Company checking identifications on all ferries. Unless Phil Smith was successful in a disguise and managed to get a professionally fake identification, he wasn't going anywhere unless he swam across the Long Island Sound.

True to their word, the FBI abandoned security at the Lance Mansion on Cliff Road. The house was now on a normal security alarm system. Bud called Allan at the security building and asked him to take extra measures on the house. Allan told Bud that Paul had already called and asked him the same thing; however, Detective Lieutenant Cronin had called before both of them and told him not to do anything different in the security detail.

Bud told Allan to follow Cronin's instructions until and if he got back to him. Bud told Paul about Cronin's instructions to Allan, and he just nodded as he looked in at Cronin's office. The detective lieutenant was with the police commissioner. Paul was sure the commissioner was threatening Cronin to resolve the case. No one was sure anymore if the unsolved killings were good or bad for the village. Yes, it had been exciting for the past eight or nine days, but if this went on too much longer, people and tourists would start to realize that if the killings were not stopped, it might not be a good place to bring the kids for a summer vacation.

Paul could see the commissioner's body motion that he was definitely giving an ultimatum to Cronin. He continued to watch because he wanted to see his famous finger-pointing before he slammed the desk with a closed fist. He only had to wait about 45 seconds until that happened. The commissioner left the office and shut the door hard, so everyone would hear it. As he walked by, everyone had their heads down in their paperwork, yet the corner of their eyes were on the commissioner as he stormed out of the precinct. Paul was only able to relax for about 20 seconds before Cronin yelled for him to come to his office.

Bud stayed at his desk and started putting all the notes together on the case in piles. He opened up his Twitter account and entered another tweet: "So you want to play the game, because you think it will bring you fame. The rules I will choose, bang you lose." This time he didn't send it to Rachelle or *Newsday*, for he already had 1,800 followers in 24 hours due to the article.

He signed off of Twitter to start to review his paperwork. His fellow cops at surrounding desks could hear him talking aloud to himself, and they started to look at each other to see if the others noticed the same thing about him. Bud was engrossed in his paperwork, going over all the details again, from notes on the interrogations of Patty Saunders and Robert Simpson to the visits to all the homes and Mather Hospital since day one. He wrote a chart almost like a family tree of all the names that had been involved or people they had come across since the case opened. The list had continued to grow in the past couple days. He picked up the phone and requested to see Patty

Saunders. She was still being held for arraignment later in the day, but Bud wanted to speak with her. A couple favors were pulled for him, and he was sitting across from her within 20 minutes.

"Do I need my attorney?" the young woman asked.

"Just answer me, left-handed or right-handed?" Bud said. "That's all I want to know. Are you ready?"

She shook her head and asked, "What's in it for me?"

"If you can't answer the question, I'll be sure to tell the judge you might have prevented another murder but you didn't want to help. So please answer the question," the detective said.

"OK," she said.

"Just answer left or right," Bud replied. "Robert Simpson?"

"Hmm, right."

"How do you know for sure?"

The young woman leaned over with a seductive smile and said, "Because when you do the things we did in bed, you are sure; you know what I mean?"

Bud ignored the question and continued with the names. "Deborah Lance?"

"Left."

"Wayne Starfield?"

"Right."

"Mason Winters?"

"Don't know."

"John Winters?"

"Don't know."

"William Lance?"

"Right."

"You?"

"Right. "

"Phil Smith?"

"Right."

The answers disappointed Bud, and he asked, "Are you sure?"

"Yes," Patty answered.

"Why are you sure about Phil and not the others?"

"Like I said, Detective, there are ways you become sure."

"Oh, great!" Bud replied. "You are living the dream of a single woman, aren't you?"

Patty smiled.

"John Winters?"

"Don't know."

"Steven Anderson?"

"Don't know."

"How do you know who Steven Anderson is?"

"Who?" she replied.

"Don't *who* me." Bud said. "How do you know him?"

"You said left or right, and I said I don't know."

"But you knew who he was."

Patty remained silent. Bud moved in a little closer to her and said, "He was sliced and diced last night by someone most likely left-handed."

"He's dead?" she asked.

"Honey," Bud replied, "he looks like a zebra with red stripes," as he pulled out a photo to show Patty of the deceased body. She put her hand to her mouth as if she was going to throw up.

"Don't throw up," Bud replied. "Throw-up makes me throw up, and someone will have to clean up twice as much." She put the other hand up to her mouth, and she was gagging.

"Hold it in," Bud said. "I just had two hot dogs with ketchup and mustard on both, and I don't want to look at it again."

She moved to the wall to face the corner to try and control her regurgitation.

"OK," Bud said.

Patty looked back at Bud and told him she wanted her attorney. He shook his head and replied, "Honey, you're lucky I'm not in the mood for your attorney. We will continue this conversation another time."

He left the room to go back to his desk, and he pounded the pencil on the top. Going down the list, he started to add names out of frustration and boredom. Bud, left. Paul, left. Cronin, right. Rachelle, right. O'Connor, right. Allan, right. Smith, not sure. Sherman, not sure. Sherry, right. Kyle Winters, right. Joey Z, right. William Powers, not sure. Simmons, left.

He threw the pencil on the desk and leaned back to stretch as he was thinking about the names. He kept going back to Phil's name. If it wasn't for the fact he was right-handed, it had to be him. No one else had a reason to have a killing spree. *Unless...* he thought. *No,* he thought, *can't be.* His thoughts turned to the letter from Phil Smith to Rachelle that no one knew about except Paul, himself, and Cronin. Then he started thinking about the figure captured on video at the hospital. The general height and weight. He crossed himself off the list, Deborah, Rachelle, the deadheads Starfield and the Winters brothers, Joey Z, Cronin, Sherry, all of them crossed off. This left Simpson, Smith, Paul, O'Connor, Sherman, Simmons, and Allan that could possibly fit the outfit. Then he crossed out Allan for not being agile enough.

Just great, he thought. *Six people on the list that possibly could wear the outfit. Can't be,* he thought. He knew he was missing something or someone as he looked at the list. He added ADA Ashley to the list, and now he knew he was getting desperate. "Gotta be Smith," he said aloud to himself as he looked at the list again. "Please, be Smith," he said, almost in a tone of wishful thinking.

He called the technician in the building and asked that the video of Patty and Simpson's interrogation be set up again. He wanted to view the whole thing once more.

Paul was with Detective Lieutenant Cronin the entire time, discussing the progress and if there was any specific plan on finding Phil Smith in what was now considered a manhunt. He also wanted Paul to visit Steven Anderson's family to see what information he could get from them. They wanted to give them a good portion of the day before they intruded, so Cronin was reviewing a list of questions with Paul, hoping some light would be shed on his killing.

Because of the short history of the case, it was easy to think Anderson was targeted because there was involvement in the kidnapping of Deborah Lance. Cronin had sent officers to their house in Stony Brook first thing in the morning to notify the family.

By the time Paul got out of Cronin's office, Bud was already in the viewing room watching the Simpson tape. When Officer Healey told Paul where Bud was, Paul started walking toward the viewing room.

He reached the door and peeked in the small window and saw Bud watching intently. Paul's eyes were going back and forth between the screen and Bud in his chair. Paul backed off to leave as he felt the wetness on the back of his head return. As he walked toward the front of the precinct, Paul asked Officer Healey to let Bud know he was on his way to the Anderson family home after a short visit to see Allan in Belle Terre in regard to the status of the mansion security.

Bud was in the viewing room for another hour, when he was told where Paul was. He sent Paul a text that he was going to stay behind at the precinct unless he wanted company to visit the Anderson family. Bud sat down at his desk again and did not like his thoughts. He began to doubt himself, thinking he was overanalyzing everything. Or was he?

He picked up his BlackBerry and sent Sherman a text asking if he was right- or left-handed. He got his answer within two minutes. Sherman answered, "Kiss my ass." Bud replied, "I knew you liked ass."

Bud went into Cronin's office and shut the door. "What's on your mind?" Cronin asked as he looked up at Bud.

Bud looked out the window as the uniformed officers, assistants, secretaries, and detectives went about their business. Then he turned around and looked at Cronin, saying, "Why do you think we can't find Smith? I mean, he can't go anywhere. It's strange to me the FBI, ourselves, don't know where he is at. Sure, a letter pops up, but we don't know if he is the one who really sent it."

"What are you getting at?" Cronin asked as he stopped doodling.

Bud frowned and looked hesitant to speak but went ahead anyway. "What if Phil Smith was dead and whoever is playing vigilante Ghost Face doesn't expect to get caught because he knows that Phil Smith will never be found?"

The detective lieutenant leaned back in his chair for a moment to cogitate on the words of Detective Johnson. Then he said, "Then why send a letter saying it wasn't you, meaning Phil Smith. It would have been better not to have sent the letter, unless you just wanted to play a game and make it more confusing for everyone. And speaking of game, are you having fun on Twitter?"

"Oh," Bud replied, "you are aware of it already? I just feel there needs to be someone else getting in the middle of this."

Cronin interrupted him, "I agree, knock yourself out, but be careful what leads, if any, you may or may not accidentally expose. Keep them cryptic, as you have. I don't need the district attorney getting nuts, plus remember you are on the hit list, and I'm not sure if you would be standing here right now if the shooter didn't want you to be."

Bud agreed and replied, "Why do you think the note about me was left for Paul?"

"That's easy," Cronin replied. "Isn't he the closest one to you? Who would be hurt most by your death, besides your immediate family? It would be Paul, right?" Cronin didn't get an answer fast enough, so he pressed more forcibly, saying, "Right?"

"Yeah," Bud said.

"It's *yes*," Cronin said, "don't *yeah* me. You sound like a rookie, and I'm too old to have someone say *yeah*."

"Yes, boss," Bud said as he walked out.

As he went back toward his desk, he stopped Officer Healey, who seemed to know most things going on at the precinct.

"Justin," Bud asked, "do we have a list of the top marksmen in the precinct?"

"Not sure about a list, but I can tell you who the top are, both handgun and rifle."

"Tell me," Bud replied.

"Officer Dugan, Summers, Smith, and Detective Waters are top in the precinct."

"Thanks," Bud said as he sat down.

"However," Healey said, "your man Powers, along with Officer Lynagh, are near the top in Suffolk County."

Bud looked up at the uniformed officer and said, "He never spoke about it to me."

"He's a modest guy," Healey said.

"However, your girl in the hospital, Sherry Walker, she was number one in all of Long Island this past year."

"OK, thanks," Bud said as he looked at some papers on his desk.

He kept staring at the same piece of paper but had no idea what was written on it. His thoughts were elsewhere. He could feel his heartbeat through his temple.

He was so engulfed in his thoughts that it startled him when his phone buzzed with a text from Deborah. He looked at his phone, and it said, "Have a nice day. Thank you again for the beautiful note." He shook his head, trying to keep his mind clear as his thoughts were taking him to a place he didn't want to go.

He sent Paul a text saying he was on his own with the Anderson family. He got up and decided to pay Allan a visit in Belle Terre. He stopped at Paul's desk and glanced over the top of it. Newspaper; paper cup; top drawer half open; articles concerning the case cut out and in a neat pile; Rachelle's tweets printed out; precinct paperwork; photos of his dad, mom, and the group that included himself, Rachelle, Allan, Timothy, Madison, and Joey Z. *Those were the days*, he thought. The photo had been taken only a month before, but now it seemed like a lifetime ago. He shook his head and went back into Cronin's office.

"Why did everyone pull security from the mansion? First you, and then the FBI."

"Because we are spending too much overtime on a house with no one there," Cronin answered.

"Why did you send Deborah and her dad to Florida?"

"I didn't send them," Cronin replied. "I asked them to leave town 'til this was over, and they complied. Any more questions?" Cronin asked.

"Yeah, I mean, yes. Is there anything you are not telling me?"

"You mean us, Detective, right? Last time I checked, you have a partner." Cronin stood up and said, "This case is a complex one, and until the photographs of the case have been developed a little bit more, there are things that should not be said."

"Photographs?" Bud said.

"Manner of speaking," Cronin said. "Until more is clear."

"OK," Bud said. "Your age is showing."

"Get the hell out of here," Cronin remarked. "Make yourself useful and find a bad guy today."

"Yes, boss," Bud said as he walked out.

He got in the car and drove to Belle Terre to see Allan. It took Bud about 15 minutes to get to the security house to see Allan. Detective Johnson told Allan he didn't want to ask the same questions as Paul, so if he could just review with him the questions he asked, it would be a big help to him.

Allan told him Paul wanted to know by whom and how many times the Lance Mansion was checked on by security. He asked if there were cameras at the security house for the grounds from Cliff Road; the answer was no. The cameras were on the road near the entrance and in the driveway at the gate. The video monitors were located in the security building. Allan told him once every hour he did a drive-by in the community. Paul also asked if they had stopped anyone that didn't live in the neighborhood, and the answer was no. He then proceeded to drive toward the mansion for a hands-on look.

"Did you leave anything out?" Bud asked.

"Don't think so," Allan replied. "You guys better end this soon, or I'm asking for a raise. This is bullshit." Allan told Bud he had missed Paul by 10 minutes.

"Anything else?" Bud asked.

"Yes, but it's personal stuff. He's my friend, remember?"

"Yes," Bud said. "He's my friend also, and my partner. Nothing you want to tell me?"

"He's hurting, that's all I'm going to say. I'm not going to break his confidence."

Bud replied quickly, "But you would if you thought he was going to hurt someone or himself, right?"

Allan was taken by surprise and asked, "What are you saying?"

"Just what I said," Bud said. "You wouldn't be silent if you thought someone would be hurt."

"He's worried about you and Rachelle," Allan answered. "And because I'm your friend too, I won't tell him what you said to me."

"Allan," Bud replied, "this is a case where this village is a firestorm of publicity. In case you haven't noticed, we are having trouble putting the puzzle together. There's never been a case like this ever on the island, and quite frankly I have not heard of anything like this in the States. Questions are going to be asked that you may not like or I may not like, but it has to be done."

Allan walked over to his desk and picked up *Newsday*. He said, "Can you believe this shit? People are buying the paper to see what Rachelle wrote. Today's tweet: 'You may think you are the star, but you won't get very far. Why? Because I know who you are.' They are printing your tweets to add to all this bullshit."

"I know what I'm doing, Allan."

"Oh, come on," Allan yelled. "You are going to get yourself killed, and that's what your partner is worried about."

"OK, OK. Calm down. I'm going to get out of your way and take a look at the mansion," Bud replied.

"Yeah, knock yourself out," Allan remarked.

"It's yes, not yeah," Bud remarked.

"Oh, fuck you!" Allan yelled. "Just go!"

Bud smiled as he went to his car satisfied that he had irritated someone else today. He got in his car to drive to the end of Cliff Street and called to check on Sherry. She was in great spirits and appreciated that Bud checked on her.

"By the way," Bud asked, "have you heard from Paul in the last couple of days?"

"Yes, I have," she answered. "He is here now, if you want to speak to him."

"No, no," Bud replied. "I just wanted to know if he had been in touch with you. By the way, I heard you were top marksman with a rifle last year."

"That's right, honey," she replied, "and it's top marks*woman* to you, so watch yourself, sweetheart."

The call ended, and they hung up the phones as Bud arrived at the end of Cliff Road, where it became a dead-end circle. He stopped the car, got out, and looked down at the harbor. It was a beautiful sight to digest. He left his car at the end and walked to the front gate of the mansion. He then walked to the second gate that guests and occupants of the pool house used. Everything looked OK, boring, he thought to himself. Maybe Cronin was right. Why spend tax dollars on house security when no one was there?

He saw the camera on him from the road and noticed the red light on the top. He took a chance that Allan was watching him, so he started dancing and waving to the camera. Allan had made it a point to watch since Bud was there, and it made him smile while adding "Sick fuck" to what he was watching.

Bud started walking to the house, when Allan noticed a shadow in the bushes near the gate. He zoomed the camera in tight to try and get a look. It was a dog, a beautiful dog. It looked like a King Charles Cavalier, and it was roped to a tree. Evidently, it had fallen asleep behind the bushes, but apparently Bud had awakened him. There was an envelope attached to the collar of the dog.

Allan called Bud on his cell, couldn't reach him, and ran to his car to block the road so Bud couldn't get by. He was in the middle of the road with his vehicle when Bud approached him. Allan yelled, "Turn around, there's a dog with an envelope on his collar." The detective turned around and drove back down, with Allan following him. They reached the second gate, and Allan led him to where he saw the dog. Sure enough, scared beyond comprehension, the dog tried to jump into Bud's arms just happy to see a human.

"Hope it's not a bomb," Bud said.

"Come on!" Allan said as he began to pet the dog. Bud took the envelope off the collar that said MONTY.

"Hey, Monty!" he said.

The dog began licking Bud, just happy that someone knew his name. Bud opened the envelope that had DETECTIVE POWERS written on the outside of it.

"It's addressed to Paul," Allan said.

"Sorry, too late," Bud said. "I didn't see it." He unfolded the paper, and it said, *"Detective Powers. I told you to stop the killing. Tell me, WHO DO YOU LOVE? I will not miss the next time."*

"What does it say?" Allan said.

"You don't want to know," Bud replied.

"I do if it involves the security of this neighborhood," Allan replied.

"No, no, my friend. It doesn't," Bud answered. "There's a phone number on the dog tag. Let's go see who the owner of this beautiful dog is."

Allan called, and it turned out Monty belonged to a 12-year-old girl who was heard crying in the background when her father picked up the phone call. The house was located just a couple blocks away on Bell Circle.

"I'm coming with you," Bud said. "I have questions."

They got to the house, and in the driveway already waiting was the father and the daughter. Bud could see from the girl's face that she had been hysterical. Allan handed the dog to her and told her how he started licking Bud when he called out his name.

Bud looked at the father and said, "What happened? Dog got loose?"

"No," the father said. "Lindsey was playing in the front yard. This guy from the road asked for directions. She was taught to stay in the yard, so she spoke to the man from about 20 yards away. He thanked her, but the dog ran to the car and, according to Lindsey, he got out and swooped up the dog and drove off."

"Did you call the security building?" Allan asked.

"Not right away, but we called the police when it happened, and they still haven't come yet."

"OK," Bud said. "Can you give me a description of the man?"

"Lindsey can," he said. She went inside the house and brought out a piece of paper that appeared to have a professional-looking sketch. She handed it to Bud.

"Shut the front door! That's Phil Smith! You drew this?" he asked Lindsey.

The father answered for her, saying, "She's in advanced classes for art."

"No shit. I mean, for sure," Bud replied. He continued, "I don't suppose you got the vehicle information, like a license plate?"

"New York plates, KNA-2388," Lindsey answered.

"How old are you?" Bud asked. "Do you want a job?"

"Bud!" Allan yelled.

"I'm not kidding, Allan, this kid is gifted. What do you want to be when you grow up?" he asked her.

"I'm going to be a judge," she answered.

"That's interesting," Bud replied. "Why?" he asked, hoping to cross her up.

"Because I like making decisions," the young girl answered right away, with a serious look on her face.

"Well, I have a feeling you are going to make it. Here's my card. You call me if you need me in 10 years or if you have any information before that time."

Bud and Allan both got in their vehicles and drove back to the security building. They went inside, where Bud looked at the sketch.

"Nice way to catch yourself," Allan said to Bud. "Shut the front door? Interesting."

"Yes," Bud said. "I did catch myself pretty good there, didn't I?"

Bud called in the license plate, and it came back as a reported stolen vehicle from three hours prior.

"It's for sure abandoned now," he said to Bud, "but where the hell is he staying? I guess the manhunt is working."

Bud sat down at Allan's desk to call Cronin and then Paul.

"Make yourself comfortable," Allan said as he was dialing.

"Thanks," Bud remarked, not noticing that Allan was being sarcastic. He spoke to Cronin and brought him up to date, and the detective lieutenant was pleased that Phil Smith was still locked in the area. He had Bud read the note to him three times.

"What are you thinking, boss?" Bud asked.

"I'm thinking we have an extra piece in the puzzle. OK, call Paul, give him the news, but I do not want this in the media. Tell no one other than Paul."

"Allan here knows, boss. He was with me and just heard me read it to you."

Cronin answered, "He needs to keep his mouth shut."

"He will, boss," Bud replied. "Hey, boss," Bud caught him before hanging up. "How did Smith know we would find the dog addressed to Paul at the mansion?"

"We are going to find out, Bud," came the reply.

"He wants to play a game. I'm going to change the rules," Bud said as he hung up without saying goodbye.

Bud called Paul and gave him the update and read the note to him. He said, "Paul, we need to get together and discuss what he means by 'who do you love?'"

"Why?" Paul yelled into the phone. "It means the people I care about are in danger!"

"Paul," Bud yelled. He heard a *click*.

"Son of a bitch! He hung up on me!"

"You are so good at aggravating people," Allan remarked.

Bud ignored the last remark and pulled out the paper with the list of names he marked *left, right,* and *don't know* and started to circle the names that fit the body profile of the masked killer who were still alive based on the video from the hospital. The names on the list that he circled, regardless if they were left- or right-handed, were Paul, Jason "Jack" O'Connor, Sherman, and Smith. Four names. He put his pen on all four and gave each thought. He turned his pen upside down and tapped each name twice. He turned to Allan and said, "Let's look at the camera film. We are going to be here a while, my friend. Let's have a pizza delivered."

Cronin was in his office going over his notes when he asked Gina to have Assistant District Attorney Ashley stop by. The assistant district attorney was in Cronin's office within 40 minutes.

"How do you like your temporary home here? Do you miss us in Yaphank?"

"You know, John, I haven't had time to miss anyone."

"What's up?" the ADA replied.

"I want to talk about Patty Saunders. Please close the door."

"Don't worry," the ADA said. "She's in for kidnapping; she's not going anywhere. In fact, after the arraignment today, we can move her to headquarters before going to Riverhead."

"That's just it," Cronin replied, "I want her out on bail."

"What?" Ashley said.

"Hear me out," Cronin said. "Be quiet and listen to everything before you interrupt. Get the judge to give her a $1 million bail so it doesn't look like a gift or setup to the perp. Now she's out on bail. We can use her to flush out Smith and/or the killer. She can cooperate with us and maybe get 10 to 15 years off for kidnapping. She'll be in for 20 years instead of life if we find who's adding to the body count."

Ashley stood up and quietly said, "You have totally lost your mind. She initiated a kidnapping that led to murders, and you want her on the street."

Cronin stood up and said, "Tell the judge it will help us further the investigation to have her out on the street."

"No," the assistant district attorney said. "You can tell the district attorney, and then you can tell the judge."

"Fine," Cronin said, "I will do that."

"You are risking your whole career if this goes south. You know that, right?" Ashley replied.

Cronin sat down again, leaned back, and said, "I've gone over this case carefully; my record speaks for itself. The only way this game will end is if she's on the street."

"You mean case, right, Detective?" Ashley said.

"Call it what you want, John, but it's a fucking game. And if we don't play it and change the rules, our careers will be over anyway."

John looked out the window at the officers and civilian personnel in their routine and turned back to Cronin. He asked, "Where would we get a million dollars from?"

Cronin answered immediately. "The bail bondsmen would need $100,000 up front, and William Lance would sign and guarantee the $900,000 if she skipped town."

"You got William Lance, the father of the girl who was beaten and kidnapped, to guarantee the bail?"

"Yes," Cronin replied.

The assistant district attorney was shaking his head as he said, "And just how the fuck, excuse my French, did you manage that?"

"I spoke to him," the detective lieutenant replied, "and I convinced him this was the only way to end this."

"Christ," Ashley said, "you're coming with me to the district attorney's office. I'm not going in alone on this."

Cronin laughed and said, "You already said that, John."

"Who else knows about this?" the assistant district attorney asked.

"No one—not the FBI, not even my detectives."

"Are you going to tell them? Are you going to tell the chief? What the hell is going on?"

Cronin looked out the window then back at Ashley and said, "I'm not telling anyone other than you, the district attorney, the judge, and Lance, who's in Florida. I've already told the commander and commissioner. I don't know who to trust, but I guarantee you, this game will be over within a few days after she is released on bail."

"She doesn't have to take it," Ashley said.

Cronin made a face at the assistant district attorney and said, "She will take it. Besides, she's probably itching at the bit to get laid. Every time we talk to her, there was another man that she notched on her bedpost."

"Damn," Ashley said. "This is absolutely crazy."

"It's a crazy case, John," Cronin answered, "but we have to do it today or tomorrow. Things are heating up, and I don't want another body found, especially one of my own."

Ashley touched his hair, tightened his tie on his shirt, and said, "Kevin, if we release this girl and she gets blown away, then what?"

"We save a few hundred thousand in taxpayers' money," the detective answered. "That's the chance they all take when they take bail. This girl does not have a lot of options. We are giving her an opportunity to help others and help herself."

Ashley shook his head and said, "Didn't you already offer her a deal to give her to the FBI on the kidnapping charges if she cooperated?"

"Yes," he said.

"Then?" the assistant district attorney asked. "So what are you doing?"

"Look," Cronin replied, "kidnapping is already a life sentence in most cases, especially this one. If we catch Smith or whoever else is killing the others, then it's worth it. Besides, she probably won't come out of this alive anyway."

"Oh, great!" the assistant district attorney said. "You really believe this is the way to go and not to tell anyone this is a setup?"

"It has to be this way," Cronin said.

"OK," the assistant district attorney answered. "I'll set up a meeting this afternoon and delay the arraignment until tomorrow so we have time to talk to the appropriate people. Do you have anything else you want to share with me? It's already been a bad day, and you have been successful at making me a nervous wreck about what we are about to do."

"So you agree with me?" Cronin answered.

"I don't have much of a choice, do I?" the assistant district attorney said.

"Well, you don't have to go to the district attorney if you disagree with me."

"True," Ashley said. "If you didn't have the reputation of a top-flight investigator, I would have told you to go screw yourself. I will call the district attorney and set something up for the afternoon."

"Thanks," Cronin said. "Get ready for the real fun."

"That's what I'm afraid of," Ashley said. "I'll be talking to you," he said as he left the office.

He got about 20 yards into the office area and turned around to look at Cronin, who was already in his paperwork. Ashley shook his head in amazement and respect at the conversation he had just had and what was about to happen. He got in his car and made a call to the district attorney's office. He told District Attorney Steinberg's secretary there needed to be a meeting later in the afternoon with him and Detective Lieutenant Cronin. The time of 5:00 pm was given, and Ashley relayed the information to Cronin's office. He started his BMW and drove to Yaphank headquarters.

Bud was still at Allan's office in the Belle Terre security building when he got a call from Cronin for an update. The detective informed his boss that they were reviewing the video from the time the young girl told him the dog was taken. When Cronin questioned him how sure he was about the young girl's time concept, Bud replied, "Boss, she's so good, we should hire her." Cronin accepted his feelings and asked for a call back in a couple hours.

Allan played back the video to the approximate time, and within five minutes, they spotted Phil Smith placing the dog behind the bushes and tying him up so he couldn't get away. After he placed the dog down, he looked up at the camera and flipped the bird, looking straight into it.

"What an asshole" Allan remarked.

Bud was squinting and still thinking about the scene he had just witnessed. Then he said, "If Phil Smith is the one wearing the mask, why didn't he just put one on, here?"

"Unless..." Allan interrupted.

"Unless what? Unless it really is someone else doing the killing," Bud answered.

Allan debated Bud and told him that he could not have worn the mask while driving around anyway, and by not wearing the mask, it only added to the puzzle. Bud was thinking about the letter again, addressed to Rachelle. Phil stated in the letter he wanted everyone to know it would be him if he killed. The letter was still confidential, so Bud didn't mention anything about it to Allan.

"When are you leaving?" Allan remarked. "You have been in my way now for over two hours. Don't you have anything else to do?"

"As a matter of fact, yes," the detective said. Bud got up to leave, when Lindsey walked into the building and gave a polite knock on the door.

"Hi!" she said in her cute girl voice. "I baked you some chocolate chip cookies for bringing Monty back to me."

"Well," Bud replied, "I guess I don't have to leave too soon."

"This is very nice," Allan said, and invited her in as he looked out in the parking lot to see if her dad was there. He was.

"Thank you so much, Lindsey," Allan remarked.

"Lindsey," Bud said, "did you ever happen to see the man you drew before?"

"Yes," she replied. "He was here yesterday but in a different car."

Bud moved closer and said, "Honey, why didn't you tell us that before?"

"You didn't ask, silly," Lindsey said.

Suddenly, Bud was brought back to reality. As smart as she was, Lindsey was still 12 years old.

"What time was he here, Lindsey?" Allan asked.

"12:04 is the time I saw him."

Bud looked at Allan before asking the young girl, "Why do you remember it was 12:04 and not 12 noon?"

"Because I always look at my watch when strangers speak to me for the first time."

"What did he say to you?" Bud asked, getting anxious.

"All he said was, 'Hello, what a cute dog.'"

Bud pushed harder, asking, "What kind of car was he driving?"

"A white Mitsubishi Montero XLS, license plate number SNY-2833."

As she answered, Lindsey's father walked in and both Bud and Allan thanked him.

As Lindsey said her goodbyes, Bud yelled, "Hey, Lindsey, what time was it today when I first spoke to you?"

"It was 11:07, Detective Johnson."

Bud nodded as they left the building, and then said, "That girl is only 12 and she scares the shit out of me." He looked at Allan and continued, "Her eyes were blue, right? They didn't turn red, did they? Damn." For the first time today, he had Allan laughing as he continued. "Is she gone yet? I have to bring her to the next party,"

Allan continued to laugh as he begged Bud to leave so he could get back to work. As the detective got in his car, he reminded Allan that Phil Smith had been in the area for the past two days and the note said there would not be a miss.

"It's your ass he wants," Allan replied.

"I guess so," Bud said. "Maybe you should hire Lindsey to watch the video feed." He started looking around again and said, "Damn, are you sure she's not looking at us?"

"Go," Allan said. "I'll call you if anything comes up."

"OK," Bud said. "Save some cookies for me."

"You don't need cookies, big man."

"Hey!" Bud yelled. "I can do four miles on the treadmill. Did Paul tell you?"

"Yes, he did," Allan answered. "See you later, Superman."

Bud nodded and said, "I guess he did tell you," as he got in the car.

Bud sat behind the steering wheel. He picked up his BlackBerry and sent Deborah a text. It said, "Did you know, just about the only thing that favors a left-hander is the toll booth?"

She answered back before he even started the car. She wrote, "You're a funny guy, Bud Johnson."

"That's what they tell me," he sent back.

She wrote back, "Call me."

Deborah's phone rang within three minutes of her text to Bud.

"Hi, there!" Deborah answered the phone.

"How's things in southern Florida?" Bud asked.

"Well, you know," she replied. "It would be better if all these strange men weren't interested in where I was and what I was doing," she said, referring to the protective detail. "Actually, I think things are pretty good. It's quiet here, and there have been no problems."

"Good," Bud said. "It was probably a good idea for you to get away."

"Are you making any progress?" she asked.

Bud spoke to her about the case in general, but he left out what had happened with the dog. There was no need to fill her mind with things she could not control.

"So tell me," Deborah asked, "what do you do with your time in the small amount of free time you have?"

"That's the problem," Bud answered. "My free time is very limited, and when I do get it, I don't want to think. I have a tendency to stare at the television and just go blank. There are so many things on my mind that I have a tendency not to focus on things that would relax me or unfortunately the most important things, such as family. There are times I don't like myself for it, and although this case is only a couple weeks old, I feel like my whole life has changed in so many ways."

"How so?" Deborah asked.

"Well," the detective went on, "it's times like these that you really get to know people. There are so many lives at stake, and each of our lives depends on the other. There are bad people out there, and some, you start to have doubts about who they are."

Deborah replied, "Does anything good come out of times like this?"

"Yes," Bud replied. "For the same reason you get to know people a little bit better, some people are brought to you by circumstances surrounding cases. This case is the one case that we will forever be linked with. There will never be a case like this again."

"When I was in the hospital, Bud, you told me about your dad, but you never said anything about your mom."

"Well," he replied, "I guess since I was working a case, I didn't think about getting personal."

"What about now, Bud?" Deborah asked. "I'd like to know more about the detective they call a 'funny guy who's a good cop.'"

"I'm not sure why," he replied, "but I'm comfortable talking to you. My mother was a good woman, so full of life. She was hard on me, but as I got older I came to realize she was very worried about me and how I'd end up. I was with her when she passed, and I spoke to her last before she went into a deep sleep. Here she is on her deathbed, and she apologizes to me for being so hard on me. I told her it was OK, that she had her reasons ,I'm sure. She replied, 'Yes, I did. I wanted you to be twice the man your father was.' So I said to her, 'Are you disappointed, Mom?' And she looked up at me as I held her hands and said, 'Are you kidding me? You have been so good to me, and I want you to know I love you more than you will ever realize.' I kissed her, and she went to sleep. The doctor told me he felt strongly her passing would be within a few hours, so I got on the phone and called the family to come back to the hospice."

Bud could not see the tears coming down Deborah's face as he told her the story.

"You know, as I talk about this, Deborah," Bud said, "I've always been a fan of poems and songwriting, and I always wanted to write lyrics that someone could put to music. I know if I sat down and focused, I could do it, just as a tribute to her. Do you think it sounds silly?"

There was silence on the other end as Deborah tried to compose herself.

"Hello?" Bud said.

"I'm here," she answered. "I think it's one of the sweetest things I've ever heard, and I want you to write the lyrics, and I want to read them. I have a feeling it will be beautiful. Please do it; if not for you, if not for your mom, please do it for me. I really want to see it, because I know how sensitive the words would be."

"Well," he answered, "maybe you are the inspiration I need to actually do it."

"Promise me you will work on it tonight," she replied.

The detective was taken aback by how important it was to her, so he asked her, "May I ask why this is so important to you?"

"It's simple," she said. "I've been disappointed by many things and people, especially these past two weeks. I want to believe in you, not only in solving this case but as a person. I've only known you a short time, and as you said, these kinds of things bring strangers together. We learn about each other, and I'm interested in learning more about you, Bud, if you are interested in learning more about me."

"Yes, I am, Deborah, but I want the case to be over."

"So," she answered, "in the meantime, please write the song."

"All this pressure," he replied with a slight laugh.

"That's what women were put here on earth for," she replied, "to keep the pressure on the men."

"Noted," he replied.

They said their goodbyes, and as Bud started the engine, Allan came back outside.

"What the hell are you still doing here?" Allan asked.

"I got tied up with a phone call," the detective answered.

"Oh, shit," Allan answered, "it's gotta be a woman."

"No comment," Bud said with a smile.

"Since you are still here, I found some film from yesterday with Smith that you should see."

Bud shut off the engine and went back inside the security building. Allan had the film set up, showing the Mitsubishi driving through different parts of the neighborhood.

"Here he is in front of Lindsey's house."

"Stop," Bud said. "What time does your camera say it was?"

"12:04," Allan said.

"Lindsey was right on, wasn't she? Smith may have met his match in a 12-year-old," replied the detective.

"Did you get results in on the Mitsubishi?" Allan asked.

Bud called in to the precinct, and of course it was a stolen vehicle from Mount Sinai. He said, "It was found in the Mount Sinai Shopping Center parked near the Rite Aid drugstore. Cronin already had the video from the Rite Aid picked up for review by two uniformed officers. They found Smith walking around buying gummy bears and Southwest Airlines gift cards, which he paid cash for at the register."

"That's odd," Allan remarked. "He still has to show identification if he gets an airline ticket with gift cards."

Bud nodded and said, "I think I want to take a ride to the store and check it out myself."

"So this time you are really leaving?" Allan remarked.

"Yes, yes, yes," Bud answered. "I'm really leaving. Let me know if anything unusual happens."

"Well then, I'll call you in 10 minutes" Allan replied. "Because this whole town has been unusual the past two weeks."

"Yeah, yeah, yeah," Bud replied. "I mean, yes, yes, yes."

Allan just shook his head and gave a final wave as Bud drove to the Mount Sinai Shopping Center, where he entered the Rite Aid drugstore.

He walked the store for a few minutes, identified himself, and asked to speak to the manager. Bud asked the manager a few questions about the footage and was told the two officers had taken the disc with the footage on it with them. Bud asked if he could speak to any of the employees who had spoken to Phil Smith. The manager led the detective to Katherine, who had rung up Smith at the register. Bud asked her a few standard questions about his mannerisms, what he had said, if anything.

"He told me I was very pretty, but I just said thank you."

"Anything else?" Bud asked.

"Well," she replied, "I don't know if it's important, but when I asked him if he had a wellness card, he said no, but he gave me a phone number that is attached to the membership number."

"That's good," Bud answered. "Can we get this transaction that shows his phone number?" The manager said he could but would need time to pull out the register tapes from the day before.

"That's OK, I will wait." Bud said. "I'll take a walk."

He exited Rite Aid and starting working his way down the sidewalk. First the Subway, the dry cleaners, the UPS store. He showed the sketch that Lindsey had drawn, and no luck. He went into the small chocolate store called Private Chocolatier, then the bagel store, the TCBY frozen yogurt store, and even the pizza parlor, Rocco's Pizza. Nothing. He kept going toward the Hallmark store and King Kullen grocery store, but first he stopped in the liquor store, Carry All, and questioned them.

As he was leaving, the young man stacking the wines at Carry All saw the sketch and said, "He comes in here every so often."

Bud got excited and said, "This is my card; I want you to call me the minute he steps in this store. When was the last time you saw him?"

The stockman said it was the previous day.

"Please show me your camera footage from yesterday."

"It will take some time to pull it up."

Bud answered quickly, saying, "I have to go down to the Rite Aid, but I'll be back in about 15 minutes. Is that enough time?"

"Yes, I'll see what I can do."

"OK," Bud said. "What's your name?"

"Ray," the young man replied.

Bud went back to the Rite Aid, where the manager had the tape transaction of Phil Smith's purchase: gummy bears, four $50 Southwest Airlines cards, a large Butterfinger candy bar. And he just had to get credit for his wellness card and gave his phone number. Bud called it right away.

"Hello," a man answered.

"I'm looking for Phil Smith."

"Why?" came the reply.

"Why do you think?" Bud asked.

"He's not here right now."

"Well, please tell me where you are, and I'll be right over to speak to him."

"No, you won't," the man answered.

Another voice came on the phone and said, "You're a dead man for calling me."

Bud was quick to answer, "And you have to be the biggest fucking asshole there is. You are so worried about getting points from Rite Aid you gave them your number. What kind of shit for brains do you have?"

The manager at Rite Aid was trying to calm down Bud and his customers at the same time, not knowing which way to turn. He was reassuring his customers while trying to get Bud off to the corner or to change his language. Bud was too engrossed in the conversation.

"You gotta be the biggest, dumb fatass there is," Bud said.

The voice came back, "Who do you love, Detective Johnson?" *Click.*

By this time, the Rite Aid manager was sweating bullets and looked comical from the episode and was very pleased when Bud thanked him and left the store.

"Sure, sure," the manager said. When Bud left, the manager was apologetic, saying, "Sorry, folks, just another crazy person."

Bud drove to the precinct to meet Cronin and called Paul, who was with the Anderson family. They agreed to meet for dinner at Z Pita to discuss the day. Bud banged the car, realizing he had forgotten to go back to the Carry All liquor store but made a note to call them. When Bud arrived at the precinct and his temporary desk, he told Cronin about the phone call with Phil Smith and the threat.

"Bud," Cronin said, "you have no immediate family here, correct?"

"Yes, boss."

"OK, you and Paul are targets, as are those you care about. Do I have to worry about anyone other than Rachelle?" the detective lieutenant asked.

"I don't think so, boss. All our relatives and loved ones are out of state."

Bud sat down and did paperwork for a couple hours before getting ready to leave for the day. Cronin was getting his jacket on when a boy came into the precinct with an envelope addressed to Bud. Bud called Cronin over as he opened the letter. In typed block letters it said, "SOMEONE ELSE WILL DIE, AND YOU'RE THE REASON WHY. STOP THE KILLING OR THE GIRL WILL DIE. SHE MAY

REMEMBER TIMES AND DATES, BUT IT WON'T CHANGE HER FATE OR FOR THAT MATTER HER COOKIE MATE." Bud stared at the note. There was silence.

"Lindsey!" Bud yelled. "Allan!" he started running with Cronin behind him. They jumped in the car with lights flashing with Cronin on the radio to get cars to the security building at Belle Terre and the home of the Wilkersons on Bell Circle. Bud was traveling at 85 miles per hour already.

"Call Paul!" he yelled.

As Bud drove, the detective lieutenant called him, and Paul left the Andersons quickly as he got the word.

"No!" Bud kept saying. "No! Not the girl! No! Not the girl!"

As they were driving north to Port Jefferson, assistant district attorney John Ashley was sitting in district attorney Barry Steinberg's office with no Kevin Cronin.

"Do you want to tell me what this is about?" Steinberg asked.

"Not really," Ashley replied. "You need both of us. Please give me a minute." He stepped outside the district attorney's office and called Cronin's cell phone. The detective picked up the phone as Bud accelerated up to 90 on Route 83.

"Cronin." Ashley calmly said, "where the hell are you? I'm sitting in the district attorney's office with my thumb up my ass."

"We got an emergency John; reschedule for tomorrow." *Click.*

Ashley stared at his cell phone in disbelief that he had just been hung up on. He went back to Barry Steinberg's office to take the wrath and to reschedule the meeting.

Bud pulled on to Cliff Street and drove to the security building, where there were three cars already.

"The girl!" Bud yelled. "Where is she?"

"On a late school bus," he was told.

"Take me to it now!"

He jumped in, and Officer Healey drove him to the bus that was surrounded by three squad cars and was waiting for authorization to be released. Paul got to the security building about five minutes later, where Cronin was inside. He walked in and saw Allan sitting in his chair with a bullet hole in his head. There was a note on the body that Cronin had with him. It read, "Stop the killing or I swear on the sky up above there will be more. Who do you love?" Paul backed off about 10 feet and started to cry. Cronin asked the other officers to leave them alone.

"You are going to have to pull yourself together and be supportive to your friend's family."

"I will be supportive. If you have any doubts, pull me off the case. Maybe it's time; we need to end it."

"Hey!" Cronin replied. "We are going to end it! But it's going to be my way, not yours! This case is bigger than all of us, and I'm going to have to be responsible for this! This is more than a kidnapping or a murder; it's gotten personal." He walked up to Paul and said, "I'm sorry, Paul, I really am, but you have to hold yourself together and get to Allan's family. I don't want them seeing him like this." Paul went to Allan's body and kissed the top of his head. Cronin turned his head to give Paul privacy for a moment.

Bud reached the school bus that was stopped on Barnum Avenue, and as he flashed his badge, the officers let him through and the bus driver let him on the bus. He saw Lindsey halfway down, and she greeted him with a hug.

"Hey," Bud said. "I'm going to bring you home. Do you want to know what's going on?"

Lindsey replied to Bud very quickly, "It's the man who took Monty, isn't it?"

"Yes, honey," Bud answered. "He was jealous you made us cookies."

"Too bad," she answered.

"Yes, too bad," Bud replied. "Listen, I'm going to take you off this bus into the squad car."

"OK," she said. "But we have to be careful. He was driving on the side of the bus before the police stopped us."

Bud looked at Lindsey and asked, "What time, sweetheart?"

"It was 4:39 pm when he was in the other lane."

"What kind of car was he driving?" Bud asked.

"A green Honda Accord, license plate number ZA-4623."

"OK, honey." Bud looked out from the window of the bus and

called over Officer Healey. He told Healey, "I'm going to take her off this bus in your car. I want the car pulled up to the side of the bus as close to the door as possible, lined up with your open window in the back. She is going to slide into the backseat of your car. First, I want traffic stopped each way. I want the officers looking outward to be sure no one unusual is watching what is going on."

"Understood," came the reply.

Bud looked around at the other kids on the bus and said, "Sorry, kids, we will be gone in a couple minutes."

Traffic was stopped in both directions on Barnum Avenue, while the other police officers put their eyes on the surrounding area as Officer Healey backed the squad car as close as he could to the door of the bus. Bud had Lindsey keep her head down while he went to the stairs of the bus at the door. The detective had the squad car lined up with the back window next to the door of the bus. As he was getting ready to move Lindsey, he got a text from Cronin that Allan was shot in the head. The look on Bud's face was apparent to Lindsey.

"Why are you so sad?" she asked him.

"People are getting hurt, honey," Bud said.

"But you are going to protect me, right?"

"Yes, of course. Nothing is going to happen to you. I promise." He took Lindsey by the hand and blocked her with his body as he told the kids to keep their heads down. He had her stay down and then got between the car and the door. Officer Healey was on the other side as Lindsey slowly made her way down the stairs. She laid out flat as Healey and Bud held her and glided her into the backseat of the car.

"I'm taking the car," Bud told Healey. "Go on the bus with the rest of the kids, see them off at each stop, then have the driver bring you back to the Wilkerson house."

Healey got on the bus as Bud drove off to Belle Terre in the squad car with Lindsey.

The bus continued on Barnum Avenue as the other squad cars disappeared. The bus made a turn up Washington Street. A gray BMW stopped as a man got out and started walking toward the bus. Healey pulled out his gun and identified himself as the police.

"Get down to the ground now!" Healey yelled.

The man hesitated, and Healey stepped out of the bus and repeated himself. "Get down on the ground, or I'll put you down permanently!" The man got down on the ground.

"Jesus Christ!" the man said. "I heard some news, and I was trying to get to my daughter."

"Daddy," one of the girls said. She started to come down the steps.

"Is this your father?" the cop asked.

"Yes!" the girl said.

Officer Healey put his gun away and said, "Sorry, sir. I'm not taking any chances for the kids."

"Can I get up now?" the man asked.

"Of course, sir," Healey answered.

"Who's going to pay for my cleaning bill?" the girl's father said.

"Sir?" the officer replied.

"I just shit my pants, and I was wondering who's paying the bill!" the father yelled. "Never mind," he said. "Let's go, Erin," He said to his daughter.

Officer Healey got back on the bus as they continued to make the rest of the stops. It was obvious to Healey that somehow the press had already gotten wind of what happened in Belle Terre and the stopping of the school bus. Parents were frantically calling the school and police about their children on the late bus. Officer Healey was a 12-year veteran of the force and a very straightforward, no-nonsense type of guy, which is why Bud chose him to ride the bus home with the kids.

The bus had only gone another couple blocks when another car flagged down the bus to get their child. This time, Healey had his hand out as a stop sign to the father. "What's the name of your child?" he asked.

"William, Billy," the father said.

Healey called out to Billy, who came up to the front. Officer Healey asked Billy if the man was his father. The boy was off the bus after he identified the nervous parent. There were eight more kids left on the bus. There was only one more interruption along the bus route from a nervous parent, but there were no incidents. Regardless,

Healey was prepared at each stop, whether it was an interruption or a regular stop, and required each child to identify each parent before letting them off the bus. Some of the mothers weren't sure whether to be grateful or mad that the officer spoke to them with one hand on his gun while it was holstered. Healey was only 5'8", but his presence in a police uniform and his serious demeanor were very intimidating to most. As the last child got off the bus, Healey looked at the bus driver and said, "Let's go home, Kato." It went right over the driver's head, so Healey was more direct, saying, "Take me back to Belle Terre before taking the bus to the yard, please."

Bud had arrived at Bell Circle and dropped Lindsey off with her family and explained the situation.

"Don't leave me," Lindsey begged Bud. "He will be back."

Bud kneeled down to her and asked, "Honey, why will he be back?"

"Because he now knows I remember everything."

"Listen, I will stay here, but in order for me to catch this guy, I will have to leave when I get a police officer here to stay with you."

"Then, Officer Healey, please," she replied as her mother held her.

"Why him?" Bud asked.

"Because I know he can be trusted, Detective Johnson."

"OK, I will have Officer Healey stay with you, Lindsey." Bud went on, "How come you were not at school this morning when Monty was taken and you baked cookies for Allan and me?"

Her father answered, "Lindsey has afternoon sessions on Mondays and Tuesdays where she takes advanced high school courses. Today she only had one class at 3:00 pm."

Bud kneeled down to Lindsey again as he looked around the area. He said, "Honey, is there anything else you think may be important in this case that you may have forgotten to tell me?"

"I don't forget anything."

Bud looked at her father who said, "Lindsey remembers pretty much everything, but you will have to ask her directly, specifically."

"OK," Bud said. "That's good to know. I'm going to bring you photos, and I will want you to tell me if you recognize or have seen anyone, OK?"

The mother, Sharyn Wilkerson, spoke up, saying, "Listen, I'm really scared and I have to say that I don't want my child involved."

Bud asked her to walk with him away from Lindsey. When they were out of earshot, he said, "Ma'am, I'm afraid to tell you that she is already involved. Somehow the people involved have found out they have messed with a genius of a girl, and they will not want a kid with what appears to be a photographic memory around for them to worry about. Our best chance of stopping this may involve your daughter. I understand your concern, but we will not let her out of our sight unless she is in the house with you and one of our officers is outside. During school, I will have Officer Healey, who she trusts, with her at all times. Ma'am, please, more important than solving the case, whoever is behind this may not want her alive. It is my belief that we have not asked her the right question yet, but when we do, it would be extremely helpful."

The mother agreed, and Bud radioed for Healey to bring his unmarked cruiser back up to the Wilkersons. As soon as Justin Healey got the message, he informed the bus driver to take him to the security building in Belle Terre. When he finally arrived, Bud told him he would be Lindsey's bodyguard during the day and rotating shifts at night. He would clear all of this through Cronin. Bud took his car back as Healey stayed with Lindsey for protection until the night shift.

As Bud got in his car, he yelled to Lindsey, "When was the first time I showed you my identification?"

"It was 11:07, Detective Johnson."

"Did you notice the number on the identification?"

"Number 1669, Detective Johnson," the girl answered.

Bud nodded and said, "That's right, Lindsey."

As he got in his car, Bud said aloud to himself, "I feel sorry for the poor bastard who marries her; he's got no chance."

Bud reached the security building as the medical examiner was loading up the body. He asked for a moment and pulled the sheet down from Allan's head.

"I'm sorry, friend. I promise you, it won't be in vain." He put his hand on the side of Allan's head for a moment and closed his eyes as if he was saying a silent prayer. He pulled his hand away and gently pulled up the sheet over Allan's head. He walked toward Cronin and asked where Paul was.

"He is with the family and will accompany them to St. Charles Hospital." Cronin showed the note to Bud that was found on Allan's body. Bud read it and slapped his leg with it.

"There was no press about Lindsey. How and why does the killer know?"

Cronin looked at Bud and said, "It means there are no rules to this game. You don't give any information other than to Paul and myself about this case. Understood?"

"What about the FBI? Sherman and O'Connor are still involved on the kidnapping angle."

"No additional information without my OK to anyone," the detective lieutenant barked. "Understood?"

"Yes," Bud answered. "I've got Healey on protection duty during the day, and I need two shifts of officers at night on Bell Circle. OK?"

"Just do it," Cronin answered. "I'm going to the district attorney's office."

"Boss, it's after 6:30 pm," Bud replied.

"He can have a late dinner," Cronin answered. "Get yourself to St. Charles to support Paul and the family. Get Lindsey squared away for school in the morning, and you and Paul meet me in the office by 11:00 am tomorrow."

Bud nodded as Cronin drove away. He got on the phone and had Officer Dugan and Franks for the next few nights outside of Lindsey's house. He went back inside to where he was just with Allan only a few hours earlier. He touched a few things and saw there were a couple of chocolate chip cookies left. He moved his fingers over them as if they were a magic wand, hoping to reverse time to when the plate was full of cookies and this had not yet happened.

He reached the door as Agents Sherman and O'Connor arrived. They expressed condolences as Bud nodded, but he wasn't in the mood to talk. He just wanted to get to the hospital, where he was sure they were being counseled by professionals. He also wanted to see Paul. The body count was getting high, and the media coverage was going to be all over this as pressure built on Cronin.

As Detective Lieutenant Cronin was driving south on 83 to Yaphank, he called Ashley and demanded the meeting not wait until the morning. There had been another murder and a threat on a 12-year-old girl, and there was not time to waste.

Ashley made a desperate plea to the district attorney and won him over when told of the murder and the possible threat to the girl. District Attorney Steinberg was already in his car and closer to Cronin's temporary home in the sixth precinct, so they all agreed to meet there in 20 minutes.

Bud arrived at the hospital and was led to a private room, where he hugged Paul and met Allan's family and two children. His widow was almost inconsolable at times and other times seemed OK. It appeared to Bud she was in shock, which was understandable. They stayed with the family for more than an hour, and Paul promised he would be in touch with them as to the case and life afterward.

The two of them drove to Z Pita as they had planned earlier in the day and took table three in the back of the restaurant so they could have privacy. They were so deep in conversation that Joey Z, who always walked around and greeted them, left them alone.

Bud grabbed Paul's hand and held it, saying, "I'm sorry, my friend." Paul lowered his head but held back the tears. "It's just us, Paul, let loose."

Paul cleared his throat and said, "Thanks, but as the boss said, I've got to hold it together, at least 'til this is over."

There was a question Bud wanted to ask Paul, but now wasn't the time. Instead, Bud replied, "Paul, that's just it. We have to get this thing solved before we have another body. We have to share the information we have with each other and Cronin. He doesn't even want us to give new information to the FBI."

"Bud," Paul answered, "I'm not sure yet about what's going on, but when we asked Rachelle about her Twitter and her writings, she told us to speak to Cronin. Deborah and her father go to Florida because of him, and now we are told not to give information to the FBI, which means we basically tell them the same thing: go speak to Detective Lieutenant Cronin." Paul continued, "We have always handled these cases, and I know this is a complex case, but I feel like we have reached a point where we are puppets and he's holding the strings."

"Listen, you have always been the voice of reason," Bud said to him. "But this case, you are different, and you know why? Because of Rachelle and now Allan. You are on this case because Cronin trusts you with our lives, but Paul, you have got to handle this as the terrific cop that you are. There's no one better than you when questioning or finding a 'badass.' We need you; I need you."

Paul shook his head and said, "Well, you are good at feeding egos, my friend."

"It's more than that, my friend, when it's the truth," Bud said. Then he looked up at Rebecca and said, "Hey, how about some coffee?"

While Bud and Paul were talking at Z Pita, Sherry was surprised by a phone call from Rachelle to see how she was doing. Rachelle reminded Sherry that she had saved her life and she would forever be indebted to her. Sherry was modest but told Rachelle they would be friends regardless and that they should get together when all of this was over.

"You have a deal," Rachelle answered.

Cronin arrived at the sixth precinct five minutes after District Attorney Steinberg and Assistant District Attorney Ashley. District Attorney Steinberg was sitting in Cronin's chair when he walked in. He slowly started to get up, but Cronin waved for him to stay put.

"OK," Steinberg said. "What was so important that both of you need to talk to me?"

"Well," Assistant District Attorney Ashley spoke. "Since this is Detective Lieutenant Cronin's idea, I thought you should hear it from the horse's mouth."

"OK," Steinberg said, "Let's hear it."

Cronin went over everything he had discussed with Assistant District Attorney Ashley about the release of Patty Saunders in a bail setup. He explained for 20 minutes the possible scenarios involving her release and flushing out the killer or killers. District Attorney Steinberg was very respectful of Cronin's presentation and stayed silent for most of it.

"I think," the district attorney responded, "It's a good idea, but a judge has to be convinced it's for the good of the investigation, and you have to get the girl to agree. She might be afraid to get out of jail."

"Her sentence is life unless she helps," Cronin said.

The district attorney nodded his head and said, "My only other concern is I think you have to up the bail to one and a half million. Someone out there who wants her dead may realize it's a setup, plus how will you explain where the bail money came from?"

Cronin replied, "Well, it will be anonymous, but I have it taken care of to avoid suspicion on where it came from."

"And?" the district attorney asked. "I assume you have given this great thought."

"Yes, sir, I have. I'm going to end this game," Cronin answered.

"You mean case, right Detective Lieutenant?"

"Barry," Cronin said, "this is a game where people will continue to die unless it ends."

"OK," the district attorney said. "Set it up." He looked at Ashley and said, "Get with Saunders and her attorney and let me know which judge is involved. Anything else, Detective Lieutenant?"

"Yes," Cronin replied. "I'd like steps taken to where the Cross Island Ferry requires identification for all passengers and have metal detectors installed for every passenger. As of now, a truck full of guns or a bomb can be in a car and loaded up on the boat with no one knowing. An asshole can wear an inflatable vest under his coat and have the boat blow up and be in the water. I can and have gone on the boat with my guns with no problem. In fact, as we know, the lack of security is how Ms. Lance was kidnapped in the first place."

Barry Steinberg stood up and said, "Wow! Anything else?"

"Well, tell me, Barry," Cronin went on, "what's the downside of doing it? You go to the airport to get on the plane, and you show identification. You show passports, you go through detectors…"

Steinberg interrupted, "You made your point, Detective. I will check into it and see what we can do. I'm afraid to ask, but is there anything else?"

"Yes," Cronin said. "On New York driver's licenses, see if you can get whether the person is left- or right-handed. It's another way to verify identification, and with technology the way it is, it will help us in investigations."

District Attorney Steinberg nodded and said, "Let's look into it," as he looked at Ashley.

"One more thing," Cronin said.

With an exasperated face, Steinberg replied, "Here we go. Now what do you need?"

Cronin ignored the remark and continued, "This plan the governor has on having a statewide DNA database is a good one. I'm sure you agree using DNA to its full potential is essential."

Steinberg smiled as he replied, "We are in agreement on this issue, Detective." They shook hands and Steinberg left the building within seconds.

Ashley looked at Cronin and said, "I'm surprised you didn't tell him you needed fingerprints on licenses."

Cronin laughed and said, "I guess I can take my chair back. The hell with it, I'm going home." He made calls to a couple of the officers on duty, including at Lindsey's house in Belle Terre, before calling it a night.

Bud and Paul finished up at Z Pita and made plans to meet at the security building and have Cronin or William Lance give permission to check the Pink Mansion. When Bud got home, he sat down alone at his kitchen table, and his eyes filled with tears. He called Deborah and apologized for calling late, but he needed to talk. She was a good listener.

When Paul got up to his apartment above Z Pita, he pushed the voice-mail button, and it was from his father. "Hey, Paul, it's Dad. I'm back in Florida, and damn it's hot. Listen, I forgot to mention to you, don't go to Morgan's Bar in the city. Can you believe they charge for a refill on a cup of coffee? Shameful. OK, son, I will speak to you. Love you." Paul half-smiled, then he got the sweat on the back of his head. He sent Cronin a text that said, "I need protection detail for my father in Florida."

Cronin pulled over on the side of the road and answered him, "Why?"

Paul replied to the text with, "Who else do you love?"

Cronin called Paul and got his father's location down in Florida. It was about an hour away from Deborah Lance in Marco but up north toward Tampa. They hung up, and the Detective Lieutenant made calls to get a protection detail on William Powers for a few days. When questioned by his counterpart about the few days, Cronin replied, "This will be over within a few days." He hung up and said aloud to himself, "I hope."

He started his car up again with thoughts about whether the day was ever going to end. He turned on his speakerphone and called William Lance's cell phone to discuss Patty Saunders' bail money.

Bud hung up the phone with Deborah after about an hour but knew he couldn't sleep with the chain of events that continued to happen with the case. He wrote himself a list that he needed to do for the morning. For the first time in years, he felt like he was getting overwhelmed. The list started off with: "meet Paul 8:00 am, verify Healey pickup of Lindsey to school, get photographs together for Lindsey, talk to Cronin about *Long Island Pulse* interview, call Sherry at the hospital, get permission to search the grounds of Lance's Pink Mansion." He put his pen down and thought he had covered everything for the morning. Little did he know his plans would be disrupted by Cronin's request to have Saunders released on bail. It was a secret as to why she would be released, but the release itself would make national news.

Bud sat down, grabbed a piece of paper, and wrote. He made some rhymes, scratched out a few lines, and started again. The man who hid behind a clown's face was thinking about the state of affairs, not only with the case but what was happening everywhere, and then he thought about his mother. She died too young, he thought. He started writing again. He wrote a tribute to her and then put the words in lyric form. "For you, Mom," he said to himself when he finished it. He made a copy of it and put it in an envelope and addressed it to Deborah Lance in Marco Island, Florida. He attached a note to it that read, "To Deborah, it's for my mother, but it's you that inspired me to write it. With Best Wishes, Bud. P.S. Thank you."

He went outside on his front porch and took in the stars. He decided to talk to the sky. "You know I've never paid much attention as to a superior being, but there has to be someone in charge of all this. Please, please give me the strength to solve this. I will do whatever I have to do to keep more lives from being lost. They say that church can be anywhere as long as you pray. If this is considered a prayer then so be it. I am asking for help and I'm asking for protection, which will allow me to keep those involved safe. We are losing good people as well as the bad. It's not fair; don't tell me life is not fair. I've never been good at this, and I may not be making that much sense, but if you are there and you are who they say you are, then you do understand what I'm saying. There has been too much hurt and too many lives changed in the past 10 days. Please allow me and the team to save lives and give peace back to these good people. I promise, sure as I'm standing here, that we will have a regular conversation if no other good person loses their life on this case. I'm sorry if I sound like I don't care about the masked killer or Phil Smith. Right now, I will take what I can get and that's to keep the good guys alive. If I never solve another case, I will be OK with it. If this is the end of the road for me, then so be it. I want—no, I need—to put an end to this, and I can't do it without your guidance. Give me the strength to continue to be determined to resolve it. No matter how long this takes, please help me keep the good souls alive. I'm here to make a promise to you and that is for you to please be here now, listening to me. Thank you. Amen. Good night. I'm embarrassed to even show you I'm not even sure how to end a prayer. But know this, I will be listening as well, and I will be closer to you but understand that while I realize that every prayer cannot be answered, I think my request deserves due attention."

Bud waved at the stars as he went into his house.

Tuesday, June 28

The alarm buzzer went off as Bud put his hand on the button to quiet the noise. He studied the time on the clock: 7:02 am. He thought Lindsey was getting to him by his new habit of checking the exact details on the time.

As he lay in bed with the television on, he thought about his speech to the stars the previous night. He remembered that while he was talking aloud that he separated Phil Smith from the masked killer. Phil Smith was responsible for the kidnapping of Deborah, the killing of Timothy and Allan, all good people. Yet, the masked killer knocked off those who were involved with Phil Smith. His thoughts continued as he shut the television off to focus more. The masked killer knocked off Steven Anderson, which had to mean Anderson had a connection with all of this. He blinked his eyes a few times to see if would clear his head of a case that had become so complex that it was cause for concern over when and how it would come to a close.

He tuned the television back to News 12, the local Long Island news station, just in time to have them announce the latest tweet from BF_TJ_GW, which had become a regular segment. Doug Geed read it, indicating it had been posted at 6:22 am. "I know you killed AGAIN, and I know you have a FRIEND, soon…it will be the END."

Bud stared at the television with his mouth open. He sent Paul a text that maybe they needed to visit her again. He continued to watch the segment where it also read some of "Detective Johnson's tweets," and as of 7:00 am, he had not posted a tweet. *This is getting out of hand*, he thought. *Or is it?*

His thoughts were becoming confusing. He turned on his laptop, and once it warmed up he signed on to Twitter and wrote, "This is just the START, When you play with someone's HEART, It's me you have to FEAR, Our date is getting NEAR." He closed his laptop while his thoughts continued. *What the fuck am I doing?*

It was past 8:00 am when Bud got himself ready to leave and meet

Paul. However, there was a text waiting for him, telling him he should go see Rachelle himself and that she may be more comfortable speaking without him there. He agreed with Paul, he thought to himself. He sent him a message back that he would meet him in Belle Terre and asked him to get the OK from the boss to look around again. Bud had also been getting emails from the editor of *LI Pulse* magazine for an interview on the case. Bud had never met Nada during the five years the magazine existed, but he started friendly email correspondence with her about the magazine. He was impressed with it and was surprised when she replied to him. He looked forward to opening the magazine each month not only for the articles but got a kick out of what kind of photo Nada would have on the editor notes page. He even amused himself thinking if only she could sing, she was the type Paul would buy a CD of, she was that pretty. Bud emailed her back and told her he would be in contact with her within 24 hours.

He gave Officer Healey a call to verify he was on the way to Lindsey's house for school, and he was already at the house waiting for her. He hung up thinking, *I should have known.*

As he was approaching his car, his BlackBerry buzzed and it was from Cronin, who said, "I need you at the precinct this morning before you get preoccupied."

Bud answered, "Is 10:00 am OK? I wanted to stop at Rachelle Robinson's place to discuss her tweet this morning."

"No," Cronin replied. "Don't worry about it. I need you and Paul to be accessible to me. Later, get photographs over to your new best friend so she can look at them after school. By the way, do you have the right officer with her?"

Bud replied, "Boss, the girl will have trouble going to the bathroom, he will be watching everything. He's the right man."

"OK," Cronin said as he hung up and thought, *It must be Healey or Lynagh.*

Bud called Paul and said he would pick him up in 15 minutes and that Cronin nixed seeing Rachelle. He was already on his way to Paul's when he got the reply from his partner that he would be ready. Although Officer Healey was a serious person, Lindsey wanted him with her at the school. Although her memory was in the top 1 percent of the population, she was also extremely aware of karma. She believed in her feelings and the waves she felt from people. She felt safe around Healey, and this gave her peace of mind. Rather than unsettle the busload of kids again, Healey put her in his squad car and took her to the Port Jefferson Middle School. Her day began there, and later she would take two advanced courses in the high school for math and science.

Healey reached the school, and proving why Bud had chosen him, scouted the grounds carefully before getting out of the car and opening the door for her. He escorted her into the school and right into her homeroom. He paid no attention to the kids who would turn around to sneak a gaze at the policeman in the back of the room while class was in session.

Between classes, Healey was right beside her and was surprised it did not make her uncomfortable. It seemed that Lindsey embraced it. Some of the kids complained when Healey had to check the bathroom before Lindsey used it. Instead of throwing the girls out when he checked, he went to the boys' room and made them leave.

During one of the classes, the principal of the school asked if he could speak to him out in the hallway, and Healey obliged only if he could see Lindsey from where they were standing through the door window. The officer was asked if there was any way to tone down the escort. The officer politely told the head of the school, "This girl is not going to be kidnapped or injured on my watch. I suggest you call our boss if you think it's a problem having a cop in the school. By the way, from what I've seen so far just today, it's probably not a bad idea to have one here anyway."

Principal Gates realized he was wasting his time and left it alone. "OK, Officer," he said, "please do your duty."

"Have a nice day, sir," Healey responded as he went back inside.

When Paul and Bud arrived at their temporary offices in the sixth precinct, they were told to go right into Detective Lieutenant Cronin's office. When they arrived, the detective lieutenant gave Bud photographs to show Lindsey. He went through them to find photos of Deborah Lance, William Lance, Patty Saunders, Rachelle Robinson, Robert Simpson, Phil Smith, and added some fillers such as

Paul Powers, Officer Dugan, Sherry Walker, Agent Sherman, Agent O'Connor, Steven Anderson, and Roger Thompson. There were also photographs of the Lance household staff that had been put on vacation since Debbie and her dad had gone to Florida.

"You get to the grounds of the mansion, take a look around. Meet Healey at Lindsey's house after school."

"Boss," Detective Johnson replied, "I think we need to speak with Rachelle about today's tweets."

"Don't worry about it," Cronin replied. "I spoke to her; it's under control." He looked at Paul. "Patty Saunders is being arraigned today. I want you in the courtroom when it happens. In the meantime, catch up on some of your reports, stay in touch with Allan's family, and let us know when the wake is and funeral arrangements."

He started to walk away when Paul replied, "Isn't that what you have a secretary for?"

Cronin turned around and said, "Yes, but I want you to do it. Get right with it or go home."

Paul just stared at the detective lieutenant and decided to go to his desk rather than lose a stare-down with him. Cronin went to the conference room where Assistant District Attorney Ashley and Patty Saunders' attorney, Al Simmons, were waiting for him.

He sat down and said, "Good morning, gentlemen."

Bud was still at his desk when Paul got back. Paul said, "Maybe this isn't for me anymore." He took out his badge and held it in his hand.

"Hey! Hey! Hey!" Bud said. "Stop this shit!"

Paul looked at him and said, "This case has changed me."

"It's changed all of us, Paul," Bud replied. "And I'm not going to let you ruin your career because you have gotten yourself in too deep."

"He has me finding out about wakes and funerals and to be a witness in an arraignment, Bud."

"OK, Paul," Bud replied, "have the secretary do it, but who do you think Allan's widow wants to hear from? The arraignment thing, he has his reasons. We have to trust him, Paul. You are the best at this I've ever seen, especially when it comes to interrogation and the courts. Cronin knows what he is doing."

Paul put his badge in his pocket and said, "I'm not going to make the call, I'm going to see them in person."

"OK," Bud replied, "but keep in touch so you can be back for the arraignment."

Cronin and Ashley explained the deal to Simmons. As of now she was in for life. They would cut her a deal if she agreed to be let out on bail and be a spy and/or bait to flush out the killer or killers.

"Gee, let me think this one over," Simmons said.

"A, go to prison for life, B, accept bail and probably be killed and if not go to jail for 25 years. Gosh, you guys certainly know how to make a sweet deal."

"With good behavior, she'll be out in less than 20," Ashley said.

"Let me talk to her," Simmons replied.

"We need to know today," Ashley said. "The body count is climbing, and we have to speak to the judge if your client accepts the deal."

Simmons waved as he left the room, and as he walked by Bud without acknowledging him, Bud began singing "You Can Call Me Al" by Paul Simon. Simmons stopped in his tracks to look at Bud, who was amused with himself that he remembered the lyrics so well. He even moved a little to make believe the music was playing. He really started moving as he got into the chorus of the classic song. Simmons stood there with his mouth open as he watched the detective perform the song for another 30 seconds until he stopped.

"Are you proud of yourself?"

"Yes, I am," Bud said. "It was a great video. I just loved it when Chevy Chase lip-synced the words."

Simmons frowned and asked, "Are you having a breakdown?"

"No," Bud replied, getting serious and losing his smile. "It's the bad guys who will have the breakdown, or the bad girls, for that matter. Have a nice day," Bud said as he walked away and sat at his desk.

Simmons went off to meet Patty Saunders to discuss the deal. Bud saw Cronin walk back to his office and told him about the *LI Pulse* interview request, and Cronin denied it unless the questions were sent in writing and they were answered by Bud and Paul under his supervision, and he wanted to add questions and answers as he felt were needed.

"I'll ask her, boss, but I don't know if that's acceptable to her," Bud said.

Cronin was getting ready to make a call as he answered Bud, "Sorry, that's the only way we will do an interview for this case. Where's Paul?"

"He went to Allan's house instead of calling."

"Good idea. Take him with you to the grounds of the Lance house, but he needs to be back in three hours for the arraignment. You have a date with Lindsey."

"On it, boss."

He met Paul at Allan's house and met with the family, where they were told the wake and funeral would be delayed because the medical examiner and the district attorney's office wanted another 24 hours. Paul and Bud spent some quality time with Allan's family, and Paul told stories from high school. Allan's wife, Linda, asked Paul to speak at Allan's wake, and he was honored to be able to do it.

They left Allan's home with the family's appreciation and headed over to the Lances' Pink Mansion with the permission of William Lance, which included the security code to open the gates and access the house. They drove up to the gate, and Bud pushed 2131, waited for a second buzzer, then pushed the same number backwards—1312—and the gates opened. "This should be fun," Bud said aloud.

As Officer Healey sat in the back of the class in silence, the teacher, Ms. Meghan, was impressed how disciplined he was while the kids were working. He never uttered one word and he was eyeballing the room, the doors to the classroom, and Lindsey. One of the boys reached over to Lindsey and whispered to her, "Your cop friend looks like a robot. I saw an old movie called *Terminator 2: Judgment Day*, and he reminds me of the mean cop."

Lindsey giggled and looked back at Healey, who winked at her then set his sights on the boy, who had a smile on his face. Healey pointed his finger at the boy and gave him a stern look, which prompted the boy to turn around quickly toward the front of the class. As the bell rang to change classes, Lindsey got up and went into the hallway, knowing Officer Healey was within 10 feet of her. As they walked in the hallway, there were many stares and whispers as the uniformed officer strolled behind her with a holstered gun tucked underneath a very light windbreaker. There was no need for the light jacket in late June, but Cronin did not want his gun visible to middle school students, especially after what had happened on the school bus. Cronin wanted a little more discretion in the hallways of the school. The principal had also expressed his concerns to the superintendent to relay the message to the Suffolk County executive, who in turn had called the police commissioner. It seems that not only did no one want to take a chance something could happen to Lindsey with the threatening letter, Suffolk executive Marshall Collins relented on the request when he found out the police escort was related to the Lance case. As a courtesy, and respect to the former county executive, Collins in turn contacted the superintendent and told him the principal would have to deal with it for a few days.

During recess, where the kids had lunch and access to go outside in back of the building, Healey told Lindsey he preferred she stay indoors, and she complied without any problems. She noticed how he had the *iPhone5,* unlike the other cops who were still using *BlackBerry's.* The day was going smoothly until they had gym class. There seems to always be someone in the crowd. The kids were doing relay races and then began dodge ball. There appeared to be one boy who needed attention and wanted to show off in front of his classmates. He took great pleasure in trying to hit Lindsey with the ball and made quite a few remarks about her appearance in gym shorts. Healey was getting restless watching the game as the boy continued, each time he got the ball, to throw it at Lindsey. Finally, he did hit her, and it struck her between the head and her shoulders. Once the game was over, the kids were going to their lockers, Healey asked Lindsey to hold up as he approached the boy.

"What's your name, son?"

"Marvin," he said. "What's it to ya?"

"You're a tough guy, aren't you?" Healey asked.

"Yeah, so what?"

"You like singling out girls, do ya?" the officer asked.

"No, just Lindsey."

Healey went closer to Marvin as the gym teacher was getting

closer and said, "Son, I'm going to check on your father's status with tickets, insurance, or any other problems going on. Then I'm going to ask him why he raised a son that likes to bully girls, and I'm going to do it in the classroom in front of all of your friends and classmates. How does that sound, tough guy?"

"Ugh!" the boy answered. "What if I don't do it anymore?"

"Then I won't do it," Healey answered. "Your choice."

The boy walked away as the gym teacher reached them and asked, "Is there a problem here?"

"Not anymore," Healey answered.

He went to the front of the girls' locker room and waited for Lindsey to come out changed and showered. He had checked it out before the girls entered to be sure there was no other way in or out. She came out about 15 minutes later as they headed off to the rest of her classes.

Sherry was getting restless in the hospital. However, the doctors were not ready to release her for at least a few more days. She was reading the newspaper about the Steven Anderson killing when she received a surprise visit from Rachelle and Madison.

"Hi there!" Rachelle said as she approached the bed and gave Sherry a hug. Sherry was excited to see Rachelle and thought she looked terrific.

"Listen," Rachelle said, "I know I said this on the phone, but I owe you my life. Thank you!"

Sherry smiled and said, "I'm just happy I found my gun."

Madison came over to the bed also and thanked Sherry and grabbed her hand while expressing it.

"Forget about me," Sherry said. "How are you doing, and what is going on with your tweets?"

Rachelle smiled and answered, "I'm doing OK. I start seeing Dr. Hunt tomorrow, a couple times a week. I guess a therapist will do me good."

Sherry noticed Rachelle didn't answer in regards to the tweets, but she let Rachelle continue. "It's been crazy, and now Steven is gone. I just don't understand why or what he has to do with this. I'm writing notes on all of this. I'm going to write a book and do articles for *Newsday* on the case when it's over or if I get out of this alive."

Madison spoke up at the remark, saying, "Don't talk like that. You have a protection detail with you everywhere you go; nothing is going to happen."

Rachelle looked at Madison and said, "I may make it through this alive, but I know something will happen. Listen," she went on, "I'm not here to be depressed, I came to give you some company."

As Bud and Paul searched the grounds of the Lance Mansion, Bud was texting Deborah where he was in the house. They were exchanging funny messages as Bud walked around the back. Paul was inside the house making sure everything was secure. They met up in the front 45 minutes later and walked over to the guesthouse. The door had been jarred open, and Paul and Bud took out their guns and walked in the entrance with guns pointed. They moved cautiously to the den as Paul looked to the right and Bud concentrated on the left. Paul yelled "Clear!" as Bud did, and they moved toward the back of the house. As they moved toward the back, they heard running out the front that came down the stairs. They ran to the front as a man got in Bud's unmarked car and started it.

"The keys!" Paul yelled. "Did you leave the keys in the car!"

"Yes!" Bud answered. They started running down Cliff Street and found another vehicle driven by a woman. They flashed their badges and took over her car. She was yelling, not clearly understanding what was going on, as they jumped in her car. It was a BMW 328 convertible, and Bud pushed the pedal down.

"Good thing we are in Belle Terre! Could you imagine doing this in a Ford Fusion?"

They went down Cliff Street at 65 miles per hour and saw their unmarked cruiser take a left on East Broadway and a right on Belle Terre Road. The chase was on.

"Who the fuck is this?" Bud yelled over the wind. Paul started calling it in that an unmarked vehicle was stolen and they were in pursuit. The Ford cruiser was crisscrossing and cutting off cars as it zigzagged to lose the pursuers. The cruiser hit 90 miles per hour as it traveled down North Country Road and suddenly turned right into the back entrance of Mount Sinai Schools. The cruiser cut through the road at a solid 60 miles per hour as the driver tried to lose the BMW in pursuit.

"Come on!" Bud yelled. "You son of a bitch! You're going to kill someone!"

"Don't lose him!" Paul yelled. Paul took out his weapon to see if he could get a shot off but decided to wait until they were off school grounds. The cruiser went through the red light on Nesconset Highway, and three cars barely missed him by turning and slamming into cars off the side of the road. "Fuck!" Bud yelled. Paul was calling for medical vehicles to the corner of Nesconset Highway and Chestnut Street. Bud had to stop, then go and wiggle around vehicles to make it onto Chestnut. He pushed the BMW to 70 miles per hour on the street as they continued the chase. The cruiser reached Canal Road and made a left and drove at 75 miles per hour to Route 83 Patchogue–Mount Sinai Road and made a sharp right and floored it to almost 100 miles per hour, going south toward the Long Island Expressway.

Bud made the turn onto Canal just as he caught the back of his cruiser turn right on to the highway. Bud got to 70 miles per hour before reaching the corner of Route 83, and like the driver of the cruiser, he gunned the BMW to 100 miles per hour, weaving in and out of cars. Paul called in for a helicopter to assist in the chase. Although Bud moved at almost 100 miles per hour, they lost sight of the cruiser as two other marked cars joined the chase. They passed the Vietnam Memorial, and Paul tried to stand up in the car to look for the cruiser.

"What the fuck are you doing?" Bud yelled. "Sit your ass down!"

Paul couldn't see anything, then suddenly yelled, "Shit! Turn around."

"What?" Bud yelled.

Paul yelled louder. "Turn around! He pulled into the Memorial plaza. Go back!"

Bud pulled off the exit, turned left, and started going up the exit northbound. He drove the mile at close to 100 miles per hour and slowed as he pulled into the left lane to enter into the Vietnam Memorial parking area, and there it was. Bud and Paul jumped out of the BMW with guns drawn as they approached the cruiser. No one was there. They ran up the hill with guns out as the tourists stood back.

They approached the memorial, and again nothing. As they walked back to the vehicles and the parking lot, it was discovered from one of the tourists that their car had just been stolen.

"Damn!" Paul said as he got the make of the car and called it in. "Follow me back to Belle Terre so we can return the BMW to the owner."

"Shit!" Bud said. "Son of a bitch."

Before leaving they started checking with the memorial visitors for a description of the driver. Again, nothing of importance.

"This guy has nine lives!" Bud yelled.

"No, he doesn't," Paul replied back. "His time is running out. I'd like to know where the hell the helicopter went."

He directed one of the officers to drive the cruiser to Belle Terre while his partner followed so he and Bud could stay together in the BMW. They drove back to Belle Terre to return the car to the owner, and when they pulled up to the house, the middle-aged woman was angry beyond words. She had called the police to report her car had been stolen by two police detectives. They transferred her call to the precinct commander, who in turn contacted Cronin as soon as he heard Belle Terre and the Lance Mansion. The detective lieutenant called Mrs. Theresa Williams and assured her she would be reimbursed for the use of the car and all liability would be handled by the Suffolk County Police Department.

"I'm sorry, ma'am," Paul said to her. "We had no choice. This is my card if you need to reach us or if there is any problem with the vehicle."

Paul jumped back in the cruiser with Bud. "We have to get the car back for prints. Let's get another car out here and let the lab boys look at this."

Bud turned to the backseat and said, "Damn it!"

"Now what?" Paul said.

"The photographs! They're gone!"

Paul got out and searched the back and underneath. Only the four masks they had gotten from Fun World were still on the backseat. "Well," Paul said, "I think it's safe to say whoever was in the car was in one of the photographs."

"We have to meet Lindsey, and we have nothing to show for the day but a stolen car and lost photographs," Bud said as he banged his open hand into the side of the car. "Asshole! That's what I am today."

"You feel like an asshole now?" Paul asked. "Wait 'til we get back and explain all of this to Cronin. "I feel like the only thing we are missing is the third stooge."

They got back in the unmarked cruiser and arrived back at the precinct prepared to face the music with Cronin.

They arrived at his office as the detective lieutenant and Assistant District Attorney Ashley were on their way to meet Judge Green about getting Patty Saunders released on bail.

They entered his office and their boss said, "Well, well, well, I'm sure you two are proud of yourselves today. You leave keys in the car, you take some lady's BMW to chase the bad guy, you lose him. Anything else I need to know?"

Bud hesitated but spoke up, saying, "The photographs you gave us to show Lindsey were taken from the car."

Cronin flipped his pen in a violent fashion to show his displeasure. Assistant District Attorney Ashley was smart enough to keep silent and let Cronin handle it.

"Anything else you want to tell me?" Cronin asked.

"Boss," Paul said, "there is a connection with all this with Robert Simpson and Phil Smith. We have to bring him in again."

"No!" Cronin yelled. "You have no evidence. Let it be for now, and by the way, Paul, how come you never talk about the Rachelle Robinson connection?"

"What's that supposed to mean?" Paul asked in a very firm voice.

"Have you read her tweets lately?" Cronin asked. "Not to mention, everyone who knows her or threatens her seems to get killed."

"That's not fair," Paul answered. "We questioned her, and she tells us to talk to you." As Paul raised his voice, he said, "Now why's that!"

"Maybe you're not asking the right questions," Cronin said, "and lower your voice before I throw you through my office window."

"OK," Ashley said, "I don't need to hear this. I'll wait for you outside, Kevin," Ashley said as he left.

"I'll go with you," Bud said as he tried to follow the assistant district attorney.

"Keep your ass in my office!" Cronin yelled as Ashley shut the door. "Listen," the detective lieutenant said, "I need you guys to do your job. The media is itching to destroy our credibility and bring in outside help with this. It may be my career, but I'm not going to let it happen. If this case is not solved within the next few days, you guys will be back in uniform the rest of your careers and mine will be over. You are going to have to accept that things are being done for a reason, and some of it you may not know about for now, but it's to protect your careers."

"What is it we don't know about?" Paul asked.

"Everything will come out in the wash. The most important thing is to find Phil Smith before he kills again. Get the car over to the lab for fingerprinting, get over to the mansion, and see if you can figure out what he was up to."

"What about the photographs for Lindsey?" Bud asked.

"I'm going that way later and can take care of it after I get a new set of photos," Cronin replied. He added, "I've got to go see Judge Green about the Saunders arraignment."

"Don't worry, boss," Bud answered. "No way she's getting bail." Cronin didn't answer as he walked by both of them.

"Boss," Paul said as Cronin turned around. "Are we OK?"

Cronin made a face before walking out, telling Paul they were.

"A real tough guy," Paul said as they looked at him meet up with Ashley. As Cronin went to the front desk of the precinct, he called Gina to have Officer Dugan bring him another set of the photos at the Riverhead Courthouse, where he would be meeting with Judge Green. They drove to exit 73, took the exit and made it to the courthouse within 25 minutes. They were brought to a little room to discuss the case. Patty Saunders' attorney, Al Simmons, was already waiting for them in the room.

"Let's talk," Ashley said. "We have about 10 minutes before Judge Green gets here."

"She'll do it," Simmons said, "on two conditions."

"Let's hear it," Ashley said.

"First," Simmons replied, "she wants to have a conversation with Deborah before she's out."

Cronin spoke up, saying, "She's down South taking a vacation."

Simmons replied quickly, "She will speak to her on the phone."

"What's the second?" Ashley remarked.

"She wants it on the record that she initiated the kidnapping of a friend in order to get ransom. She made a deal that no one would get hurt whether the ransom was paid or not. While she recognizes that she is responsible for the repercussions of her actions and it will probably make no difference in the eyes of the jury, it will in the public's eyes, and she wants it known there was no intent on her part the way this has escalated."

Cronin and Ashley whispered in each other's ears for a few moments, then Ashley answered Simmons, "We will recognize in court her intent, as long as you recognize it won't make a difference in the eyes of the law as to the kidnapping. Also, this deal is contingent upon her flushing out Phil Smith and anyone else who may be involved. The people of the state of New York will ask for a reduced sentence for the murders and request manslaughter in the second degree. The kidnapping charges stay. It's a good deal, considering everything that has happened. We now have the murders of two good, innocent people as well as the six dirtbags that have been killed in the past nine days. She should take the deal."

Simmons opened his briefcase and said, "You realize, of course, she is also putting her life at risk by doing this."

Cronin spoke again. "I would say she doesn't have much of a choice. She can stay in jail the rest of her life or try and help solve it and be out of jail in 20 to 25 years."

"Let's not jump the gun," Ashley spoke up. "This is all contingent upon Judge Green being OK with this. He is not exactly the easiest judge to deal with, as we know." There was a knock on the door, and it was Officer Dugan bringing Cronin the envelope full of photographs. Both Ashley and Simmons did not ask about what had just happened. The detective lieutenant put the envelope down on the table without saying a word.

"So," Simmons said, "how is the singing detective doing?" The grin on his face was not appreciated by Cronin and neither was the question in front of the assistant district attorney.

"I have no idea who you are talking about," the detective lieutenant answered. The grin came off of Simmons' face quickly.

Cronin turned to Ashley and said, "What's the story with this judge?"

"Serious judge," Ashley replied. "No one has ever seen him smile or crack a joke. Very old-fashioned. About 65 years old, looks about 75. We need to be careful, but quite frankly this is an unusual request, and I don't know any judge who wouldn't have reservations about doing this."

They sat in silence for a few minutes, and Cronin sorted through the photos during this brief intermission. He stared a little longer at the photos of Robert Simpson, Phil Smith, and Paul Powers. His thoughts filled his head with so many scenarios that he was starting to get a headache. He pulled out a few more photos as Ashley went through some papers and Simmons pushed buttons on his BlackBerry. Cronin looked at all the photos again and marked an X on the back of one of them. He then picked them up and tapped the table with them so they were all even as he shoved them all in the envelope again. He then picked up his phone and called Officer Healey at the school to see how things were going with Lindsey. There were no problems at the school, and Cronin told Healey to stay with her longer today until he got there to show her photographs. He would see them in about two hours. He hung up with the officer and started getting restless.

"The nice thing about being a judge," Cronin said, "is that everyone has to wait for you."

"Welcome to my world," Simmons answered as he put his BlackBerry down.

"They're busy," Ashley said.

"Don't use that word around me," Cronin said, looking at both of them. "*Busy* is a four-letter word. When someone tells me they're busy, it insinuates to me that I'm not busy, and I am busy, so tell me many things but don't tell me you've been busy."

"OK," Ashley replied. "Take it easy."

"Just stating the facts," Cronin said. "Are you a busy person?" Cronin asked, looking at Ashley.

"Yes," the assistant district attorney said.

"We all are," the detective lieutenant replied. "Have you ever heard me tell you I haven't returned your call because I'm busy?"

Ashley looked around the room for acceptance as he said no.

"You're damn right," Cronin said. "Don't insult me with the word *busy*. It's about priorities. Speaking of which, my priority is solving this case, and I have now been waiting for this judge for 20 minutes."

"I'll see what's going on," Ashley said as he held his hands up.

"No," Cronin said, "let's wait another five minutes. You just pushed a sore button with me."

"I can tell," the assistant district attorney answered.

Simmons was sitting there actually enjoying the exchange between them. There were about 20 seconds of silence before Judge Green stepped into the room. He was a gray-haired man, hair combed back neatly, and about six feet tall. And Ashley was right, he looked about 75 years of age as he walked slowly to his chair, sat down, and started to talk.

"I apologize for the delay, gentlemen. Things have been a little challenging today. I'm sure all of you are as busy as I am, so let's get right to it. What exactly is this about? You have 10 minutes." He had already made points with Cronin by his comment that all must be busy.

Ashley stood up and reviewed the entire eight days as an outline that included eight murders with one, possibly two, perpetrators still on the loose. This took the entire 10 minutes that Judge Harold Green had given him, but he sat silently as the assistant district attorney continued to make his pitch to release Patty Saunders on bail for $1.5 million to flush out the remaining killer or killers. When he finished, the judge sat with a stoic look on his face for about thirty seconds before he spoke.

"So let me get this straight. You want me to release someone who is responsible for kidnapping her best friend, which has indirectly led to eight murders in the last eight or nine days, because we think it will flush out who we want in this entire mess? Do I have that right?"

Ashley spoke again, saying, "You would, of course, be giving a realistic bail of $1.5 million to avoid suspicion."

"Oh," the judge said. "Thanks for that bit of information."

He sat silently again and looked at Cronin before asking, "As the detective in charge of this case, what do you think of that idea?"

"I think it's a damn good one, Judge, which is why I brought it to the district attorney's office."

The judge looked at Simmons and stated, "I assume you and your client are accepting of this."

"Yes, Your Honor," Simmons answered.

"Why?" the judge asked.

"It's her best chance to have some kind of life other than prison," Simmons answered.

The judge looked confused by everyone's agreement on this and brought his attention back to Ashley. "I assume your boss is OK with this?" he asked.

"Yes, Judge," Ashley answered.

The judge sat idle for another few seconds before commenting, "Maybe when we release her we should put a big bull's eye on her backside to help whoever is killing everyone find her."

Simmons started laughing as he remarked, "Ashley said you never crack a joke," as he continued laughing.

"I don't," the judge answered as he looked at Simmons with a stern look. The attorney quickly stopped his giggling as the judge looked at Ashley.

"The nature of this crime is shocking, and a release on bail may cause a public outcry that will reach levels we have never seen before. The violence level here is beyond anything seen on Long Island, ever. More than the Long Island Sniper case, more than the Smithtown murders. Ms. Saunders is a cunning woman who it appears will do anything to anyone to get what she wants. I need to be convinced the safety of the public will not be in danger if we do this and that there is no other way to solve this case."

Cronin spoke, saying, "Judge, I agree with what you are saying. However, I worked the Long Island Sniper case; this case, as you mentioned, is much more complex than that and the other murders.

I can attest to you that this case is dependent upon you releasing her on bail."

The judge was silent as he contemplated a bit more before saying, "We are not on Candid Camera or, what do the kids say today, being punked, are we?"

Simmons started laughing again as the other three stared him down to force him to be quiet.

"No, Judge," Ashley said. "This is for real."

Judge Green spoke again. "And who in the hell is going to guarantee the bail and put 10 percent down to the bail bondsman?"

Ashley began to speak, but Cronin interrupted him, saying, "It's anonymous."

"Anonymous?" the judge said.

"Anonymous," Ashley said.

"Anonymous," Simmons said weakly.

"Is there an echo in here?" the judge asked. "You guys are willing to risk your careers on this?"

"Yes, sir," Cronin answered. The judge looked over the file that was handed to him on the Saunders case for a few minutes before looking up at them again.

"I want to talk to the district attorney, and I will give you my answer in 24 hours. There are many things to consider here, and before I open Pandora's Box, I want to think it over a bit. I realize this case is esoteric in regards to the norm, but I need to evaluate the law and the possible repercussions from it."

"Judge," Ashley spoke up, "while I respect your feelings and your comments, under the law, everyone is entitled to some kind of bail."

The judge stood up and said, "Yes, however, the law also allows me to have a bail so high it's impossible to release her. Let me think about it."

"Yes, Your Honor," Ashley answered.

The judge left the room as the three men looked at each other.

"Well," Ashley said, "that went over well. He will call Steinberg, and we should get this done." The three of them shook hands as Cronin asked Ashley to drop him off at Lindsey's house in Belle Terre on the way back from Riverhead.

On the way out of the building, Cronin asked Simmons, "Who's paying you to defend Patty Saunders?"

"You are," Simmons answered as he walked away.

Cronin looked at Ashley and said, "What the hell?"

Ashley put his arm around him and replied, "He's doing this pro bono. He knows a good thing to put on his resume of cases. He'll write off his expenses, which means savings on taxes, which in effect we all pay. He's just fucking with you."

Cronin replied, "Did you see the look on the judge's face when he stared down Simmons for laughing at his remarks?"

"You have to admit," Ashley started smiling, "the judge was unintentionally funny, but I think we shook him up a little by the request." They both were laughing as they got in Ashley's car. The assistant district attorney spoke up about Simmons' remark about "the singing detective." "You were a bit defensive," he said to the detective lieutenant.

"Yes, I was," Cronin replied. "He's off the wall, but quite frankly there isn't a better person to be on a case like this. If my life depended on it, I would want him with me. He did save my life a few years ago, and we are all a little nuts; he's just not afraid to show it. He needs protection because of what police protocol is used to, but he is a damn good cop who gives 110 percent. They both are. This case is not something they have ever experienced before."

Ashley interrupted, "And that's why you've gotten involved in the field on this one?"

Cronin replied, "If I didn't, we would have the FBI everywhere, and O'Connor and Sherman would eventually have consultant roles in upcoming movies."

Ashley was quick to respond, "Who cares as long as the case gets resolved?"

"It's our problem eight people are dead, and I don't want the FBI running my household," The detective lieutenant replied.

"Any theories?" Ashley said.

"I know who is behind this," Cronin answered.

Ashley slammed on the brakes and moved to the side of the road. "Excuse me!" he remarked. Cronin gave him a stare, and they both looked at each other until the assistant district attorney spoke up.

"What the hell are you doing?" Ashley asked.

Cronin stared out the window and spoke, saying, "You just get Saunders released on bail, and I'll get my evidence."

The Assistant District Attorney continued to look at the detective staring out the window before he asked, "Are you going to tell me anything?"

"Not now," Cronin replied. "As I said to the chief, I don't know who to trust when it comes to this case."

The assistant district attorney pounded on the steering wheel of the car and said, "What about you, Detective? What about trusting you?"

Cronin turned his head back to Ashley and said, "This is my case until your office convinces the district attorney or the chief to take it away from me. You don't have much of a choice."

He started to turn his head back toward his window again when Ashley put his hand on the detective's shoulder.

Ashley said, "Your whole career and your life are on the line. If you don't get yourself killed, never mind about flushing out the killer; your career will be flushed down the toilet."

Cronin nodded and answered, "Did you ever notice, when you flush the toilet, the water goes round and round in circles 'til it finally goes down the drain?"

Ashley looked forward with confusion on his face as he spoke. "I never thought about it, but now that you mentioned it, yeah, I guess so."

"Well," Cronin replied, "that's life. Life is a circle, and we all end up being flushed away."

Ashley stared at the detective before speaking. "You know you are starting to sound like Detective Johnson now."

Cronin laughed and said, "Good ol' Bud."

"What about Detective Powers?" the assistant district attorney asked.

"Paul?" Cronin replied. "Don't get on his bad side."

"Is that a hint?" the assistant district attorney asked.

"No hints," Cronin replied. "You get Saunders released on bond. If Judge Green tells you tomorrow she will be held without bond, you and the district attorney push. I don't give a shit. This case will drag for weeks unless she's out there."

"OK, Ashley said, "but you told me William Lance was putting up the bond money, and then you tell the judge it's anonymous."

"Officially," Cronin replied, "it will be, but just wait. It's all going to fall into place. Even if I don't make it through this, it will come into place for you to end it."

"Words like that," Ashley replied, "tell me you trust me."

The detective shook his head and said, "I trust you will do the right thing, but you have no need to know the rest of my thoughts at this time. It's for your own safety as well as others' for now."

Ashley started to put his car in drive but took his hand off the shifter. "Kevin," he said, "are you sure you know what you're doing? There has to be another way."

"No" Cronin replied. "This is the way it has to be. It's a game, and the one who's standing or alive at the end of the game wins."

"How much of what you're thinking do your detectives know?" the assistant district attorney asked.

Cronin took a deep breath before answering, "They know enough to keep them in the game. I need them involved to keep the other players safe, and now we have a 12-year-old in this."

There was silence in the car. Ashley could hear the sounds of the trucks and cars whizzing by on the Long Island Expressway.

"Well?" Cronin replied. Ashley wasn't ready to move yet.

"The girl, how does she play in all of this? Shit," he replied, "now you have me talking your language."

The detective lieutenant laughed as he replied, "She's a key right now. I know they want her eliminated."

"Wait," Ashley said. "You said 'they.' Are you convinced there's more than one person involved at this point?"

Cronin replied, "My friend, to play a good game, you need a few players."

"What?" Ashley raised his voice. "Two maybe, maybe three, everyone else is dead."

Cronin took his seat belt off and spoke. "Get Patty Saunders out on bail, and you may have more than three players playing."

"And you?" Ashley asked. "You know how to play?"

"With an adjustment to the rules, yes," Cronin replied.

"And the girl?" the assistant district attorney asked.

"She's in good hands," the detective lieutenant answered. "Healey is barely letting her use the girls' room in private, and according to Bud, he's the most serious cop on the beat. Anybody touches that girl, he'll tear their arm off and beat them to death with it."

"Can he stop a bullet?" Ashley asked.

"No, he can't," Cronin replied. "But God help them if Healey catches them, hit or miss. He's the right man for this, and she knows it."

Ashley put on his confused face again and asked, "How does a 12-year-old know something like that?"

"You haven't met this girl yet," Cronin replied. "These poor bastards had no idea they would kidnap the dog of a girl genius."

"Maybe I should talk to her then," Ashley said.

"Let me know when," the detective lieutenant replied. "I'll set it up with Healey, or you can come with me now. That's where you were dropping me off."

"Sounds good," the assistant district attorney answered.

"Just as well," Cronin replied. "This way it will be easier for you with Healey around if you're with me."

The detective lieutenant proceeded to tell the assistant district attorney about what had happened with one of the girl's parents on the school bus, and you could hear their laughter if you were standing outside the car.

"So," Cronin finally said, "anything else you want to say before we get on the road? We would have been there by now if we didn't have this chat for the past 30 minutes."

Ashley put his hand back on the shift while looking at the detective and said, "I'll give you the same courtesy. I'll trust that you will do the right thing."

The detective smiled as he spoke, saying, "Fair enough."

Cronin put his seat belt back on as a police cruiser flashed its lights behind them.

"Oh, great," Ashley said.

Cronin smiled and said, "What did you expect? He probably thinks we are having sex or making out, we have been parked here for so long."

Ashley shook his head and said, "Now I really know where Bud gets his training from."

The officer approached the vehicle asking for registration and license, and instead they showed identification and the badge of the detective. The officer verified the photos and Cronin's badge number and suggested to them the parking area would be safer to talk rather than a breakdown lane on the Long Island Expressway.

"Noted," the assistant district attorney said as they drove off to Belle Terre. Cronin called Healey and said that they would be arriving late and reviewed the day at school with Lindsey. The officer reported there were no problems during the day and they were now home waiting for them. The detective lieutenant told Healey they would be there in about 15 minutes.

As he disconnected the conversation, Ashley spoke. "Can't wait to speak to your girl," he said in a voice of sarcasm. Cronin just smiled.

Paul and Bud were finishing up at the mansion with an extensive search of the guesthouse. This time, Bud took the keys out of the car. Paul got a call from the lab that the man who had taken the vehicle was Phil Smith. Bud thought to himself as to the reasons why Smith wouldn't care if his fingerprints were left in the car but went to great lengths not to leave prints if he was wearing the Ghost Face mask. He decided to express his thoughts to Paul and then added they must be two different people.

Paul replied, "Maybe he wants us to think they are two different people. Maybe he wants to frame someone else. We should take a look at the video on the grounds here also."

Bud pushed a little harder, saying, "I think somebody is after the 3 million in cash that is still in the house. That's what started all of this."

Bud got out his BlackBerry and sent William Lance a text asking if the $3 million in cash was still in the house. As they walked around a bit more, Bud had not received an answer. He sent Deborah a message asking if her father was with her in the house in Florida.

She answered, "Yes, why?"

Bud replied, "No worries, but tell him to check his phone."

She answered, "OK, anything else?"

"Yes," he said. "May I call you later?"

She wrote back, "If you don't, I'll have another detective assigned to the case."

He smiled as he looked at Paul, who was searching the rest of the guesthouse. His BlackBerry buzzed with a text from Cronin to meet him at Lindsey's house.

They got in the car as Paul remarked, "Oh, looky here. Our car is still here."

"Smartass," Bud said as he pulled out on to Cliff Street. He drove to Bell Circle in three minutes, where the assistant district attorney and Cronin were walking up to Lindsey with Healey by her side and her parents in the background on the front lawn. Bud checked his watch; it was 4:27 pm. They walked up to everyone as Healey continued to look around as they spoke and an additional police cruiser was parked on the side of the road about 30 yards away. Cronin had already finished introducing Lindsey to Assistant District Attorney Ashley, who asked her some routine questions.

"A beautiful village you live in," Ashley said to the 12-year-old. "How large is it?" he asked as he smiled to Cronin.

Without hesitation, she answered, "Belle Terre is 0.9 square miles, Mr. Ashley." The smile was erased quickly.

"Is that land and water, Lindsey?"

"Yes and no," she answered. "Belle Terre is 0.9 square miles of land and 0.0 square miles of water, therefore its total is land and water combined, but none of it is water."

"OK," Ashley said, as Bud was smiling.

"Well," Detective Johnson remarked, "the numbers on Belle Terre are rather easy to remember. It's not like we asked you the size of Long Island or anything," he said with a funny smirk.

The young girl squinted her eyes at Bud as she replied, "Long Island is 1,401 miles long and 23 miles wide at the farthest points. Its coordinates are 40.8°N 73.3°W with a population of 7,568,304, according to the 2010 census. Is there anything else you would like to know?" she asked as she turned her head at an angle.

Bud pointed at her and said, "You're just messing with me."

"Look it up," the young girl answered with a smile.

Cronin interrupted, "Bud, you better quit while you're this far behind. Lindsey, may I speak to you alone for a moment?" he asked.

They walked away from the crowd of people except for Healey, who followed about five feet behind them. Close enough if there was a problem, yet far enough not to hear their conversation. Bud and Paul watched intently as Cronin took her over by the car and pulled out the envelope full of photographs. Paul turned to talk to Ashley, but Bud kept his eye on Cronin. The detective pulled out one photograph and showed it to Lindsey. It was killing him he could not hear what was going on.

"Yes," Lindsey said to Cronin. "I have seen him before."

"Where, Lindsey?" Cronin asked. "And when?"

"I saw him speaking with the man who took my dog in Mount Misery Point on Sunday at 2:29 pm."

"What were you doing there, Lindsey?"

"I love going there in the summer. The view is beautiful, and if we can't go far, we go there for a walk."

Cronin asked, "*We* being you and your dad?"

"Yes," Lindsey answered.

Cronin then asked, "Did you ever see the man who took your dog with anybody else?"

"No," she replied.

The detective pushed on, asking, "How long did you see them talking to each other?"

"It was an uncomfortable feeling to me, so I asked my dad if we could leave. He trusts my feelings, but it was four minutes by the time we left."

"OK," Cronin said. "Thank you very much. You can go back with Officer Healey now."

Cronin turned around with his back to everyone and looked at the photo. It was the one he had put an X on the back. Bud was still staring at Cronin and wondering why he had only showed Lindsey one photo from the batch.

He began to walk toward the detective lieutenant when his Black-

Berry rang. It was from *LI Pulse* magazine.

Oh, Bud thought, *finally a chat with Nada.*

"Hello, Detective Johnson?"

"Yes," he answered.

"This is The Shannyn T, and I'm calling for Nada to tell you a list of questions will be faxed over to your precinct for the interview. Please try and get them back to me over the next 48 hours so we can get them published."

"OK," the detective said, "and your name again?"

"Oh, this is The Shannyn T; I am an intern here helping out Nada and the staff."

"OK," the detective answered. "Do I call you 'The' or 'Shannyn'?"

"Neither," the girl answered, "but you can call me 'The Shannyn T.'" Bud held out his BlackBerry to see if it would help him interpret the girl better, but it didn't help.

"Fine, The Shannyn T," he answered. "We will get back to you once I get the questions from the precinct."

"Thank you, sir," she said as she hung up.

Bud sent an email to Nada asking who the hell The Shannyn T was, and she replied back, "She is a terrific intern who works as The Shannyn T, and remember, it's a *Y* in Shannyn not an *O* or *A* or an *E*." He answered her, "The world is filling up with crazy people." She answered him immediately, texting, "You should see the way she treats her pet goldfish, Pocky, on her desk. You would think it's a dog." He laughed as he walked up to Cronin.

"Anything you need to tell me?"

"No," the detective answered.

"What about the mansion, anything?"

"We didn't see much, but it's obvious someone was looking for the 3 million if it's there. Cronin nodded, and Bud continued, saying, "I asked William Lance through text if the money was still in the house, and he didn't answer me. I find that odd."

Cronin nodded but didn't say anything. "What are you working on tonight?" he asked Bud.

"We have the wake for Allan tonight and a funeral tomorrow," Bud said.

"I'll be there," Cronin replied.

He left Bud standing there and walked over to Healey to tell him the girl was not to go near the wake or funeral the next day. Healey nodded. Bud stood by the car and looked at the envelope full of photographs as Cronin kneeled to get at Lindsey's level of eyesight.

"Our conversation is between me and you for now, OK?"

"No problem," Lindsey answered.

Bud thought about reaching in the front seat but thought better of it. Cronin walked back to Bud and told him to get to the precinct after the funeral the next day.

"We have the *Pulse* interview questions anyway, boss," he answered.

"Another busy day," Cronin replied. "I have things to take care of as well."

Paul walked over to the car with Ashley as Cronin looked at him. "Get with Anderson's wife and see if you can find out anything more about him. It's likely she doesn't know much, but if there were problems, she might be willing to talk. Then check the *Now* offices and go through everything. Maybe he left a clue unintentionally in all of this."

Cronin then turned his attention to Ashley and said, "And what are you doing tomorrow?"

"You forget?" he replied. "You and I have a date with the judge."

"Oh, yeah," he replied as he looked at Bud. "Get to the precinct early so we have time to review the questions."

"How did it go today on Saunders' arraignment?" Bud asked.

"She's not out on bail as of now," the assistant district attorney answered for Cronin.

"Told ya," Bud replied as if he were a peacock. He looked over at Lindsey and her parents heading into the house.

"Hey, Lindsey, what time was it when you saw Assistant District Attorney Ashley for the first time?"

"4:29 pm," she replied.

"Ha ha! Gotcha!" he laughed. "It was 4:27 pm. I checked my watch."

The girl stopped at the porch to turn around and said, "Your watch is two minutes slow, Detective Johnson. Bye for now."

Bud looked over at Ashley, Paul, and Cronin and said, "There's no way she could be the Ghost Face killer, right?"

"Yeah, right, she's too short. OK."

"Ready, Paul?" Bud asked.

They all started to laugh except for Paul, who had Allan's wake on his mind. Rachelle was in seclusion, Allan was dead, Bud was being threatened, his father had protective detail. He wasn't exactly feeling good about his life at the moment. Bud dropped Paul off in the back of Z Pita and told him he would be back in a couple hours to attend the wake with him.

When Paul reached the top of the stairs to his apartment, he felt he was too exhausted to shower and go to a wake, but he had no choice. He had to do it. He knew he was in trouble emotionally, for everything happening around him was putting him in a state of depression. The safety of himself and those around him were in jeopardy, and he started to wonder if he should not have let Bud talk him out of quitting.

He picked up the phone to speak to his father, who was always his rock. "This shall pass, son," his father told him. "I didn't raise you to give up. Never, ever give up. There is a reason you are in the middle of this."

Paul accepted his dad's advice and asked if the Florida police were doing a good job for him. His dad answered they were but it was tough on his love life. Finally, Paul laughed as they hung up, and he got himself ready for the wake. Paul had about 40 minutes until Bud was going to pick him up, so he went downstairs to Z Pita to get something to eat quickly and had a chance to sit with Joey Z for a few minutes. A new server by the name of Rosie came by for his order.

"All righty, now," she said with a smile that could light up a dark room. He gave her an order for sweet potato fries and a roast beef wrap, and she replied, "Our whole-wheat wrap is healthier, OK?"

"OK," Paul said. He looked at Joey Z as she walked away.

"Don't ask," the owner said. "I'll tell you some other time."

They spoke for a few minutes until Paul's food was served. Usually Joey Z would get up to allow his friends and patrons to enjoy their dinner, but this time Paul asked him to stay so they could talk.

"You know," Paul said to the owner, "there was a time when you used to tease me, saying you would like to switch places with me because you live here in the restaurant, this place has become your life. I haven't heard you say it to me the past week and a half."

Joey Z smiled at Paul and said, "You know, my friend, you will never hear me say that again. Too much shit has happened, and I'll be satisfied making sure the food and service is to everyone's satisfaction. I do not have a problem having a boring life."

"I know what you mean," Paul replied.

Rosie came by the table to check on them and asked, "Anything else for you tonight?"

"No," Paul replied, "thank you."

"Very good, honey," the new server replied.

Paul looked at Joey again as the owner replied, "The customers love her personality and smile. What can I say?"

They both began to speak at the same time, then Paul let Joey speak. Joey said, "Is it ever going to be the way it was again?"

Paul sipped on his coffee and replied, "I think over time we will begin to live our lives again, but for it to be the same again, well, that's a big question. I have thought about resigning because I feel the escalation of this is my fault. I got my friends, people I trust, involved, and their lives were put in danger, and Rachelle's life will never be the same."

Joey Z made a signal to Tina to give him a cup of coffee as he began to speak. "Rachelle is a writer. She would not have gotten involved if she thought some maniac would try and kill her." Paul nodded as Tina poured Joey Z's cup of coffee. "And look at her now," Joey Z continued. "She's writing for *Newsday*, writing tweets to antagonize the killers. Why? That's not Rachelle. She would not do anything to hurt you. If she's doing it, it's to help you."

"Help me?" Paul replied. "How can her doing this help me?"

Joey Z took a sip of coffee and lost track for a second, saying, "What do you think of these new coffee cups? Everyone wanted bigger cups to feel like they were drinking a real cup of coffee."

"Joey," Paul said.

"OK, listen," the owner remarked. "Whatever she's writing, it's my belief she either thinks it will help you find these bastards or prove something about you."

"Prove what about me?"

"You tell me," Joey Z replied.

Paul started to get that wetness in the back of his hair again, in his neck area, and tried to change the subject, asking, "How's business been?"

"Other business places have been affected a little bit," Joey answered as he continued. "The teenagers and young adults enjoy the excitement and mystery, so we are getting new customers with our medium-priced menu. However, the higher-income older adults are staying away until it's over. I personally think when the craziness is over, we will have more curious tourists visiting the village."

"Interesting," Paul replied.

Rosie dropped the check at the table. "Take your time, now," she said and walked away.

"Where are you off to?" Joey Z asked.

Paul told him, "Moloney's Funeral Home on Route 112 in Port Jefferson Station across from the Jefferson Plaza strip center, for Allan's wake."

Joey acknowledged his sympathy and said he would also stop by for a few minutes. Paul put his credit card in the check cover, and they continued to talk about the state of things in the world, not just Port Jefferson, when Rosie brought back the check and slip for him to sign.

As usual, Bud's timing was right on. He had gone upstairs but found no one in the apartment. Since he did not get a message from Paul, he went down to the restaurant, and sure enough, he was there. Bud greeted Joey Z and sat with them for a few minutes until they were ready to go.

"You know," Paul said to Joey, "I think this is the longest time we have ever held a conversation before."

"I'm not a talker, Paul," the owner replied, "but I'm concerned about you and Rachelle. I don't know the others involved in this, and I'm sure they are good people, but I'm worried about the two of you."

I may only be the owner here, but I've circled this restaurant thousands of times over the past few years. I see more than my customers enjoying their meals and my staff working hard. Get this thing to end so we all can move on with our lives."

Paul nodded and said, "OK, Joey. Thanks."

"OK," Joey Z answered, "you paid the bill, so you can leave now" and smiled.

When he walked away, Bud put his arm on Paul and asked, "Ready, my partner?"

"Yes," Paul said as they walked through the front door.

As with most destinations in the Port Jefferson area, it only took about five minutes to drive to Moloney's Funeral Home. They signed in and walked in to the closed casket of Allan Jones. There were pictures on the casket of Allan and even more on a board 15 feet to the left of the casket that Paul noticed when he walked in. He paid his respects to his longtime friend and greeted his widow and family. He hugged Linda and did the same to the children before heading over to the board with all the photos on it. As he looked at the photos, Bud was extending sympathy to the family. Paul looked at the photos with sentimental emotion. There were at least three photos of just him with Allan, and one of them was slightly curled enough that he could tell it had some writing on it. He bent the photo even more to see if he could read it. It said in Allan's writing and said, "Paul and me 1999—A true friend is felt, no words need be spoken, your eyes can see it, your heart can feel it."

Paul's eyes began to tear up as he read it over and over again. He felt a hand on his shoulder and turned around to see Rachelle, who was slightly smiling until she saw the tears in his eyes.

"I'm sorry, Paul, about Allan," she spoke. He nodded.

"Me too," he said as he wiped his tears. "Thank you. How are you doing, Rachelle?"

"Don't worry about me right now; I'm concerned about you."

"Well," Paul answered, "life is complicated right now."

He walked over to Linda while Rachelle went to a seat and kneeled in front of her as he took her hand. "Linda, I would like very much to have one of the photos of Allan and myself. I would like to carry it with me and have it on me when we catch this guy. It will help me emotionally and give me strength."

Linda answered, "You take the photo and one of his family. You show him the family he destroyed, and if he goes to jail, you make sure those photos are in his jail cell so he has to think about us every day, and Paul, you get your strength through prayer. The good Lord will help you."

"Yes, ma'am," Paul replied. "I'm not sure he will make it to jail, but I will make sure he sees the photos."

As he walked away, he did not even notice Bud was listening to him speak to Linda. Bud watched Paul walk over to Rachelle as she was sitting in one of the chairs in silence. She looked at him as he walked up to her, kissed the top of her head, and walked away. He noticed that she too began to have a tear trickle down her cheek. Bud acknowledged Rachelle in silence as he walked out to meet Paul.

"Are you holding it together?" Bud asked.

"Get real," Paul said. "No one is holding it together. He's going to have to be taken out before he kills Rachelle, Deborah, you, me, and the girl."

"Stop it," Bud said, "I'm the crazy one here. Stop this shit! Look at me! This is going down legal!"

Paul nodded and replied in a calmer voice, "I need to get back and decide what I'm going to say tomorrow before the funeral. Damn, I forgot the photographs. I'll be right back."

"Paul!" Bud yelled. "You get in the car, I'll get them."

"Just calm down," Paul said, and told him which ones he wanted. Bud went inside to get the photos from the board. Rachelle was still in her seat but this time with her head down. Bud went over to her and sat down next to her and put his arm around her.

She leaned her head on his shoulder and said, "I don't know what to do anymore, everything is so screwed up."

Bud moved his head to see her face and replied, "Rachelle, I have to get back to him. Before it's too late, you need to tell him how you feel about him. He's not himself without you. I'm still not sure about the Twitter thing, but you're both miserable without the other. Even when you pretended to be good friends, things seemed OK." He kissed her on her forehead and got up.

He was 10 feet away when she called to him, saying, "About Twitter, speak to Cronin."

It wasn't the first time she had mentioned it, and Bud decided he was going to push the issue the next day.

He got back in the car, gave the photos to Paul, and said, "Let's get some sleep. Another long day tomorrow."

Wednesday, June 29

Paul rolled over in bed at 6:30 am. He wasn't looking forward to speaking at the funeral, but he knew he had to. Bud had given him the photos from the previous night's wake, and he promised himself he would have them on his person when he finally had the one who was ultimately responsible for this.

He got up and ran down the stairs to pick up his *Newsday* that was left at the door every morning. He looked for the section that carried Rachelle's daily tweet. Today it read, "Soon you will be off the CASE, for you will get a TASTE. There's nowhere to HIDE. It's the changing of the TIDE." Paul shook his head and started to call Rachelle but caught himself. "Damn!" he yelled to himself as he entered the bathroom.

Bud was at the apartment at 7:30 am to pick up Paul. The Port Jefferson United Methodist Church was a short distance away, and Bud wanted to keep an eye on his partner as much as he could. In his mind, he wasn't sure which was the main reason he wanted to keep an eye on him. Bud had already read the latest tweet from Rachelle and knew his tweet from this morning would be in his paper.

As he sat in the car with his BlackBerry, he typed in on Twitter, "I will win the GAME, you will not have your FAME. The next thing you DO, I will be behind YOU." Bud pushed the *send* button. He knew his tweets were escalating his status as the next target. It was Rachelle that he was still having trouble understanding. Either way, it was going to end soon. For him, for all of them, or a few more. The village could not absorb much more publicity at this point.

Paul ran out to the car in his dark blue suit and tie with his white shirt.

"Handsome guy," Bud said as he backed out to drive to the church.

Inside there were about 200 people paying their respects to Allan Jones. A few people, including his cousin and his brother from Georgia, spoke, and then it was time for Paul to get up and speak. He went behind the podium and stared into the filled seating area. There were so many faces that he did not notice that Detective Lieutenant Cronin was there or even Rachelle.

Finally, he spoke, saying, "I feel like expressing my friendship with Allan to all of you is a contradiction of what he believed in. In this case he would forgive me. You see, being Allan's friend was something you felt in the heart. It was something you expressed by your actions. It was something you could see without saying anything. I know this because of my friendship with him over the last 20 years, and I know this from the words he wrote on the back of this photo. I'm ashamed to say that although I was his friend, I did not always share in his feelings, and I did not always appreciate the kind of man he really was until now. But I can show my appreciation to him by my heartfelt actions to his loved ones and telling all of you here not to let life pass you by without some attempt to make it worthwhile for you and your loved ones. Have your goals, have your dreams, give it your best shot to attain them, but always remember, it won't mean anything if someone you love or someone you care about is not there to share them with you. Allan Jones was a good man, a good husband, a good father, a great friend, and a man of strong faith. I will miss you, my friend."

Paul walked away from the podium and did not notice the women and some men seated who where wiping their eyes with tissues. The minister came out with last words as the casket was slowly moved to the front, with Paul and Bud being two of the pallbearers. The funeral procession to Mount Sinai Cemetery took about 12 minutes. There, some last words were spoken before everyone started heading to their cars. Rachelle saw Paul and Bud going back to the car but thought it best not to interrupt them. When Paul got in the car, his BlackBerry buzzed. It was a text from Rachelle. It said, "Your speech was so beautiful and so true."

He answered back, "Thank you, Rachelle. XOXO."

He looked over at Bud and asked, "Where to now?"

"The precinct." We have some questions to answer for the *Long Island Pulse*."

"How can we do that?" Paul asked. "We don't have any answers yet."

It took Bud another 20 minutes to get to their temporary home, which seemed like it had been a month instead of under two weeks. Once they entered the precinct, Paul stopped at his desk while Bud went straight into Cronin's office and shut the door.

"I guess you would like to speak with me?" the detective lieutenant said.

"Is that a problem?" Bud replied.

"My door is always open," the boss said, "so to speak."

"I'm concerned that Rachelle Robinson, when questioned about her tweets again, told me the same thing again, and that is to see you. Now why is that?"

Cronin looked at Bud and said, "Maybe the same reason when the chief of police asks people here about your tweets, they tell him to see me."

Bud moved closer to his desk and said, "If the chief of police asked me personally about my tweets, I would answer him and not tell him to see you."

"You will now," Cronin replied.

"And why is that?" Bud pushed.

Without even looking up at Bud, he replied, "Because I am the boss, and that's how I want it handled. Dismissed."

Bud walked out to his desk, and laying there was an email sent to the precinct via his attention from The Shannyn T of the *Long Island Pulse* with questions. Bud gave it to Cronin's assistant, telling her he might want to take a look at how he wants to answer the inquiries.

Bud no longer had a desire to be involved. Suddenly he was feeling like a puppet on a string, and Cronin was the master. He looked at the stack of paperwork on his desk and got himself to sit down and sort through it. Cronin looked over the questions sent in from the *Long Island Pulse* and crossed out a few before handing the sheet back to his assistant for his detectives to answer. He told Gina to tell Powers and Johnson to get it back to him by 3:30 pm. The magazine would be out next week, so they needed to get the answers back today in order to meet the deadline. The Shannyn T wrote a note at the bottom that she would be calling around 4:00 pm to check on the status of the questions and answers. Gina brought the interview back to Bud with Cronin's instructions.

"I'm really getting nuts with all of this," Bud remarked.

Paul looked over at him and said, "Wasn't it you who wanted to do the interview in the first place?"

"Yes, but he has his hands in everything!"

Paul leaned forward and said, "We have to play this out, Bud. Together we will get it done."

Cronin's phone rang from the judge's office, telling him to meet him in the chambers in one hour with Assistant District Attorney Ashley and Saunders' attorney, Al Simmons. Cronin got up to leave, when Ashley came in.

"How the hell did you get here so fast?" Cronin asked.

Ashley laughed and said, "Steinberg told me about his phone call with Judge Green last night. He told me to meet you here so we could go in together."

Cronin smiled and said, "This should be fun," as they headed out the door.

"See you guys later," he said, as he waved to Bud and Paul.

Bud looked over the questions from the *Pulse* and started reading them to Paul. They agreed on most of the questions, and where they didn't agree they wrote separate answers from each of them. It was during this rehearsal of questions and answers that Bud sent Deborah a text.

"May I call you?" he texted.

Deborah was lying on the beach with her protection detail about 20 feet behind her, sitting on a blanket, when her phone buzzed.

She smiled and wrote back, "Yes, but only if you call me now."

Her phone rang within two minutes, but she answered, "What took you so long?"

Bud laughed and told her he just wanted to check up on her and see how she was doing. She told him she had not been so relaxed in quite a while, and the same went for her father.

"That's good," Bud replied.

Deborah continued, "I'm a little nervous about Patty getting out on bail, though. I'm not ready to speak with her."

Bud answered quickly, "You have nothing to worry about. First of all, she's not getting out, and if she did, she won't be able to leave the state 'til her trial."

"No," Deborah replied. "They are working on some sort of bail deal to get her out but Patty only agreed if she gets to talk to me first."

Bud's face flushed as he listened to Deborah.

"Hello? Bud, are you there?"

"Ah, yes," he replied. "Deborah, I will call you back; I need to check on something."

"OK," she answered, and the call went *click* before she could say goodbye.

"This fucking game is getting out of hand! I'm going to the courthouse! Are you coming?" he said to Paul.

"Are you going to tell me what this is about?" Paul asked.

"You better come! You may need to stop me from shooting someone!"

They jumped in the car as Bud told him what he had found out from Debbie. A deal was in the making for the release of Patty Saunders, and Cronin had kept them in the dark. They were about 20 minutes behind the detective lieutenant and the assistant district attorney, and Bud was hoping old Judge Green would keep them waiting a bit.

While they were driving out to Riverhead, Paul called Sherry to check in on her. The hero officer told Paul she would be going home the next day. Seven days and going home. Not bad. Sherry told him that Rachelle would be stopping by her room for a visit after her therapy session upstairs.

"Tell her I said hello. Bud's driving but wants to say hello. Putting you on speaker."

Bud started singing, and Sherry just said, "Oh, Lordy," and hung up.

"Well, I guess she's getting better," Paul said.

They pulled off of exit 73 and got to the courthouse but were too late. Cronin and Ashley were already in Judge Green's chambers. Bud stood by the outside office and would not move. The judge's clerk buzzed Judge Green as he started to speak to Simmons, Ashley, and Cronin. His Honor looked up at Cronin and told him he had two restless detectives waiting outside for him.

"They can wait, Your Honor," the detective lieutenant replied.

"OK, then, I have considered this very unusual request, understanding that this is an unusual case. I will give Patty Saunders bail on arraignment but not for one and a half million dollars but for two million dollars, and she must have an ankle monitor and a bulletproof vest when she leaves the house. In addition, I don't want the money given to the bail bondsman to be anonymous. I want a name attached to it. Take it or leave it. I'll give you five minutes to discuss it. I'll be right back; coffee goes right through me."

Ashley started speaking first.

"I don't think Steinberg thought the judge would raise the stakes," Simmons spoke.

"We are still agreeable, it's you guys that have to come up with the money."

They both looked at Cronin for his thoughts. He looked at Ashley, "It's agreeable, do it."

Ashley pulled him aside to whisper to him,

"Does Lance want his name in this?"

"It won't be his name." Cronin replied.

"Listen!" Ashley said in a loud whisper. "Whose name will be on the bail?

Cronin smiled, "It will be Robert Simpson"

Ashley pulled Cronin again. "Our careers are on the line here"

Cronin said it again, "Simpson, Robert Simpson" as he stepped away from Ashley

Judge Green came back to his office and was told they were in agreement. The judge told them the arraignment would be in four hours and to get Saunders ready for release. Simmons spoke to Ashley and Cronin as they were walking out about the phone call that was needed between Patty and Deborah Lance before the arraignment. Cronin said he would take care of it through the father.

As they hit the hallway, Bud walked up fast toward Cronin, interrupting their conversation. He said, "Just what the fuck is going on?"

Paul came up behind Bud to ensure he wouldn't do something foolish to the boss. Bud continued, "You are not telling us everything, and you may be jeopardizing this case and lives! What's going on?"

Cronin calmly looked at Detective Johnson and said, "Just do your job; you will understand."

"No!" Bud replied. "You understand something. I will do my job, and I will figure it out, no matter who it hurts."

"I'm counting on it," Cronin replied.

Bud started to walk away, when Cronin called out to him, "Detective!"

With his back still to him, Bud stopped as Cronin spoke. "Don't call Debbie Lance anymore until this case is over. Get right with it or go home, understood?" Bud didn't answer but started to walk away as Paul looked at Cronin.

"This is not you. Why?" Paul asked.

"I've told you everything I can. Get back to the precinct with Bud. Later, check on ballistics on Allan's bullet and the Anderson family. We will have a meeting after Saunders' release around 3:30 pm to discuss how we are going to handle her."

Paul just looked at him as well as the assistant district attorney and Simmons, nodded, and walked away. Cronin dialed a number while Simmons and Ashley heard him speak to William Lance about having his daughter speak to Patty in about three hours. He disconnected the call to tell both Ashley and Simmons it was a done deal.

Deborah got to her house on Collier Boulevard, where her father was waiting for her. He spoke to her about why it was important she speak to Patty. After about 30 minutes of yelling and crying, she finally agreed to do it.

Officer Healey was, as usual, on time to relieve Dugan from being Lindsey's escort to take her to school, when he got the call from Cronin.

"Sir," Healey answered the phone.

"Officer, get in plainclothes. You are now moving into Lindsey's house and will be responsible for her safety 24 hours a day 'til this case is over. Got it?"

"Yes, sir," Healey replied. No questions, he understood.

Cronin disconnected and called Lindsey's father to request Officer Healey's presence at all times because of where they were in the case. The father was only too happy and told him the guest room was next door to Lindsey's. They disconnected as Cronin looked out the window. Ashley was trying to look at him while he was driving.

"Anything to say?" he said to Cronin.

The detective lieutenant looked at Ashley and said, "This is where the game gets interesting. There's no going back now, my friend." Ashley just shook his head.

Cronin spoke again, saying, "Have them bring Patty down to the precinct. I'd like to hear the conversation."

"I'll bring the popcorn," Ashley remarked. Then he paused before speaking again. "Your man, Bud Johnson, is getting a little worked up."

"We all are," the detective lieutenant answered. "They are not used to me being so active in a case. They are good cops, but I've been through a few difficult cases in my career as well. The publicity and pressure needs my involvement, whether they want to admit it or not; hopefully they will understand when it's over."

The assistant district attorney nodded and said, "I agree with your experience and taking the active responsibility on a case such as this, but it's clear, no one knows everything you are doing, and that tells me you're not sure if you can trust them."

Cronin nodded and said, "Let me just say, we are going to find out who can be trusted in the next 24 to 48 hours."

Ashley continued, "What about Healey?"

Cronin laughed and said, "I trust him to keep the girl protected, and I feel sorry for the poor bastard who attempts anything on his watch. He's so gung-ho I'm surprised he doesn't have a couple knives in his socks somewhere. His job is the girl. He's not involved in any other part of this case."

Ashley went into the precinct with Cronin, and they were informed by Gina that Patty would be brought to the interview room within 25 minutes.

Cronin was in his office when Bud came in with the *Long Island*

Pulse questions and answers.

"Thank you," Cronin said. "Just leave them on the desk, I'll take a look at it and let you know."

As Bud reached the door to exit, Cronin spoke, saying, "Bud, Patty Saunders is going to have a conversation with Debbie Lance. You are welcome to listen to it so we can discuss her release at the arraignment today."

Bud turned around slowly and looked at the detective lieutenant before he asked, "You are really going to do this?"

"Yes. Do you want to listen in on the conversation?" Cronin replied.

"Who managed to work out a release for her?" Bud asked.

Ashley spoke up, saying, "We made the arrangements, but it was his idea," pointing at Cronin.

"Why am I not surprised?" Bud said.

"Yes or No?" Cronin asked.

"Yes," Bud said.

"OK," Cronin said. "She will be sitting in the interrogation room with the speakerphone on. We will be in the room, but we guaranteed we would not interrupt or speak during the conversation. Can you keep your promise?"

"Yes," Bud replied.

"One more thing," Cronin replied, starting to leave the room. "Don't bring your gun or your car keys in the room with you."

Cronin went to Paul's desk as he left Bud in the room with Ashley. Bud stared at Cronin as he spoke to the assistant district attorney. "Was that a joke? Was he trying to be funny?"

"Yes," Ashley said, smiling. "I thought it was humorous."

Bud looked at him and said, "I still have my gun, smartass."

Ashley's smile was erased as Bud pointed his finger at him and said, "Gotcha," and laughed all the way to his desk. Cronin had just finished telling Paul to get officers assigned to the outside of the Wilkerson house from 8:00 pm to 7:00 am while Healey was inside the house during the night.

"Once you get the schedule, go down to the school and go over it with Healey, see if he is comfortable with your selections. Give him a voice, he is the one with the girl's life in his hands."

Paul got up to look at the duty roster and schedules for the next couple nights as Patty Saunders was led to the interrogation room.

"OK, everyone. Time to put on the seat belts," Cronin said. "There's no going back after this. By the way," he whispered in Bud's ear, "the deal struck with Saunders is discussed with no one as of now. No one. I know Paul knows, but no one else."

"Understood," Bud answered.

When they got to the interrogation room, Simmons was sitting with Patty, and Bud, Cronin, and Ashley each took a seat as Patty dialed Deborah's cell phone number. It rang four times before Deborah Lance picked up.

"Hello, Patty. I didn't want to pick up, but a promise is a promise."

"I know, Debbie. I know you won't believe me, but I never thought it would be like this. I swear. To prove it, I only have my life to lose and only a few years shaved off my prison sentence if I make it. I'm doing this to help finish this case for everyone but mostly for you."

"Don't do anything else for me, Patty. You not only almost cost me my life, but you took my dignity, my relationship with Robert, and almost my father. And for what! You call yourself a friend?"

Deborah started to cry as Patty said, "I'm sorry. I hope when my life is over, you will see it as a token from me to try and make what I can right."

"You have my attention, Patty. What else do you want?"

"I want you to know that no matter what happens from this point on that I know I was wrong and I will regret losing you as my friend because of this."

"Hello? Reality check," Deborah answered. "Patty, this one thing you thought would be so smooth and end so quickly cost eight people their lives already! And it's not over."

"It will be, Debbie," Patty replied. "I just wanted to hear your voice one last time. I know you can never forgive me, but I wanted to say it."

Deborah was crying and said, "You have hurt me beyond what anyone who considered me a friend could do. I have to go now. Good luck, Patty. I don't want to see anything happen to you, but I think it's fair to say you brought it on yourself."

"Yes, you are right, Debbie. This will be over, and you can come back to Long Island soon."

"Goodbye, Patty."

"Bye, Debbie. Thank you for speaking with me." *Click.*

As Deborah disconnected, she covered her face to hide her tears.

"OK," Patty said, "I'm ready."

"First," Cronin said, "I would like to have a private conversation with Ms. Saunders."

"Hold on," Simmons balked.

"Counselor," Cronin said, "her rights are protected; however, she's not going anywhere without a couple minutes with me. You can look through the glass windows if you wish, but I believe it's important to the case to speak privately with her."

"It's OK," Patty remarked.

They walked into Cronin's office as Bud, Ashley, and Simmons looked at the two of them.

"What the hell is this?" Simmons remarked.

"Hey," Bud said, "things could be worse. How about a song?"

Simmons raised up his hand and said, "Stay away from me, you freak."

As Cronin spoke privately with Patty, Bud sent Deborah a text asking her if she was all right. She answered back, asking him to call her. He shook his head and wrote back to her that he was directed not to speak to her until the case was over.

"I'm sorry," he wrote. "I lost my temper with the boss about you having to speak with Patty."

She wrote back, "I'm sorry too. Don't forget about me."

He answered back, "This will be over soon, and I want you to come back and spend some time with the funny man."

"Promise," she wrote. "I'm OK now, thank you."

Bud's thoughts were interrupted by Simmons, who said, "Hello to earth! Anybody home?"

Bud started singing "You Can Call Me Al" again just to see if he could get a rise out of the attorney, at the very least annoy him a bit more.

Simmons looked over at Ashley and said, "He must be getting laid tonight."

"Where did you say you lived?" Bud asked.

"I didn't," Simmons said, with his smile gone.

"Oh, that's right. Guess I'll have to look it up," Bud said as he went to his desk.

Simmons looked at Ashley and asked, "He's not dangerous, is he?"

"Well," Ashley said, "he did shoot Kyle Winters in the groin."

"Funny," Simmons said. Bud sat at his computer and signed on to Twitter and sang more lyrics from the song. The ADA and Simmons walked away while Bud continued until he signed off and started looking at the pile of paperwork.

Healey was sitting in the back of the room during history class. He sat in amazement as Lindsey led the class through the Revolutionary War period. She was so far ahead of her class that some of the teachers had her "teach" as part of her grade. Some had wanted to push her to high school; however, Ms. Meghan, her favorite teacher from this particular class, felt strongly that, as smart as Lindsey was, she was emotionally immature and convinced her parents she would regress to age 12 with the older kids. As a compromise, she stayed in the sixth grade but took math,science and history classes on the senior level one day a week at the high school.

Healey watched the girl he was becoming very fond of and was concerned about whether he could keep her alive. He had no doubt whoever put a bullet in Allan's head would eliminate her in a second. As fond as he was of her, he had not spoken much in conversation with her, but she let him know she felt protected with him. As the class continued, he noticed Paul outside the door waving to him to come out in the hallway. Healey wrote a note and held it up for him to read. It read, "She's not leaving my sight. Please come in."

Paul opened the door as the whole class turned their heads.

"Sorry, class," Paul said as he sat down with Healey.

Ms. Meghan came to the back to greet Paul and said, "Hello there. I assume this is really important to interrupt my class."

"I'm sorry, ma'am, but my partner in crime here did not want to lose sight of Lindsey, so I had to come in."

"Well," the teacher replied, "next time you want to come to my classroom, please knock and let me know what is it you wish to do. It's only a courtesy that I ask."

"Yes, ma'am. I'm sorry."

"Please don't call me 'ma'am,'" the teacher replied.

"What is your name?" Paul replied.

"In this class, you call me Ms. Meghan."

"Oh," Paul replied. "I apologize, Ms. Meghan. It won't happen again."

As she walked away, Healey was smiling. Ms. Meghan was actually a young thirtyish woman who, although very pretty, would not take any shit from anyone, especially when it came to respecting her classroom. Most of the teachers used their last name at the school but Meghan preferred using her first as long as they respected her using Ms in front of her name. Apparently, she expected the same when it came to the adults in her class. Healey amused himself with his thoughts. *she is so pretty, if I asked her out for a drink, I wonder if she would still make me call her Ms. Meghan.* His thoughts were interrupted by the sound of Paul's voice.

"I'm getting shit from everyone today," Paul said. He pulled out the schedule for overnight duty in the car for the next few days and nights. It showed Dugan from 5:00 am to 5:00 pm, Chapman from 11:00 am to 2:00 pm to give Dugan a break between. Paul had Officer Franks from 5:00 pm to 5:00 am with O'Brien overlapping and giving Franks a break from 11:00 pm to 2:00 am. Healey looked over the list silently while Lindsey continued reviewing the writing of the Declaration of Independence.

"I would be more comfortable," Healey spoke, "if Dugan and Franks switched shifts. I'd rather have him outside while I'm trying to get some sleep, if you don't mind."

"No worries," Paul answered. "Consider it done. This starts now." Paul sent a text to the precinct to inform them of the schedule and to send Franks over to the Wilkerson house and for Dugan to get some sleep.

"How's the girl doing?" Paul whispered.

"She is the most amazing girl I've ever met," Healey answered. He continued, "Just have a conversation with her; you'll see what I mean. A real gift to anyone who knows her."

Paul nodded and said, "Or dangerous."

Ms. Meghan dismissed the class, and Lindsey came to the back to Healey and to greet Paul.

"Hello, Detective Powers."

"Hi, Lindsey, how are you doing?" he asked her.

Her attention went back to Healey, and she said, "I have a surprise for you." Healey just stared at her. She pulled out a sketch she had drawn of the officer while he was in the back of the class.

"How did you do this without looking at me?" Healey asked.

Lindsey giggled and said, "From memory, silly. Let me get my books."

Paul and Healey just looked at each other.

"See?" Paul said. "Dangerous."

Paul walked with Lindsey and Healey to her next class and decided to have the conversation with her as her escort suggested.

"You're pretty smart, aren't you?"

Lindsey smiled and said, "I think I'm fairly intelligent. Well, I think you're pretty smart also." Lindsey laughed.

"Who," Paul continued, "do you think is the smartest person in the world?"

"Christopher Langan," she answered, "his IQ has been measured between 195 and 210. He developed his own theory of the relationship between mind and reality, which he calls 'the Cognitive-Theoretic Model of the Universe.'"

"Interesting," Paul said. "When we have more time, will you tell me more about him?"

"Yes," she answered. "I think you will find him interesting. He rose to prominence right here on Long Island."

As Lindsey reached her next class, Paul spoke again. He said, "Lindsey, the photo Detective Cronin showed you at the car. You remember, right?"

"Yes, of course," she answered.

He bent down to her and said, "Can you draw me a sketch of who the person was?"

Lindsey looked up at Healey then back at Paul. "Um, I'm not sure. Um, Detective Cronin asked me not to tell anyone."

"You wouldn't be telling me, Lindsey. You would be drawing me a sketch."

"Well, I suppose it would be fine as long as he wouldn't get mad at me."

"No," Paul said. "He won't get mad at you, I promise. If he gets mad, it will be at me. And besides, Officer Healey is here to be sure no one gets mad at you."

She smiled and agreed to draw him a sketch that he would have the next day. As intelligent as she was, there still could be manipulation at the age of 12.

"Thank you very much, Lindsey. Enjoy the rest of your day." As she walked into class, Paul looked at Healey, who kept his eyes on her, and said, "You got your hands full, my friend."

Healey smiled and said, "Tell me about it," as he walked into the class.

Paul walked outside to begin his ride over to the lab to check on the ballistics of the bullets, and then he was going over to the Anderson home. The funeral was today, and Paul was thinking maybe of holding off until the morning. He checked his Twitter and saw Bud's tweet. He thought, *Please, this has to end soon*. He promised himself he would do everything to be sure it would come to a conclusion.

After a few minutes of conversation, Cronin opened the door to his office and told Patty, "Good luck at the arraignment."

She met up with Simmons and a police escort until the arraignment with Judge Green in a few hours. Simmons wanted to review some things with her.

Ashley walked in Cronin's office and shut the door. He said, "I suppose you are not going to tell me what the hell is going on?"

"Believe me, my friend," the detective lieutenant answered, "you don't want to know, at least not now."

Ashley raised his hands in the air and said, "You're right, I don't. But I do have to do my job and uphold the law, Kevin."

The detective lieutenant stopped what he was doing and looked at the assistant district attorney and said, "Have I ever asked you to do anything other?"

"No," Ashley said, "but you have me scared on this one."

"It's all going to work out. Simpson will go through with the bail money, and you make sure Judge Green doesn't take a coffee break during the arraignment."

Ashley shook his head and said, "I'll take care of it. Who's going to keep an eye on her once she is released?"

"Bud and Paul, for starters," he answered. "Then we will pull them off her and put uniforms on her."

"OK, I'm leaving," the assistant district attorney said. "I can't hear any more of this."

Cronin laughed as he shut the door. He picked up the phone and pushed Robert Simpson's cell phone number. He answered.

"You're on. Don't screw it up, or I'll send Officer Lynagh over there to spend a few nights with you. Patty will be released in about four hours."

He disconnected and then called William Lance, who picked up within a couple rings. "OK, Mr. Lance. The game will be reaching the climax soon. Please deposit the money to the bail bondsman, $200,000,. Thank you and don't forget to call our friend."

William Lance had agreed to do what Detective Lieutenant Cronin wanted him to do because Cronin had convinced him this was the best way to stop the bloodshed.

Cronin walked over to Bud as he was shuffling his papers and said, "Make sure you are going to the arraignment today. Stay with Patty and get her settled the first few hours."

As he walked away, Bud began talking to himself, saying, "Do you want me to clean the bathroom, shine your shoes, and feed your pets also?"

Cronin's voice bellowed from the other side of the room. "Not now, but if you screw this up, you may need a new job."

Bud couldn't believe he had heard him and said, "Sorry, boss," as he gave Paul a call to see what was going on.

Cronin sat down at his desk and looked at the *Long Island Pulse* interview with Paul and Bud. He had asked his secretary to furnish him with additional information on the magazine with an issue. He looked through it and thought it was very well put together. It was an older issue given to him from Gina, dated March, 2011, that had NBC news anchor Soledad O'Brien on the cover. It was an easy read and very informative about local events on Long Island. Almost like the *Port Jefferson Now* except that was a newspaper form with this being in the form of a magazine.

Under the words *Publisher* and *Editor* was the name Nada Marjanovich, who had been in occasional communication with Bud through email over the years. He also noticed the names under *Intern* and saw The Shannyn T, while everyone else had a regular name. He smiled and noticed in the back of the issue why Bud enjoyed reading it so much. A page filled with interesting facts or great trivia appeared to be a regular feature called "Pulse Rate."

So, he thought to himself, *this must be a source of all his trivia shit.* He was surprised to read that 75 percent of all gold in use across the world has only been out of the ground since 1910. He looked at the notes Gina gave him, and it stated the magazine had a 100,000 monthly circulation and was published 10 times a year. He was satisfied to let the interview be published in the issue as he started reviewing the questions and answers.

They were all pretty basic, such as, "How does it feel to be involved in the highest-profile case in Long Island history?" Both Bud and Paul had each answered the questions well, and he saw no problem with the interview until the last question.

"Do you have any potential suspects in the case, and when do you estimate it will be resolved?" Bud had answered, "We have people of interest in the case and those we are checking carefully. We believe, based on the evidence we have compiled, this case will be coming to a close soon." Paul had answered, "I expect the case to be resolved shortly. Our goal is to stop the killing as soon as possible."

Cronin wrote down his answer: "We know who is responsible for the killing of innocent people, and the case will be over by the time this article is published. As for the killings by the person wearing the Ghost Face mask, we hope to have it resolved once we arrest the person responsible for killing three innocent people."

He handed it to Gina to type and send back to the offices of the *Long Island Pulse*, Attn: The Shannyn T. As Gina typed she stopped as she read what Detective Lieutenant Cronin had written.

She pushed her speakerphone button and asked, "Sir, are you sure this is what you want me to send?"

"Yes," Cronin answered.

He sat there with his thoughts and knew he should have checked with legal before sending it in, but he knew they would have stopped him. He had never felt so strongly about a case. He knew this was the right thing to do, and he knew that the *Long Island Pulse* would get it out sooner than the release next week. He thought to himself, *Let the games begin. Now let's separate the men from the boys.*

Gina was finished within five minutes and walked in to her boss's office and said, "Sir, I'm ready to send it through email."

"Go ahead," Cronin said. "It's OK, Gina."

She sat down at her desk and pushed *enter*.

The Shannyn T was talking to her pet fish, Pocky, when the email came in, and when she got to the last question that had Cronin's statements, she started flapping her hands in a violent motion, which was common when she was either excited or extremely nervous. She read his answer three times, and it didn't change. She printed it out and ran into Nada's office to show her the interview.

"Read the last question!" The Shannyn T yelled.

As Nada read it, her face turned red. She looked up at her intern and said, "If you were getting paid, I'd give you a raise," and they both laughed.

Nada picked up her cell phone and called the precinct to speak to Kevin Cronin. She was put through to him right away.

"Thank you, sir, for the information. As you know, our issue is not published until next week. However, due to the nature of your statement, I would like to release it to the networks right away."

Cronin paused for a moment then said, I had a feeling I would be hearing from you. Thanks for asking. I would be fine with you releasing it, but it would be helpful if you released it to the networks tomorrow morning."

Nada replied, "Tomorrow morning it is. If I may," she continued, "why release this to us instead of a *Newsday* or a *New York Post*?"

"Well," Cronin answered, "Bud told me that, although he never met you, you were always cordial and always replied to him with every email, no matter what the contents were. I like that in a businessperson. We are all getting so caught up in our lives that we need to give some time to those who have shown us we are in their thoughts. You never asked him for a story or an interview. I think he appreciated it, and I wanted to respect his opinion on giving you the information."

Nada was appreciative of his remarks and promised she would hold it until the morning. Cronin disconnected and turned on the little television that was in his office.

Phil's disposable cell phone rang, and he picked it up before it rang for the second time.

The voice on the other end began talking, saying, "Patty Saunders is going to be released on bail today."

"What?" Phil interrupted.

"Shut up and listen!" The voice on the other end said. "You are going to meet three guys at the McDonald's in Miller Place at 8:00 am tomorrow morning. They will be giving you instructions and what is going down. Their names are not important; you will know who they are."

Phil was getting angry and said, "You are going to have to tell me more than this. Who the fuck are these guys, and how the hell can we trust them? And even if we can, there are only so many ways to split the five million. Besides, I know there is really only three million in cash at the house."

The voice on the other end got louder and said, "Leave the worries to me. The three guys you are meeting don't want the cash. They want considerations in return that only I can give them. Simpson is going after the cash to get Saunders on bail. He will have to put $200,000 down today, which means there is $2,800,000 left somewhere. He has to be eliminated as well as Patty, Rachelle Robinson, and the girl." There was silence on Phil's end.

"So," the voice on the other end spoke again. "You got a problem with taking a 12-year-old out?"

"No," Phil answered. "What I have a problem with is taking out four more people in the next 24 hours while they have protection."

"That's what my people will explain to you when they see you. They will help you. The girl remembers every date, every minute, and every detail that she experiences. She cannot be alive when this is over. As for Simpson, I will take care of him myself. He screwed me and now wants to bail out that bitch, and the one no one can seem to kill wants a piece of the action. So they all have to go."

"OK," Phil answered. "I will meet your guys. But one other thing. What about the guy running around as Ghost Face?"

"No problem," the voice said. "First of all, they have a lead on who it may be and think it may possibly be you trying to frame someone. Either way, we don't have to share the money with as many people."

"True," Phil answered. "But how am I going to get off Long Island? They have my photo plastered in print and on the news."

The voice replied, "Not to worry. I will make sure you get off the island. Once Saunders is out on bail, she will contact Simpson for the cash. She has to be wasted before she spends all of it getting her ankle monitor off and trying to disappear. One last thing," the voice said, "just what in the hell are you doing in a Rite Aid store buying Southwest Airline cards for?"

"I thought," Phil replied, "it would be a backup insurance plan to have them if I needed them."

The voice laughed and said, "You still have to give a name and show identification. You are seen on surveillance video, and then you leave a phone number for your membership points."

"It was a disposable phone," Phil said in defense.

"You got rid of it, right?" the voice asked.

"Yes," Phil answered.

"Just keep using the one I gave you," the voice said. "You need me alive to help you, and I need you alive to get rid of the witnesses or anyone that can hurt us."

"In that case," Phil said, "I want that son of a bitch Johnson. I want to put a bullet between his eyes like his friend Allan whatever the fuck his last name was. You should have seen his reaction when he saw me just walk in like a Sunday stroll. It was quite a surprise for him."

"How did the girl get away?" the voice asked.

Phil replied, "Very difficult to explain. She was there in the office with Jones, I saw her, but she was nowhere in sight when I shot him."

"Well," the voice said, "you made me look bad because I had sent a note to the precinct saying their lives were over. You should have seen that asshole running from the precinct to his car when he figured out a simple riddle."

Phil laughed, "He's gotta go before we get out of this place."

"Oh, I have a feeling he will die a slow death," the voice said.

"All right," Phil replied, "let me get ready, and I'll meet your boys."

"Where are you staying?" the voice asked.

"Between the gym for showers and using our friend Anderson's office and the place you let me use on occasion, it's not easy. The *Now* offices are closed temporarily, the gym never checks for more than my gym number. I walk in and rattle off my number with no identification, so I've been washing there. The cash you gave me helps with local motels, so I'm getting by waiting for the big payday."

The voice replied, "Well, you were the smart one. You were the only one who wanted to listen to me, and now look. They are all dead, and you are still here in line to disappear and head for the hills." the voice continued, "But there is more work to be done. Once this wave of killing starts over the next 24 hours, the FBI will take over the entire case for sure. What's the first thing you are going to do with your share?" the voice asked.

Phil answered right away. "I want to get myself to Las Vegas and disappear. No one cares who you are there, as long as you have money. I want to stay at Caesar's Palace, move over to the Bellagio for a few days, head over to the Venetian for a bit, and then even go downtown for a bit."

"So what's your plan?" the voice asked. "To blow your share in a week?"

Phil laughed and said, "No, maybe a few weeks. I won't have a long life anyway. Our plan was to get much more money for the ransom, but I made the mistake of letting John Winters run the show."

"That's right," the voice answered. "All of you should have listened to me from the beginning."

"Well," Phil said, "you have to admit it was a little difficult to realize we could trust you."

"And now," the voice said, "you are the only one left alive as well as the three guys who will meet you tomorrow. They have been listening to me the past year."

"OK, OK," Phil answered. "I understand."

The voice replied, "They will be your contacts from now on. When this is over and we have the cash, you will be sent instructions on where to meet. Good Luck. I almost wish you could take a video of some of this. Ha! Ha!"

Phil moved the phone away from his ear to look at it from a distance with a puzzled look on his face.

"You are a little crazy, aren't you?" Phil replied.

"We all are, don't you think?" the voice asked. "See you in a couple days or on the other side." The phone went *click*.

That's comforting, Phil thought to himself as the man who was the voice to Phil on the phone call checked the battery life left on his disposable phone. He was thinking that Phil was right about one thing, and that was that he would not have a long life. He would make sure of it. The man who was the voice considered Phil a liability that could no longer be afforded. He had already instructed his three messengers to take care of Phil Smith once the task at hand was completed.

Kevin Cronin picked up the call from Assistant District Attorney Ashley asking him if he really was going to skip the arraignment, and the detective lieutenant told him he thought from a national news point of view, it would be best if he wasn't around. He also told him Detective Bud Johnson would be at the arraignment. The assistant district attorney accepted his answer and said he would stop by later, and maybe the two of them would get a drink. Cronin disconnected the call, thinking maybe he should have that drink before the *Long Island Pulse* released the interview the next day. It might be his last chance, he thought.

He called Gina in to have her find out where everyone was. "Everyone" meaning the team assigned to this case. That included the four additional officers that would be stationed outside the Wilkersons' house on Bell Circle in the cruisers, so Healey could be with Lindsey on a 24-hour basis inside and outside the house.

Within five minutes, Gina gave him the locations of everyone on the case. He looked at it and then asked Gina for the number to Sherry at the hospital and Rachelle Robinson's home phone number. He called both and spoke to each of them for about five minutes before disconnecting and turning on the television again in his office.

It was a short day for Lindsey at school. Her advanced class teacher was ill, and she got the OK to study at home. The principal was not about to resist considering her academic skills and the whole "escort thing." While he thought it was much better Officer Healey was now wearing civilian clothes, he was concerned over the distraction of the students.

As Lindsey was walking to the car with Healey, it was simply too intimidating for most of the girls and all of the boys to approach Lindsey with Healey's stare-down as they got close to her. He opened the car's passenger door for her and then jogged around the front into the driver's seat. Healey had her at her house within 10 minutes.

As she got out of the car, he asked her to hold up while he got a suitcase of his belongings out of the trunk. He waved to Officer Chapman sitting in the cruiser with a cup of coffee. As they entered the house, Monty came running up to greet Lindsey and wouldn't let her greet her parents. Lindsey's father told Officer Healey he would show him his sleeping quarters and Lindsey's room.

Healey was sometimes considered extreme, but in this particular case he did not care. He told the father the doors must be locked and Lindsey was not to go outside the house while she was out of his sight. The house was to be locked at all times, day and night. Healey noticed the windows were already closed and locked for the air conditioning.

When they reached the top of the stairs, Mr. Wilkerson showed Healey Lindsey's room. He walked in and looked at the photos she had on the wall. On one side there was mathematicans, Archimedes,

Einstein, Robert Osserman, and famous historical women mathematicians, Sophie Germain, Hypatia, Ada Lovelace. On the other side the musical groups the Strokes, the Killers, 3oh3, and Muse. *Interesting*, he thought. *Who the hell is Robert Osserman? She is 12 years old on one side of the room, and a genius on the other side.*

He laughed as he looked out her window, which was above the front lawn, and he could see the cruiser parked on the road. Her dad, Walter, then showed him the room he would be using, which was the guest room. It was convenient and next door, with a private bathroom. He told Walter that Lindsey should be in the guest bedroom so she would not have to go into the hallway to use the bathroom. If she balked at the idea, then the officer asked him for a cot to be used in the hallway outside her door. He would only be a certain distance from her, to where he could hear anything, and the cot would allow him to be within a foot of her door yet still give her privacy. In addition, if she had to use the bathroom in the middle of the night, it would awaken him and he would stay awake until she was back in her room.

Lindsey told her dad she wanted to stay in her own room, which meant they had to pull a cot they had from the attic for Healey to use during the overnight hours. Justin Healey unpacked his clothes in the guest room and went back downstairs as Lindsey's mom prepared a late lunch.

Healey received a call from Officer Chapman that Bud was on his way to the front door. Lindsey greeted him with a huge hug, as did Monty.

"Boy," Bud said, "this is such a great welcome."

"You're just in time for lunch," Mrs. Wilkerson said.

"Oh, wow, thank you. I love to eat," Bud replied. "I just came to speak to Officer Healey about today."

"You have to eat your lunch!" Lindsey said.

"Actually, this is perfect," her father said. "Sharyn and I have to go down to BJ's Wholesale Club to pick up a few things with our additional guest, and you guys can have lunch with Lindsey until we get back."

"Sure, Mr. Wilkerson," Bud replied.

"Please, call me Walter."

"Thank you," Bud answered.

They were gone within five minutes as the three of them sat down with the lunch of sandwiches and salad Sharyn Wilkerson had left for them.

"How did the day go?" Bud asked, looking at them.

"Smooth day," Healey said. "School, no problems, Paul stopped in to go over the schedule of officers outside."

Bud nodded and said, "Good, good. So you had a chance to speak with Detective Powers for a change."

"Yes," Lindsey answered. "He's a very nice man, and I must say he's very handsome."

"Hey, now," Bud replied. "You're 12 years old. What do you know about being handsome?"

She laughed and said, "You're a funny guy, Detective Johnson."

"Yes," he said with a smile. "That's what they tell me." Bud remembered that Lindsey would not volunteer information, so he was thinking about the next question for her.

"Did Paul ask you any questions?"

"Yes," Lindsey answered, "he asked me five questions."

Bud nodded and said, "Five questions. Could you tell me the questions he asked you?"

Lindsey replied, "In order or random?"

Bud tilted his head and asked, "Are you showing off right now with me?"

Lindsey laughed and said, "OK, I'll tell you in order. First question: 'You're pretty smart, aren't you?' Second question: 'Who do you think the smartest person in the world is, Lindsey?' Third question: 'When we have more time, will you tell me more about him?' Fourth question: Lindsey, the photo Detective Cronin showed you at the car, you remember, right?' Fifth question:'Can you draw me a sketch of who the person was?' These were the questions in order, Detective Johnson."

Bud stared at her in amazed silence as he said, "Lindsey, that's great. When you finish the sketch, I want you to show it to Officer Healey first so we can save time and he can call both myself and Detective Powers."

"OK," she replied.

Once again, Bud remembered the first time he had met Lindsey. She could remember everything, but she would not volunteer information or process what is important to say if she wasn't directly asked.

"Lindsey," Bud said, "did you see Allan get shot?"

He saw the girl start trembling, so he took her hand.

"It's all right, please tell me."

"Yes," she said.

"You never told anyone?" Bud said as a tear rolled down her cheek, her voice trembling.

"No one asked me." Bud looked up at Justin Healey, who promptly started checking the ammunition levels of his gun.

"Tell us what happened," Bud said. As Lindsey began to talk, the detective sent a text to Gina to get with Cronin and have Paul be at the arraignment, that there had been a development with Lindsey. He wrote, "She is safe, but we may have to increase security."

Lindsey spoke, saying, "I was going to school late so I walked over to see Allan. He was so nice to me and he told me how much the two of you loved my cookies."

"Yes," Bud said, "go on." "We were playing checkers, and I was making him laugh by showing him eight moves in advance if I was going to win, and then…" The young girl started to stutter.

"It's OK," Bud said, "we are here."

And then she continued, "Allan looked up and saw someone running toward the front door. He said, 'Quick! Hide! Don't say a word, no matter what happens.' I crawled inside the opening of the desk, and he slid his chair with his legs into the desk opening, totally hiding me. The man came in and said, 'Where is the girl? Where is the girl? Where is the girl?' Three times."

As Lindsey started to cry, Bud squeezed her hand as Healey started looking out the windows. Finally she spoke again, saying, "'She just left to bake me more cookies,' Allan told him. Then the man shot him in the head, looked around, and went to the video monitor. He took the recording and shot the machine. Then he said, 'Come out, come out, wherever you are.' I was having trouble breathing without making noise, but he finally left. I waited another 10 minutes before I could move."

"Then what?" Bud asked.

"I got up and had to push Allan's chair out a bit so I could get out. I put my hand on his face and I said I was sorry to him, and I...I kissed the side of his head and began to run home. I was afraid if the man saw me he would shoot me and my dog."

"Wait," Bud said, "why your dog?"

"Well," she said, "he took my dog and shot Allan. Why wouldn't he shoot my dog?"

Bud could see Healey was getting more and more antsy as her story unfolded.

"Lindsey," Bud said, "did you see the man's face?"

"No," she answered. "But it was the man who took Monty. I remember voices as well as images and numbers." Bud looked up at Healey as Lindsey spoke again.

"I have to use the bathroom, Officer Healey."

"Go ahead, Lindsey," he said as she walked into the bathroom and shut the door.

Justin Healey started talking right away to Bud, saying, "We need another person here, and I want a shotgun to have in the house, and I assume the cruiser outside has a shotgun."

There was no objection from Bud as he started to make a call to the precinct. He had hung up by the time Lindsey came back to the table.

"So," Bud said, "the man in the sketch you are going to draw for Detective Powers. Is it the man who shot Allan?"

"No," Lindsey said.

"Had you ever seen the man before?" Bud asked. "Can you draw the sketch now?"

"I'm sorry," she replied. "I'm too tired, and it won't be good if I do it now, but yes I have seen the man before, which I told Detective Cronin."

"OK, OK," Bud said.

Officer Healey spoke up, saying, "I'm going outside to speak with Franks. He's back from his break, and I want to bring both Chapman and him up to date while they are here. I'll call Dugan after I'm finished speaking with them."

Bud nodded as Lindsey spoke to Healey in a nervous tone, asking, "Where are you going?"

He came back to her and kneeled, saying, "Listen, honey, I have to bring the other officers the new information so everyone understands how serious this is. You understand, right? Detective Johnson is not going anywhere 'til I get back. I will only be in the front yard."

"OK," she replied with a smile. As the front door shut, Bud looked at Lindsey looking at the empty space by the door.

"You like Officer Healey, don't you?"

"Yes," she replied. "He's a good protector; I trust him."

"Yes," Bud answered. "He's a good cop and a good protector. So when Paul asked you who the smartest person was in the world, who did you answer?"

A smile came back on her face, and she said, "I told him Christopher Langan, his IQ is very high.."

"Ahh, he must be Irish. So tell me," Bud said, "does the smartest person in the world believe in God?" The question surprised Lindsey, but she was up to the challenge.

"Well," she said, "Christopher Langan has been quoted as saying that he believes in the theory, which means he believes that evolution including the principle of natural selection is one of the tools used by God to create mankind. He believes that there is a level on which science and religious metaphor are mutually compatible."

Lindsey went on that when she went to his website that Christopher Langan wrote, quote, "since biblical accounts of the genesis of our world and species are true but metaphorical, our task is to correctly decipher the metaphor in light of scientific evidence also given to us by God."

Bud asked, "And when did you visit his website?"

"March 6, 2010," She answered.

"Are you sure?" Bud teased her.

"No doubt in my mind," she laughed.

"You, Lindsey," Bud asked. "Do you believe in God?"

"I believe there is a superior being that is connected to our source of knowledge. Our soul or being spiritual is what makes us whole. When I think about what causes high tide and low tide of the ocean each day, it makes me think there is a God that gives us the knowledge as to why these things happen. When the Earth rotates 180 degrees in 12 hours and the moon meanwhile rotates six degrees around the Earth in 12 hours. It helps with my faith that someone is the director."

Healey walked in as Bud was telling Lindsey what an amazing girl she was as well as a baker. Bud excused himself and walked over to Healey and said, "The extra shotgun will be sent with Dugan tonight. That way you have one in the cruiser and one in the house. I assume you are qualified?" Healey shot him a look with cross-eyes.

"Yeah, I guess you are," Bud said.

"OK," Healey said. "But we should have someone from emergency service with an MP5 over here."

"If," Bud replied, "we knew for certain they were going to make an attempt, yes, but let me discuss it further with Cronin. Listen," Bud continued, "I will come over tonight for a few hours, then Paul will relieve me or we both will be here for about six hours so you can get some shuteye. Tomorrow night we will work something out, maybe even bring Dugan in the house so you can get some sleep during the night." Healey nodded.

An MP5 is a select switch-type machine gun that has one bullet round, three bullet rounds, and a setting for a full-round burst, and Bud was not sure if they would want a weapon like that in a residential home.

"You won't be alone, Justin. I know this changes a few things, but what the hell? Between Sherry, Rachelle, and now Lindsey, the taxpayers have a heavy cost with this one." Healey looked over at Lindsey at the kitchen table then back at Bud.

"I've been doing this a long time, I'm worried about who we are dealing with here. This is not going to be pretty, I feel it."

Lindsey interrupted them, saying, "I also am very good at hearing."

Bud turned around and asked the girl, "Is there anything you can't do?"

"Yes," she replied. "I can't swim. I'm afraid of the water."

"Well," Bud answered, "I'm sure you could write a thesis on the scientific reasons why you can't swim."

Lindsey gave him a face and answered, "I'd rather write the scientific reasons why a plane should not be able to fly based on the way they are built," and she stuck her tongue out.

"Ah," Bud said, "we are going to have to have that discussion later before I fly to Los Angeles next month. Until then, can you go in the bathroom for a few minutes and turn on the fan. This is serious police business."

Lindsey huffed and puffed as she went into the bathroom and shut the door. Bud looked at the door and spoke. "That kid is really going to have a husband one day and a family, I hope I'm around to see that."

Healey answered, "I hope we are all around.

"Listen," Bud said, "I have to get to the courthouse and see what's going on, but we will be back. I think over the next 24 to 48 hours we should consider whether we want the parents going out on their own."

"Yeah, I agree," the officer replied.

Bud said, "Let me say goodbye to Lindsey, and I'll see you later."

As he walked toward the door, it opened. "Were you listening to us?" he asked.

"No," she smiled. "I heard footsteps coming toward the door." He looked back at Healey then looked back at the young girl.

"You like playing with me, don't you?"

"Yes," she smiled. "You're a funny guy."

He nodded again and said, "That's what they tell me." He smiled and said, "I'll see you later." Lindsey smiled back.

"Bud," Lindsey said, "it is faith that sometimes gives you the extra incentive or power to do more than what you originally intended to do."

The detective stared at her for a moment and was very touched by her comment. He walked back to Lindsey and gave her a hug. "I'll see you later, special girl."

"OK," she said. As he walked out the door, Lindsey yelled, "Hey, Officer Healey, how about I teach you how to play Angry Birds?" Bud waved to Franks as he got in his car to drive to the arraignment. He called Paul to find out if he was in the courtroom awaiting Judge Green, and his partner answered he was. Assistant District Attorney Ashley, Saunders, Simmons, as well as FBI Agents Sherman and O'Connor were in the courtroom as well.

"OK," Bud said, "thanks for getting there for me. I'll explain when I get there what's going on now. As Cronin would say, 'The game just got a little more challenging.'"

Before he turned on the car, Bud looked up to the sky. "I hope you don't mind that I did some verifying today. If you are all right with Lindsey, then you're OK with me also. Please remember my request, and I will keep my word."

He turned on the ignition and started driving out to Riverhead. As usual, when Bud drove alone, he had time to fill his mind with many thoughts. On this particular drive he was wondering why Cronin only showed Lindsey one photograph. His BlackBerry buzzed with a text from Nada thanking him for the terrific interview and the exclusive. He sent her a quick text back—"YW," for "You're welcome"—while he was driving. Of course, he had no idea what she was so excited about. Like everyone else, except, of course, Cronin, no one else knew. Yet in the morning, the whole world would know that the Suffolk County Police Department, through the words of Detective Lieutenant Cronin, knew who was responsible for all of this.

Bud lost so much track of time that he was at exit 69 on the expressway before he knew it. He noticed the radio was playing "Teenage Dream" by Katy Perry. Normally he would be singing along with it, but this time his mind was too distracted. He spoke aloud in the car, saying, "Too much going on."

It was another 10 minutes before Bud turned off the Long Island Expressway on exit 73 and drove to the court building. It was 3:50 pm by the time Bud met Paul in the courtroom, and his timing was perfect. Judge Green was delayed with other *State of New York vs. People* arraignments, and the Patty Saunders hearing was just getting under way.

Bud whispered to Paul, "More problems. Lindsey witnessed Allan's murder. Your friend was also a hero; he hid her inside the desk opening with his legs. This is why he was sitting there. If he got up to fight off Phil, she would have been seen. We'll talk after this."

Paul looked at Bud and put his hand to his forehead. His thoughts were with his friend, Allan, who had saved Lindsey's life.

The bailiff started talking, saying, "The People versus Patricia Saunders." Assistant District Attorney Ashley began talking to Judge Green for the People's recommendation of bail for $2 million, the surrender of her passport, and the wearing of an ankle monitor.

Judge Green looked over at defense attorney Simmons and asked, "Any comments?"

"No, Your Honor," he replied.

"Excuse me, Your Honor. I'm Special Agent Sherman, this is Special Agent O'Connor. We would appreciate a delay on the bail arraignment."

The judge looked at Agent Sherman and asked, "On what grounds?"

Agent Sherman replied, "We have been requested by the U.S. Attorney to delay this until he can get here to discuss with you."

The judge shrugged his shoulders and asked, "So where is he?"

"He should be here by tomorrow, Your Honor," Agent O'Connor replied.

Judge Green sat in silence as he looked at Ashley and Simmons. Ashley was starting to get a sinking feeling, when the judge surprised himby saying, "I haven't heard a thing. No one from the U.S. Attorney's office has sent me a note, given me a phone call, or even an email about this. Instead, the two of you come into my courtroom and basically object and ask for a delay until it's convenient for him. I don't operate that way. So consider your objection denied. We will proceed unless, of course, the U.S. Attorney walks in during this."

Bud sent Deborah a text during all of this, saying, "This is probably inappropriate, but I wanted you to know I was thinking about you."

She answered back, "Thank you. It makes me feel good that you were, because I think about you."

Paul looked over at Bud's smile as the court proceedings continued and whispered to him, "What are you looking like a proud peacock who's showing his feathers for?"

Bud looked over at him and said, "That obvious, eh?" as he smiled again.

Paul and Bud were actually enjoying watching Judge Green interact with the two attorneys. Bud even waved at O'Connor and even gave him the ASL sign for "sorry" about being denied the chance to delay the hearing. ASL stood for American Sign Language for deaf children and adults. "Sorry" in ASL is closing your hand like a fist over your chest and moving it in a circular motion.

"You forgot the bulletproof vest," Green said to Ashley, regarding the release.

"It will be taken care of, Your Honor," Ashley replied.

Judge Green set bail at $2 million, contingent upon the ankle monitor and bulletproof vest. The judge asked who was posting bail, and the name Robert Simpson was given. Bud stood up as he heard the name. Paul tried to pull him down.

"Wait," Bud yelled.

"Who the hell are you?" Judge Green asked.

"Detective Johnson," Bud answered, as he walked up to Assistant District Attorney Ashley. "He's using the money from the house to get this bitch out on bail," he said to the assistant district attorney.

"Let it go," Ashley said to him in a loud whisper.

"What?" Bud replied.

The judge interrupted them, saying, "Sit down, Detective, before I find you in contempt."

Bud waved at the judge to speak to Ashley again and said, "Listen to me; he's going to use the cash from the mansion."

Ashley moved closer to Bud as Paul came up behind him. The ADA said, "Stop right now and go speak to Cronin. We know what we are doing."

Paul grabbed Bud as his partner yelled, "Cronin again! What the fuck is going on!"

The judge stood up, saying, "You are in contempt. Take this detective into lockup! Bailiff!"

Paul put his fingers on Bud's mouth as the court officer took Bud away. He turned to Ashley and said, "John, we can't help if we don't know what's going on."

"Listen," the assistant district attorney answered, "I don't know everything going on, but there's one thing I do have that you and Bud need to get, and that's faith in your boss. You guys do as you're told, and you might just get out of this case alive. Now if you want me to get Bud out, I'm going to have to find more money for bail."

Paul spoke up again, saying, "So Cronin is aware that Simpson is putting up the bond for her?"

"Talk to him!" Ashley said as he walked away.

"I'm coming with you," Paul said as they walked to the holding cell. "The girl witnessed Allan Jones' murder."

Ashley stopped and turned around, asking, "Who's watching her?"

"We have Justin Healey staying with her. There's no one better. They have no chance getting to her unless they rush the house with 20 suicide-mission guys, and even then it's not a sure thing. We also have a car outside and unscheduled stops at the house."

O'Connor and Sherman walked up to them in the hallway. "We will want to question her," O'Connor said.

"What for?" Paul asked.

O'Connor made a face and looked at Sherman, who said, "She witnessed a murder by someone responsible for the kidnapping of Deborah Lance. I think that gives us the right to interview her. We will make arrangements with your chief if Cronin doesn't want to help. Meanwhile, I think your boy needs you."

Paul stood there looking at them as they walked away. "Interesting," the detective said out loud.

"What?" Ashley said.

"All in due time," Paul said. "Let's get Bud the hell out of here."

"Let's go talk to Judge Green first; it's our best chance," Ashley said.

They walked into Judge Green's office with Assistant District Attorney Ashley beginning the conversation. "I apologize, Judge, on behalf of the Suffolk County District Attorney's Office and Police Department, but I would like to explain the circumstances behind it."

The judge leaned back as he spoke and said, "I can't wait to hear this one," as he looked at Paul. "And you are?"

"I'm Detective Sergeant Powers, Your Honor. Bud Johnson is my partner, and I must apologize also, but please understand that when you said Robert Simpson would be paying the bond on Patty Saunders, he knew where the money was coming from."

"So?" the judge said.

"Well," Paul continued, "the money being used for the bail is the same that was intended to be used for Deborah Lance."

"I suppose you have proof of that?" the judge said.

Paul raised his voice and said, "Your Honor, Robert Simpson does not have 10 percent of $2 million for the release. It's obvious where the money is coming from!"

"One more raised tone from you, and you will be in the cell with your partner," the judge replied.

"Sir," Assistant District Attorney Ashley said, "it is imperative to this case that Detective Johnson be released to serve your contempt charge at another time."

"Give me a good reason," the judge replied.

Paul spoke up again, saying, "A 12-year-old girl is a witness in this case that can break it wide open. She is in protective custody at her house now, and Detective Johnson is one of only a few people this girl trusts. If he is kept here, her life could be in jeopardy."

The judge grumbled some inaudible words and told the assistant district attorney he could get his detective.

They went into the hallway as Paul called Cronin to inform him what happened at the courthouse.

Robert Simpson's cell phone rang, and it was William Lance on the other end.

"Mr. Lance," Simpson said, "Debbie won't take any of my calls. You have to believe me, I had nothing to do with any of this."

"I suppose not," William Lance answered, "except betrayal."

"That was over a year ago," Simpson answered. "Patty even approached you, from what I hear. Please, I would never have anything to do with hurting Debbie in this way."

"This is not why I called you," Mr. Lance spoke. "Whatever issues you and Deborah have, you will have to either work out between yourselves or move on; it will be her decision."

There was a pause, and then Simpson asked, "My job?"

"Robert," Lance replied, "You know I can't have you at the house while Deborah is with me; it would be too uncomfortable." Then he spoke again, saying, "But I have had time down here the past few days to consider a few things, and I would like to offer you an opportunity to stay in the guesthouse and tie up any loose ends with your belongings and such. Someone will be in the house, and it will give you a chance to get things right in your mind. I'm doing this, Robert, because I've been told from Detective Lieutenant Cronin you had nothing to do with Deborah's kidnapping or the killings."

"Thank you, Mr. Lance, it's a very nice gesture on your part," Simpson replied. "Will we be able to talk when you get back?"

Deborah's father spoke again. "We can always talk, Robert, but no promises. My daughter is my world."

"Understood," Robert replied. "I will go in today. I assume the codes are the same?"

"Yes," William Lance replied. "Just give me a couple of hours to notify Detective Lieutenant Cronin that I have authorized you to go back in until we return."

"Thank you, sir," Simpson replied.

"OK, Robert," Lance replied. "Just make sure all your things are packed up and ready to move when we get back. We will give you a couple days' notice when we plan to arrive."

They disconnected, and Robert let out a long sigh of relief before he started pushing the buttons on his cell phone.

As the phone rang, Robert Simpson was getting nervous there would be no answer. Finally before voice mail picked up, Rachelle picked up. Robert spoke, saying, "I'm back in at the house for a few days. I will be moving in tonight. Tomorrow I will be packing up the rest of my things and taking care of our 'needs' during the evening."

"Good," Rachelle answered. "Meet me Friday morning at the same location, and we can discuss the rest of our 'needs.' Just make sure everything is taken care of."

"No problem," Simpson replied. He hung up and started on a hunt to get some boxes so he could finish his move once and for all.

Once Bud was released and met up with Paul and Assistant District Attorney Ashley, they decided to get back to the precinct, since Cronin had been calling for them. They also had to ride back in separate cars. While Bud was driving back, he called in to Dugan to get a Remington 12-gauge shotgun to Healey at the house.

"Also," he said, "see if the precinct commander can spare Officer Lynagh at the house from 2:00 am to 6:00 am so Healey can get some sleep, as well as Paul and myself. I would like to see if we can get him for Thursday morning as well." Dugan said he would confirm and get back to him.

As Bud drove back to the precinct, he was conflicted over his feelings about what had just happened. He was thrown in jail for contempt because of arguing with the judge and assistant district attorney over Robert Simpson paying the 10 percent of the bail to the bondsman. He knew Simpson didn't have the money, and it was clear he knew where the money was. Instead he was told to speak to Cronin, just like Rachelle had told him to do.

Bud called William Lance in Florida during the drive back to the precinct and asked him if he knew where Simpson was getting the money to pay the bail. William Lance promptly told him it would be best if he spoke to Cronin, before he hung up.

Bud started banging the steering wheel as he was told to speak to the detective lieutenant again. He started to get a headache trying to figure out why everyone was telling him this. He made up his mind during the last 10 minutes of the drive that he was going to find out. Bud reached the precinct and was handed two messages from Gina. One was from Officer Dugan that he had brought the extra shotgun to Healey and confirmation that Officer Lynagh would be in the house from 2:00 am to 6:00 am. The second message was from Detective Lieutenant Cronin to come to his office right away.

As he stepped in the boss' office, Bud decided to try a different approach with Cronin and just stay calm. "OK," the detective lieutenant said, "let's have it. What's on your mind?"

Bud paused, then spoke in the calmest voice he could. "I'm working this case. Every time I begin to make progress, I'm told to speak to you. I'm tired of hitting dead ends."

"That's it?" Cronin asked.

"No," Bud replied. "All this tells me you are keeping things from us. Why? Do you not trust us? We have been on your team for a while. Why are you not telling us things and keeping us informed?"

Cronin sat back and replied, "Bud, you are a good cop and a

much better investigator than most realize. I've said this before, and I'm going to say it again. This is all a game, and you just happen to be a terrific player. But it's not about trusting you or anyone else right now. You are going to have to trust me. Some of the moves I'm making are to get the game to end the way I need it to end, and some of the moves I'm making are to protect your careers and to keep you in the game. I need your trust for another 24 to 36 hours. As for not keeping you informed, I could say the same for you. You schedule Lynagh from 2:00 am to 6:00 am, and you told me you couldn't make the court appearance because of a development, then you made it and got yourself thrown in jail because you decided to fuck around with Judge Green."

"Boss," Bud replied, "Simpson is using Lance's money for the bail."

"Let it ride, let the game play out," Cronin replied.

Bud just sat there and shook his head at the boss and said, "Is it going to be worth it?"

"I hope so, Detective," he answered. "I certainly hope so."

"One last question," Bud said. "The photo that Lindsey picked out for you…"

Cronin interrupted him, "Now is not the time to go there, but soon it will be."

"OK," Bud said. "I'm going to share all of this with Paul. Any problem with that?"

Cronin smiled and said, "He's your partner; you should be sharing all of this with him."

As Bud reached the door, he turned around and spoke. "Did we accomplish anything by this talk?"

"I think so," Cronin said. "We came to an understanding."

Bud tapped the frame of the door as he walked out and went to his desk. As he reached his desk, Paul walked in.

As Paul sat down, he spoke, saying, "Sherry is going to be released tomorrow. Isn't that great news?"

"Yes," Bud replied.

"Listen," Paul replied, "I think you and I need to go over all our notes and make sure we both know the same things. You have been off doing things as I have, and we need to get together and match a few things up."

Bud had been scribbling with his pencil on his desk when he suddenly stopped and started to speak. "I think we do, I agree, but the key to this is the girl, not Rachelle, not Deborah or that asshole Simpson or even the bitch we just let get out on bail. The girl can ruin them."

"Them?" Paul said.

"Yes," Bud said, "them."

"I agree," Paul replied, "but to a point. Releasing Saunders will move things along faster."

"And who," Bud replied, "is going to keep an eye on her? We have 24/7 on Lindsey, Rachelle, Deborah, and your father in Florida, and now this. And more important, we have a masked killer eliminating the bad guys."

Paul moved forward and said, "How do you know he's not eliminating partners? The pot is only $3 million. The masked killer has eliminated Starfield, the three Winters brothers, and Anderson. There's a big savings in killing five partners."

"Yes," Bud replied. "He lets Deborah, Rachelle, and Sherry live, and it's fair to say he saved their lives. Doesn't sound like the same person to me."

"Unless," Paul answered, "he wanted us to have the conflict and the confusion."

"Or," Bud said as he looked at Paul, "someone wanted to frame him."

Paul started to feel the sweat on the back of his head as he answered Bud, saying, "Do you really think someone would go to that much trouble?"

"I think," Bud said, "a killer would."

He picked up the phone and dialed the lab and left it on speakerphone so Paul could hear him.

"Hey, Ross. This is Bud Johnson. The video we have of the masked killer from the hospital in the Kyle Winters killing. You indicated from the body structure and height that it's possible it was Phil Smith."

"Yes," came the reply.

"OK, I'm going to give you additional names."

"OK," Ross replied.

"Are you ready?"

"Yes," the lab technician replied. "Go ahead."

"Myself," Bud continued, "Kevin Cronin, Paul Powers."

"Sir?" Ross interrupted.

"It's OK," Bud answered as he looked at his partner, "it's all in a day's work. Robert Simpson, Al Simmons, Agent Jason 'Jack' O'Connor, Agent Sherman, Officer Healey. Any questions?" Bud asked.

"Only a comment," Ross answered. "I can eliminate you, Sherman, and Cronin right away because of obvious body structure, weight, and the age of Cronin. There is no way at the age of 48 he could perform some of the things I saw on the video, and certainly not as quickly."

As Bud continued to eye Paul out of the corner of his eye, he said, "Are you saying I'm too chunky to be the masked killer?"

"Well," Ross replied, "that's a nice way of putting it."

"OK, so take a closer look at Simmons, Powers, Healey, Simpson, and O'Connor for possible matches."

The lab technician replied, "I'm also going to eliminate Simmons because he was too thin and a bit too tall. I will study the photos of Simpson, Powers, O'Connor, and Healey and get back to you."

Bud replied, "Also add Lynagh and ADA Ashley to the list." The phone went *click* as Bud looked at Paul.

Paul got up and said, "I'm leaving. I hope you're proud of yourself for wasting taxpayers' dollars."

He started to walk toward Cronin's office, when Bud yelled, "I gave my name as well as yours. I have to tell you, I don't agree the one going around shooting people is the same person. They can't be that smart. The victims being killed by the Ghost Face mask killer are the bad guys. These are vigilante killings in response to what happened to Deborah and Rachelle. What better vigilante person than someone in law enforcement who doesn't want to see a long trial or their loved ones go through suffering on the witness stand? I think you know I may be right."

As Paul stepped into Cronin's office, he turned and looked at Bud, saying, "Knock yourself out."

Paul began to get lightheaded as he sat down in Cronin's office.

"Are you OK?" his boss asked.

"I'll be fine," Paul answered. "I want to talk more about what happened in the courtroom today, and I'm not discussing it with Bud right now, so let's talk."

Patty Saunders left the Riverhead Correctional Facility and raised her hands above her head and started yelling about the fresh air.

"Don't get too excited," Al Simmons said. "You have an ankle monitor on you, and they will be able to tell if you leave the Port Jefferson area. Even now, you have two hours to get there before they come looking for you and throw your ass back in lockup. So what are you going to do first?" he asked.

"Hmmm," she said. "That's easy. I need to get laid quick, before I bust."

"Well," he replied, "good luck. You will have to take off your bulletproof vest for that."

"Ha, ha," she replied, "no kidding."

As they were talking, Officer George Lynagh walked up to them and said, "Ma'am, I'm here to take you to your apartment."

"Oh, thank you, Officer," she replied. "Do you have any plans later?"

"I'm a married man," he replied.

"Oh, even better," she said as she looked back at Simmons with a wink.

"Hold on," O'Connor yelled to Patty as she was walking. Simmons also walked toward Patty to be sure there were no issues with the FBI. Agent Sherman was also present as O'Connor began to speak. O'Connor said, "Ms. Saunders, you are the instigator in a major kidnapping trial that involves the states of New York and Connecticut. It is the FBI that will be keeping an eye on you, not the Suffolk County Police Department. Just be aware of it."

"Whatever," Patty remarked. "Who's taking me home?"

"I am," Lynagh said. "You guys want to watch her, go ahead, but

I have my orders, and they're not from you," he said as he gently put his hand on Patty and steered her toward the car.

Sherman spoke, saying, "Sounds like you need an attitude adjustment, Officer Lynagh."

"Give it your best shot," the cop replied. "After all, I'm only part of the Suffolk County Police Department. You should be able to handle that." He got in the cruiser to drive to Patty's apartment in Port Jefferson.

As Patty sat in the backseat she suddenly realized there was a cell phone in her pants pocket. Lynagh was already on the expressway, heading west, when Patty was still wondering where she had gotten the cell phone. Her thoughts were filled with confusion and apparently had seen too many movies because she promptly reached from the backseat and threw it out onto the Long Island Expressway from Lynagh's window.

"What the hell was that?" Lynagh spoke up.

"I threw out a cell phone," Patty answered.

Lynagh pulled over his cruiser and turned around. "You listen to me. You don't throw anything from this vehicle. If you can't follow directions or stop from doing dumb things like that, I will turn around and take your ass back to Riverhead. I don't give a shit what the judge says. Do you understand me? Now why are you throwing out a cell phone on the highway?"

"Because I don't know how I got it, and I was afraid."

Lynagh started backing up his cruiser at a fast speed in the emergency lane to the approximate place she had thrown out the phone, then got out of the car and looked at Patty. He said, "You stay in this car, or I will make your release a living hell." He locked her in the vehicle, took out his shotgun, and opened up his badge as he started motioning for cars to stop.

Another police cruiser happened to drive up within a couple minutes from the courthouse and assisted Lynagh is stopping traffic before the cell phone was run over. The second cruiser parked sideways on the Long Island Expressway, and the officer got out of the car to hold traffic. Lynagh had his shotgun because he wanted to be more intimidating to the drivers to get them to cooperate with him, and he was right. Pointing at them with one hand and holding the shotgun in the other worked. His dark sunglasses were the icing on the cake. They all were at a standstill as the traffic backed up about 200 yards very quickly.

Officer Lynagh's persistence paid off. He had searched the open area of the Long Island Expressway but continued toward the parked cars in the lanes. He searched the first few rows of the vehicles that were at a standstill and feared one of them had run over the cell phone. As he searched through the vehicles with his eyes to the ground, with quick glances at who was in the cars. It was the shotgun he was carrying that had everyone's attention. It was a very intimidating sight as he brushed aside each of the cars. Having a second officer parked in the middle of the Expressway holding another shotgun was only an added form of intimidation.

Officer Lynagh made it to the sixth row of vehicles and located the cell phone about two inches from one of the tires of the vehicle. He picked it up and opened it up to see if it worked, and thanks to the leather cover, it still operated properly. He thanked the assisting officer as he ran back to his cruiser. He sat in the cruiser and called in to Bud about what had happened, and in turn Bud went into Cronin's office to let him know what had happened.

Paul was still there talking to him as Cronin answered Bud, saying, "Tell Lynagh to give the phone back to Patty to use, bring her home, and then get some sleep before his 2:00 am shift tonight."

"The FBI also told Lynagh that they will be watching Patty, not the Suffolk County Police Department," Bud replied.

"OK," the detective lieutenant replied. "Sounds good to me."

"Very good," Bud replied as he shut the door.

"Getting interesting, isn't it?" Cronin said as he looked at Paul.

Lynagh sat there to be sure the assisting officer moved his cruiser out of the middle of the Long Island Expressway without any incidents. Once Officer Waters turned his vehicle around and waved to Lynagh, he turned on his cruiser and waited a couple minutes before moving. He was surprised how a five-minute delay looked like it caused a backup of more than 100 vehicles.

He turned around to Patty and said, "This is your cell phone.

Please keep it on you. Someone has gone to the trouble to be able to reach you if they need you."

"That's why I threw it away in the first place, genius," Patty remarked.

Lynagh kept looking straight ahead as he said, "You were released on bail to help us catch a killer, not have a vacation. Keep the cell phone."

Patty became silent and didn't say another word as Lynagh started up the car and drove back to the village that had become famous throughout the nation. It took Officer Lynagh about 25 minutes to reach the Fairview Apartments. He escorted her to her apartment and looked around to be sure there were no problems.

"I think you are OK," he told her. "If you decide to go out, remember to wear your vest."

"Wait," she said. "Will they be able to tell if I'm having sex with an ankle monitor on?" Lynagh didn't smile but answered, "Why don't you let me know next time I see you."

As Lynagh left the front door of her apartment building, he noticed there was an unmarked car about 60 yards to the right. There was no doubt in his mind it was the feds. "You can have her," he said aloud to himself as he got to the car. He was now alone in the car and he did what was requested of him directly from Cronin in a text.

"Officer Lynagh, before you hand over the phone to Patty Saunders, get the number for me, and tell no one."

Lynagh texted the number of the cell phone directly to Cronin's phone. He turned on his vehicle and, instead of driving out of the complex, made a u-turn and drove up alongside where the unmarked vehicle was. He rolled down his window as he pulled out his 9mm Glock and kept it on his lap. There were two men in the vehicle.

"What's up, boys?" Lynagh spoke. The two men looked at each other like it was beneath them to even speak to a Suffolk County police officer.

Finally one of them spoke up, saying, "FBI surveillance of Patty Saunders."

"How about some identification?" Lynagh spoke again.

"Are you busting our balls?" the other man asked.

Lynagh smiled and said, "No, sir. I dropped Ms. Saunders off from the courthouse, and before I leave I want to be certain she is safe."

"And if I don't feel like it?" the man in the passenger seat answered. Lynagh took a deep breath then looked back at the two men. This time he had no smile.

He said, "Then I will think you are not part of the FBI, and you don't want me thinking that, because then we will have a problem. Identification please."

The two men looked at each other again and went into their lightweight jackets as Lynagh raised his 9mm toward the bottom of the window. Their identifications came out of their pockets as they extended their arms out of the window.

"Thank you, sirs," Lynagh said. "You have a nice rest of the day now, you hear."

As he pushed the button to raise his window and drive away, he muttered "assholes" to himself. He pulled out of the complex and drove to Crystal Brook Hollow Road to get some sleep before his shift that night at the Wilkerson home. His house was only about eight minutes away from the house on Bell Circle in Belle Terre. He arrived at his house and figured if he got four to five hours of sleep he would be OK for the 2:00 am shift so Healey could get some shuteye. He checked his phone to be sure there were no messages from anyone before he shut it off.

Bud was watching Fox News from the precinct and was getting ready to leave when he looked at the bottom of the screen of the television. It showed 5:04 pm, and he looked at his watch, which said 5:02 pm. Lindsey had been right, it was two minutes off. He was shaking his head when he told Cronin he was going home to get some shuteye before he headed over to the Wilkerson home about midnight. If Healey could get six hours of sleep between Bud and Lynagh relieving him, he thought it would be a big help to the officer who had Lindsey's life in his hands.

"Where's Paul?" he asked Cronin.

"He needed to take care of some things," the boss answered.

"What about the ballistics on Allan?"

"He gave them to me," Cronin answered. ".22 caliber shot from about two feet away. A gun from Ohio, bought by a man in 2006 that somehow ended up dead here on Long Island last year."

"Names?" Bud asked.

"We are checking, won't know 'til morning, computers are down."

Bud said good night as Cronin held a paper in his hand. The computers were not down. He looked at the name on the piece of paper; it was all starting to come together. As Bud walked past his desk, he stopped Officer Henderson to contact Fun World to send over images of every costume they had associated with the Ghost Face mask. He wanted to take a look at the differences in the styles based on what was sold in stores everywhere and the one from the hospital video. He got in his car and sent Deborah a text before starting the car.

He wrote, "I hope you are OK and I can speak to you soon!"

She answered him within minutes, writing, "I miss talking to you. I look forward to being able to come home."

He pulled over his car to text back to her, typing, "Me too!"

He reached his apartment, took a shower, and climbed into bed for a three-hour nap. Usually he would be texting or calling Paul, but he didn't want to. He felt a change in the air. He wasn't comfortable about how he was feeling. He didn't feel the need to call him, and evidently Paul felt the same way. He laid in his bed for more than an hour before he dozed off.

The Wilkerson home was in good hands. Officer Dugan was sitting in his cruiser looking at the beautiful homes in this tiny village. He scanned all the yards and looked at every vehicle that drove by. Every hour or so he would get out of the car with his shotgun and walk a bit just to stretch his legs. He would even call Healey in the house just to tease him that he had gotten the better end of the deal.

On the inside, the Wilkerson family was having dinner at the kitchen table, but only after Healey had moved the portion of the table they would be sitting at away from the window. Healey also sat about 12 feet away from them, just in case there were any problems. It was Lindsey who kept bringing food over to him. She was almost motherly to him, the way she wanted to please him.

"I'm OK, Lindsey," he said, and smiled at her.

Both her parents were surprised at how well Lindsey was handling all of this but felt she truly felt protected by his presence.

After they finished dinner, Lindsey wanted to watch the History Channel but decided not to. When asked why she had changed her mind, she told Officer Healey that she had enough on her mind for now and did not want another 60 minutes of history in her head forever.

He raised his eyebrows as if to say he almost didn't believe her, but based on everything he had seen, he gave her the benefit of the doubt. He got up and looked out the window and saw a shadow on the front lawn. He picked up his shotgun and sent Dugan a text to wave if it was him. A few seconds later Dugan waved at the front window. Healey sent him a note to text from then on when he was taking a walk.

Cronin was still in his office at 7:00 pm when he contacted Assistant District Attorney Ashley. He gave him the cell phone number that found its way to Patty after she was released from the correctional facility.

"I will need all the numbers in and out on this phone, John, as they happen."

"I'll get right on it," the assistant district attorney replied. He got up and said good night to Gina, who never left until he did. He got in his car and drove over to Rachelle's house. He got out of his car and waved to the officers sitting in their car on Prospect Street. He knocked on the door, and Madison greeted him and let him into the house to speak to Rachelle.

"I'll be in my room, Rachelle, if you need me," she said to her sister as she gave them their privacy. Once the door was shut, Detective Lieutenant Cronin began talking.

"How's it going?" he asked.

"It's going," she answered.

The Detective replied, "The woman who started all of this with the kidnapping of Debbie Lance is now home. She's only five minutes away from here, but she has an ankle monitor. Her movements are constantly watched. I have reason to believe her release will bring all of this to a climax. I would prefer that you did not go out for the next 24 hours at least."

Rachelle started to interrupt him by starting to speak about Twitter, but he put his fingers up to her lips. He shook his head no to tell her silently not to talk about that subject at this time.

"Just stay in and know they have FBI agents watching her place at Fairview. I will be in touch with you. Just be cool over the next 24 hours. If you need anything, give me a call or send your sister out, but really, stay indoors." She nodded her head as he said good night.

As he approached the door, he looked at Rachelle and said, "You know, Rachelle, if you didn't have love for someone in your heart, you wouldn't be feeling the pain that you have."

She smiled at the detective lieutenant as she shut the door behind him.

Paul gave his father a call to check up on him, and everything was fine. In fact, he said to him, "Son, I don't think the state of Florida can afford to watch me."

"Well, Dad," Paul replied, "they are going to have to find a way for now. OK, time for my nap. I have to get up in a few hours so Bud is not alone tonight."

"Be careful, son, you are all I have."

"OK, Dad, talk tomorrow." Paul put the phone down and sent Rachelle a text.

"Hi," She answered back, "were your ears ringing? We were just talking about you."

He texted back, "Really? That's nice. Have a good night."

He put the charger on his BlackBerry and lay down on his bed after setting the alarm for 10:30 pm. He wouldn't see Rachelle's reply to him saying, "I miss our talks," until after he woke up.

Paul woke up at 10:31 pm and lay in bed until it was almost 11:00 pm. He put on his blue jeans and a white shirt. He strapped on his backup gun and then put on his main weapon underneath his shirt. He washed his face to help him wake up and combed his hair as he headed toward the door to go downstairs. He remembered his phone, came back, pulled out the battery charger, and saw Rachelle's text as he got in his car to head up to the Wilkerson house.

He decided to stop at Rachelle's house on the way, and she appeared to be happy when she walked up to him at the door.

"Hi! Come on in, Paul, it's so wonderful to see you."

Madison came out to greet Paul and offered him a drink.

"No, no thank you," he replied. "I'm going up to give relief at a home for a few hours and just wanted to see how things were going."

"It's fine, thank you," Rachelle said.

Madison added, "You missed Detective Lieutenant Cronin a few hours ago."

Paul seemed surprised and said, "Oh, really? What did he want?"

"I guess the same as you," Madison said. "He was checking on things. What brings you here so late?" Madison asked.

"Well, I thought you would be up since the lights were on."

"Oh," Madison replied. "I guess that was a sign," she said as she laughed.

"OK," he said, "I have to get going. I'm glad everything is OK."

"Thank you, Paul," Rachelle said as she shut the door. When the young woman started walking back to her room, Madison couldn't help herself and asked, "Are you still hurting for him?"

Rachelle just turned her head with a pained look on her face and said good night.

Paul arrived at the Wilkerson home at 11:15 pm, and Bud was already there conversing with Lindsey. They were having a debate about the age of judges. Bud did not believe that Judge Green was only 65 years of age. He thought at least 75, which would make him one of the oldest judges in the nation. Lindsey laughed and said no way.

"Judge Wesley Brown is the oldest in the nation at 104 years old in Wichita, Kansas. He was appointed by President John F. Kennedy."

"Bud," Healey said, "do you really think you can win a debate with her?" Bud nodded.

"Hey, Lindsey, time for bed. You and Officer Healey need some sleep for school tomorrow."

"Good night, Bud," she said. "Good night Paul. I will have the sketch for you tomorrow."

"Thank you," Paul replied.

Bud walked up to Healey and said, "Why don't you sleep in the guest room instead of a cot in the hallway? Paul and I will be here 'til

Lynagh gets here and Dugan is here 'til 6:00 am."

"I know," Healey replied. "I just feel I should be outside her door, but thanks."

"OK," Bud replied.

"Night guys," Healey said as he went upstairs. It was awkward, as Bud and Paul were in the living room and kitchen not saying much to each other. Bud was becoming uncomfortable about Paul, and the same was happening to Paul about Bud. Paul was so uncomfortable that he decided to go outside and see what Dugan was doing. He waved to him as Dugan got out of the car and they had the conversation that Bud and Paul would normally have. Bud looked around the house at the expensive furniture and accessories in the house. He thought that the sofa was more expensive than his entire house.

"Damn," he said aloud to himself, "there is a lot of expensive shit in this place." His BlackBerry buzzed. It was a text from Lindsey.

"Bud, don't swear; it's not nice." He looked puzzled as he read the text. He went upstairs, and Lindsey was in the hallway as Healey settled himself in the cot.

"You heard me from up here?"

"Yes, so be careful," she laughed.

"Good night, smart…" he caught himself…"girl."

"That's better," she replied. He looked at Healey as he pointed down the hallway.

"Parents' room?"

"Yes," Healey answered. Bud headed downstairs as he put on the television with low volume. Paul was outside with Dugan for more than an hour before he came in.

"Are we going to talk?" Bud asked.

"I have nothing to talk to you about right now," Paul replied.

"OK," Bud replied, "let's just try and get through this, then." Paul didn't reply as he headed into the kitchen and poured himself some water.

Bud thought to himself, *Thank God this is only 'til 2:00 am.*

As 2am approached, Bud received a text from Dugan that Lynagh was approaching the front door. There was a slight knock as Bud opened the door to greet him. Bud reviewed the house with him as

Paul stayed in the living room. Lynagh walked around the house with the shotgun in his possession and finally said good night to the two detectives. As Paul walked to his car Bud yelled, "Good night, Paul." Paul kept walking to his car but raised up his hand to say good night. He went back to his apartment and climbed into bed, not knowing his life would not be the same the next day.

Thursday, June 30

Paul woke up about 7:00 am and as he always did, turned on Fox News. It was perfect timing because the Fox and Friends broadcast was interrupted by a breaking news segment. The announcer went to a press conference that was about to begin with Nada Marjanovich, the publisher and editor of *Long Island Pulse* magazine. She stepped right up to the microphone and began to speak.

"Good morning, everyone. I have a brief statement to make. *Long Island Pulse* magazine conducted an interview with Detective Bud Johnson, Detective Sergeant Paul Powers and Detective Lieutenant Kevin Cronin a few days ago that will be in its full text when our issue comes out next week. However, we believed it was important to release certain excerpts from the interview now."

Paul woke up fast and sat up to get a closer view of his television as Nada continued. "When we posed the question of if and when the people responsible for the kidnapping and murders would be caught in what has become known as 'the Face of Fear Investigation,' Detective Lieutenant Kevin Cronin answered, 'An arrest will be made before the publication of next week's issue.' This strong statement is the reason we are releasing this news now. Not only to calm fears of the people of Port Jefferson but to be a responsible news source and let the public know now instead of waiting another week." The questions from her fellow peers were nonstop, and Paul could not make out what they were trying to ask Nada. She simply put her hands up and tried to interrupt them.

"Please! Let me try and answer your questions."

She pointed to someone who asked, "If the Suffolk County Police Department knows who is involved, why don't they arrest him now?"

Nada was a pro. She answered, "Detective Lieutenant Cronin stated clearly he knows who they are and arrests will be made. I assume this means anytime."

The other channels quickly picked up her news conference and within minutes were playing it on ABC, NBC, and CBS as well as CNN and the Local News 12 Long Island station. Paul was switching back and forth and only saying three words: "Oh my God, oh my God, oh my God."

He attempted to put his slacks on too fast and tripped to the floor. Once he got his pants on, he ran down the stairs saying the same thing, "Oh my God, oh my God."

He was in his car before he realized he didn't have a shirt on. He ran back up the stairs, saying, "Oh my God, oh my God." He put on his shirt and ran downstairs again and drove to the precinct within 12 minutes. There were rows of reporters waiting outside for a press conference. Paul had to politely shove his way into the front door, where Officers Chapman and Franks were guarding the door to be certain the precinct was not overrun by reporters. As he approached his desk, he saw Cronin sitting in his office calmly doing paperwork. He knocked on his door and opened it.

"Kevin, is there anything we need to talk about?"

"No, Paul," the detective lieutenant answered. "Not yet. Have you spoken to Bud?"

"No," Paul replied. "We have hit a rough patch."

Within two minutes Assistant District Attorney Ashley walked in and walked right into Cronin's office and sat down as Paul walked out. There was silence for a few moments and then he spoke.

"You really did it this time. We did everything you wanted in this case, but you couldn't let me know the statement you were going to release."

The detective lieutenant moved his papers to the other side of the desk and answered Ashley. "I wanted to see everyone's reaction to the statement."

"Including your own team of detectives?" Ashley replied.

"Yes," Cronin replied. "Even my own team of detectives."

Bud looked up to see Police Chief Jameson and the precinct commander walk at a steady pace all the way to Cronin's office. He slammed the door behind him and stared at everyone in the room.

He pointed at Cronin and began to speak.

"Don't say a word, don't say anything, just listen. I really don't know what the bloody hell you are doing or what you are thinking, but now that you have released this statement, you have 24 hours to close this case or I will see to it that your career is over. Jesus, Mary, and Joseph, I have to go outside and explain this, and I have no choice but to support you and say this will be over soon. And it will be over soon, right? Right!"

Cronin politely asked, "I can speak now?"

Jameson slammed his fist on his desk and said, "You better speak or I'll rescind the 24 hours."

Kevin Cronin looked at Ashley, then at Jameson, and said, "It ends in the next 24 hours, one way or another. My career, my life. It's going to end. Hopefully it will end for the bad guys."

"Just what the hell do I tell the reporters?" Jameson bellowed.

"Tell them," Cronin said, "to be patient. They will know why, who, and when shortly in regards to my statement."

The chief looked Detective Lieutenant Cronin up and down before saying, "Don't embarrass us, Kevin. This time I want it to be over. You don't want to see me again in this temporary office of yours."

With that, he walked out and did exactly what the detective suggested to him. Officer Henderson came over to Bud and gave him a CD of images of the costume styles used with the Ghost Face mask over at Fun World. He studied the styles very carefully and matched them up with images from the hospital. It was totally different. The killer has a sleek black outfit almost looking like it was customized yet at the same time not tight enough to see total body build. All black yet it looked like the chest had a stylish leather design on the front. The black gloves were also sleek leather where the costume from Fun World was all loose nylon fabric. He opened the *Newsday* where Rachelle's tweet messages were more prominent. It was like she had a crazy cult following. He went on to Twitter to see what she wrote today. It said, "Today, it is the END, I won't say it AGAIN, I know who you ARE, you won't get very FAR."

Bud read it to Paul and then asked, "Now why would she write something like that?"

"Why don't you ask her?" Paul replied.

"I think I will," Bud replied. He felt a bad energy coming from Paul, and he decided that it had to get resolved before it got worse.

"We need to talk," he said to Paul.

"Not now. Let's get through this for now," Paul responded.

Phil Smith walked into the McDonald's off of Nesconset highway in Miller Place with a baseball cap on and looked around to see if three men were sitting together. No one fit the description, so he walked up to get a cup of coffee. The man behind him said, "Here, it's on me," as he paid for his coffee. "Please join us over here." Phil looked over at the table and joined the two men already sitting there in the back booth. Phil sat down and shook their hands. He asked for their names, and the leader of the group said it didn't matter.

"We are here to help you," he said. "The voice brought us up to date on everything. Everything happens today and tonight, and then we are out of there."

"I don't agree," Phil answered. "Have you seen the news today? The cops have said they know who is behind this and an arrest will be made."

"Let's get real," the leader said. "First of all, they know you, no one else, and yes if they could find you, they would arrest you. This is what we are here for. Today, the girl will be killed at the school. You will not even be around. There will be such a distraction, they won't even care or be thinking about you. Second, our contact is back living at the mansion as of last night. We will get the money tonight. You will help us, we will split everything and we go our separate ways." Phil rubbed his forehead.

"The voice said you guys were getting considerations not money. Plus if the girl is killed today, don't you think they will have a clue that we are making our move?" The leader spoke again as the other two stayed silent.

"We can't wait, the longer this goes the more difficult it will be to get the money for you and the voice, but you won't enjoy it as long as the girl is alive. The voice says now. Quite frankly, you are the only one that anybody really cares about. Be at the mansion tonight at 1:30 am. It's going down. This is my number to the disposable phone I have. The girl will be in school from about 10:00–2:30 pm. Be ready for anything in case we need you." Phil got up and left the table.

The leader, whose name was Ron Buckner, looked over at his two friends, Brian Thompson and Eric Pierson.

"When we finish the girl and get the money, the voice will set it up to where Phil is eliminated in a manner he will get the blame for most everything. He wants to eliminate Bud Johnson and expose his partner to the world as well." Ron Buckner was a tall man about six foot three inches tall and in very good physical condition. He had been involved in a few things over the years with the voice but nothing of this magnitude. Brian Thompson had been a tag along of Ron's for years and made most of his living as a contractor. Business had been so slow with the recession that he did side jobs with Ron over the past few years. Eric Pierson was new to the group and the voice called him "the killer." He was proud he had killed five people across the country over the past ten years and had never been caught. It was Eric who was going to kill twelve year old Lindsey today and it didn't bother him in the least.

"Let's get ready, men," Ron said.

Robert Simpson's cell phone rang, and it was Patty.

"Hello, handsome," she said. "I haven't had sex in a week, so why don't you come over here and we can mix business with pleasure."

"Patty," Robert said, "I've got too many things on my mind, quite frankly." Patty got a little more serious.

"You better have how much share I'm getting from the house on your mind."

"Oh, you too," he said. "Everybody wants a share."

"Who else?" she said.

"Gee," he answered, "you have the voice, Rachelle, you, Phil, me, and who knows who the hell else."

"We will see about that," she answered.

"Patty," he said, "you have a monitor on your ankle; you are not in a position to tell people how much you want."

"Oh, yes I am," she said. "You will all help me, or I'll bring all of you down."

"Patty," Robert replied. "You can't come to the house you will bring all the cops here with you having the monitor on you."

"That's right," she answered, "you tell the voice to call me this morning or I will show up where and when you least expect it." The phone disconnected.

Ashley was still with Cronin in his office when the Detective Lieutenant picked up the phone and called Healey's cell phone. The officer answered the phone,

"Healey."

Cronin said, "Keep the kid home from school today, understood?"

"Confirmed and noted," was Healey's answer. He knocked on Lindsey's bedroom door and as she answered he told her she would be staying home from school today. She questioned him as to why when Cronin called the cell of Healey again.

"Put her on, please."

"Hello Detective Lieutenant Cronin," Lindsey said. He continued,

"Have you done it yet?"

"Yes," she said. He replied, "does it match the photo you showed me?"

"Yes," she said.

"OK, I want you to put it in a manila envelope, seal it with tape and give it to Healey."

"OK," she said, "but if they ask me for it?" He answered her,

"Tell them you are doing what I told you to do."

"OK I will," she answered.

"Good," he said, "give me back to Officer Healey."

"Yes, sir," Healey said. Cronin told him she would be handing him the manila envelope, sealed and it was not to be opened by anyone other than himself or Assistant District Attorney Ashley in case anything happened to him." He disconnected the phone and looked at Ashley. The assistant district attorney just shook his head as he spoke.

"If you think you are going to leave me to handle all this bullshit you have another thing coming."

"You heard the chief," Cronin replied. "I've now got 24 hours." Ashley stood up to leave,

"I believe in you, Kevin. See you tomorrow."

As the assistant district attorney left, Cronin whispered to himself, "God willing." He then went to Gina and asked her what time Lynagh was back on duty. Gina told him since he was on the 2am to 6am shift, he would be back on duty about 7:00 pm.

"Tell him as soon as he is on to check on Saunders and report to me before going back to the Wilkerson house."

"Yes, sir," she replied as she made a note in her book to call Officer Lynagh around 2:00 pm.

"OK," Cronin said, "where are Powers and Johnson?" he thought it had a nice ring to it. "Sounds like a Starsky and Hutch episode but only better."

"Sir," Gina said, "they are here in the precinct. They were worried about you since the *Long Island Pulse* released your statement."

"Yes Gina, thanks, I know you were also, please send them to my office." He walked in and shut the door which he rarely did in his office when he was alone. He checked his voicemail and it was District Attorney Steinberg.

"Kevin, I really don't know what to say other than I wish you had warned me what you were going to do, but it's behind us now. I know you think you know what you are doing and I hope you are right. Take care." As he cancelled the message, Paul and Bud came in.

"Good morning again Powers and Johnson, I just noticed how good that sounds." There was no comment from either one of them, so Cronin continued. "Any problems last night?"

"No," they both answered at the same time but Bud continued,

"All's quiet on the Belle Terre front." Cronin replied,

"I don't know what you have planned for today, but I'm going to give you a schedule if you don't mind. I want you guys to check on Saunders this morning and see what she is doing. I know the FBI is watching her but I still want to know. Then get yourself over to Rachelle's house and make sure she's not going anywhere for the next 24 hours. Tell Chapman or whoever is in the cruiser to be alert. Check on Healey and Lindsey by 2:00 pm today. I want people to see police going in and out of the house all day. In between, I want you to go to the school where Lindsey was supposed to be today. Let me know if you see anything unusual. Get yourself in bed by 5pm so you guys will be ready to rock and roll by midnight tonight. Keep in touch with me at least every hour today 'til you catch some shut eye."

"What about you?" Paul said. "When are you going to catch some sleep?"

"I'll pull the drapes and catch ninety minutes here and there," the Detective Lieutenant answered. "Gina will be keeping an eye on me. Any questions? OK, good, see you later, Bud stay here for a moment." The door shut behind Paul and Cronin started to speak immediately.

"What's up Detective?"

"I think," Bud said, "when this is all over, it will be best to have a new partner."

"What is the issue?" Cronin asked.

"Trust," Bud answered. "We used to tell each other everything, now it's different, this case has changed us. I can't remember the last time I smiled or cracked a joke to control the levity."

"It's your decision," Cronin replied. "We will see when it's over, in the meantime, you better work together for the next twenty four to forty eight hours or more lives could be lost." Bud nodded as he walked out of Cronin's office and sat down at his desk. Finally, Paul stood up and said he was going to Patty Saunders apartment and if he wanted to tag along he was welcome. Bud answered,

"I'm coming, but I'll take my own car."

Deborah Lance went out to the mailbox to get the mail and was very excited to see something had arrived from Bud. She dropped the rest of the mail on the kitchen table and took the envelope to her bedroom to insure she would have total privacy. She pulled out the 8 ½ x 11 sheet that had a post it note attached to it. It read, "The song is for my mother but it's you that inspired me to write the words. Deborah read the lyrics to the song called "I'm Missing You."

"I'm Missing You"

Verse 1 If you could feel my heart
          And touch the tears to my pain
          Then you'd know how much you were a part
          Of dreams that never came

Verse 2 Life is never fair...to some of us it's true
          But I feel you in my prayers at night
          When I am missing you

Chorus I'm missing you
         I'm missing you
         I'm missing you
         I'm missing you
         I miss your smile
         I miss your touch
         I miss the way
         You loved so much

Verse 3 (Violin Verse) We never said goodbye
                        After all these years I cry
                        So when I smile with a tear in my eye
                        It's when I think of you

Verse 4 The gift you gave to me...was a heart that could see
          So I know that you'll be with me...
          Even though I'm missing you

Chorus I'm missing you
         I'm missing you
         I'm missing you
         I'm missing you
         I miss your kiss
         I miss the nights
         I miss the way...you held me tight

Solo Instrumental

Verse 5 Life must go on
          And it's you that makes me strong
          So my gift to you is this song
          'Cause I am......missing you.

Verse 6 Wherever I may go
          Or whatever I may do
          Just know I will always love you
          Cause I'm missing you
          Yes, I am missing....you.

Deborah cried as she read the lyrics that were so touching to her. She picked up her iPhone and sent a text to Bud.

"You are a kind and gentle soul. Thank you for sending me those beautiful lyrics." She held the paper to her chest as she closed her eyes and let her thoughts run free with what she was feeling at this moment. She got herself together and went back downstairs to where her father was reading the morning newspaper.

"Father," she said, "when do you think we are going back to Long Island?" He answered without even looking up at her.

"By the looks of this new tweet from Rachelle, maybe within a few days." Her tweets were now carried in over three hundred newspapers across the country and her face was becoming more and more recognizable simply by her having over one hundred thousand followers and growing every day since *Newsday* started giving her a featured presence in the paper. He showed her the paper and said that maybe she would call her later to see how she was doing. She did try her about ten minutes later but was told her number was disconnected. She sent Bud a text to ask her about her number and if he saw her. He acknowledged that he would and told her he was on his way to see Patty Saunders. She wrote back, "don't tell her hello from me." Bud pulled up to Patty's Fair View apartment and was not surprised to see two FBI agents sitting across the street. He went over to the car as Paul pulled in and parked near Bud.

"What's going on folks?" Bud shouted as he approached the car.

"Just doing our job, Officer Johnson. Hey, isn't Johnson slang for dick?" one said as they started laughing.

"Never heard that one," Bud replied, "and it's Detective and I wouldn't do jokes about dicks if I were you because according to Officer Lynagh, you two don't have any dicks." As Bud started imitating them in an exaggerated way only he could do.

"Here's my identification! I've got it here officer! Don't shoot me! Please don't shoot me! I'll miss my Mommy!"

"That's not the way it went down!" Agent Barnes yelled.

"Well," Bud said "watch the funny jokes about dicks then or I'll do a YouTube video you wouldn't believe. Paul walked up to the car,

"Any problems here?"

"No, Detective Sergeant," Bud said as he walked away. Agent Barnes spoke up again.

"You got a pretty sick partner."

"Yeah," Paul answered. "It's what we like about him." Paul caught up with Bud as they knocked on Patty's door. She answered within a couple minutes and invited them in.

"How's it going?" Bud asked.

"It's fine," Patty answered. "I don't think I need everyone watching so close. Why would anyone come out for me at this point when they know I'm being watched?"

"Well," Paul said, "let's see how much someone wants you dead." Bud looked at Paul and thought the remark was strange coming from Paul.

"Ms. Saunders," Bud spoke, "do you wear your vest when you go out?"

"Yes," she answered. "I'm wondering if I should be back in jail, there is no privacy, and how do I know the apartment isn't bugged?"

"If it is, it's for your safety," Paul replied. Patty just shrugged it off.

"If I want to get laid, I don't want the whole world listening to my screams and moans."

"Well," Bud said, "just be happy there isn't a camera here," as he laughed and continued, "or is there?"

"Very funny," Patty answered. Paul's BlackBerry as well as Bud's buzzed at the same time. It was another tweet post by Rachelle. This time it was a photo of Ghost Face imposed over a mountain of money. The caption read, "You may think it's FUNNY, but I don't want the MONEY. It's TRUE, I only want YOU."

"What the," Bud caught himself and looked at Paul who was surprised he didn't finish the sentence. Bud replied to his look,

"I'm trying to watch my language." "Lindsey has an effect on you like that." Paul nodded.

"Who the fuck is Lindsey," Patty asked.

"It doesn't matter," Paul answered her. "You have our numbers, just be careful. Come on Bud, we have to go to our other assignment." As they left the building, they looked at the tweet sent in from

Rachelle again. It was the Ghost Face costume from Fun World posing with its arms out on a pile of money. There was a legal description in the bottom left corner that read sightingsghostface.com. Paul called it in for Officer Franks to find out information about the website. Normally he would have called a detective to find out but he was instructed from Cronin to try and limit the involvement to those already working the case. Bud looked at Paul as he made the calls about *Sightings Ghost Face* and was getting more and more curious about why Rachelle would send a tweet like that. It was obvious the money at the Lance mansion was an issue and the statement YOU in capital letters was meant for someone that Rachelle knew.

"See you at the school," Paul said without even turning around to Bud. Paul walked to his car, got in and drove away as Bud stood in front still entertaining his thoughts. The two FBI agents were sipping coffee as Johnson walked by. Agent Barnes asked him how it went. Bud continued to walk by saying,

"Kiss my ass." Barnes said to his partner,

"No thanks, dickhead." Bud drove away and headed down to Port Jefferson High School. Paul was already waiting for him by the front door when they walked in and visited the principal and asked if there had been any problems. There had been none. They visited with the teachers and found out what time recess was and when the kids normally went outside since the school year was coming to an end and it was the last week of session. The kids were also allowed to go outside during their lunch break. Paul and Bud stayed and looked at the outside area where Lindsey would normally be.

Eric Pierson waited patiently with his binoculars waiting for Lindsey and her guardian officer to pull up in his unmarked car so he could take her out. He decided he would take out Officer Healey for free as well. After about an hour and all the school buses came and went, he slammed his binoculars down and made a call to Ron Buckner.

"The little angel didn't come to school today."

"OK," he answered, "Let me call the voice and see what he wants to do." He called back Eric within five minutes to tell him they would all go to the house tonight and eliminate all of them. He told Eric the plan was for tonight. Elimination of Lindsey and her family, the same with Phil Smith and Patty Saunders as well as Bud Johnson and Rachelle Robinson. Tonight the bloodbath would take place. Eric asked Ron about Deborah Lance and the answer was,

"Who gives a shit about her as long as we get the cash and we frame the right person to take the fall." Eric disconnected from his call and drove away. He was never observed or seen by Paul and Bud. They left the school and were each on their way to see Rachelle when Bud got a text from Paul that he was going back to his apartment and it was probably best if Bud checked on Rachelle himself. Bud received the text when he parked his car on Prospect Street as he was walking toward the front door. He waved to the officers sitting in the police cruiser about twenty yards away and knocked on the door. Rachelle had just blow dried her hair and was quite stunning with no makeup and blue jeans. She invited him in and he asked where Madison was. She laughed and told him.

"Remember she has to work," and told him she had dancing classes and that some school districts were already out for the summer so her busy season was almost in full swing. Rachelle asked where Paul was and Bud told her the truth.

"He thought you would be more comfortable without him being here."

"Oh," she answered. Bud could see the look of disappointment on her face.

"Rachelle, Cronin has sent us here, I mean me, to insure you stay put inside the house for the next twenty-four hours." She folded her arms and shook her head.

"Yes, I know. I've been here writing. I only go out to the hospital to see my therapist and Sherry." Bud replied,

"I know, Sherry is being released today but you can't see anyone, just for a day or so, and speaking of writing, we have been talking about your tweets in the past, but this time, now you put the Ghost Face character with a message from a website called Sightings. What's this about Rachelle? Let me help you please." Rachelle's head looked down on the floor and with a broken voice said,

"I can't, I simply can't right now."

"Rachelle," Bud replied "don't tell me you are involved with this." She looked at him.

"Don't you understand? In order to protect everyone, I can't tell you. Not yet."

"Rachelle," Bud answered, "I'm going to pray tonight as I have the past few nights. My prayers tonight will be about you. I have been praying that no more innocent people are killed. My prayer tonight will be that you are one of those innocent people. Do you know what I'm trying to say?"

"Yes," she answered. "You are telling me if I'm not innocent, you won't lose sleep if something happens to me."

"No," Bud said. "Not true, but I'm putting my faith on the line for those who are not up to their asses in being worried about the money. There is a twelve year old girl mixed up in all of this. We have lost Victoria, Timothy, Allan and almost lost Sherry and you. My priority will be saving the lives of those innocent. By the way, how did you find this Sightings website?" Rachelle looked away from Bud and spoke,

"I think it's time you spoke to Detective Lieutenant Cronin." Bud replied,

"I was wondering when we were going to get to that. OK," he continued, "stay inside." He went to the door and looked back at Rachelle with her arms folded and looking away. "Bye Rachelle." She turned her head to look at him and he could see the tears of pain in her eyes as she said goodbye. As the door shut, she spoke aloud to herself.

"I'm only doing this to help prove his innocence." She walked to her room and fell on her bed and curled up like an infant in her mother's womb.

Bud was going to drive over to Z Pita and see what Paul was up to but decided to go to the Wilkerson house in Belle Terre without him. He drove up, waved at the cruiser and was let in the house by Lindsey's mother Sharyn. He wasn't in the door two minutes when Lindsey walked up to him and gave him a big bear hug. Healey came up behind her and waved to Bud.

"Lindsey," Bud spoke, "can we speak for a few minutes?"

"Sure, let's get some breakfast," she answered. They sat down at the kitchen table and Bud was asked if he wanted coffee and breakfast from Sharyn Wilkerson.

"No, thank you Ma'am," Bud replied. "Coffee and a bagel is just fine, kind of watching my calorie intake." Lindsey couldn't help but speak up.

"Actually, Detective Johnson," He interrupted her with a,

"Oh God, here we go again," as Healey and Sharyn laughed. Lindsey ignored his comment and continued,

"The calories in a bagel depend on the size and the diameter of the bagel. We have mini bagels here that have seventy-two calories in them, the average deli bagel is three and a half to four inches in diameter which has over two hundred and eighty nine calories and that's without any condiments. They are a carbohydrate rich food and will give you plenty of energy to help you with your daily tasks." She continued as Bud just kept silently nodding his head looking at her as if she had Eveready batteries inside of her.

"If you're on a strict, fat loss diet, you may want to forego them altogether because to burn off a bagel you would have to do thirty-one minutes of jogging, twenty-eight minutes of cycling or thirty-three minutes of basketball. Now when you compare them to muffins and donuts, which cops are famous for, they are the better choice because they limit saturated fat. Donuts in addition to calories have from two to five grams of saturated fat and two to five grams of trans fat. That's a quarter to one half the recommended daily limit for saturated fat." Bud looked at Sharyn Wilkerson and said,

"I'll take coffee with a plain mini bagel." Lindsey nodded,

"Good choice. Now since you want to lose weight, you should eliminate five hundred calories a week. But if you eliminate two hundred and fifty calories per day and exercise it is a much healthier way for you to lose weight." Bud's phoned buzzed as Lindsey wanted to continue.

"Saved by the phone," he said as the other adults were amused. It was Officer Franks informing him of the website *Sightings Ghost Face*.

"It's run by a company Red Dot Media which calls it a social photo sharing application for iPhone and iPad. It allows fans to interact with the movie fan community, get the latest news, view movie trailers and combine photos with dramatic poses of Ghost Face to create a sighting and share through Facebook." Franks continued, "Let me fax over the features to you." Bud asked Sharyn Wilkerson if they had a fax machine and she answered no. Lindsey spoke up,

"Have them scan it and email it to you." Officer Franks gave it to Gina and she emailed it over to Bud within a few minutes. Bud looked at the features offered which included combining favorite photos with over twenty poses of Ghost Face. Now the question in Bud's mind was where did Rachelle get a photo of a mountain of cash to combine Ghost Face with it? He called back Franks. Once he got him on the line, he asked him to get with Sherman and O'Connor to find out who paid for the application and to start looking where the photo came from.

"Bud," Officer Franks replied. "Why don't you go to the person who posted it in the first place?"

"I did that," Bud replied, "just check this out for me." He disconnected and sipped on his coffee as Lindsey just stared at him. "You enjoying watching me eat?" Bud asked.

"Yes," she answered.

"Maybe you should go try and disprove Einstein's theory of relativity, now that will keep you busy," he said as he smiled at her.

"Actually," she replied, "I have a theory I'm working on and believe that I may be able to do just that if I'm not beaten by Jacob Barnett. He has an IQ of 170 which is higher than mine and he believes he is only a few mathematical equations away from disapproving."

"Sorry I mentioned it," Bud replied. "Well," he continued, "do you have the sketch you promised us today?"

"Yes," the young girl replied, "but I'm not allowed to give it to you." Bud put his coffee down.

"What do you mean?" Lindsey replied,

"Detective Lieutenant Cronin asked me to put the sketch in a yellow envelope, seal it and give it to Officer Healey." Bud looked at Healey.

"Justin, you are kidding me."

"No," the officer replied. "He said to give it to him or Assistant

District Attorney Ashley if anything happens to him." Bud was upset and said he felt like eating steak and eggs now.

"No," Lindsey said. "That's the worst time to eat, when you're upset." Bud put down his coffee cup and thanked Sharyn Wilkerson for the hospitality.

"OK," he said, "I've got to take care of a few things before I get back here tonight." He said his goodbyes and got in his car and drove to Mather Hospital to see Sherry before she was released during the day.

Agents Barnes and his partner, Agent Payton were getting ready to leave from their shift at 2pm when they noticed a group of people getting out of three different cars to head for the apartment building door. It was about six or seven people, men and women grouped together laughing amongst themselves as they entered the main building.

"Let's check it out," Barnes said to his partner Edward Payton. They walked in the building and went to Patty Saunders door and knocked. She answered the door and smiled,

"Wow, more men."

"Is everything all right Ma'am?" Barnes said.

"Not really," she said, "but I'm OK if that's what you mean."

"OK," the agent said. "There will be someone outside, we are leaving in a couple of minutes." She shut the door and within thirty seconds there was another knock.

"I told you I was fine," as she opened the door. There was no one there. She put her head out to the hallway saw nothing and she began to walk back into her apartment when a figure from the hallway put a black bag over her head as she tried to scream in terror.

"Shhh," the man said. "Quiet, before I break your neck. If I tighten this bag, you won't have much time for air so just listen." The man spoke in a whisper as he got close to her ear. "Who the hell do you think you are making phone calls demanding money. You have been one fuck up after another. A simple kidnapping turns into the biggest murder case in Long Island history. Oh wait, excuse me, don't know if there will be more bodies found on Ocean Parkway at Jones Beach dumping grounds yet. You listen to me you bitch, you will go down to the Port Jefferson Jazz Club tonight and be out 'til 2am in the morning. You let them monitor you down in the Village. You make a call to Simpson around 1am and tell him you want him to come meet you about the money. Do you understand?" As he tightened the bag, Patty struggled to talk but managed to tell the man she had a curfew with her ankle monitoring of 11pm.

"Then you let them come looking for you. It will take them a couple hours to realize you have purposely broken the curfew and come get you. I would have you leave Port Jefferson Village but no, you and your fucking monitor are tying our hands behind our backs. When this is over, I may decide to leave you alive. Do this right and maybe you will have a long life in jail. Just nod yes if you understand. I know you are running out of air and shouldn't speak. OK, now that I have your attention, be a good girl and decoy some of the police tonight and maybe I won't tie you up and start cutting off your fingers one at a time, then your toes, then your tongue. You will die a long suffering death if you betray me, I promise you." "You take this bag off in ten seconds or I'll come back and start with your first finger," the man said. Suddenly he was gone. Patty was shaking and crying so hard it was past ten seconds before she took the bag off her head. She fell to the floor breathing hard as she was crying.

The lab technician called Detective Lieutenant Cronin direct as per his instruction and said, "You better get down here right away." Cronin drove to the Yaphank station and met with Gary Osborne, the lab technician he had assigned to keep an eye on the Saunders apartment. "Take a look at this," Osborne said. He played him the tape of the intruder that put the bag over Patty's head and spoke to her while she was shaking.

"What are we going to do with this?" Osborne asked.

"Nothing," Cronin answered. "We are going to let this game play out."

"Wait," Osborne said. "We have to inform the FBI, Assistant District Attorney and," Cronin interrupted him.

"We tell no one. It's not admissible anyway. I just changed the rules today."

"Sir," Osborne said. "Are you telling me the surveillance camera was installed illegally?"

"No," Cronin answered, "I'm not telling you anything. Just do your job, I'll take the responsibility." Osborne looked at the piece of film and kept turning his head to Cronin then back at the film.

"Shit," he said to himself as Cronin left. As Cronin got in his car, he sent Bud a text.

"Your visit today was successful." Bud received the text and knew immediately what it meant. Cronin could not be specific in a text but he had asked Bud to install a small wireless surveillance camera on top of the doorway in Patty's apartment when he was there. It was not easy figuring out the different frequency that was needed to insure what happened in the apartment was captured. Patty had an ankle monitor, a computer and television but with the help of Gary Osborne they figured it out. His BlackBerry buzzed again, it was another alert from Rachelle, for the second time in a row it was a so called "Sighting" of Ghost Face, this time the image was superimposed next to a bank safe that was open and had no money in it. The caption read, "It's too LATE…It was your FATE. Soon you will SEE… that it's all for ME."

"What the shit is she doing?" Bud said aloud to himself. He sent Paul a text. "Where the hell are you?"

He called the precinct asking if Paul was there since they left. He was connected to Gina who told him he had not been back. He drove to Z Pita, knocked on the back door and went up the stairs to find Paul was not around. He walked around the front, entered into the restaurant to sit down for a cup of coffee and was greeted by Rosie.

"How are you doing, honey? What can I get for you now?"

"A cup of joe, err, I mean coffee and Joey Z."

"All righty now," the smiling server replied. Joey Z walked over to Bud and sat down. Bud started talking right away.

"Have you seen Paul?"

"No, not since breakfast this morning," the owner replied.

"If you see him, you tell him he better call me like yesterday." Rosie brought over his coffee.

"Here you go, honey," and walked away. Bud looked back at her, "I can't believe she is still here, she seems nuts." Joey Z laughed.

"That's what they say about you, my friend, besides, it was difficult getting used to her personality but now we have parties of six, eight, ten or more that specifically request her. She's like a breath of fresh air." Bud shook his head,

"I guess you can't always go by first impressions."

"No, my friend," Joey Z replied, "you most certainly cannot. What do you think of the new wall décor and paint colors of the place?" Bud looked around and didn't want to say he had not noticed but he said it was very nice. Joey Z continued,

"Rosie and Tina did not like the mirrors at first without drapes but they came around." Bud was getting anxious to leave. He loved Joey Z but he had a murder on his mind as well as the whereabouts of Paul.

"OK," Bud replied as he got up. "It will be a late night tonight. I better get some rest." He wrote a note to Paul and gave it to Joey Z to give to Paul. He suspected he would come in for something to eat before he went upstairs to get some sleep before the shift tonight. Bud got in his car and drove to the precinct to speak with Detective Lieutenant Cronin about the footage before heading back to his place. He arrived at 4pm and as he headed to the Detective Lieutenant's office, Gina stopped him to tell him he was taking a sixty minute nap. The curtains were drawn and his phone was directed to ring at Gina's desk. Bud looked at his watch and asked how much longer would it be before his nap reached sixty minutes.

"Another thirty minutes," she answered. "Please wait." Bud was chomping at the bit. He needed to talk to Cronin about what was captured on film in Patty's apartment. He was praying it was someone he didn't know. When 4:30pm arrived, Gina woke up the boss and Bud walked in and shut the door. Paul walked in to the precinct and was told that Bud and Cronin were in his office.

"OK," he replied, he walked over to Gina and told her to tell Bud to pick him up at his apartment at midnight if he wanted to go to the Wilkerson house together.

Bud walked out of Cronin's office about ten minutes later and was told by Gina that Paul was there, left, and gave him the message about the pickup. He went back into Cronin's office and spoke,

"If this asshole can get inside Patty's apartment with the FBI watching her from the outside, how the hell is she going to be protected when she goes to Port Jazz tonight?"

"I know," Cronin spoke. "However, she got herself into this mess and she agreed to the deal. She has already flushed out one of them and we have him on film. We will put Chapman on detail at Port Jazz tonight just to see what goes down if anything." Bud nodded.

"See ya later boss." He tried to leave but held himself back. He turned around and looked at the man he had admired so much these past few years. "Are you sorry boss?"

"About what?" Cronin replied.

"The decisions you made," Bud answered. "The statement made to *Long Island Pulse*?"

"No," the Detective Lieutenant replied. "I've been doing this a long time and I won't regret my decisions. I believe that to protect my team and to end the game, I had to be personally involved in this one." Bud nodded.

"See you later."

"OK, Bud, get some rest," the boss replied. Bud drove back to his apartment and texted,

"I miss you," to Deborah. He wasn't sure why he did. He really didn't know her that well, but the short time they had together, he felt there was a connection not to mention a chemical reaction on his part. He wanted to be a better person every time he thought about her. He wanted to be a better cop when he was around her. He laughed to himself when he thought how happy he was she didn't have the memory of a Lindsey. He was going to call the Wilkerson house when he received a text from Deborah that said,

"Thank you for telling me that." He wrote back and said,

"You're welcome" and felt a little foolish for expressing himself that way until about two minutes later, he received a text from her saying,

"I miss you as well." They began to exchange texts until Bud realized it was almost 7pm before telling her he had to get some sleep for the shift tonight. Before he went to bed he wrote a note to Deborah to her in case something happened to him. Cronin felt strongly something was going to happen Thursday or Friday night, due to his statement. He thought they have all felt strongly about things in the past that never happened but the intense scrutiny of the case was forcing the hand of those who were after the cash. Bud sat on his bed with his thoughts spinning. "Who are you working with Phil Smith? It's true the camera adds ten pounds to you."

William Lance called Robert Simpson at the mansion to tell him they would be coming home Sunday and to please be out by Saturday to avoid awkward moments with Deborah. Simpson acknowledged he would be out but told his former employer he was not giving up on Debbie. William Lance replied that would be up to his daughter to decide that. He hung up the phone and within thirty seconds Simpson called the number and the person they referred to as the voice answered.

"It's tonight or tomorrow," Simpson said. "I have to be out by Saturday."

"You just be there tonight," the voice said and he heard the tone indicating the caller hung up. Ron Buckner also received a call and was told,

"Tonight you wipe out everyone in the Wilkerson house. You don't leave until the girl is dead, and you listen to me. You check her pulse, because if she's not dead, she'll be able to say what time you shot her and what color socks you were wearing. Do you understand?"

"No worries," Ron replied as he heard a click. He sent text messages to Eric and Brian to meet and discuss the plan.

Paul had entered Z Pita at 4:45pm and ordered a Greek salad and take out of Joey's famous eggplant skordalia to have upstairs when he woke up later. Joey sat down and spoke.

"Listen to me, I don't know what's going on and I don't want to know, but, as for you, you as a person and a friend, you're scaring me. These past two weeks have been hell I know, that's your job, but you have people that care about you just remember that. Have you spoken to Rachelle?" Paul was served his Greek salad from his favorite waitress Tina, when he answered Joey Z.

"No, I haven't spoken to her in what seems ages but it has only been about twenty-four hours. We never went more than a few hours from communicating in some way. I guess you could say she is the closest woman I've ever been with without being intimate," he said as he smiled. Joey Z shook his head.

"Is that supposed to be funny?" Paul stabbed his salad with his fork.

"No, I guess not," he said.

"You take care of this, Paul, and you remember, don't do anything you will regret because the ones who care about you will be the ones who are hurt."

"I hear you," Paul said as he sipped on his iced tea mixed with cranberry juice. Normally Joey Z would get up and walk around the two sides of the restaurant but this time he was compelled to sip on his coffee and stay with Paul in case he wanted to talk. The Detective Sergeant started to reminisce with Joey Z about the past few years and the funny moments they have had with the wait staff and other customers. Joey Z even told him the story of the new server Rosie who went outside to greet people who were looking at the chalkboard on the sidewalk and a man who was questioning whether he wanted to try the restaurant or just go down to the pizzeria. Rosie started playfully hitting the man's chest telling him how great Z Pita was and after the third time the man finally said,

"Ma'am, please, I have a pacemaker."

"It was all I could do to keep from exploding with laughter." Joey said.

"Too bad Bud wasn't there to see it," Paul remarked. "He would have peed his pants." Joey Z and Paul shared a few laughs like the old times before he went upstairs to bed. He called his Dad and got his voicemail and decided to just say,

"I love you, Dad, thanks for being my father." He put his BlackBerry in the charger and lay on his bed with the television on. He set the alarm for 11pm and slowly went into a sleep by 7pm.

Lindsey was watching the History Channel with Monty when Healey approached her parents Sharyn and Walt.

"How are you holding up?" Her Mom was putting the dishes away as Walt stood by the counter.

"I'm just looking forward to this being over and going back to our normal lives." Healey looked at Lindsey on the couch and replied,

"With a girl like that, I'm not sure how normal you think it's going to be." They all laughed as she sat quietly in the living room. Healey then walked over to Lindsey and said,

"What were they talking about four minutes thirty two seconds ago Lindsey?" The young girl looked up at him and said,

"Ford Focus, a commercial was on." Healey stopped in his tracks, smiled and said,

"Bud was right about you." She laughed as he petted Monty on his head as he was on her lap.

"He's a beautiful dog," he remarked. The young girl told him that Monty was going to be a father and she was going to get three puppies from the owner of the female. The breeder was going to sell them for over a thousand dollars apiece. Healey nodded,

"And what are you going to do with three puppies?" Lindsey was quick to answer.

"I'm going to give them to you, Bud and Paul for taking care of me." Healey put his hand on the side of her face.

"You are a sweet, sweet girl Lindsey. I noticed your posters of the famous mathematicians in your room, who is Robert Osserman?" The young girl smiled and replied

"He was also a mathematician who wrote the book *Poetry of the Universe*. It changed the way I look at the world. Read it and you will understand what I mean"

Healey nodded with a smile as he walked over to the front window, looked out and saw Officer Dugan standing outside the cruiser. As he looked at Dugan, his mind was someplace else. It was the gesture of kindness bestowed upon him from a beautiful twelve year old girl who had gotten mixed up in this mess. He turned his head and looked at her totally engrossed in the program and wondered what it would be like to remember just about anything you've seen. His thoughts wondered to the sketch that was inside the manila envelope. He went upstairs into the guest room and unlocked the closet door that he had a special lock put on it. He pulled out the Remington 12 gauge shotgun and brought it to the cot that was outside Lindsey's bedroom. He slit it underneath the small mattress to have there for the evening. He looked over the railing as Lindsey was kissing Monty. As he walked down the stairs, he thought about how he too couldn't wait for this to be over. He had made up his mind that no one would touch this special girl unless they were successful in taking him out as well.

"What is this about?" he said to her.

"It's the Revolutionary War," she replied. "I've seen it before but it is so good."

"I'm afraid to ask," Healey replied, "but if you remember everything, why would you need to watch it again?"

"You are silly," she replied. "I don't watch it to remember, I watch it to be entertained and to see the actual vision and picture that relates to the dates."

"So," he said, "when did you last see this then?"

"April 24, 2010," she replied.

"I'm calling Bud on you," he replied as they both laughed. Walt and Sharyn came into the living room as the laughter stopped.

"10:15, 10:30 Lindsey for bed OK," her Mom said. Lindsey saluted her Mom as they said good night to Officer Healey. It was now 10pm.

"When's this show over?" he asked Lindsey.

"It's over at 11pm," she answered, "but it's OK, I'll go to bed at 10:30. I remember how it ends." Healey thought to himself,

"No shit."

Officer Healey walked toward the stairway with Sharyn and Walt as he spoke. "May I ask when did you realize you had a special girl on your hands?" Walt stopped on the second stair up as Sharyn was at the bottom and replied first.

"We knew pretty much from the time she was eighteen months old that she was above average in intelligence. When she started to speak extremely clear by the age of two, we had her tested. We were told Lindsey most likely had eidetic memory which is perfect recall. Most call it photographic memory but there is more than the ability to recall images, sounds or objects with extreme precision. Her hearing is way above the normal range. As you know, she can sketch from her memory. If she studies an image or face for at least thirty seconds, she will maintain a nearly perfect photographic memory on it forever with extreme precision and abundant volume." Healey nodded as he replied.

"Have they explained to you why or how?" Walt came down a step to speak.

"They can give you all the scientific explanations they feel they need to explain. I find they tend to do it with most things today, but when it comes to the miracle of birth and the first thing that develops is the brain, you can't tell me the good Lord doesn't have anything to do with it. There are reasons why you are who you are and why Lindsey has her gift. Her gift is not a scientific gift, it's a gift from God. Thanks for being here and watching over our child." With that, Walt Wilkerson started going up the stairs as Sharyn and Justin Healey looked at him as he reached the top of the stairs, turned right down the hallway and into the master bedroom. Sharyn turned to Officer Healey.

"That goes for me too. This has been difficult for us and although Lindsey is gifted, she is still twelve and I'm not sure if she quite understands the danger she could be in." Healey turned his head to look at Lindsey and Monty on the sofa.

"Oh, I have a feeling she knows, but she loves her parents so much that she just doesn't want to worry and upset you more. See you in the morning." Sharyn smiled and thanked him again as she went up the stairs. Officer Healey walked over to the young girl and could see she was falling asleep.

"Come on girl. You've got too much going on in that brain of yours and it's making you tired."

"Monty," the girl said, "shut the television off please." With that, the dog got off the sofa and went to the television and pushed the button to shut off the television. Healey's mouth dropped.

"You had to show off didn't you? The remote control was too easy. You just had to show how smart Monty was." Lindsey laughed as she got up to go to the stairs.

"I was saving that for Bud but it seemed perfect to do it now. Good night."

As Robert sat down on the sofa in the guesthouse to watch some television, a hand reached over his mouth with the other hand holding a gun to his temple.

"Hello, Mr. Simpson. I'm Mr. Phil." He was very amused with himself that he said that line in the tone of the horse from the Mr. Ed classic television series.

"I will not waste any time. Give me the money now and I will leave you alive to explain to "the voice" how you lost it to me. Make your decision now. 5-4-3-2"

"OK," Simpson replied. "I'll give it to you," with that he got up as Phil Smith followed him into the bedroom. He tore off the mattress and inside the spring mattress was a section cut out to where the suitcase fit. He lifted it up and gave the suitcase to Phil. As Phil took the suitcase he said,

"I'm not sure if you're smart or dumb. But here are some Southwest gift cards. Use them, get out of town if you want to live. I will say you are lucky because if I didn't need you to deal with the police and the voice, you would have a bullet in your head right now. Have fun tonight to face the music." Robert Simpson seemed startled as Phil Smith left. He started shaking and wasn't sure what he should do. He pulled out his phone and started making calls. Phil Smith got in his car parked on the side of the road on Cliff Road and drove toward the exit which led to East Broadway. As he passed Bell Circle he waved,

"Bye, it's been nice knowing you." He started laughing as he pulled on to East Broadway and drove away.

Patty arrived at Port Jazz at 10:45pm and ordered two martinis with three olives to sit at the bar. She knew it would be a short time before the police would be looking for her with the monitor on her ankle. She pulled out her phone and sent Phil a text. "I'm here." When Phil looked at the message he received, he laughed again. "Dumb bitch," he said to himself.

Robert Simpson was shaking as he tried to call Rachelle. There was no answer. He pushed his buttons again and called Detective Lieutenant Cronin as he explained what happened.

"Did you do what I told you to do and separate five hundred thousand from the 3 million?" asked the Detective Lieutenant.

"Yes," Simpson said.

"Then you have nothing to worry about. Just stay there and act like nothing has happened," the Detective Lieutenant continued to speak, "if you blow this, I will shoot you myself." Simpson disconnected and decided he would do as he was told by the detective. He tried to contact Rachelle again and just like the first time, there was no answer. Rachelle stared at her iPhone as she let the call from Simpson go to her voicemail. She stared at Detective Lieutenant Cronin who was standing in her living room and instructed her not to pick up the call.

"Phil made his move a little early," he said. He figured out he would be a target and got to the house early. He sent Patty to Port Jazz as a decoy. That means as I suspected the game ends tonight." Madison walked down the hallway and held on to Rachelle as Cronin spoke.

"Don't leave this house for any reason Rachelle."

"She won't," Madison answered. The Detective Lieutenant walked outside and walked over to the protective detail on Prospect Street.

"Keep your eyes open. If Rachelle leaves the house, you will be a security guard at Kohl's Department Store next week, understand?"

"Yes sir,' the officers replied. Cronin walked away and got into his unmarked vehicle and called Assistant District Attorney Ashley.

"You know what to do if I'm not here tomorrow, whether alive or not as a cop."

"Kevin," Ashley replied. "There's no one better at playing a game."

"Gee," Cronin replied. "I'm not sure how to take that but thank you. Take care, John."

"You too," the Assistant District Attorney replied. He turned on the ignition and drove away. The two officers in the cruiser decided that maybe one of them should be outside the vehicle and be closer to the house. They didn't want to take any chances that someone would get in or out of the house. Inside the house, Rachelle was sitting in her chair and looking at photos from her media file on her iPhone. She couldn't believe how many photos there were of her and Paul that she had saved. She dropped her phone and told Madison she needed to go to sleep and wake up in the morning and find out this had all been a dream.

"Me too Sis. I'll see you in the morning," Madison replied.

Ron, Eric and Brian all met in the Mount Sinai Shopping Center parking lot. Ironically, near the very same Rite Aid drug store that Phil had been captured on film.

"Let's go over the plan," Ron said. "Let's get one thing clear, we don't leave 'til the girl is dead." They all nodded their heads in agreement as Ron started reviewing where the girl's room was and where the police should be. He was still reviewing the plans as Officer Lynagh left the twenty-four hour King Kullen Supermarket in the same parking lot with snacks to bring to the house while Healey slept. So close yet so far they were less than one hundred yards apart when Lynagh got in his car. As he drove toward the exit, he was less than forty yards away from them. All their lives would change in less than two hours.

The alarm went off at 11:01 and Paul felt like he only had two hours sleep instead of four. He took a shower, came out and looked out on Main Street. He was surprised to see cars still going by past 11pm on a Thursday night. From his window he saw Joey Z walk out to the sidewalk. It wasn't unusual to see him on the front sidewalk but not at 11:15pm. He leaned out the window and asked if everything was OK. Joey Z waved back and told Paul he was late tonight doing an inventory and wanted some fresh air. Paul told him he had a late shift tonight and would be leaving soon. Joey Z made one of his famous quotes,

"Whose got it better then you?" to Paul.

"I'll be here 'til about 12:30am my friend."

"OK," Paul said, "have a good night." It really is fascinating how life can be affected by the small events in our life. Paul didn't realize it but the fact that Joey Z picked this particular night to do his inventory at a restaurant helped shape the destiny of what was to come. Bud got up at 11:25pm, showered and put on his jeans and Hawaiian shirt and was out the door by 11:55pm. He sent Paul a text that he would be there to pick him up by 12:15. As Bud drove, his thoughts wanted to be of Deborah but they kept going back to Paul. So many things, so many thoughts going through his mind.

12:10 AM JULY 1

He reached the back parking lot behind Z Pita, knocked lightly and went up the stairs. Paul was looking over some papers with his back to Bud as he spoke.

"So you decided to be a partner at least 'til this is over."

"Do I have a choice?" was Bud's answer. Bud continued to stare at Paul as his back was turned to him. He had started to dislike himself for the things he was thinking about Paul but his instincts were telling him things he didn't like. He looked around the apartment and noticed the Ghost Face mask that was always hanging on the coat rack there was not there.

"Where's the mask that hung there for years Paul?"

"Not sure," Paul answered as he opened his drawer to get a shirt. Bud pulled out his 9mm and pointed it at Paul. Paul turned around as he lifted his shirt.

"Don't move," Bud said. "You Fuck! You son of a bitch! You couldn't do this the right way. You had to be a hero vigilante and wipe them out!"

"Bud," Paul said.

"Shut the fuck up! You listen to me, I will shoot and I will be angry at you and myself for handling it this way, but it won't change things. I will shoot, you bastard!"

"Are you going to let me speak?" Paul replied. As Bud continued to hold aim on him, Paul spoke.

"Bud, you are mistaken, this is not what you think or it appears to be. I am not the vigilante."

"Shut up," Bud answered. "You really piss me off. You throw everything away for the sake of the girl!" "I watched the interrogation you did with Simpson three times. You never even brought up the hospital video. The night Rachelle was attacked, where the fuck were you? I'll tell you where you were, on the front lawn killing Winters."

"Bud," Paul said, "Shut Up!" as he held the 9mm steady.

"Where were you while Deborah was saved and Mason Winters was being stabbed? I could never reach you while this was going on! The attack of John Winters in the abandoned building. I was with Cronin and where the fuck were you! I got a call from the lab on the body type possibility for the masked figure. Guess who was on the list that could have done what he did in the hospital? You, you Paul were on the list. I kept putting if off thinking, no, not Paul. And then the note from whoever shot at me in front of the building and killed Allan. The note said stop the killing Detective Powers. It wasn't about you being a detective to solve the crime and stop the killings, no, it was about you. You! You! To actually stop killing. You risked everyone's lives in this case to get vengeance for Rachelle." Paul started to move towards Bud. "Stop, Paul, I swear don't make me shoot you. Get your hands up."

"Now what," Paul replied.

"And now," Bud said, "the mask. The mask that you love so much that never left this coat rack is not where it's supposed to be. Why because it has blood splatter on it? There are too many things that happen that point to you. I won't even get to your sweats. That's right, I know you. Every time you get stressed out and nervous, the back of your head gets wet. Where's your piece?"

"Bud," Paul said.

"Don't go there," Bud answered. He took out his handcuffs. "Lock yourself to the opening of this bedpost." He watched Paul lock himself in as Bud searched the apartment for his gun. He found it in a small box inside his closet. "Where's your back up?" he asked.

"Under the bed in a box." Bud found it in the middle underneath.

"I guess I'll be going to the Wilkerson house alone tonight," Bud said.

"I'll be calling for an officer to come over and pick you up. Don't make this harder for everyone Paul. If you're not here when I get back, I will find you and I will shoot you."

"Bud," Paul said. "Don't do this, you are making a mistake Bud!" His partner started walking toward the stairs as he turned around and looked at Paul.

"Was it worth it Paul? By the way, it's just a coincidence you are left handed also. It's past midnight already, I gotta go." Bud started running down the stairs as Paul started yelling,

"Don't do this Bud!" It was to no avail as Bud slammed the door as he left.

Paul started banging the headboard against the wall and began jumping up and down as best as he could. He remembered that Joey Z was downstairs late doing inventory and was trying to make such a racket that he would want to see what was going on. For ten minutes, he banged, and he hopped up and down and was so exhausted he almost gave up when he heard Joey Z locking up the front door. Paul grabbed the now famous coat rack with his free hand and drove it through the front window. As the pieces of window crashed over the sidewalk Joey Z threw himself toward the front of the building to avoid the falling glass and held onto his chest to make sure he wasn't having a heart attack.

"Joey!" Paul yelled. "I need you Joey, come up!" Joey Z ran around to the back through the small alley way that separated the buildings on Main Street and found that the door was locked. He pulled out his key ring, unlocked the door and ran up the stairs to find the apartment a mess and the bed half torn apart because Paul was locked to a heavy bedpost.

"What the hell," Joey Z remarked.

"Joey!" Paul yelled, "my gun, there's a small box underneath the sink in my bathroom. Please bring it to me!"

"Paul," Joey Z remarked. "Why are you locked up in handcuffs?" Paul replied,

"If I tell you, will you bring me the box?"

"Before I pee my pants try me," Joey Z said.

"Bud thinks I'm the masked Ghost Face doing the killings of the kidnappers."

"Ugh," Joey said. "OK, that makes me feel safe, maybe I will pee my pants," as he went to get the box.

"I'm not a kidnapper," Paul said to Joey as he handed him the box. Paul opened the box with his free hand and out came a small 22 handgun.

"Oh shit," Joey Z said, "almost too late to hold it." Paul ignored Joey Z as he fired into the chain that held him.

"I've got to get out of here before the officers come to pick me up." He ran to his closet and tore apart the bottom drawer as he pulled out an older 9MM Glock from a combination box. He put on his shirt, got his car keys and ran down the stairs.

"Thanks Joey," he said as the restaurant owner and landlord was now standing in the middle of the apartment he said to himself aloud, "maybe it's time for a new tenant." He looked around the apartment in disbelief, then walked into Paul's bathroom and shut the door.

Bud had called it in for an officer to go to Paul's apartment to bring him to the precinct as a person of interest. He was afraid of a total blow up of the media if he said anything else before they had a chance to formally question him. Bud pulled up to the driveway of the Wilkerson's and met with Officer Dugan. Status was all good with no problems as Bud went to the front door. Lynagh opened it before he knocked which startled Bud.

"How's it going?" he asked Lynagh.

"Quiet, which is good," Lynagh answered.

"Healey and the girl are upstairs sleeping."

"OK," Bud answered "I would go up there but knowing Healey he would shoot me so I'll just stay down here." Lynagh didn't crack a smile.

"Good idea."

Ron, Eric and Brian drove to Cliff Road and parked the car about one hundred yards away from Bell Circle. Ron and Eric had handguns called Grandpower R100 Slovak semi-automatic pistols while Brian carried a pump action Remington 870 Shotgun. They walked in the still of the night and stopped about twenty five yards away from Officer Dugan now sitting in the cruiser. The three of them split up to their assignments while Ron attached a silencer to his gun. Ron walked to the left of the road and was given four minutes to peacefully cause Dugan to take a walk or to get outside of the car. The plan was to eliminate him before he could request back up. Once he was taken out, they figured they had five minutes to decoy what would be happening about a mile down the road to allow Simpson, Phil and the voice to secure the cash. The only thing that the three of them didn't realize was Phil had already beaten them to the money. Ron began his walk in front of the house and true to form Dugan got out and stood by his car. What the three intruders didn't realize was Dugan had texted Lynagh there was a pedestrian on the road before he got out of the car. Lynagh told Bud and the detective started looking out the front window. He had started to tell Lynagh to get his shotgun but he heard the officer already pull the gauge back.

"Probably nothing," Bud said, "but let's be ready."

"Excuse me, sir," Ron said. Officer Dugan spoke,

"Kinda late for you to be walking the streets alone, even in Belle Terre." As Dugan spoke, Eric was able to quickly climb from the side of the house to the front bedroom window where Lindsey slept. The twelve year old girl had heard noises on the house but was used to creaks and noises, especially from the heating system. This time her gifted hearing heard someone working quietly to open her window. Lindsey began getting nervous but was too startled to even run. She started throwing her plush pigs she always slept with against her room door to awaken Healey. By the time the window was open, she had thrown her last and final pig against the door. As she started to pull the covers over her head, Eric was already sitting inside the window ledge. He pulled out his knife in order to keep it as quiet as possible and even liked it that Lindsey covered her face with the covers. He noticed the door slowly opening and he pulled his gun out from his sleeve and pointed it at Lindsey just as he saw Officer Healey standing there with his 9mm Glock on him.

"So," Eric said. "You are truly the good bodyguard. How did you hear us?" Healey stood there. No words but with the gun focused on the intruder. Lindsey lowered the covers and without moving her head, her eyes were rotating from Eric to Healey. Eric continued to speak. "Looks like we have a problem, I'm not leaving here 'til she's not breathing and you will most likely shoot me, so either way, you have failed because she won't be alive. You have failed, Officer." Still, the officer with his arms straight out would not respond. The silence was uncomfortable to Eric but he continued to speak. "You shoot me, I will still pull the trigger. The question is who will shoot first." Healey focused on Eric's eyes without saying anything. Finally, the twelve year old girl spoke in words barely audible.

"I trust you," as she finished those words, Monty who was sleeping under the bed let out a small sigh. Eric's eyes quickly glanced to the bed and Healey took his shot. The bullet hit him squarely in the head as he fell through the window onto the secondary roof and on to the ground.

Dugan turned around and Ron fired twice hitting Dugan in the back and his leg. Healey's shot was heard as Lynagh started to run upstairs but was held up by Bud.

"No! Stay here! Call for backup! If there are more of them, you need to be down here! Justin! Justin!" Bud yelled.

"I have the girl!" Healey yelled from upstairs.

"Get the family all in one place!" Bud screamed, "Now!" He saw Dugan on the ground in the circular driveway, he looked back at Lynagh.

"Nobody gets upstairs! You hear me!" Lynagh nodded as he stood against the wall with his shotgun pointed up. He had called for back up thirty seconds prior but it already seemed like ten minutes. Bud left the front door and reached Dugan to pull him to cover. As he looked down at the fallen officer, he could see he was still alive from wearing his vest. As he pulled Dugan toward the car, Ron had moved to the opposite side of the cruiser when Eric had fallen out the window. Bud tried to save Dugan, but he was about to realize it was a mistake. Ron crawled around the front of the car, stepped around the side and by the time Bud knew what was happening it was too late. Ron raised his gun and shots were fired. As Ron stood there, he looked down at his stomach and chest and saw blood coming out. As the blood started coming out of his mouth, he fell to the ground. Bud held on to Dugan and held out his gun as the figure started walking out of the darkness into the motion light of the driveway. It was Paul. Bud yelled,

"What the fuck are you doing here!"

"Saving your fat ass! ," Paul yelled.

"I'll accept that," Bud replied. Paul crouched down to look at Officer Dugan who was bleeding heavily. Paul started wrapping his leg from a cloth scarf that was in the cruiser when they heard shotgun blasts in the house.

"Fuck!" Bud said, "Where is the back up!"

"Stay here with Dugan" Paul replied as he ran into the house. "Lynagh, it's Detective Powers! I'm coming in!"

Lynagh was behind the sofa, and he had fired a round from seeing Brian come in through the side door. Paul started moving around the back of the dining room to get over to the side. He looked at Lynagh as he spoke.

"What are you doing?"

"I'm staying here, he needs to get upstairs and this is the best place to be."

"You!" Paul replied, "Are a sitting duck!"

"It is what it is," Lynagh answered. "He's not getting upstairs this way!" Upstairs, Healey moved the girl to the large bathroom and put her in the hot tub. By now, the mother Sharyn, was screaming and Walt was holding on to her. Healey grabbed them and moved them to the bathroom and had all three of them in the hot tub.

"Monty!" Lindsey started yelling. "They will kill my dog." Healey put his hand out to her.

"Wait! You are not going anywhere!" He looked at the father and gave him the shotgun.

"Anybody but me coming through the bathroom door you shoot to protect your family, do you understand?"

"Yes," Walt replied as his hands shook. Healey crawled out into the hallway with his handgun and stated yelling to Lynagh.

"I'm in the hallway upstairs! Who else is in the house!" Paul answered.

"Justin, you have me and Lynagh and we know of one in the house downstairs! We don't know how many more are here. Two dead outside. Dugan is badly injured." Lynagh spoke up.

"I've got the stairway covered. I can't speak for upstairs!" Healey started calling for Monty as the dog looked out of Lindsey's doorway but was afraid to leave the room. The officer crawled all the way to Lindsey's room and grabbed Monty as the dog whimpered. It was too uncomfortable to crawl back with the dog in his arms so he stood up and started running for the bathroom.

Brian couldn't resist. He fired his shotgun at the running officer and it struck Healey down as Lynagh started firing his shotgun toward the wall where the shots came from. Three rounds he fired as he moved closer to the wall.

"Lynagh," yelled Paul. "Get under cover."

"He's not getting upstairs!" Lynagh answered.

"What if there's more in the house!" Paul answered. Bud heard the shots inside and it was killing him but he was afraid Dugan would not be able to defend himself. His BlackBerry buzzed as he grabbed it. It was a text from Cronin to get to the Lance mansion right away. "What the fuck," Bud said.

"Go," Dugan said. "Leave me with my shotgun. I'll either bleed to death or kill someone. Either way I'm a hero." Bud called Paul, and he answered.

"Bad time to work out our problems partner. Cronin needs me at the mansion, this was a decoy. Dugan is out here with his shotgun. Are you OK with me leaving. Back up will be here any second."

"Go," Paul said. "But it looks like Healey is down. I've got to get upstairs to the girl."

"OK, I'll compromise. I'll wait 'til back up is here then I'll take the car with me to the mansion."

"Deal," Paul said as he disconnected.

"Justin!" Paul yelled upstairs. "Justin! I'm coming up if you don't answer!" Lynagh, still lying on the floor with his shotgun ready just stared waiting to hear a response.

"No one," Justin Healey responded. "No one comes upstairs, I'm not dead yet." The officer was bleeding from the pellets that hit him in the shoulder, arm and leg. His vest had prevented further damage as he crawled to the bathroom with Monty. As he entered the bathroom, he let the dog go which went straight for Lindsey. Healey crawled inside bleeding as the young girl started crying when she saw him bleeding. Monty was not shot and was trying to lick Lindsey but she was visibly shaken by seeing Officer Healey laying on the floor bleeding and not breathing regularly.

"It's my fault," Lindsey said crying.

"No honey," Healey replied. "Just stay in the tub," as he took the shotgun from her father.

"All of you just stay in there, I'm here." He crouched up against the back wall of the bathroom with his legs stretched out and held the shotgun barrel toward the door. He looked at the father who was in the tub with his family.

"You know how to use my gun if something happens to me?" The father nodded as Lindsey tried to get to Healey but Sharyn held her back.

"No." Lindsey was shaking as her mother held on to her tightly to keep her from going to Officer Healey. Healey looked at Lindsey.

"It's going to be OK, but you need to be quiet, OK? It's going to be fine." Lindsey just stared at him and tried to hold back her tears. Her face told the story of how frightened she was, but not for herself, for the policeman who was injured trying to save her life. Sharyn Wilkerson held on to her daughter tight to control her shaking and the volume of Lindsey's cries.

Downstairs, Paul continued to move toward the wall that Lynagh obliterated with his shotgun blasts. He started talking to the intruder.

"You are not going to get out of here alive. We will have no problem killing you, so why don't you just surrender right now, your friends are gone. There were only three of you, right?"

"That's what you think," the answer came back.

"If there are more of you," Paul spoke again, "then why are they not here to help you?"

"Maybe they are somewhere else asshole," Brian answered. Paul got on his cell and called Bud outside.

"Get to the Lance mansion now. The others are there. We will hold the fort here 'til back up gets here." Bud left Dugan with the shotgun and as he ran onto Cliff Road, three police cars and two ambulances came roaring down the road. Bud held up his badge and directed two squad cars and both ambulances to the Wilkerson house while he jumped in the car with Chapman who left Port Jazz on the call to go to the Lance mansion. Paul started speaking inside the house again while Lynagh was still lying on the floor with his shotgun ready to burst again.

"Back up is here, there is no way out. Don't become a dead man and dumbass at the same time." Brian sneaked a peek and saw

Lynagh lying on the floor and knew he didn't have much of a chance with Eric and Ron gone but he still felt he wouldn't be a failure if he got the girl.

As back up officers and medics attended to Dugan, Brian started blasting toward the floor at Lynagh as the officer started firing back. Lynagh rolled over twice as Brian ran up the stairs, Lynagh got up and ran firing toward the stairway with Paul firing from his handgun. The blasts hit Brian halfway up the stairs as he fell sideways taking the railing with him.

"Christ!" Paul yelled. He could smell the wood like it was burnt from the splinters in the house from all the blasts of gunfire. The cops outside had all their firearms out as they entered the house. Paul and Lynagh were standing there as Paul told them to secure the premises as they all scattered about. They started to walk up the stairs toward the bathroom as Paul grabbed Lynagh.

"Let's be careful here. He will bleed to death before leaving the girl if he thinks she is still in danger." Lynagh nodded.

"Not to mention shoot us if he's not sure it's us."

"Justin," Paul said. "It's Powers and Lynagh. It's all over in the house. We got them, all three of them. We are coming in with no guns drawn. Do you understand?"

"Yes," the answer came back.

"You recognize my voice, right?" Healey looked at Lindsey as she nodded yes.

"I want to hear Lynagh's voice," Healey spoke back.

"It's me Justin," Lynagh replied. "We need to get you to a hospital." The officer looked at Lindsey and she nodded it was his voice.

"Come on in," he replied to Paul and Lynagh. They slowly pushed the door open showing their hands in the doorway hoping Healey did not have a quick trigger finger. He was laying there badly bleeding from the shotgun wounds. Healy dropped his shotgun when he saw it was Paul and Lynagh. Paul started yelling for the medics to come upstairs and tend to Healey as he looked at the family in the hot tub.

"Come on," he said as he stretched out his hand to help them. Lindsey jumped over the tub herself and went straight to Healey holding his hand as she began to cry again. Paul warned the parents the house was practically destroyed downstairs and there was a dead body near the stairway. Most of all, he warned them it may not be over just yet.

"I'm going to have four officers stay outside to secure the premises. Lynagh will still be here while we take Officer Healey to the hospital."

"I'm going with him," Lindsey said as she stayed by his side.

"Lindsey," her Mom said. "Lindsey answered still crying.

"I'm not leaving him Mom. He didn't leave me and I'm not leaving him," she replied in her shaken voice. Paul looked at the parents, then Lynagh.

"Let her go, she will ride in the ambulance with Officer Healey and Lynagh. I'll have an escort take you behind the ambulance." He waited for Sharyn and Walt Wilkerson to acknowledge, but spoke again.

"It's probably safer for you there while we finish this." Sharyn Wilkerson replied,

"I can't say no to her." Healey was put on a stretcher and carried down as Paul spoke to Lynagh. "Don't let the girl out of your sight and keep the shotgun visible. Make anyone think twice before getting close to her, remember Phil Smith is still not in custody." Lynagh jumped in the back of the ambulance as Lindsey got in and continued to hold his hand as the medics worked on him. Sharyn and Walt got in a cruiser and followed it to Mather hospital. Paul yelled to the ambulance driver."take him to Stony Brook hospital!" The trip was an extra 10 minutes but Stony Brook was a trauma center and Paul felt it was the right thing to do for Healey. He stood outside the Wilkerson House and noticed how wet the back of his head was. When they arrived at Stony Brook Hosptal, it was quite a sight to see. Between the 2 cruisers that escorted the ambulance and Lynagh jumping out of the back with his shotgun. There were so many lights, it looked like a scene from a movie. Officer Dugan had already been at the hospital for 15 minutes and Mayor Margot Garant of Port Jefferson Village was on her way to the Hospital to extend her support to the injured police officers.

Simpson had the suitcase of money with him on the grounds between the mansion and the guesthouse when Agents Sherman and O'Connor pointed their weapons at him.

"Where are you going?" O'Connor said.

"Nowhere," Robert said. "I'm just doing what I was told." Agent Sherman moved around the other side for a different angle while he pointed his gun at Simpson.

"Who told you to take the money?" Sherman asked. "The voice," Simpson replied.

"Who told you to try and leave the grounds with it?" O'Connor asked.

Simpson put the suitcase down and said, "Detective Lieutenant Cronin told me to leave the grounds with it tonight."

Sherman looked at O'Connor and asked, "Now why the hell would he tell you to do that?"

"Because," Cronin said as he stepped out from behind a tree. "Because I wanted to see who would show up here."

"What's that supposed to mean?" Sherman replied. "This is a kidnapping that crossed state lines, involving $3 million in cash."

"How," Cronin continued, "did you know to be here tonight?"

"It's a funny thing," O'Connor said. "We are called investigators, we have leads, and we even read Twitter, Detective Lieutenant Cronin. You have a statement published that you know who is behind this, and it's all over the fucking news. It doesn't take a genius to stake out the house."

"True," Cronin replied as he called out Officer Chapman's name. The officer came out with his gun on Sherman, and before O'Connor could react, Cronin was pointing his firearm at O'Connor.

"Now this is what I call interesting," Cronin said. "You have guns on Simpson here, and we have guns on you." Sherman moved his gun toward Chapman.

"I don't know what the fuck is going on, but I will defend myself." O'Connor moved his gun toward Cronin.

Simpson spoke, saying, "Since nobody has a gun on me, can I leave if the money stays?" He was ignored, as Cronin started to get closer to O'Connor.

"Jason 'Jack' O'Connor, or should I call you 'the voice'? You almost had everyone fooled, but you see, I'm better at playing games than most people. Now drop your weapon before you stop breathing within the next 10 seconds."

O'Connor started to laugh as he held the gun on the detective.

"How did you know?" O'Connor said. With that remark, Sherman moved his gun to O'Connor.

"Well," Cronin said, "where do I start? Let's see, how about the letter from Phil to Rachelle. The only three people that knew about it were Paul, Bud, myself, and your partner, yet you brought it up when we spoke to Anderson. When Bud called in to the precinct requesting a list of who had blue cars from the Twitter messages, you were there. Somehow, Bud got in the middle of a hail of bullets. I had Rachelle change her cell phone number, yet you as an FBI agent still checked on how to reach her; your cell phone dialed the same number Phil gave to the Rite Aid store. You were interviewing William Lance when all of this started at his home and were the first one to know about the $3 million in cash. Oh yeah, besides me setting you up with Mr. Simpson here and Rachelle, I have a 12-year-old witness who happens to have a photographic memory who can place you with exact time and place speaking to Phil Smith. It just isn't your day…or night, I should say."

Bud was standing behind a tree watching about 10 yards away with his gun drawn, listening to Detective Lieutenant Cronin put the case together, and he began to understand why he was not sharing information.

O'Connor put his gun down as he put his hands up and said, "What about the girl, Rachelle? Her tweets prove she was involved with me."

"No," Cronin replied. "That was me. I took over her account and password. She had nothing to do with it. I only had her have lunch here with this asshole," pointing at Simpson, "to throw confusion as to who was involved and how deeply."

"Hey," Simpson remarked, "I resent that."

"Shut up!" Chapman yelled. "Only talk when we tell you to!"

"Now," Cronin continued, "take out your backup." As O'Connor bent over to take out his backup, a shot was fired from Bud, and it struck O'Connor in the backside. He keeled over in pain as Bud walked up to him, which startled everyone.

He looked at Cronin and said, "Sorry, boss, I thought he was going for his backup, and besides, I always wanted to shoot him in the ass."

O'Connor was on the ground yelping, "You shot me in the ass, you shit! You shot me in the ass."

Bud pulled Simpson away as Sherman picked up the money. Cronin kneeled over O'Connor as he lay on the ground and said, "You see, Mr. Voice, it's one thing to bend the rules of the game, but when you start cheating, the details start being overlooked. And let's see, shall I continue? Agent Sherman, did you tell your partner about the letter, yes or no?"

"No," Sherman replied.

"Agent Sherman," Cronin replied "when Paul and Bud requested that the masks you took out of Starfield's house be sent to the precinct, why were they never brought?"

Agent Sherman kept his gun on O'Connor as he answered, "My partner here said he would take care of it."

As Cronin moved a little closer, he spoke again. "What really screwed you up with the details was telling Paul about the girl witnessing the murder in Belle Terre. No one at the courthouse from the FBI could have possibly known at the time you mentioned it. Your greed has gotten the best of you. When Detective Powers wanted to reenact the kidnapping on the ferry, I let him do it expecting nothing to happen. There was no reason for the kidnappers to expose themselves, they had the girl, now all they wanted was the money. Yet somebody in charge wanted to get rid of his accomplices, to take the blame, and to keep a bigger share of the money for himself. Your greed got the best of you Mr Voice."

He looked up at Chapman to take him to the hospital.

"Bud!" Cronin yelled. "You had to shoot him in the ass, didn't you?"

"Sorry," Bud replied, "I missed again."

"Get to Patty Saunders; we have another killer on the loose," Cronin replied.

Bud suddenly thought of Paul and started running for the cruiser that he drove up in with Chapman. Bud yelled at Chapman, "Put him in Cronin's car! I'm taking the cruiser!"

It was at this moment that they all remembered Patty had been sent to Port Jazz to be a decoy. It was good odds Phil Smith was being drawn out.

Patty left Port Jazz and started texting at 1:30 am to Phil Smith. He should have had enough time to secure the money and be safe. As Patty walked down Main Street toward her car, a dark figure with the Ghost Face mask ran into her and grabbed her by the hair and cut off her ponytail. Patty started screaming as she got up and ran straight ahead toward the end of the street. She stumbled twice as the masked figure didn't care about the few pedestrians up this late. Both men and women rushed to be out of harm's way as the mask with the blood splatter continued to chase Patty.

Bud drove as fast as he could down Cliff Road and was heading toward the front of the house when Paul flagged him down. He got in the car as Bud stepped on it again to get to Port Jazz.

"I thought I was going to prevent you from killing Saunders in a mask," Bud said to him.

"Let's just get her," Paul said.

As Patty continued to scream, the masked figure continued to catch up to her and give her a slice of the knife each time. He wanted her to suffer. Patty made it to the dock of the ferry where it all started, and although she was wearing a vest, the killer knew where to put the knife. Deep into her neck, which silenced Patty as she dropped in the water. Before Bud turned left to go up Main Street, Paul saw the figure by the loading dock.

"There!" Bud turned right instead and stopped the car as they got out. Bud took his Glock and yelled for him to stop. "Don't shoot!" Paul begged Bud. "Don't shoot!" He looked at the masked killer. "It's over. Don't give him a reason to shoot you. All you have done is kill the bad guys; the public will be sympathetic to you."

Finally, the masked killer spoke, saying, "There is one left."

"No, it's over," Paul said, as he got closer. The masked killer started to run as Paul threw himself on him. Bud ran up with his gun.

"Don't shoot!" Paul said as Bud put his gun away and held on to the hand with the knife. He secured the knife, and they could hear the crying. He took off the mask with the blood splatter on it. It was Madison. Bud was shocked beyond belief.

"What? Why?" he said as he bent over in disbelief.

"My sister," she replied. "They changed her life, and I wasn't going to put her through years of trials or to look over her shoulder the rest of her life."

"Maddie," Paul said. "The hospital with Kyle Winters, Anderson, John Winters. How did you know where to find them?"

She answered through her sobs, "It's amazing what people tell you to try to save their own lives. Kyle Winters told me things and Mason Winters told me where everyone was before I killed them."

"Why Patty?" Bud asked.

"She started this," Madison answered. "None of this would have happened."

"Listen to me," Paul said. "We are bringing you in; don't say another word without your attorney. Listen carefully, the people you killed were not innocent, plus you saved lives with Deborah, Sherry, and Rachelle. Do you understand?"

"Yes," Maddie answered as he put her in the back of the cruiser.

Paul looked at Bud. "Don't look at me," Bud replied. "I didn't hear a thing. I was looking for the body that fell in the water." Paul nodded.

Bud looked over at the officers who had just arrived at the scene and said, "Sorry, guys, someone has to get the body in the water, and it's not going to be me."

The hospital brought Healey into surgery right away, as Lindsey had to be consoled when they took him away from her. Bud and Paul brought Madison to the precinct as they called Cronin, who in turn picked up Rachelle to bring her down to see her sister. Bud called Al Simmons, Patty's attorney, on what happened to her and told him he had a new client by the name of Madison Robinson.

"It's 3:00 am," Simmons replied.

"Yes," Bud replied. "Some of us work for a living," he said as he disconnected.

As they rode back to the precinct, Bud looked at Paul and said, "I suppose you want an apology from me."

"No need," Paul replied. "You'll make it up to me."

Bud looked puzzled and asked, "What's that supposed to mean?"

"You'll see," Paul answered, "and thanks for not shooting."

"You?" Bud said.

"No, Maddie," Paul answered. "I knew you could never shoot me." Bud turned his head toward the front. He had nothing to say because he knew Paul was right.

"Cronin," Bud answered. "He took us to school on this one. He set all of this up, from Rachelle's Twitter account to having Patty released, to not giving us certain information to protect us in case something went wrong. I feel like such a, such a..."

"Student," Paul finished.

"And you?" Bud went on. "Did you figure out it was her?"

"I had my suspicions. Rachelle and her were both in my apartment when my mask went missing, but I wasn't sure until maybe a day or two ago."

"So where were you when I couldn't reach you for hours yesterday?"

Paul glanced over at Bud and said, "I was with Allan's kids. They needed some company."

"And your sweats?" Bud asked.

Paul nodded and said, "I kept thinking about Madison, but because I was too involved, my judgment was clouded."

Bud put his hand on Paul's arm and said, "You saved my life tonight. Thank you."

Paul smiled and replied, "It's what partners do."

Maddie lay in the backseat curled up, which she was able to do because they didn't put handcuffs on her. As they brought her into the precinct, Al Simmons was already there. He was in his pajamas, but he was there. They took her to a room where he could speak with her. Ten minutes later, Rachelle came in and ran to Paul, crying uncontrollably.

Cronin pulled Bud aside and said, "Let's not forget Phil Smith is still on the loose with the money."

Bud nodded and asked, "Where's O'Connor?"

"Well," Cronin replied, "he's at the hospital being watched by his old friends because you shot him in the ass. They are doing a bedside arraignment on one murder charge with additional charges pending. Turns out O'Connor was lucky. The bullet hit his ID in his wallet, and struck the gleuteus maximus which is the strongest muscle in the human body."

"I couldn't miss," Bud said as he walked away.

"Listen," Cronin said to Bud, "I forced Simpson to do things to have this play out the way I wanted it to. If I'm not here in a day or two, I want you and Paul to know it's been a pleasure." Bud shook his hand.

"Did you ever suspect us?"

"The evidence made me cautious about you two, but I let it play out because I knew the only ones that had to be afraid of the Face of Fear Investigation were the bad guys. If it wasn't Paul or you, then I needed your help. See you in the morning."

Bud said good night, and Paul stayed with Rachelle while she spoke to Maddie and then dropped her back at her place. It was already 4:00 am when he dropped her off.

Phil Smith was in the barn on Morgan Lane in Port Jefferson Station with his cash. He had found the place about two days prior, and it seemed that no one came in and out of the place. He had been sleeping for a few hours and missed all the excitement of the prior six hours. A pebble hit him in the neck area as he finally opened his eyes. Standing in the shadows was a figure wearing a flesh-colored mask with long gray fabric, cutout eyes, and a red tongue coming out of the mouth.

"Who the hell are you?"

The man behind the mask answered in a whispered tone, "Does it really matter?"

"How did you find me?" Phil asked.

The masked man whispered again, saying, "Technology is a wonderful thing, especially when your case of cash is bugged with a transmitter."

"What do you want?" Phil asked.

The man moved closer and said, "I want you to go to hell. You have caused hell, created hell, and now, it's time for you to go to hell."

"That means," Phil answered, "that you would have to kill me."

"Oh, we've got Einstein here," the masked man replied.

"What are you going to do, come after me with a knife like the other masked killings?"

"No," he replied. "Like I said, technology is a wonderful thing."

With that he pulled out his weapon and fired a single shot to the head of Phil Smith, but it missed. Smith reached for his gun, but the masked man fired again and this time hit Phil Smith in the throat. He fired again, and the bullet entered his cheek. He was dead within a minute. The shooter left the building with the money and disappeared before daylight broke.

Nine o'clock in the morning came fast, with very little sleep for all those involved. The *Long Island Pulse* magazine had made an announcement that Detective Lieutenant Cronin was true to his word. Arrests had been made of FBI agent Jason "Jack" O'Connor, and three of his accomplices—Ron Buckner, Brian Thompson, and Eric Pierson—were all killed in a gun battle in one of the homes in Belle Terre. In addition, the body of Phil Smith was found in a storage building on Morgan Lane in Port Jefferson Station. It was strongly suspected that one of the three accomplices with Agent O'Connor had killed Phil Smith and had planned to go back for the cash, which was never found.

Police Commissioner Jameson came out to the podium with Detective Lieutenant Cronin, Assistant District Attorney Ashley, and detectives Paul Powers and Bud Johnson. The commissioner made his opening remarks and turned the podium over to Detective Lieutenant Cronin. He was clearly uncomfortable and didn't want to answer too many questions, but he understood the situation.

The questions started with *Newsday* asking about the masked killer in the Ghost Face mask. Detective Lieutenant Cronin answered it was most likely the result of a vigilante killing spree from the sister of one of the victims. He gave her name as Madison Robinson, the younger sister of Rachelle Robinson, who was one of the intended victims in the Face of Fear Investigation.

Fox News asked, "What would most likely happen to her since they were vigilante killings?" And Detective Lieutenant Cronin answered that he would not speculate on the question and that it would be up to the district attorney's office as to the handling and recommendations. The questions continued from NBC and CBS regarding the vigilante killings until Cronin reminded everyone that the kidnapping of Deborah Lance was the genesis of the case and innocent people were also killed and wounded during the investigation. He continued answering questions for another 10 minutes until he said it was time to wrap things up.

"What now?" asked The Shannyn T, the young intern from *Long Island Pulse* magazine. "What are your plans?"

"My plans?" Detective Lieutenant Cronin answered. "I'm going to Disney World," he said as he walked away from the podium. Most in the crowd laughed with a puzzled look on their faces, but those who knew him best knew he wasn't kidding. Disney World was a place he visited two to three times a year to relieve stress, sometimes with his family and sometimes without.

Cronin walked to his office, and within a few minutes, Bud and Paul walked in. They waited for Gina to leave with some papers before speaking.

"We need to talk," Paul said.

Cronin looked up at his two detectives and asked, "Does it stay in this office, or do we need to be on record?"

Bud and Paul looked at each other, and Bud spoke up, saying, "It can stay in this office." Paul nodded in agreement.

"OK," the boss said, "what's on your mind?"

"You manipulated almost everything," Bud said. "I heard you at the Lance Mansion."

"It worked, right?" Cronin answered.

"You forgot a few things while you were checkmating O'Connor," Bud answered.

"Like?" Cronin asked.

"You were the one who got William Lance to leave town, not to mention offer the bail to get Patty released. It was you who purposely called off security at the mansion, and it was you who got Simpson to agree to be a player in this, including lunch with Rachelle. You kept all of this to yourself."

"No," Cronin answered. "Simpson was threatened by me to be a part of this. Rachelle wanted to help, but I told her she couldn't speak to anyone about it. I made her change her number and knew O'Connor would find a way to get her number once the tweets started coming out on Twitter."

Paul moved closer to his desk as he asked, "And why the use of the Ghost Face photo applications?"

Cronin looked at Paul and said, "Because the only uncertainty I had was just how involved you were, Paul. Your judgment was clouded from the minute Rachelle's life was in danger, and I was going to draw you, Madison, or Phil out by getting Patty released on bail and leaving antagonizing messages and photos on the Internet."

Bud spoke up, asking, "Yet you kept Paul on the case with me?"

"Yes," Cronin said. "First of all, I didn't know how much you knew and were hiding and if Paul was the vigilante. I knew he wouldn't hurt you or Rachelle, so yes I kept him on the case. The vigilante killer was imperative to the kidnapping and the murder case."

"Why," Bud continued, "did you not want us to see the sketch Lindsey drew?"

Cronin replied, "What was the point? Lindsey identified him already to me. I needed this to play out, and by not showing you, I still controlled the moves. I felt strongly about not having other opinions cloud my judgment. I was going to live or die with my decisions. Assistant District Attorney Ashley would have received the envelope and been in charge of an arrest if something had happened to me."

With that, the detective lieutenant pulled out the envelope he had received that morning from Officer Lynagh and opened it up to see a perfect sketch of Jason "Jack" O'Connor.

"What about him?" Paul asked.

"He's going away for the rest of his life," Cronin answered. "The FBI and Sherman have been extremely cooperative and will continue to be. The three men that you guys took care of at the Wilkerson house were cronies of O'Connor and did special projects for him. It's likely they killed Phil Smith and stashed the money somewhere. He just couldn't resist when he found out about the cash. He had no idea the vigilante Ghost Face would be a factor in the case and in reality destroy any opportunity he or they had in getting away. Anyway, guys, I have a meeting with Assistant District Attorney Ashley in five minutes. Good job. We will be moving back to Yaphank next week, then I will be taking a week off."

"Does that mean class is dismissed?" Bud asked with a smile.

Cronin looked at both of his detectives and said, "Is that a sarcastic or respectful comment?"

"Well," Bud said, "I guess it's a little of both, Professor."

Paul said, "We are going to have dinner tomorrow night with everyone at Z Pita to celebrate the end of this. Would you like to join us?"

"No," the boss replied. "You guys enjoy; you don't need me around. I will be with the police commissioner, District Attorney Steinberg, and Ashley at Cavenaugh's having a few beers and burgers. Get your paperwork in order, guys."

Bud and Paul walked over to their desks, and Bud told Paul he would be back, that he had something to do. As he walked out of the building, Internal Affairs officer Steve Rubelli walked in to Cronin's office.

"Now what?" the detective lieutenant asked.

"You're kidding, right?" Rubelli said. "You guys destroy a house and kill three guys last night, and you ask me that question. I'm not even going to go there. It's Bud Johnson, your detective. First he shoots Kyle Winters in the groin, then he shoots O'Connor in the ass. Anything to say? Or does he just have a sick sense of humor?"

Cronin replied, "He probably saved their lives by injuring them."

Rubelli spoke again, saying, "O'Connor claims that Johnson made the comment, 'I always wanted to shoot you in the ass.'"

Cronin stood up and said, "I didn't hear him say that. I was too busy trying to prevent more killings of innocent people and fellow cops."

Cronin stared at Rubelli, hoping he would get the message. The IA detective thought about Cronin's words and said, "I agree with you. Enjoy Disney World."

With that he did an Elvis and left the building.

Bud got in his car and called Officer Lynagh to find out what was happening with Healey at the hospital and Lindsey. The officer told Bud that the young girl fell asleep at the hospital and they took her home.

"I need a favor," Bud told Lynagh.

As Detective Johnson pulled on to Cliff Street, he stopped on the side of the road near the security building where Allan had worked and died.

"Rest in peace, Allan. We will miss you." He called Deborah to tell her the case was over and hoped she didn't mind he was speaking with her.

"You really are funny," she answered. "We will be at the house tomorrow."

"Good," he said. "You can have dinner with us tomorrow if you would like."

As he sat on the side of the road, Lynagh drove up with his cruiser, with Simpson in the back. It was evident that the officer had picked up Simpson and brought him to Bud. Lynagh walked up to Bud's car as Bud sat in the backseat with Simpson alone.

"So what are your plans, Robert Simpson?"

"You're kidding, right?" Simpson answered. "This is the fifth time Lynagh has brought me somewhere. I'm going to sue your department. Cronin threatened my life, my whole being, to flush these guys out. I didn't want any part of this, and he put me in the middle of it against my will. He even told me evidence might get mixed up and a jury would find it hard to believe I wasn't involved. I will have his career."

Bud slapped his face as Lynagh turned his back to them. Bud said, "This is what I'm telling you is going to happen. I'm not going to let you ruin a good cop's career. Me I don't care about. When asked, you are going to say you willingly participated in this to bring the kidnappers to justice. If you say anything else, I will see to it that your life is fucked up forever. I have a lot of friends inside and outside of the jail. Think about what I am saying. I will have no problem putting a bullet in your ass as well as screwing the rest of your life up. Do you understand me?" Simpson was in shock and was silent as Bud spoke again. "Do I have to slap you again?"

"No," Simpson replied. "I understand."

Bud gently patted the side of his face and said, "Good boy. Now I'm going to have Officer Lynagh over there take you back to the Lance Mansion so you can finish packing up the rest of your things so you are out 100 percent by tomorrow, and I don't want to see you again unless Deborah calls you."

With that, Bud walked over to Lynagh sitting in his vehicle, and they switched places again so Lynagh could take him back to the mansion.

Bud drove back to the precinct to find Paul still working on his paperwork. He saw Assistant District Attorney Ashley speaking with Cronin and wished he could hear what they were talking about. Inside the room, Ashley was privately telling Detective Lieutenant Cronin interpretation of the laws and what he expected during the trials of Jack O'Connor and Madison Robinson.

"Green for the Robinson trial," Cronin said. "He is sensitive to public outcry and sympathy."

"He still has to follow the law, Kevin," Ashley replied.

"Yes," Cronin replied, "but maybe he will remember that laws are made by the people, and people are often wrong."

Paul got up from his desk to go check in on Rachelle and then Healey at the hospital.

"Later," Bud said.

As soon as Paul left for Mather Hospital, Bud called to speak to Lindsey to see how she was doing. Once Paul arrived at the hospital, he was told Officer Healey would recover within the next seven to ten days. He was lucky that many of the pellets had hit his vest, but he had been caught in the spray of fire in the shoulder, arm, and leg. Paul was thinking how lucky Lynagh actually was because he wasn't hit at all lying on the floor. During his visit, Healey told him Lindsey had been sending messages to him at the hospital.

"Looks like you have a friend for life," Paul replied.

"Looks like I do," the officer replied.

After seeing Officer Healey, Paul walked into O'Connor's room and stared at the agent under arrest for a couple of minutes. Without saying a word, he pulled out photos that he had been carrying with him. He said, "Take a look at these. These are the photos of people and families you ruined." O'Connor moved his head and looked at the photos without saying a word.

"Why do you think I care?" O'Connor replied.

"I know you don't," Paul replied, "but I keep my promises. Once you are in your jail cell, I will do everything I can to make sure these photos and more are hanging on your walls."

The agent started laughing and said, "Good luck with that. Even prisoners have rights."

As Paul started to leave, O'Connor said, "Your friend shot me in the ass."

"Sorry," Paul answered. "I'm sorry. No, wait, I'm not. I want to see you live and have years in prison looking at the images of families that you ruined on your walls. I don't want you thinking about anything else the rest of your life," he said as the door shut.

Paul left the hospital and drove to Prospect Street to check on Rachelle. She answered the door and greeted him warmly.

"Rachelle," Paul said, "I know it's difficult, but I will be here to help and advise you through this if you need it. One thing is for certain, Madison will be away for a bit, but if you need me, I will be here."

Rachelle hugged him, thanked him, and shed a few tears. She told him the whole *Newsday*, Twitter thing would be placed on hold and that she would be returning to Z Pita while thinking about her future. Paul told her they would be at the restaurant the next night with a few people, including Deborah Lance, and it would be nice if she was there. She thanked him again but told him she needed time to think about how she was going to help Madison for a while.

Before he left, Paul had to ask, "Rachelle, why did you agree to take the calls, make the calls, have lunch with Simpson, and let Cronin take over your Twitter account?"

She looked at him directly in the eyes and said, "To prove your innocence, but mostly because I believe in you." Paul was touched by her words and hugged her very tightly before leaving.

Bud walked outside of the precinct at 8:30pm for it had taken him the entire day and evening to file his paperwork on the case. It was starting to get dark as he looked up at the stars. "Thank you, I guess I need to make good on my promise that no other innocent person died since my last talk with you. I know I have a ways to go, especially with my language, but a promise is a promise. I will speak to you more and I will work hard on what I say. I hope you don't mind that I ask Lindsey questions here and there. She has more faith than anyone I know and it had to be someone like you to make a special girl like that. The only thing is have mercy for her future husband. OK, that's it for now. Peace and thank you."

Saturday, July 8 One Week Later

Bud and Paul were requested to stop by the Wilkerson house from the family and as they walked in the house which was still in disarray from the gun fire, Lindsey told them to come in the den. Inside was the mother of the puppies that Lindsey had talked to Officer Healey about.

"They are too young to give away now," Lindsey told them, "but in two to three weeks, I want to give one to you Bud, you Paul and Officer Healey." The detectives were very touched by her gesture and they whispered to each other for a few seconds then Paul spoke.

"Lindsey, we are very honored that you would want to give these to us but if it's OK with you, we know someone who would not only appreciate them but will need company for a while. It's Rachelle and she will be alone because of everything that has happened. Is it OK with you if Bud and I give ours to her to take care of?" Lindsey thought for a moment and said,

"They are yours, you do what you want as long as she gives them a good home." They hugged her and spoke with her parents for a few minutes before going to Rachelle's house to give her the news.

Rachelle was touched by the gesture and hugged them both and told them how much she liked the attorney Bud set up with her for Madison. After about fifteen minutes with her, they got in the car and as they drove to the precinct, Bud looked at Paul in the passenger seat,

"I owe you."

"Paul replied, "I'm your partner."

"No," Bud said. "I handcuffed you and was having you picked up. You responded by saving my life, Dugan's life and quite possibly Lynagh's life by backing him up while he wouldn't move from the floor. I really owe you."

"Well," Paul said, "since you insist," he took out an envelope and gave it to Bud. "Don't open it 'til dinner tonight. You have a chance to make things even." He put the envelope in Bud's shirt pocket. As Bud kept turning his head in disbelief at Paul,

"You were prepared for this?"

"Yes," Paul said as they both started to laugh. "One more thing," Paul added, "don't think I didn't notice that you knew Kellie Martin was in *Life Goes On*. Bud looked down with a smile, then over at Paul.

"You got me my partner, but you have to admit, she was adorable in that show."

Paul nodded as he spoke again. "The moral of the story, it's simple, good never get's old."

"I like that," Bud said. "Good never gets old." "Can I trademark that?"

"Good luck," Paul replied.

Dinner at Z Pita was bittersweet. Joey Z put a table together for Paul, Bud, Sherry, Lynagh, Chapman, Lindsey, her parents and Deborah. They were missing Rachelle as well as Healey and Dugan to injury as well as Detective Lieutenant Cronin who was at Cavenaugh's in Blue Point on the south shore of Long Island. It was a dinner of thanks as well as a dinner of toasts and they were all treated to a special conversation between Lindsey and Bud. As she grabbed her fork to eat, Bud said,

"You are left-handed?"

The young girl smiled and said, "Yes I am."

"And how rare is that?"

Lindsey replied, "A two percent probability."

Bud threw his arms up in the air. "I got you! It's more like ten to fifteen percent probability. Yay! Got you!" Lindsey just stared at him and replied,

"Are you finished? Both my parents are right handed which makes it a two percent probability I would be left handed. And as for the ten to fifteen percent of the population that are left handed there are more boys than girls that are southpaws."

"OK," Bud said, "I won't ask where the term southpaw comes from."

"Actually," Lindsey said.

"Oh God," Bud said. As everyone was laughing Lindsey continued,

"The baseball diamond was usually developed to protect the batters from the late afternoon sun so the pitcher faced west and that meant if he was left-handed, he was known as a southpaw."

"Would you do me a favor?" Bud asked. "Make sure you invite me to your wedding. I would really love to meet the lucky man." Lindsey just gave him a face as the table continued to laugh. Paul spoke up.

"OK Bud, open the envelope, read it and tell me if you want to make things up to me." Bud took the envelope out, opened it up and read it. Bud's reaction had everyone puzzled while Paul was laughing.

"No! Don't do this to me! Please! You are so cruel!" He kept shaking his head. "OK, OK. I have no choice. Three weeks from tonight everyone make yourselves available at Danfords. Healey and Dugan will be out of the hospital and I'm sure Rachelle will be back. Everyone promise?" They all couldn't wait to see what it was so they all agreed.

When Deborah got home, her father was waiting for her to show her a note, it said in letters cut out from magazines. Here is your money minus $300,000 to help in the defense of Madison Robinson. I hope you don't mind. Your discretion would be appreciated. William Lance thought it was the least he could accept considering Madison saved his daughter's life.

Sunday, July 9

Al Simmons got home to his apartment after a long day with Madison Robinson. It didn't matter it was a Sunday. He dropped his briefcase on his desk and noticed a package on his chair with a note on it cut out from magazines. *"Here in this package is $300,000 dollars toward the defense of Madison. Use it well, do your best, work hard and be discreet."*

Three Weeks Later Epilogue July 30

District Attorney Steinberg made good on his word to John Ashley and Kevin Cronin to have Judge Green handle the trial. Normally this is not normal protocol but he did pull enough strings. Al Simmons was working hard preparing for Madison's defense and he had won over the respect of Detective Powers and Johnson during these past few weeks.

The Attorney believed strongly that with the notoriety of the case and the public outcry for Madison to be treated with sympathy rather than anger was something he would take advantage of. He sat down with Rachelle and explained to her patiently the argument he was going to make. He explained to her that Madison would definitely go to jail, for the last thing the police department could ever condone is a vigilante running the streets. He studied the penal code and found section 125.25 subdivision 1A which states,

> There is an affirmative defense, when the defendant acted under the influence of extreme emotional disturbance for which there was a reasonable explanation or excuse. The reasonableness of which is to be determined from the viewpoint of a person in the defendants situation under the circumstances as the defendant believed them to be. Nothing contained in this paragraph shall constitute the defense to a prosecution for or preclude a conviction of manslaughter in the 1st degree or any other crime.

Simmons knew he had his work cut out for him but he thought he had a strong argument that would constitute a mitigating circumstance reducing murder to manslaughter. With no prior criminal records on Madison and the fact she actually saved Deborah Lance's life. Simmons thought it was realistic that the B Felony and Judge Green's history she could be looking at 5-15 years in prison. William Lance was supportive and if the Attorney needed anything, which already included an assistant law clerk to be by his side. Detective

Powers was available for "off the record" phone conversations that could be of help to the defense. Even Bud Johnson was available when needed, over drinks.

During these past weeks, it was discovered that Madison most likely saved Rachelle's life as well. Steven Anderson had tape recorded a phone call from the voice offering him 1 million dollars to arrange Rachelle coming to the *Now* offices for her elimination. Since Rachelle was being followed by police officers, Al Simmons would argue that Madison saved their lives as well, if not serious injury, by killing Anderson. He had kept the tape in the *Now* offices safe. It was ironic that he saved the tape for "insurance" purposes but he didn't count on Madison finding out about him from one of the other cronies of O'Conner. Simmons knew the prosecution would be arguing that Madison tried to frame Paul by using his mask from the coat rack, but his client swore to him she was never returning the mask and only wanted to create confusion over taking it and wearing it during the vigilante killing spree. Simmons smiled as he sat through his pile of notes for the upcoming trial. Something so complex was simply just that. They got in over their heads that they couldn't remember the simple details. Madison would most likely be in protective custody isolation, protected from the general population due to the notoriety of the case. As for the former Agent Jason "Jack" O'Connor, he waived his right to a felony exam to go straight to a Grand Jury hearing. There was no bail allowed and he was awaiting trial for murder and kidnapping in the first degree. The DA also had O'Connor on suicide watch.

It was 8:30pm upstairs at Danford's Brookhaven Room and it was the first time everyone involved in the Face of Fear case, which it had now become known as, were together. This included Detective Lieutenant Cronin, Rachelle, as well as Dugan, Assistant District Attorney Ashley as well as Healey who missed the dinner three weeks prior due to his injuries. Even William Lance was there. They were all there at the request of Bud. He walked up to the DJ from PJ from Rantin Ravin Entertainment and spoke to him that he was now ready. Bud went to the center of the floor and asked for everyone's attention. "Folks, I owe this to Paul. Hit it." The music came on provocative and sexy as Bud began dancing. The singing began and it was none other than Olivia Newton-John's song called *I Need Love*. It was easy to see that Bud had practiced the song. He was perfect and his lip syncing was so good that he had the full attention of everyone in the room as the song continued. If there was one thing that Bud never dreamed he would do in his life, it would be dancing and lip synching to a song about sex by Olivia Newton John in front of an audience.

It was a song most had never heard from Olivia Newton-John but they were impressed with not only Bud's performance but the song. When it was over, everyone was clapping, whistling and stomping. Paul gave Bud a hug and said,

"OK, we are even." Lindsey gave Bud a kiss and said,

"Great job, even if you said the word sex." It was about 11pm when Rachelle needed to get home and she started to say good night to everyone when Paul asked her if he could walk her home. She said it would be great and she had something home she wanted him to see.

Paul walked her home and she brought him inside. She took his hand and walked him over to the kitchen. In a small cage were two young puppies whimpering and ready to drink again.

"Oh, so cute," Paul said. "When did you get them?"

"A couple of days ago," she replied. Paul started petting them.

"Did you give them their names?" he asked.

"Yes," she said. "I wanted to name them Benjamin and Franklin."

"Oh wow, that's so you," Paul replied.

"But," she said, "I thought that maybe you would help me raise them so I thought it would be cool to name them Wes and Craven." Paul just looked at her and gave her a hug.

"You are sweet," as he continued to hug her. He pulled away and started walking to the door and hesitated when his hands were on the door knob.

"What's up Paul?" Rachelle asked. He turned around and walked toward her and stopped in front of her.

"Rachelle, I'm tired of pretending." She put her hand on his face and said,

"Me too." They kissed on the lips for the first time as Rachelle started to unbutton his shirt. Bud was sitting outside in his car looking at the figures in the shadows kissing inside. He was smiling as he looked over at Deborah sitting in the passenger seat.

"How would you like to have lunch with me at The Red Onion Café tomorrow? You know they don't charge me since I shot the bad guy in the groin." Deborah started laughing as Bud said, "I know, I know. I'm a funny guy."

"No," she answered. 'You're an amazing guy," she said as she leaned over to kiss him. "I will have lunch with you tomorrow, if you go to Vegas with me next weekend."

"Sounds fun," he said, "Vegas?"

"Yes," she answered, "I go there three times a year to escape and see Gordie Brown at the Golden Nugget hotel."

"Who is he?" Bud asked. Deborah smiled. "You won't be asking that once you see him." "You won't stop smiling and laughing once the show starts, he is the world's greatest impressionist."

"You're on." he said. She pulled out a small wrapped package from her pocketbook and gave it to him. "What's this?" he said.

"It's a gift for you," she replied. He opened it up and it was a CD called Freedom from Michael W. Smith. She could tell by the way Bud said thank you that he wasn't sure why he was given this particular CD.

"Consider it a belated birthday gift, it was July 9 right?" She spoke again, "Listen to track three, a song called *Carol Ann* and read your lyrics you sent me to this music." He shook his head puzzled.

"How?" "How could you find an instrumental that would match my lyrics?"

"God works in mysterious ways Bud," she replied. In the corner of his eye, he noticed that the four Ghost Face masks he had received from Fun World were still there in the back seat. He turned them upside down as he began to kiss Deborah again.

"You know," Bud said to her, "the first time I saw you in Starfield's home, I wanted to hold you, hug you, and give you comfort but I was afraid of how inappropriate it would have been." Deborah smiled as she replied and touched his hand,

"What about now?" Bud smiled back as he kissed her again.

Kevin Cronin and John Ashley were going to their cars at 11:30pm as the party was starting to break up. When they reached the parking lot, Cronin looked around and said,

"It's nice to be back to normal." Ashley replied,

"Is it?" Cronin looked at him as Ashley spoke again.

"The medical examiner informed you three weeks ago that the body temperature of Phil Smith and conditions of the barn was such that he may have been killed a few hours after O'Connor's men were killed by Lynagh, Powers, and Healey. It's very possible that O'Connor's men didn't kill Smith."

"Are you going to do anything about it?" Cronin pulled out his car keys as he approached his car.

"Kevin?" Ashley replied. Are you going to investigate it further?"

"Do we want to go down this road John?" Cronin replied.

"You know," Ashley answered. "I can't tell you anything else." Cronin looked up at the sky as he spoke reluctantly.

"I will take care of it."

"When were you sure about O'Connor," Ashley asked.

"I was always suspicious since the game began," Cronin replied. "I knew for sure when Paul told me he confronted you guys at the courthouse about Lindsey witnessing a murder. No one who knew told him about it."

"OK," Ashley said, "now what?"

"John, do we have the tax dollars to investigate the killing of a cold blooded killer?" Ashley had started to walk away when he turned to face the Detective Lieutenant. There was silence between them as the stare down continued.

"I will keep my word," Cronin said. "I promise." John Ashley took a step closer to the Detective Lieutenant as he spoke again,

"Not only is the elimination of Phil Smith a question, the mystery continues. We know Anderson didn't kill him for he was already taken care of from Madison. Yet the gun that killed our dirt bag in the barn was traced to Anderson. Isn't that interesting? I wonder who found that gun and used it on Smith?" Cronin spoke quickly,

"Assuming of course it wasn't one of O'Connor's three stooges that were killed at the Wilkerson house, right ADA Ashley?" It was the first time in years that Kevin Cronin was formal with John and he noticed it. Ashley spoke again,

"You're not uncomfortable with the way Phil Smith was eliminated, or the fact some of the money was not recovered?" Kevin looked over at the back of the corner building on East Main and Main Street,

"This village has enough notoriety and now they announce the Long Island Music Hall of Fame will be there next year."

Ashley ignored the comment and started to walk away, but turned around and spoke again,

"I will hold you to your word Kevin." Cronin dangled his keys at the top of his car to the point that it was almost annoying. He looked in the opposite direction to gather his thoughts before turning his head back to John Ashley. His piercing blue eyes almost glowed in the dark under the Trader Coves overhead street lamps as he answered the ADA.

"Like all things in life, and like all games that we play," he paused for a second before continuing, "there comes a time when it just has to end."

Author's Note

My respect for the Suffolk County Police Department in Long Island is evident in this story. While it is a fictional story, I have had the pleasure and honor of being good friends with many of them over the years.

There is always a chance when they leave their homes in the morning that they will not return to their families. Many of us, including myself, could not handle the stress of uncertainty such as this.

Police officers all over the country have lost their lives and continue to lose their lives in the line of duty, leaving their families behind. During the writing of this book, Long Island resident and NYPD officer Peter Figoski lost his life, leaving behind four daughters.

Below are the names of Suffolk County police officers who have lost their lives in the line of duty. In honor of them, 5 percent of the author's profits from this book will be donated to the SUFFOLK COUNTY POLICE MEMORIAL FUND. If you have enjoyed this book and/or you could never imagine leaving your family to continue their lives without you, I encourage you to make a donation to your local police department's memorial fund to help their families and children for the remainder of their lives for the sacrifices of their mother or father in uniform. Thank you.

Suffolk County, Long Island, NY, police officers who have died in the line of duty:

Police Officer Jack C. Burkhardt
Police Officer Carmelo A. Cattano
Police Officer William V. DeRosa
Police Officer Vincent J. DeVivo
Detective Lieutenant Joseph H. Hawkins
Police Officer Edwin Hernandez
Police Officer John Jantzen
Detective Carmine M. Macchia
Deputy Inspector George A. McMullen
Police Officer John J. Nolan
Police Officer Henry J. Stewart
Police Officer Albert A. Willetts
Police Officer Frank D. Cataldo
Police Officer Glen Ciano
Sergeant Lawrence J. Devine
Police Officer George A. Frees
Sergeant Timothy J. Henck
Sergeant James Hutchens
Deputy Chief Alfred C. Kohler
Police Officer Ralph Sorli
Police Officer John J. Venus
Detective Dennis J. Wustenhoff

About the Author

R.J. Torbert has been a key figure of all things Ghost Face behind the scenes since 1996. He is responsible for the legal baptism of the name "Ghost Face," amending the original copyrights that officially linked the image and name together forever, as well as having the Icon of Halloween trademarked. R.J. lives with his family not far from the village where this story is based. He continues his responsibilities as director of licensing for properties such as Ghost Face as well as product development, which has resulted in creating hundreds of toys seen in stores worldwide for Easter, Valentine's Day, and St. Patrick's Day.

R.J. is also co-creator of the limited-edition 24 karat gold records of Elvis Presley sold at Graceland and catalogs worldwide. He loves to travel with his family when not traveling for work. He is proud to say he is a veteran of our armed forces.

Powers and Johnson will return-----